From the

THE COLLECTE

GUY DE MAUPASSANT

She felt herself drowned in the scorn of these honest scoundrels, who had first sacrificed her and then rejected her, like some improper or useless article. She thought of her great basket full of good things which they had greedily devoured, of her two chickens shining with jelly, of her *pâtés*, her pears, and the four bottles of Bordeaux; and her fury suddenly falling, as a cord drawn too tightly breaks, she felt ready to weep.

(from "Ball-of-Fat," pages 40–41)

"When I know how people love in a country, I know that country well enough to describe it, although I may never have seen it."

(from "Marroca," page 62)

We are quite different in our dreams to what we are in real life.

(from "The Awakening," page 83)

"Big Sister, I do not want thee to be unhappy. I do not want thee to cry all thy life. I will never leave thee, never, never! I—I, too, shall never marry. I shall stay with thee always, always, always!"

(from "The Confession," pages 94–95)

If, however, his life had been complete! If he had done something; if he had had adventures, grand pleasures, successes, satisfaction of some kind or another. But now, nothing. He had done nothing.

(from "Regret," page 100)

"He married her—he married her—as one marries—well, because he was a fool!"

(from "The Artist's Wife," page 115)

With women there is neither caste nor rank; and beauty, grace, and charm act instead of family and birth. Natural fineness, instinct for what is elegant, suppleness of wit, are the sole hierarchy, and make from women of the people the equals of the very greatest ladies.

(from "The Necklace," page 130)

"I yield to her charm, and I only approach her with the apprehension that I would feel concerning a man who was known to be a skillful thief. In her presence I have an irrational impulse toward belief in her possible purity and a very reasonable mistrust of her not less probable trickery. I feel myself in contact with an abnormal being, beyond the pale of natural laws, an exquisite or detestable creature—I don't know which." (from "Yvette," page 172)

From all her experiences she had never known either a genuine tenderness or a great repulsion. (from "Yvette," page 203)

"That was perhaps the only woman I have ever loved. No—that I ever should have loved. . . . Ah, well! who can tell? Facts master you. . . . And then—and then—all passes."

(from "The Wreck," page 233)

Ah, if we had only other organs which would perform in our favor other miracles like that miracle of music, what new things we should discover all about our lives! (from "The Horla," pages 241–242)

THE COLLECTED STORIES OF
GUY DE MAUPASSANT

*With an Introduction and Notes
by Richard Fusco*

GEORGE STADE
CONSULTING EDITORIAL DIRECTOR

BARNES & NOBLE CLASSICS
NEW YORK

ℬ

BARNES & NOBLE CLASSICS

NEW YORK

Published by Barnes & Noble Books
122 Fifth Avenue
New York, NY 10011

www.barnesandnoble.com/classics

See Original Publication Data in the back of the book for
original publication dates and venues.

Published in 2008 by Barnes & Noble Classics with new Introduction, Notes,
Biography, Chronology, Original Publication Data, Inspired By,
Comments & Questions, and For Further Reading.

The Collected Stories of Guy de Maupassant
ISBN-13 978-1-59308-222-2
ISBN-10 1-59308-222-3
LC Control Number 2008929047

Produced and published in conjunction with:
Fine Creative Media, Inc.
322 Eighth Avenue
New York, NY 10001

Michael J. Fine, President and Publisher

Printed in the United States of America

QM

1 3 5 7 9 10 8 6 4 2

FIRST PRINTING

GUY DE MAUPASSANT

The French short-story writer and novelist Guy de Maupassant was born on August 5, 1850, on the coast of Normandy in northwestern France. His parents were affluent but unhappy. When Guy was ten, they separated, and he and his brother moved with their mother to the seaside village of Étretat in the picturesque Norman region of Pays de Caux. There Maupassant developed an attachment to the sea and to the provincial towns that were to become an inspiration for many of his stories. When he was thirteen, his mother enrolled him in a seminary school in nearby Yvetot; he rebelled against the school's disciplined, religious atmosphere and was expelled five years later for writing offensive poetry. While he was in college in Rouen, Maupassant met his mother's childhood friend and the most influential figure of his literary career, the great French novelist Gustave Flaubert.

In 1869 Maupassant moved to Paris to study law, but upon the outbreak of the Franco-Prussian War in 1870, he left school to join the French army as a private. After the war, he renewed his acquaintance with Flaubert, who took the young man under his wing, giving him creative guidance as well as access to a Parisian literary circle that included Émile Zola, Ivan Turgenev, and Henry James. During these years, Maupassant supported himself by working as a civil servant, first in the ministry of the navy and later in the ministry of education.

In 1880 Maupassant's short story "Boule de suif" ("Ball-of-Fat") was published in the anthology *Les Soirées du Médan* (*Evenings at Médan*), which also included contributions by Zola and J. K. Huysmans. With this publication, Maupassant gained immediate recognition as a major talent. The 1880s were a prolific and rewarding decade for Maupassant; besides publishing more than 300 short stories, he wrote six novels, several travel books, a volume of verse, and numerous newspaper articles. But it is his mastery of the short story that has made him one of France's most famous writers. Maupassant's stories cover a wide range of subjects, from peasants in Normandy, through the Franco-Prussian War, life in bureaucratic ministries, and Parisian society, to prostitutes.

Though the success of his writing made him rich and famous, Maupassant was increasingly harrowed by the debilitating effects of syphilis. In 1887 he published "Le Horla," a horrific story of a man afflicted by hallucinations and madness. Meanwhile, his own syphilitic neuralgia was becoming more pronounced. When his brother died of syphilis in 1889, Maupassant felt that his own insanity and death were imminent. He published his final novel, *Notre Cœur* (*Our Heart*), in 1890 and his final short story, "Les Tombales" ("Graveyard Sirens"), the following year. By 1891 Maupassant had grown increasingly deranged, and in January 1892 he attempted suicide by cutting his throat. He was committed to a sanatorium in Paris, where he spent the next year and a half suffering the painful and debilitating symptoms of late-stage syphilis. Guy de Maupassant died on July 6, 1893.

TABLE OF CONTENTS

THE COLLECTED STORIES OF
GUY DE MAUPASSANT

The World of
GUY DE MAUPASSANT

1850   Henri-René-Albert-Guy de Maupassant is born on August 5
in Fécamp, on the Normandy coast. His mother, Laure (née
Le Poittevin), is a childhood friend of French novelist Gustave Flaubert (1821–1880). French author Honoré de Balzac
dies.

1852   Russian author Ivan Turgenev publishes *The Hunter's Sketches*,
a collection of short stories about the lives of Russian serfs.

1856   Flaubert's first published novel, *Madame Bovary*, sparks con-
troversy because of its depiction of adultery. Victor Hugo
publishes a collection of poems, *Les Contemplations*.

1859   The Maupassant family lives briefly in Paris, where Guy's father, Gustave, works in a bank. English novelist Charles
Dickens publishes *A Tale of Two Cities*. English philosopher and
economist John Stuart Mill writes his essay *On Liberty*.

1860   Maupassant's parents permanently separate, and Guy and his
brother move with their mother back to Normandy, where
they live in the seaside village of Étretat. Abraham Lincoln is
elected president of the United States. German philosopher
Arthur Schopenhauer dies; his writings will become a great
influence in Maupassant's life.

1863   Maupassant enters a seminary school in Yvetot in northern
Normandy. Théophile Gautier publishes his novel *Le Capi-
taine Fracasse*.

1867   German philosopher and revolutionary Karl Marx publishes
the first volume of his critique of capitalism, *Das Kapital*.
French poet Charles Baudelaire dies.

1868   In May, Maupassant is expelled from the seminary school for
writing offensive poetry. He enters college in Rouen, where
he meets his mother's old friend Flaubert, who will become

his friend and literary mentor. Russian novelist Fyodor Dostoevsky publishes *The Idiot*. The Impressionist style of painting develops in France with works by Claude Monet, Paul Cézanne, Edgar Degas, and Pierre-Auguste Renoir.

1869   Maupassant begins to study law in Paris. Flaubert publishes *L'Éducation sentimentale* (*A Sentimental Education*); French poet Paul Verlaine publishes *Fêtes galantes* (*Romantic Feasts*).

1870   The Franco-Prussian War begins, and Maupassant volunteers for the French army. Napoléon III's imperialist Second Empire collapses and the democratic Third Republic is established. Prussia begins a siege of Paris in September.

1871   France signs an armistice with Prussia in January, ending the ten-month conflict; Adolphe Thiers is named chief executive of France's provisional government. The citizens of Paris, refusing to disarm, form the Commune of Paris, which rules the city for two months until it is defeated by loyalist troops in May. Maupassant returns to Paris and reconnects with Flaubert, who invites him into a literary circle that includes Turgenev, French novelist Émile Zola, and American author Henry James. English novelist George Eliot begins serial publication of *Middlemarch*. French novelist Marcel Proust is born.

1872   Maupassant works as a civil servant in the ministry of the navy. Turgenev writes his play *A Month in the Country*. French author Jules Verne begins serial publication of *Le Tour du monde en quatre-vingts jours* (*Around the World in Eighty Days*).

1877   Henry James publishes his novel *The American*; Zola publishes his novel *L'Assommoir* (*The Drunkard*) to huge commercial success.

1878   Maupassant is transferred to the ministry of education. He works as an editor for several well-known magazines and newspapers, and continues to write in his spare time.

1879   James publishes his novella *Daisy Miller*.

1880   Maupassant's story "Boule de suif" ("Ball-of-Fat") is published in the anthology *Les Soirées de Médan* (*Evenings at Médan*), which also includes stories by Zola and French novelist J. K. Huysmans. "Boule de suif" is an immediate success and propels Maupassant to literary fame. He begins contributing stories to the newspapers *Le Gaulois* and *Gil Blas*. Flaubert dies.

1881   *La Maison Tellier* (*The Tellier House*), Maupassant's first collection of stories, is published. James publishes *The Portrait of a Lady*. French writer Anatole France publishes *Le Crime de Sylvestre Bonnard*. Dostoevsky dies.

1882   The first edition of Maupassant's story collection *Mademoiselle Fifi* is published. As he often did with his anthologies, Maupassant reissued *Mademoiselle Fifi* several times in later years, adding new stories to the collection.

1883   Maupassant's first novel, *Une Vie* (*A Woman's Life*), is published, as well as his story collection *Contes de la bécasse* (*Tales of the Goose*). Turgenev dies. German philosopher Friedrich Nietzsche publishes *Thus Spoke Zarathustra*.

1884   Maupassant publishes the collections *Clair de lune* (*Moonlight*), *Les Soeurs Rondoli* (*The Rondoli Sisters*), *Miss Harriet*, and *Yvette*. Mark Twain publishes *The Adventures of Huckleberry Finn*.

1885   Maupassant's novel *Bel-Ami* and two story collections, *Toine* and *Contes du jour et de la nuit* (*Stories of Day and Night*), are published. Dutch post-Impressionist painter Vincent van Gogh paints his first major work, *The Potato Eaters*. Victor Hugo dies.

1886   Maupassant's collection *La Petite Roque* (*Little Roque*) is published.

1887   His story collection *Le Horla* is published; the title story is a horror tale about a man's madness and eventual suicide. His novel *Mont-Oriol* also comes out during this year. Zola publishes *La Terre*.

1888   Maupassant publishes the story collection *Le Rosier de Madame Husson* (*Madame Husson's Rosebush*) as well as his controversial novel about adultery, *Pierre et Jean*.

1889   French philosopher Henri Bergson publishes *Essai sur les don-
        nées immédiates de la conscience (Time and Free Will)*. Construc-
        tion of the Eiffel Tower is completed in Paris, over the
        protests of Maupassant and many other literary figures. Mau-
        passant's story collection *La Main gauche (The Left Hand)* is
        published.

1890   Maupassant's last novel, *Notre Coeur (Our Heart)*, is published.
        American psychologist William James publishes *The Princi-
        ples of Psychology*. Van Gogh dies.

1891   Maupassant's last story, "Les Tombales" ("Graveyard Sirens"),
        is published.

1892   In January, Maupassant attempts suicide by cutting his throat.
        He is committed to an asylum in Paris.

1893   Guy de Maupassant dies on July 6. He is buried at the Mont-
        parnasse Cemetery in Paris.

INTRODUCTION

Eternal and Wretched Exile:
Maupassant and the Craft of the Short Story

During the early morning following New Year's Day in 1892, Guy de Maupassant attempted suicide by cutting his throat. The syphilis that he had contracted fifteen years earlier was now well into its tertiary stage, violently consuming his life and sanity. The once brilliant and ambitious writer who had injected bravado into every aspect of his existence was now peevish and sullen. What rationality that remained had accepted his doom, but that resignation could not brace him for the continual agony of the disease. His memory continually failed him. As happens with the dementia suffered by the old, he sometimes lost himself in the memories of his remote past. Episodes of seizures became increasingly harrowing. A parade of delusions and hallucinations corrupted his personality. He saw ghosts. He thought himself back in the military, fighting Germans during the Franco-Prussian War of 1870. He imagined his brain was liquefying and seeping into his nasal passages. The latter illusion was in reality an effect of the syphilis, caused by gummas, soft tumors, growing in his mucous membranes. In his prime, he had embraced life ferociously, but now he needed constant watching by a loyal valet, who served as his nurse and keeper.

He had just returned from a fitful New Year's visit to his mother and brother's widow in Nice. His servant, François, had escorted him back to Cannes and managed to get him to bed. Alone, shortly after 2:00 A.M., Maupassant did the deed. What prompted Maupassant to take a razor to his throat one can only speculate. Perhaps it was yet another syphilitically inspired apparition that urged him to do so. Perhaps in a moment of waning sanity, he recalled all the pain he had suffered and anticipated all that was yet to come—and in that rational moment, fearing the return of diseased madness, seized an opportunity to control life by ending it. Perhaps he had an experience like that of his character M. Leras in "Promenade" (1884) who, after a random encounter with various pleasant sights along the Champs-Élysées, suddenly realizes how vapid his life is and impulsively hangs himself with his braces.

Maupassant survived the suicide attempt. Hearing his master stirring, François went to see what he needed. Bleeding, Maupassant confessed: "See what I have done. I have cut my throat[;] it is an absolute case of madness."* François and another servant bandaged the cut and then procured a physician, who stitched the wound of the now passive patient. As is the case in some suicides, had his hand balked at the last moment and subconsciously missed the carotid artery? Or had his syphilitic eyes merely missed the mark? Certainly the same animal survival instinct that he had studied so often in his stories had prompted him to yield to François's ministrations. In much of his fiction, killing oneself seems to be such an easy act, often captured by a single painless sentence. M. Leras's resolve to die manifests itself offstage. In "Le Champ d'oliviers" (1890; "The Olive Orchard"), the Abbé Vilbois's suicide is similarly a brief and decisive act.

But Maupassant's real-life experience was different. Death was not instantaneous with the decision to die. That night proved to be long and arduous, somewhat reminiscent of his mentor Gustave Flaubert's measured description in the 1857 novel, *Madame Bovary*, of Emma Bovary's slow death after consuming poison. Although his physical body did not die that night in 1892, for all practical purposes Maupassant became dead to the world. The day after, attendants of Dr. Émile Blanche strapped Maupassant into a straitjacket and escorted him to a sanatorium in Paris. He lived another year and a half in increasing isolation, his family and friends finding the situation too horrific to repeat visits. When he finally died in 1893, many who had

---

* Reported by biographer Francis Steegmuller in *Maupassant: A Lion in the Path* (New York: Random House, 1949), p. 340.

known him well felt relief. His American friend Henry James confessed that he had already shed a "crystalline tear" for him long ago.

This death ended a remarkable decade of literary production. He had composed more than 300 short stories, six novels, and a wealth of material in other genres, most of which was published between 1880 and 1890. Despite his early desire to be a poet, which Flaubert dissuaded, and his later ambition to be a great novelist, which death thwarted, he earned a place in literary history as one of the four great practitioners of the short story in the nineteenth century, the others being the American Edgar Allan Poe (1809–1849) and the Russians Ivan Turgenev (1818–1883) and Anton Chekhov (1860–1904). All four men had peers in their respective countries who occasionally produced a superior short story; but Poe, Turgenev, Maupassant, and Chekhov each composed a body of work that quickly found an international audience, which greatly shaped the development of short fiction as it moved from its immediate antecedent (the essay) through the tale to the short story. Considered by his countrymen a hack composer of macabre tales, Poe found a sympathetic translator in French Romantic poet Charles Baudelaire (1821–1867), whose renderings subsequently helped to inspire movements such as European Symbolism and the Gothic revival of the 1890s. Not only did Turgenev's *The Hunter's Sketches* (1852) contribute to the cultural changes that led to the emancipation of serfs in his native Russia, it also blueprinted the perimeters of the local-color literary phenomenon worldwide. Constance Garnett's translations into English of Chekhov's stories became the artistic archetype for fiction appearing in leading periodicals such as *The New Yorker* from the 1920s to the 1950s. Maupassant's career belongs sandwiched between Turgenev's and Chekhov's. Like most French writers of his day, he studied Poe. He knew the older Turgenev personally, benefiting greatly from the friendship. And his *contes* (stories) inspired Chekhov as the latter honed his approach to the short story.

As they did with the fiction of Poe, Turgenev, and Chekhov, subsequent writers around the world would study Maupassant's texts for the way he shaped and developed plots, deftly infused his images with symbols and concepts, and used language with precision and re-markable concision. Similar to those of his American and Russian col-leagues, his works quickly found willing (if not always competent) translators, including Lafcadio Hearn and Jonathan Sturges in the United States. Curiously, as was the case with the other three mas-ters, Maupassant embraced the short-story form at a time of per-sonal adversity. Poe tried with meager success to ease his continual money problems by selling tales at bargain prices. Turgenev's rebel-lion against his family's ownership of serfs led to his personal and fi-nancial estrangement and produced *The Hunter's Sketches*. Chekhov's literary endeavors initially counterbalanced his life as an often unpaid physician. And Maupassant wrote with a syphilitic sword of Damo-cles precariously strung over his being.

Some critics consider it a scholarly blunder to suggest strong links between an author's works and his life. That caution is certainly valid if a biographer tries to glean life facts from fictional texts, for while writers often tap into their experience for inspiration, they just as often transfigure it for artistic and philosophical effect. But I wish to assert a different sort of connection. I find it interesting not only that four men turned to the short story at times of great personal adver-sity but that these circumstances also facilitated their embrace of the form. In Maupassant's case, then, practicing the short story allowed him to indulge his anxieties about and to seek psychological relief from his disease.

Maupassant's biographers report that he contracted syphilis in 1877. Thus, his decade of munificent creativity from 1880 to 1890 had the continual pall of venereal disease qualifying its intensity and future. I liken Maupassant's situation to the allegory Poe presents in his poetically macabre "The Masque of the Red Death." In the tale, revelers seek refuge from a devastating plague in a castellated abbey. For most of each hour, they waltz away their anxieties of death, but at the end of that hour, an ebony clock tolls to remind them that an inevitable death approaches one hour nearer. Such a fragmented ex-istence produces a stagnant world that defines itself by momentary divertissements. Likewise, Maupassant waltzed amid the realms of short fiction to find diversion from contemplating his looming death sentence. On one level, the act of storytelling had long been a vital part of Maupassant's social persona. Besides enjoying its literary benefits, Maupassant valued being a member of Flaubert's salon during the 1870s because of the comradeship of writers such as Turgenev, Émile Zola (1840–1902), Henry James (1843–1916), Alphonse Daudet (1840–1897), and Edmond de Goncourt (1822–1896), many of whom swapped stories in an energetic contest of male bravado. Just as such get-togethers often pleasantly while away a day, so too can the composition of a story occupy the mind, thus momentarily sublimating the cares of life.

On a second level, each short text has the potential to enshrine one small aspect of the human condition. Such insights befit the character of Maupassant's sensibilities. He pursued life as a consumer of moments. An infamous womanizer, he boasted of the parade of conquests, affairs, and prostitutes, but he never cultivated a satisfying, lifelong sexual relationship with a woman. Likewise in his fiction, insights about the sustained meanings and patterns of human existence often eluded him. Such global perspectives belonged more properly in the novel. Although Maupassant turned increasingly toward the novel after 1883 to build his literary reputation (eventually completing six), he did not live long enough to master the form to the degree achieved by his mentor, Flaubert. As intriguing as his novels are, most critics agree that his short stories compose the core of his achievement and are best suited his temperament. In the rapidity of his life, Maupassant had little room for reflection and well-pondered philosophy. In most of his stories, he celebrates the instant of insight—what Aristotle called *anagnorisis*—and thus each text becomes a momentary synthesis of concision, of diction, of syntax, of plot, of symbol, and of meaning.

In effect, Maupassant saw the universe in meaningless decay. His country's humiliating defeat in 1871 at the hands of the Germans vexed an entire generation of young Frenchmen into political and personal disillusionment. His parents' loveless marriage and subsequent separation as well as his father's infidelity motivated him to reject the family as the prime unifier of life. (While he maintained a close relationship with his mother and brother, his detached relationship with his children born out of wedlock never became truly paternal.) And, again, his disease robbed him of health and fated an end devoid of personal meaning. Finding little to appreciate in contemplating long perspectives, such as human destiny, Maupassant chose to lose himself in disconnected moments of insight.

Thus, existence became a series of brief illusions of discovery, each braving a temporary escape from the horrors of a nonsensical world. Such moments are unique, illuminating, but vestigial. Among all the forms of prose fiction, the short story most suitably captures such transient events. The writer and his reader share the flash of insight and then allow it to fade without any attempt to integrate it into a larger aesthetic or philosophy. As in the Poe tale, we can intellectually waltz away an hour blindly ignorant that we have danced one step closer to death.

Freed from the burden of weaving insights into a consistent philosophical fabric, as a writer often does in a novel, Maupassant used his more than 300 short stories to explore the panorama of human behavior and experience. As a whole, these texts defy critical synthesis in their plots and perspectives. In "La Parure" (1884; "The Necklace"), Mathilde Loisel's life turns farcical when she discovers that jewelry she thought priceless is made of paste. Meanwhile, in "Les Bijoux" (1883; "The False Gems"), M. Lantin's existence disintegrates when he learns that his dead wife's supposedly costume jewelry is made of precious stones. In "Mouche" (1890) Maupassant paints a rowing club's cavalier treatment of a woman in very wide chauvinistic strokes, while in "L'Inutile Beauté" (1890; "Useless Beauty"), he sketches the Countess de Mascaret's plight with the passion of an ardent feminist. In his local-color fiction of his native Normandy, he savages many of its inhabitants for their parsimony, ignorance, and inhumanity while quietly commending others for their patriotism and patient endurance of harsh lives. Maupassant saw a world ruled by chance and so used his stories to isolate numerous opposing forces. As his friend Henry James once noted, Maupassant was a raconteur without a moral center. Nor did he have a true aesthetic or literary one. Consequently, Maupassant's stories *ensemble* took census of the length and breadth of nineteenth-century French society, recording how the innocent and the depraved, the heroes and the cowards, the truly passionate and the dilettantes, and other human dichotomies fare against the incivilities, the injustices, and the abandonments that plague modern experience.

Maupassant's youth helped to shape this sensibility of a world in irredeemable decay. Henri-René-Albert-Guy de Maupassant was born on August 5, 1850, in Normandy. His parents, Gustave and Laure (née Le Poittevin) de Maupassant, fought often over the husband's frequent infidelities and the wife's difficult temperament. By the time they separated in the early 1860s, their incessant bickering had indelibly influenced their son's attitudes toward marriage and relationships in general. Ironically, despite the growing ambivalence between father and son, the adult Guy would later emulate and subsequently surpass Gustave's womanizing. After her son was left in her care, Laure and a cleric friend attempted to tutor Guy at their home in Étretat, but the increasingly rambunctious twelve-year-old proved taxing to her hypersensitive psyche. Therefore, in 1863, she dispatched him to a boarding school in nearby Yvetot that stressed discipline but where his rebellious nature fully erupted, eventually prompting his expulsion.

Most of Maupassant's later teen years are characterized by freedom and indulgence, especially regarding his sexuality after he lost his virginity at age sixteen. Fancying himself a poet, his early literary interests were furthered by fortuitous meetings with Algernon Swinburne (1837–1909), the Pre-Raphaelite English poet whom Guy saved from drowning; Louis Bouilhet (1822–1869), a French poet and playwright who had been Laure's childhood friend; and Flaubert, the greatest novelist of his generation. But his mastery of fictional technique was to be put off a full decade, for in 1870, the Franco-Prussian War broke out. Thus, at the end of his youth, the nineteen-year-old Maupassant left his studies, as did many of his generation, and eagerly enlisted in the army to defend the honor and soil of France. This romantic misconception, however, was dashed by the initial inactivity and subsequent flight of his ill-prepared regiment. The conflict proved to be a military, political, and cultural debacle for France, leaving in its wake disaffected and cynical young men. More than any other writer, Maupassant spoke for this generation, chronicling the search for remnants of meaning in a vapid universe.

One consequence of this pursuit can be found in his deceptively simple prose style. Beneath the lean sentence structure, the economical but rich use of symbols, the deft word choices, and Spartan plotting resides a plethora of perspectives, sampling diverse aesthetic traditions and philosophies. At the core of Maupassant's style and thought are three profound influences: Gustave Flaubert, Ivan Turgenev, and Émile Zola. I am hard-pressed to recall any other neophyte writer in the history of literature who had so many brilliant and accomplished mentors.

Gustave Flaubert (1821–1880) had been an intimate childhood friend of Maupassant's mother, Laure, and her brother, Alfred Le Poittevin (to whom Flaubert posthumously dedicated *La Tentation de Saint Antoine* [*The Temptation of Saint Anthony*] in 1874). After Alfred's death as a young adult reinforced Laure and Flaubert's friendship through shared mourning, Laure arranged for her seventeen-year-old son to meet the celebrated novelist. That initial contact eventually began a contest regarding the direction the young man's obvious artistic talents would take. On one side was another of Laure's friends, the poet Louis Bouilhet, who encouraged Maupassant's fervent early interest in poetry. After Bouilhet's death in 1869, Flaubert persistently dissuaded Maupassant from such a career. Poetry had nurtured the young writer's gifts with language, but his mentor directed him to apply such abilities to select *le mot juste* in prose. Despite the cultural impact of the new poets of French Symbolism, Flaubert judged that France's chief literary production of his age would be in prose. *Madame Bovary* became the textual paradigm for this generation of French writers. The mentor abhorred the idea of artistic schools. Consequently, he would advise Maupassant through years of intense editorial scrutiny of the young man's prose experiments, but Flaubert never insisted upon mere imitation of the forms and practices in *Madame Bovary*—instead, he guided his pupil to find his own fictive voice.

During the 1870s, Maupassant became a regular visitor to Flaubert's Sunday salons, a planned gathering of established writers, which included Turgenev, Zola, Daudet, Goncourt, and Hippolyte Taine (1828–1893), as well as many aspiring ones, such as the young Henry James. Conversation ranged over a wide variety of topics from the literary discursive to ribald jokes. Hearing such diversity among authorial voices encouraged Maupassant to cultivate his own.

From Flaubert himself, however, the fledgling writer grew to appreciate the artistic consequence in his mentor's Spartan realism, defined by its exacting prose, uncluttered images, and a zealous objectivity in narration. A curious dynamic occurred during these tutoring sessions. The principles that Flaubert applied with consciously laborious attention Maupassant absorbed so wholly that he could apply them with much less deliberation. Thus, with a similar commitment to describe everyday life, the pupil was eventually able to crank out elegant prose in quantities beyond the capacities of his teacher, although Maupassant's initial fictive vision lacked the broad expanse of Flaubert's sensibilities. In many ways, he applied Flaubert's lessons to all aspects of writing: economy of prose and the avoidance of poetic excesses spilled over into economies of plot, character, and image—three of the properties of well-crafted short stories. Try as he eventually did, Maupassant could never surpass Flaubert's excellences in the novel, but as a short-story writer, he possessed an intuitive deftness that his teacher and peers never equaled. Years later, Henry James recorded in his journal his intention to follow his friend Maupassant's example in composing a story in which concisions of plot, character, and language were virtues. Nevertheless, the resulting text of "Glasses" (1896) grew from James's planned few thousand words to some 20,000 in the published version.

Although he had seen a few sketches in print beforehand, Maupassant's first substantial notoriety as a writer arrived with the issuing of an anthology of mostly emerging writers, *Les Soirées de Médan* (1880; *Evenings at Médan*), which included his contribution "Boule de suif" ("Ball-of-Fat"). It appeared weeks before Flaubert's unexpected death from a stroke. *Les Soirées de Médan* had been organized by another literary giant of the period, Émile Zola, through whose influence Maupassant would encounter realism's chief challenger in the literary world—naturalism. As opposed to the perceptual objectivity of realism, literary naturalism philosophically presupposes a deterministic universe in which humans lack control over the conduct of their lives. Based in part upon his understanding of English naturalist Charles Darwin's (1809–1882) scientific conjectures, Zola was predominantly interested in how animal instincts such as sexual impulses deprive the conscious mind from exercising any command over one's environment. Alongside such biologically based determinism were the impediments arising from external forces—a proto-Marxian sensibility that postulated how political, social, and other outside influences deprive individuals of free will. Such perspectives in literature combine to construct dark fictive worlds such as the implosive interpersonal tensions we find in "Boule de suif," where sexual traps and the horrors of war compel hypocrisy, moral cowardliness, and duplicity among French travelers attempting to flee from the German invasion in 1870. In his famous biographical essay on his friend (published in *Partial Portraits* in 1888), James declared that "the sexual impulse [. . .] is none the less the wire that moves almost all M. de Maupassant's puppets." Although Zola and his disciple would grow to have aesthetic and other sorts of differences over the next decade, Maupassant still integrated several aspects of such naturalist assumptions into the fabric of many of his subsequent stories and novels.

Another extraordinary writer that Maupassant met at Flaubert's salon was Ivan Turgenev, author of *Fathers and Sons* (1862) but whose more profound impact upon Western literature was through *The Hunter's Sketches*, perhaps the most culturally significant short-story collection published during the nineteenth century. This anthology of twenty-five stories chronicles the diverse existences of Russian serfs, fusing sympathetic and harshly critical assessments of their plights. These fictional accounts influenced the calculations of Czar Alexander II in his 1861 decision to free the serfs after centuries of servitude. *The Hunter's Sketches* also marked the incipient moment of the local-color movement in fiction, when realistic writers accentuated locality and characterization over plot in their works.

In portraying the poor and the middle class of his native Normandy, Maupassant adopted such values. Similar to the ambivalent responses Turgenev had to his subjects, Maupassant found much to love, deplore, exalt, and pity in his Norman neighbors. At the lower part of the spectrum, he detested the self-denying miserliness and cruel avarice that dominated the day-to-day pursuits of the French poor. At the upper end, in "Les Prisonniers" (1884; "The Prisoners"), a lone Norman peasant proves to be extraordinarily cunning and brave in capturing enemy soldiers, an act that Maupassant positions in stark contrast to the incompetence of the French military during the Franco-Prussian War. In one story Maupassant could manipulate a reader into laughing at the ridiculous plight of "Ce cochon de Morin" (1882; "That Pig Morin"), and in the next we are compelled to pity a wife's impasse in "Première neige" (1883; "First Snow"). In effect, Maupassant renders the citizens of Normandy as if they were members of one imaginary family, who each has the capacity to exasperate and to enthrall, to disappoint and to charm us. We embrace them for their simple virtues while simultaneously yearning to abandon them for their susceptibility to folly. All in all, Maupassant experienced an intense loyalty and revulsion to the region. Like those to family, one's ties to one's neighbors can be complicated and disconcerting.

Influences less direct than Flaubert, Zola, and Turgenev but equally powerful abound in Maupassant's work. Certainly, he was one of the inheritors of a short-story tradition in France that Prosper Mérimée (1803–1870) had advanced. A more significant authorial model, however, had been a practitioner in the United States. Promoted by

Charles Baudelaire through translations and literary criticism, the tales and poems of Edgar Allan Poe had a sizable effect upon the direction of French artistic sensibilities during the last half of the nineteenth century. Using Gothic motifs and techniques, Poe explored what resided beyond the boundaries of human rationality, in effect studying abnormal psychology when medical science had yet to formalize a practical approach to the subject. Maupassant's life and imagination were replete with real acquaintances and fictional characters who existed on the fringes of sanity. Informed in part by his anxieties regarding his own mental health, he composed narratives from a disintegrating first-person point of view that are as horrific as any other *fin de siècle* text. As with Poe's narrators of "Ligeia" and "The Tell-Tale Heart," the unnamed narrator in Maupassant's "Le Horla" (1887) painfully recounts the ebbs and flows of his battle against madness, only to succumb in the end to a frenzied apocalypse of the self. For Maupassant, the greatest potential horrors in life were forever lurking in the darker recesses of the individual mind.

Baudelaire and Poe had another, more circular path of influence toward Maupassant. Their theories and approaches to poetics reinforced the aesthetic preferences of the Symbolists, a loose school of French poets that had for its headmaster Stéphane Mallarmé (1842–1898) and boasted prized pupils such as Arthur Rimbaud (1854–1891). Not only were the Symbolists interested in the utility of symbols in art, they advocated how the artist himself was empowered to create new ones. For instance, Mallarmé composed eulogistic sonnets for the tombs of Poe and Baudelaire in which he enshrines the artistic contribution both poets made to the world of the intellect.

Learning much from the Symbolist's ability to pack intense meaning into a word or phrase, Maupassant would often indicate the symbolic center of a story through its title. "Le Horla" names the omnipresent mental possibility that may unexpectedly drive us mad. "La Ficelle" (1883; "The Piece of String") identifies the seemingly insignificant moment or object that destroys the quality of life. "La Parure" (1884; "The Necklace") represents the folly of social pretentions and vain self-sacrifice. In effect, Maupassant's narratives have the muscle to embed symbols in our memory as indelible as those created in any lyric poem. I, for one, cannot look upon any woman wearing a gaudy diamond choker without recalling Mathilde Loisel, the egotistical protagonist of "La Parure."

The works of Poe, Mérimée, Baudelaire, and Mallarmé are but a few of the many literary models that Maupassant borrowed from in some cases and rebelled against in others. And these influences extended beyond the realms of fiction and poetry. Among philosophers, Maupassant became a particularly devoted reader of Arthur Schopenhauer (1788–1860) and Herbert Spencer (1820–1903). Philosophically foregrounding Freud's assumptions about the id and literary naturalism's pessimism regarding the absence of free will, Schopenhauer saw the sexual impulse as a mechanism that can never be satiated; Maupassant treated this subject in stories such as "Le Rendez-vous" (1889; "The Rendezvous"), where we see the vicious circles in courtship rituals. For Schopenhauer, the boredom with or despair of life that sexual compulsion generates can be relieved only by a Romantic escape in which an artist imagines an aesthetic alternative that intellectually supplants the banal images of everyday life.

During Maupassant's lifetime, Spencer was Western civilization's most famous public intellectual; his prolific philosophical, social, political, and cultural commentary attracted much notice among literati searching for new ways to look at human existence. In *The Philosophy of Style* (1852), Spencer advocated that a writer should invest as much energy as possible in constructing elegantly lean and syntactically nimble sentences so as to facilitate the reader's effortless comprehension of their content. Certainly, this rhetorical preference reinforced the years of Maupassant's lessons under Flaubert's tutelage. Although considered somewhat passé by sociologists nowadays, Spencer's social Darwinism—Spencer, not Darwin, coined the phrase "survival of the fittest"—provided some of the framework for the fierce confrontations between human beings in Maupassant stories such as "Aux champs" (1882; "In the Country").

Advancements in other artistic disciplines also shaped Maupassant's approach to fiction. The 1880s, the decade of his literary productivity, saw the reluctant acceptance by critics of the aesthetic and perceptual revolution effected by Impressionist painters such as Édouard Manet (1832–1883), Edgar Degas (1834–1917), Claude Monet (1840–1926), and Pierre-Auguste Renoir (1841–1919). Maupassant learned from the techniques of these men that one can create striking images in an audience's memory without relying upon a fanatical eye for photographic detail. Like the careful strokes from Manet's brush, Maupassant uses swaths of words to paint with skill and insight the personalities of his characters amid the imagistic realities in which they exist:

> The Countess de Mascaret came down just as her husband, who was coming home, appeared in the carriage entrance. He stopped for a few moments to look at his wife and grew rather pale. She was very beautiful, graceful, and distinguished looking, with her long oval face, her complexion like gilt ivory, her large gray eyes, and her black hair; and she got into her carriage without looking at him, without even seeming to have noticed him, with such a particularly high-bred air, that the furious jealousy by which he had been devoured for so long again gnawed at his heart ("L'Inutile Beauté," p. 299).

As did Degas, Maupassant became well aware of the transforming powers of light. In fact, he titled an 1885 compilation *Contes du jour et de la nuit* (*Stories of Day and Night*). Quite often, the shifting physical lighting effects upon a scene parallel movement in moral light. Thus in "Le Lit 29" (1884; "Bed No. 29"), the eerie atmosphere in a hospice following the Franco-Prussian War forces a military officer to see his dying former lover in a bizarrely different patriotic light. Like his Impressionist cousins, Maupassant sought for that one moment in human life that was pregnant with meaning—an epiphany that explains the banality, futility, or truth permeating an individual's entire existence.

Maupassant synthesized these disparate artistic, social, philosophical, and political forces into an uncompromising personal conception of a world filled with occasional brutality, frequent despair, and
continual irony. In "L'Inutile Beauté," a story infused with Schopenhauer's assumptions, which he composed toward the end of his writing career, Maupassant could finally articulate his vision of the proper
place of the artist in a world ill-wrought by God:

> "It is sufficient to reflect for a moment, in order to understand
> that this world was not made for such creatures as we are.
> Thought, which is developed by a miracle in the nerves of the
> cells in our brain, powerless, ignorant, and confused as it is, and
> as it will always remain, makes all of us who are intellectual be-
> ings eternal and wretched exiles on earth" (p. 312).

In effect, Maupassant believed himself to be an intellectual expatriate who seldom physically left his native France. There were no
permanent escapes from Zola's pessimism about deterministic existence, from Poe's horror of the maddening threats to rationality,
from Spencer's theory that animalistic qualities dominate human in-
stitutions, or from Schopenhauer's grief about how sexual urges
deprive life of meaning and purpose.

More so than his efforts with the novel and poetry, Maupassant
sought in more than 300 short stories temporary moments of Romantic escape from the ennui that dominates life, especially by studying how civilization repeatedly thwarts human aspirations. Many
subjects that he broached in his fiction were the qualities of life that
exasperated him the most. The lasting ignominy he and his generation felt at their 1871 defeat at the hands of the Germans surfaced as
themes in stories such as "Boule de suif," "La Mère sauvage" (1884;
"Mother Savage"), and many other attempts to fathom the war's impact upon the national psyche. His fear of the debilitating effects of
syphilis injected itself in terse examinations of creeping insanity in
efforts such as "Le Horla," "Fou?" (1882; "Mad?"), and "Un lâche"

(1884; "A Coward"). The symbiotic pride and loathing he had for the Norman poor became a frequent ambivalence in his regional stories, appearing in "La Ficelle" and "Le Diable" (1886; "The Devil"), among many others.

Most of the stories selected for this volume involve in various ways another focus that fascinated and frustrated Maupassant greatly—women. On one hand, women aroused the subconscious desires that Schopenhauer thought diminished the quality of existence. On the other, they inspired in Maupassant idiosyncratic ideals of beauty to which male artists should aspire. Dante had his Beatrice, Petrarch his Laura, Shakespeare his dark lady, but Maupassant was incapable of synthesizing his vision of woman to a single body. His own sexual exploits were legion and infamous, even amid the decadence of nineteenth-century Paris. Each conquest became an illusionary epiphany that quickly dissipated its explanatory power. In a way, reading a Maupassant story resembles achieving a similar momentary intellectual pleasure—grasping the impressionistic truth underlying a character's situation before the sensation diffuses, returning us to our own commonplace realities.

Maupassant's study of women in his fiction allowed him to explore the extremes of all human relationships and the intricacies of his own reactions to them. As one of his characters in "Réveil" (1883; "The Awakening") quips, "women are really very strange, complicated, and inexplicable beings" (p. 86). Maupassant could at one moment portray a woman caustically, as he does with the self-important socialites in "Boule de suif," and at the next moment tenderly, as he does with the ingénue in "Yvette" (1884). He could play the part of the emphatically chauvinistic author, who in stories such as "Mouche" rendered women as iconic sexual playthings. Or he could become the surprising feminist who penned "L'Inutile Beauté," in which a wife rebels against becoming a "brood mare" for her possessive husband. This capability to immerse himself into so many different gender roles would inspire writers across the Western world, including American Kate Chopin (author of *The Awakening*, 1899), who used

Maupassant's work as a catalyst to her own sexual liberation in fiction.

Through his at times hesitant and at other times embracing sketches of the plights and wiles of women, Maupassant strove to comprehend the meaning of all existence. Sometimes his insights are tantalizingly irresolvable. Are Maupassant's contemporary readers to feel pity or pride for Irma, the former lover of Captain Epivent in "Le Lit 29," who boasts on her deathbed that she deliberately infected German invaders with her syphilis during the war? Do we celebrate the rescue of young Yvette from her suicide attempt, or do we resign ourselves that her life will follow the path of her courtesan mother? Often, Maupassant constructed stories unsympathetic to female sensibilities, sometimes even asserting that women are deviously calculating. Told from the viewpoint of a socially experienced woman, "Le Baiser" (1884; "The Kiss") investigates the unromantic, often farcical, mechanics of lovemaking. A woman in "Le Modèle" (1883; "The Model") exploits her departing lover's guilt-filled humanity to trap him into marriage, which displaces his devotion from pursuing art to caring for his self-crippled wife. For Maupassant, one's compulsive pursuit of the feminine ideal had the power to destroy the pursuer. In "La Femme de Paul" (1881; "Paul's Mistress"), for instance, when a woman leaves the protagonist to rendezvous with her lesbian lover, the once pretentious young man experiences a suicidal spiral of emasculation. Had they not been linked by the poetic blueprint of Maupassant's terse, symbol-laden prose style, a reader could find it difficult to believe that one writer was capable of empathizing with so many antithetical perspectives.

Thus, among his short stories, women often became the metaphysical conceit by which Maupassant struggled to comprehend human experience. The fathomless depths of his subject prevented direct and logical observation. Consequently, each story attempts to discern one dimension, and the assembly of hundreds of such glimpses surrounds the center of an overwhelming, illusive secret. Like Schopenhauer, Maupassant sought relief from the insipid routines of life by seeking for the beauty that exists beyond the capacities of nature. In "L'Inutile Beauté," during an intermission at a theater, dilettante Roger de Salnis delights from afar at the sight of the self-liberated, impeccably coiffeured, elegantly dressed, socially dazzling Gabrielle de Mascaret and muses:

> "As to ourselves, the more civilized, intellectual, and refined we are, the more we ought to conquer and subdue that animal instinct, which represents the will of God in us. . . .
> "Look at that woman, Madame de Mascaret. God intended her to live in a cave naked, or wrapped up in the skins of wild animals, but is she not better as she is?" (pp. 312–313)

If women, beauty, truth, and the ideal are all one and the same, then they represent the artifices by which artists seek to evade the will of God for a moment; so Maupassant welcomed the decadent mood of his generation because every insight in fiction proved vestigial, never offering sustained relief from his eternal and wretched reality. But his drive to search for meaning nevertheless fueled his ten-year frenetic composition of hundreds of stories, each of which invites us to share a somber moment of anger, regret, wonder, or irony with a skilled and discerning observer of mankind. For Maupassant, only disease, insanity, and death could still his quixotic search for beauty, which cruelly and mercifully ended in a lonely asylum on July 6, 1893.

RICHARD FUSCO received his Ph.D. from Duke University in 1990. Since 1997 he has taught at Saint Joseph's University in Philadelphia, where he is currently an associate professor. A specialist in nineteenth-century American fiction and in short-story narrative theory, he has published monographs about the works of a variety of American, British, and Continental literary figures, including Edgar Allan Poe, Guy de Maupassant, Henry James, Kate Chopin, Ambrose Bierce, O. Henry, Nathaniel Hawthorne, Jack London, John Reuben Thompson, Thomas Carlyle, Charles Dickens, Wilkie Collins, Arthur Conan Doyle, Dashiell Hammett, and Raymond Chandler. His major works of criticism include *Maupassant and the American Short Story: The Influence of Form at the Turn of the Century* (Pennsylvania State University Press, 1994) and *Fin de millénaire: Poe's Legacy for the Detective Story* (Enoch Pratt Free Library, 1993). He also composed the introductory essay "Stephen Crane Said to the Universe" and the notes for *The Red Badge of Courage and Selected Short Fiction* (Barnes & Noble Classics, 2004). From 2004 to 2007, he was coeditor of *The Edgar Allan Poe Review*. He dedicates this introductory essay to the memory of Wallace Fowlie, teacher and friend.

THE COLLECTED STORIES OF
GUY DE MAUPASSANT

BALL-OF-FAT

FOR MANY DAYS NOW the fag-end of the army had been straggling through the town. They were not troops, but a disbanded horde. The beards of the men were long and filthy, their uniforms in tatters, and they advanced at an easy pace without flag or regiment. All seemed worn-out and back-broken, incapable of a thought or a resolution, marching by habit solely, and falling from fatigue as soon as they stopped. In short, they were a mobilized, pacific people, bending under the weight of the gun; some little squads on the alert, easy to take alarm and prompt in enthusiasm, ready to attack or to flee; and in the midst of them, some red breeches, the remains of a division broken up in a great battle; some somber artillery men in line with these varied kinds of foot soldiers; and, sometimes the brilliant helmet of a dragoon on foot who followed with difficulty the shortest march of the lines.

Some legions of free-shooters, under the heroic names of "Avengers of the Defeat," "Citizens of the Tomb," "Partakers of Death," passed in their turn with the air of bandits.

Their leaders were former cloth or grain merchants, ex-merchants in tallow or soap, warriors of circumstance, elected officers on account of their escutcheons and the length of their mustaches, covered with arms and with braid, speaking in constrained voices, discussing plans of campaign, and pretending to carry agonized France alone on their swaggering shoulders, but sometimes fearing their own soldiers, prison-birds, that were often brave at first and later proved to be plunderers and debauchees.

It was said that the Prussians were going to enter Rouen.

The National Guard who for two months had been carefully

reconnoitering in the neighboring woods, shooting sometimes their own sentinels, and ready for a combat whenever a little wolf stirred in the thicket, had now returned to their firesides. Their arms, their uniforms, all the murderous accoutrements with which they had lately struck fear into the national heart for three leagues in every direction, had suddenly disappeared.

The last French soldiers finally came across the Seine to reach the Audemer bridge through Saint-Sever and Bourg-Achard; and, marching behind, on foot, between two officers of ordnance, the General, in despair, unable to do anything with these incongruous tatters, himself lost in the breaking-up of a people accustomed to conquer, and disastrously beaten, in spite of his legendary bravery.[1]

A profound calm, a frightful, silent expectancy had spread over the city. Many of the heavy citizens, emasculated by commerce, anxiously awaited the conquerors, trembling lest their roasting spits or kitchen knives be considered arms.

All life seemed stopped; shops were closed, the streets dumb. Sometimes an inhabitant, intimidated by this silence, moved rapidly along next the walls. The agony of waiting made them wish the enemy would come.

In the afternoon of the day which followed the departure of the French troops, some uhlans, coming from one knows not where, crossed the town with celerity. Then, a little later, a black mass descended the side of St. Catharine, while two other invading bands appeared by the way of Darnetal and Boisguillaume. The advance guard of the three bodies joined one another at the same moment in Hotel de Ville square and, by all the neighboring streets, the German army continued to arrive, spreading out its battalions, making the pavement resound under their hard, rhythmic step.

Some orders of the commander, in a foreign, guttural voice, reached the houses which seemed dead and deserted, while behind closed shutters, eyes were watching these victorious men, masters of the city, of fortunes, of lives, through the "rights of war." The inhabitants, shut up in their rooms, were visited with the kind of excitement that a cataclysm, or some fatal upheaval of the earth, brings to us, against which all wisdom, all force is useless. For the same sensation is produced each time that the established order of things is overturned, when security no longer exists, and all that protect the laws of man and of nature find themselves at the mercy of unreasoning, ferocious brutality. The trembling of the earth crushing the houses and burying an entire people; a river overflowing its banks and carrying in its course the drowned peasants, carcasses of beeves, and girders snatched from roofs, or a glorious army massacring those trying to defend themselves, leading others prisoners, pillaging in the name of the Sword and thanking God to the sound of the cannon, all are alike frightful scourges which disconcert all belief in eternal justice, all the confidence that we have in the protection of Heaven and the reason of man.

Some detachments rapped at each door, then disappeared into the houses. It was occupation after invasion. Then the duty commences for the conquered to show themselves gracious toward the conquerors.

After some time, as soon as the first terror disappears, a new calm is established. In many families, the Prussian officer eats at the table. He is sometimes well bred and, through politeness, pities France, and speaks of his repugnance in taking part in this affair. One is grateful to him for this sentiment; then, one may be, some day or other, in need of his protection. By treating him well, one has, perhaps, a less number of men to feed. And why should we wound anyone on whom we are entirely dependent? To act thus would be less bravery than temerity. And temerity is no longer a fault of the commoner of Rouen, as it was at the time of the heroic defense, when their city became famous. Finally, each told himself that the highest judgment of French urbanity required that they be allowed to be polite to the strange soldier in the house, provided they did not show themselves familiar with him in public. Outside they would not make themselves known to each other, but at home they could chat freely, and the German might remain longer each evening warming his feet at their hearthstones.

The town even took on, little by little, its ordinary aspect. The

French scarcely went out, but the Prussian soldiers grumbled in the streets. In short, the officers of the Blue Hussars, who dragged with arrogance their great weapons of death up and down the pavement, seemed to have no more grievous scorn for the simple citizens than the officers or the sportsmen who, the year before, drank in the same *cafés*.

There was nevertheless, something in the air, something subtle and unknown, a strange, intolerable atmosphere, like a penetrating odor, the odor of invasion. It filled the dwellings and the public places, changed the taste of the food, gave the impression of being on a journey, far away, among barbarous and dangerous tribes.

The conquerors exacted money, much money. The inhabitants always paid and they were rich enough to do it. But the richer a trading Norman becomes the more he suffers at every outlay, at each part of his fortune that he sees pass from his hands into those of another.

Therefore, two or three leagues below the town, following the course of the river toward Croisset, Dieppedalle, or Biessart, mariners and fishermen often picked up the swollen corpse of a German in uniform from the bottom of the river, killed by the blow of a knife, the head crushed with a stone, or perhaps thrown into the water by a push from the high bridge. The slime of the river bed buried these obscure vengeances, savage, but legitimate, unknown heroisms, mute attacks more perilous than the battles of broad day, and without the echoing sound of glory.

For hatred of the foreigner always arouses some intrepid ones, who are ready to die for an idea.

Finally, as soon as the invaders had brought the town quite under subjection with their inflexible discipline, without having been guilty of any of the horrors for which they were famous along their triumphal line of march, people began to take courage, and the need of trade put new heart into the commerce of the country. Some had large interests at Havre, which the French army occupied, and they wished to try and reach this port by going to Dieppe by land and there embarking.

They used their influence with the German soldiers with whom they had an acquaintance, and finally, an authorization of departure was obtained from the General-in-chief.

Then, a large diligence,* with four horses, having been engaged for this journey, and ten persons having engaged seats in it, it was resolved to set out on Tuesday morning before daylight, in order to escape observation.

For some time before, the frost had been hardening the earth and on Monday, toward three o'clock, great black clouds coming from the north brought the snow which fell without interruption during the evening and all night.

At half past four in the morning, the travelers met in the courtyard of Hotel Normandie, where they were to take the carriage.

They were still full of sleep, and shivering with cold under their wraps. They could only see each other dimly in the obscure light, and the accumulation of heavy winter garments made them all resemble fat curates in long cassocks. Only two of the men were acquainted; a third accosted them and they chatted: "I'm going to take my wife," said one. "I too," said another. "And I," said the third. The first added: "We shall not return to Rouen, and if the Prussians approach Havre, we shall go over to England." All had the same projects, being of the same mind.

As yet the horses were not harnessed. A little lantern, carried by a stable boy, went out one door from time to time, to immediately appear at another. The feet of the horses striking the floor could be heard, although deadened by the straw and litter, and the voice of a man talking to the beasts, sometimes swearing, came from the end of the building. A light tinkling of bells announced that they were taking down the harness; this murmur soon became a clear and continuous rhythm by the movement of the animal, stopping sometimes, then breaking into a brusque shake which was accompanied by the dull stamp of a sabot upon the hard earth.

The door suddenly closed. All noise ceased. The frozen citizens were silent; they remained immovable and stiff.

---

* Stagecoach (French; unless otherwise noted, translations are from the French).

A curtain of uninterrupted white flakes constantly sparkled in its descent to the ground. It effaced forms, and powdered everything with a downy moss. And nothing could be heard in the great silence. The town was calm, and buried under the wintry frost, as this fall of snow, unnamable and floating, a sensation rather than a sound (trembling atoms which only seem to fill all space), came to cover the earth.

The man reappeared with his lantern, pulling at the end of a rope a sad horse which would not come willingly. He placed him against the pole, fastened the traces, walked about a long time adjusting the harness, for he had the use of but one hand, the other carrying the lantern. As he went for the second horse, he noticed the travelers, motionless, already white with snow, and said to them: "Why not get into the carriage? You will be under cover, at least."

They had evidently not thought of it, and they hastened to do so. The three men installed their wives at the back and then followed them. Then the other forms, undecided and veiled, took in their turn the last places without exchanging a word.

The floor was covered with straw, in which the feet ensconced themselves. The ladies at the back having brought little copper foot stoves, with a carbon fire, lighted them and, for some time, in low voices, enumerated the advantages of the appliances, repeating things that they had known for a long time.

Finally, the carriage was harnessed with six horses instead of four, because the traveling was very bad, and a voice called out:

"Is everybody aboard?"

And a voice within answered: "Yes."

They were off. The carriage moved slowly, slowly for a little way. The wheels were imbedded in the snow; the whole body groaned with heavy cracking sounds; the horses glistened, puffed, and smoked; and the great whip of the driver snapped without ceasing, hovering about on all sides, knotting and unrolling itself like a thin serpent, lashing brusquely some horse on the rebound, which then put forth its most violent effort.

Now the day was imperceptibly dawning. The light flakes, which one of the travelers, a Rouenese by birth, said looked like a shower of cotton, no longer fell. A faint light filtered through the great, dull clouds, which rendered more brilliant the white of the fields, where appeared a line of great trees clothed in whiteness, or a chimney with a cap of snow.

In the carriage, each looked at the others curiously, in the sad light of this dawn.

At the back, in the best places, Mr. Loiseau, wholesale merchant of wine, of Grand-Pont street, and Mrs. Loiseau were sleeping opposite each other. Loiseau had bought out his former patron who failed in business, and made his fortune. He sold bad wine at a good price to small retailers in the country, and passed among his friends and acquaintances as a knavish wag, a true Norman full of deceit and joviality.

His reputation as a sharper was so well established that one evening at the residence of the prefect, Mr. Tournel, author of some fables and songs, of keen, satirical mind, a local celebrity, having proposed to some ladies, who seemed to be getting a little sleepy, that they make up a game of "Loiseau tricks," the joke traversed the rooms of the prefect, reached those of the town, and then, in the months to come, made many a face in the province expand with laughter.

Loiseau was especially known for his love of farce of every kind, for his jokes, good and bad; and no one could ever talk with him without thinking: "He is invaluable, this Loiseau." Of tall figure, his balloon-shaped front was surmounted by a ruddy face surrounded by gray whiskers.

His wife, large, strong, and resolute, with a quick, decisive manner, was the order and arithmetic of this house of commerce, while he was the life of it through his joyous activity.

Beside them, Mr. Carré-Lamadon held himself with great dignity, as if belonging to a superior caste; a considerable man, in cottons, proprietor of three mills, officer of the Legion of Honor, and member of the General Council. He had remained, during the Empire, chief of the friendly opposition, famous for making the Emperor pay more dear for rallying to the cause than if he had combated it with blunted arms, according to his own story. Madame Carré-Lamadon, much younger than her husband, was the consolation of officers of good family sent to Rouen in garrison. She sat opposite her husband, very dainty, petite, and pretty, wrapped closely in furs and looking with sad eyes at the interior of the carriage.

Her neighbors, the Count and Countess Hubert de Breville, bore the name of one of the most ancient and noble families of Normandy. The Count, an old gentleman of good figure, accentuated, by the artifices of his toilette, his resemblance to King Henry IV., who, following a glorious legend of the family, had impregnated one of the De Breville ladies, whose husband, for this reason, was made a count and governor of the province.

A colleague of Mr. Carré-Lamadon in the General Council, Count Hubert represented the Orléans party in the Department.[2]

The story of his marriage with the daughter of a little captain of a privateer had always remained a mystery. But as the Countess had a grand air, received better than anyone, and passed for having been loved by the son of Louis Philippe, all the nobility did her honor, and her salon remained the first in the country, the only one which preserved the old gallantry, and to which the *entrée* was difficult. The fortune of the Brevilles amounted, it was said, to five hundred thousand francs in income, all in good securities.

These six persons formed the foundation of the carriage company, the society side, serene and strong, honest, established people, who had both religion and principles.

By a strange chance, all the women were upon the same seat; and the Countess had for neighbors two sisters who picked at long strings of beads and muttered some *Paters* and *Aves*.* One was old and as pitted with smallpox as if she had received a broadside of grapeshot full in the face. The other, very sad, had a pretty face and a disease of the lungs, which, added to their devoted faith, illumined them and made them appear like martyrs.

---

* That is, Our Fathers and Hail Marys, common Christian prayers.

Opposite these two devotees were a man and a woman who attracted the notice of all. The man, well known, was Cornudet the democrat, the terror of respectable people. For twenty years he had soaked his great red beard in the *bocks* of all the democratic *cafés*. He had consumed with his friends and *confrères* a rather pretty fortune left him by his father, an old confectioner, and he awaited the establishing of the Republic with impatience, that he might have the position he merited by his great expenditures. On the fourth of September, by some joke perhaps, he believed himself elected prefect, but when he went to assume the duties, the clerks of the office were masters of the place and refused to recognize him, obliging him to retreat. Rather a good bachelor, on the whole, inoffensive and serviceable, he had busied himself, with incomparable ardor, in organizing the defense against the Prussians. He had dug holes in all the plains, cut down young trees from the neighboring forests, sown snares over all routes and, at the approach of the enemy, took himself quickly back to the town. He now thought he could be of more use in Havre where more entrenchments would be necessary.

The woman, one of those called a coquette, was celebrated for her *embonpoint,* * which had given her the nickname of "Ball-of-Fat." Small, round, and fat as lard, with puffy fingers choked at the phalanges, like chaplets of short sausages; with a stretched and shining skin, an enormous bosom which shook under her dress, she was, nevertheless, pleasing and sought after, on account of a certain freshness and breeziness of disposition. Her face was a round apple, a peony bud ready to pop into bloom, and inside that opened two great black eyes, shaded with thick brows that cast a shadow within; and below, a charming mouth, humid for kissing, furnished with shining, microscopic baby teeth. She was, it was said, full of admirable qualities.

As soon as she was recognized, a whisper went around among the honest women, and the words "prostitute" and "public shame" were whispered so loud that she raised her head. Then she threw at her

---

* Portliness.

neighbors such a provoking, courageous look that a great silence reigned, and everybody looked down except Loiseau, who watched her with an exhilarated air.

And immediately conversation began among the three ladies, whom the presence of this girl had suddenly rendered friendly, almost intimate. It seemed to them they should bring their married dignity into union in opposition to that sold without shame; for legal love always takes on a tone of contempt for its free *confrère*.

The three men, also drawn together by an instinct of preservation at the sight of Cornudet, talked money with a certain high tone of disdain for the poor. Count Hubert talked of the havoc which the Prussians had caused, the losses which resulted from being robbed of cattle and from destroyed crops, with the assurance of a great lord, ten times millionaire whom these ravages would scarcely cramp for a year. Mr. Carré-Lamadon, largely experienced in the cotton industry, had had need of sending six hundred thousand francs to England, as a trifle in reserve if it should be needed. As for Loiseau, he had arranged with the French administration to sell them all the wines that remained in his cellars, on account of which the State owed him a formidable sum, which he counted on collecting at Havre.

And all three threw toward each other swift and amicable glances.

Although in different conditions, they felt themselves to be brothers through money, that grand freemasonry of those who possess it, and make the gold rattle by putting their hands in their trousers' pockets.

The carriage went so slowly that at ten o'clock in the morning they had not gone four leagues. The men had got down three times to climb hills on foot. They began to be disturbed, because they should be now taking breakfast at Tôtes and they despaired now of reaching there before night. Each one had begun to watch for an inn along the route, when the carriage foundered in a snowdrift, and it took two hours to extricate it.

Growing appetites troubled their minds; and no eating-house, no wine shop showed itself, the approach of the Prussians and the passage of the troops having frightened away all these industries.

The gentlemen ran to the farms along the way for provisions, but they did not even find bread, for the defiant peasant had concealed his stores for fear of being pillaged by the soldiers who, having nothing to put between their teeth, took by force whatever they discovered.

Toward one o'clock in the afternoon, Loiseau announced that there was a decided hollow in his stomach. Everybody suffered with him, and the violent need of eating, ever increasing, had killed conversation.

From time to time some one yawned; another immediately imitated him; and each, in his turn, in accordance with his character, his knowledge of life, and his social position, opened his mouth with carelessness or modesty, placing his hand quickly before the yawning hole from whence issued a vapor.

Ball-of-Fat, after many attempts, bent down as if seeking something under her skirts. She hesitated a second, looked at her neighbors, then sat up again tranquilly. The faces were pale and drawn. Loiseau affirmed that he would give a thousand francs for a small ham. His wife made a gesture, as if in protest; but she kept quiet. She was always troubled when anyone spoke of squandering money, and could not comprehend any pleasantry on the subject. "The fact is," said the Count, "I cannot understand why I did not think to bring some provisions with me." Each reproached himself in the same way.

However, Cornudet had a flask full of rum. He offered it; it was refused coldly. Loiseau alone accepted two swallows, and then passed back the flask saying, by way of thanks: "It is good all the same; it is warming and checks the appetite." The alcohol put him in good-humor and he proposed that they do as they did on the little ship in the song, eat the fattest of the passengers. This indirect allusion to Ball-of-Fat choked the well-bred people. They said nothing. Cornudet alone laughed. The two good sisters had ceased to mumble their rosaries and, with their hands enfolded in their great sleeves, held themselves immovable, obstinately lowering their eyes, without doubt offering to Heaven the suffering it had brought upon them.

Finally, at three o'clock, when they found themselves in the midst of an interminable plain, without a single village in sight, Ball-of-Fat bending down quickly drew from under the seat a large basket covered with a white napkin.

At first she brought out a little china plate and a silver cup; then a large dish in which there were two whole chickens, cut up and imbedded in their own jelly. And one could still see in the basket other good things, some *pâtés*, fruits, and sweetmeats, provisions for three days if they should not see the kitchen of an inn. Four necks of bottles were seen among the packages of food. She took a wing of a chicken and began to eat it delicately, with one of those little biscuits called "Regence" in Normandy.

All looks were turned in her direction. Then the odor spread, enlarging the nostrils and making the mouth water, besides causing a painful contraction of the jaw behind the ears. The scorn of the women for this girl became ferocious, as if they had a desire to kill her and throw her out of the carriage into the snow, her, her silver cup, her basket, provisions and all.

But Loiseau with his eyes devoured the dish of chicken. He said: "Fortunately, Madame had more precaution than we. There are some people who know how to think ahead always."

She turned toward him, saying: "If you would like some of it, sir? It is hard to go without breakfast so long."

He saluted her and replied: "Faith, I frankly cannot refuse; I can stand it no longer. Everything goes in time of war, does it not, Madame?" And then casting a comprehensive glance around, he added: "In moments like this, one can but be pleased to find people who are obliging."

He had a newspaper which he spread out on his knees, that no spot might come to his pantaloons, and upon the point of a knife that he always carried in his pocket, he took up a leg all glistening with jelly, put it between his teeth and masticated it with a satisfaction so evident that there ran through the carriage a great sigh of distress.

Then Ball-of-Fat, in a sweet and humble voice, proposed that the two sisters partake of her collation. They both accepted instantly and, without raising their eyes, began to eat very quickly, after stammering their thanks. Cornudet no longer refused the offers of his neighbor, and they formed with the sisters a sort of table, by spreading out some newspapers upon their knees.

The mouths opened and shut without ceasing, they masticated, swallowed, gulping ferociously. Loiseau in his corner was working hard and, in a low voice, was trying to induce his wife to follow his example. She resisted for a long time; then, when a drawn sensation ran through her body, she yielded. Her husband, rounding his phrase, asked their "charming companion" if he might be allowed to offer a little piece to Madame Loiseau.

She replied: "Why, yes, certainly, sir," with an amiable smile, as she passed the dish.

An embarrassing thing confronted them when they opened the first bottle of Bordeaux: they had but one cup. Each passed it after having tasted. Cornudet alone, for politeness without doubt, placed his lips at the spot left humid by his fair neighbor.

Then, surrounded by people eating, suffocated by the odors of the food, the Count and Countess de Breville, as well as Madame and M. Carré-Lamadon, were suffering that odious torment which has preserved the name of Tantalus. Suddenly the young wife of the manufacturer gave forth such a sigh that all heads were turned in her direction; she was as white as the snow without; her eyes closed, her head drooped; she had lost consciousness. Her husband, much excited, implored the help of everybody. Each lost his head completely, until the elder of the two sisters, holding the head of the sufferer, slipped Ball-of-Fat's cup between her lips and forced her to swallow a few drops of wine. The pretty little lady revived, opened her eyes, smiled, and declared in a dying voice that she felt very well now. But, in order that the attack might not return, the sister urged her to drink a full glass of Bordeaux, and added: "It is just hunger, nothing more."

Then Ball-of-Fat, blushing and embarrassed, looked at the four travelers who had fasted and stammered: "Goodness knows! if I dared to offer anything to these gentlemen and ladies, I would—" Then she was silent, as if fearing an insult. Loiseau took up the word: "Ah! certainly, in times like these all the world are brothers and ought to aid each other. Come, ladies, without ceremony; why the devil not accept? We do not know whether we shall even find a house where we can pass the night. At the pace we are going now, we shall not reach Tôtes before noon tomorrow——"

They still hesitated, no one daring to assume the responsibility of a "Yes." The Count decided the question. He turned toward the fat, intimidated girl and, taking on a grand air of condescension, he said to her:

"We accept with gratitude, Madame."

It is the first step that counts. The Rubicon passed, one lends himself to the occasion squarely. The basket was stripped. It still contained a *pate de foie gras,* a *pâté* of larks, a piece of smoked tongue, some preserved pears, a loaf of hard bread, some wafers, and a full cup of pickled gherkins and onions, of which crudities Ball-of-Fat, like all women, was extremely fond.

They could not eat this girl's provisions without speaking to her. And so they chatted, with reserve at first; then, as she carried herself well, with more abandon. The ladies De Breville and Carré-Lamadon, who were acquainted with all the ins and outs of good-breeding, were gracious with a certain delicacy. The Countess, especially, showed that amiable condescension of very noble ladies who do not fear being soiled by contact with anyone, and was charming. But the great Madame Loiseau, who had the soul of a plebeian, remained crabbed, saying little and eating much.

The conversation was about the war, naturally. They related the horrible deeds of the Prussians, the brave acts of the French; and all of them, although running away, did homage to those who stayed behind. Then personal stories began to be told, and Ball-of-Fat related, with sincere emotion, and in the heated words that such girls sometimes use in expressing their natural feelings, how she had left Rouen:

"I believed at first that I could remain," said she. "I had my house full of provisions, and I preferred to feed a few soldiers rather than expatriate myself, to go I knew not where. But as soon as I saw them, those Prussians, that was too much for me! they made my blood boil with anger, and I wept for very shame all day long. Oh! if I were only a man! I watched them from my windows, the great porkers with their pointed helmets, and my maid held my hands to keep me from throwing the furniture down upon them. Then one of them came to lodge at my house; I sprang at his throat the first thing; they are no more difficult to strangle than other people. And I should have put an end to that one then and there had they not pulled me away by the hair. After that, it was necessary to keep out of sight. And finally, when I found an opportunity, I left town and—here I am!"

They congratulated her. She grew in the estimation of her companions, who had not shown themselves so hot-brained, and Cornudet, while listening to her, took on the approving, benevolent smile of an apostle, as a priest would if he heard a devotee praise God, for the long-bearded democrats have a monopoly of patriotism, as the men in cassocks have of religion. In his turn he spoke, in a doctrinal tone, with the emphasis of a proclamation such as we see pasted on the walls about town, and finished by a bit of eloquence whereby he gave that "scamp of a Badinguet" a good lashing.

Then Ball-of-Fat was angry, for she was a Bonapartist.[3] She grew redder than a cherry and, stammering with indignation, said:

"I would like to have seen you in his place, you other people. Then everything would have been quite right; oh, yes! It is you who have betrayed this man! One would never have had to leave France if it had been governed by blackguards like you!"

Cornudet, undisturbed, preserved a disdainful, superior smile, but all felt that the high note had been struck, until the Count, not without some difficulty, calmed the exasperated girl and proclaimed with a manner of authority that all sincere opinions should be respected. But the Countess and the manufacturer's wife, who had in their souls an unreasonable hatred for the people that favor a Republic, and the same instinctive tenderness that all women have for a decorative, despotic government, felt themselves drawn, in spite of themselves, toward this prostitute so full of dignity, whose sentiments so strongly resembled their own.

The basket was empty. By ten o'clock they had easily exhausted the contents and regretted that there was not more. Conversation continued for some time, but a little more coldly since they had finished eating.

The night fell, the darkness little by little became profound, and the cold, felt more during digestion, made Ball-of-Fat shiver in spite of her plumpness. Then Madame de Breville offered her the little foot-stove, in which the fuel had been renewed many times since morning; she accepted it immediately, for her feet were becoming numb with cold. The ladies Carré-Lamadon and Loiseau gave theirs to the two religious sisters.

The driver had lighted his lanterns. They shone out with a lively glimmer showing a cloud of foam beyond, the sweat of the horses; and, on both sides of the way, the snow seemed to roll itself along under the moving reflection of the lights.

Inside the carriage one could distinguish nothing. But a sudden movement seemed to be made between Ball-of-Fat and Cornudet; and Loiseau, whose eye penetrated the shadow, believed that he saw the big-bearded man start back quickly as if he had received a swift, noiseless blow.

Then some twinkling points of fire appeared in the distance along the road. It was Tôtes. They had traveled eleven hours, which, with the two hours given to resting and feeding the horses, made thirteen. They entered the town and stopped before the Hotel of Commerce.

The carriage door opened! A well-known sound gave the travelers a start; it was the scabbard of a sword hitting the ground. Immediately a German voice was heard in the darkness.

Although the diligence was not moving, no one offered to alight, fearing some one might be waiting to murder them as they stepped out. Then the conductor appeared, holding in his hand one of the lanterns which lighted the carriage to its depth, and showed the two rows of frightened faces, whose mouths were open and whose eyes were wide with surprise and fear.

Outside beside the driver, in plain sight, stood a German officer, an excessively tall young man, thin and blond, squeezed into his uniform like a girl in a corset, and wearing on his head a flat, oilcloth cap which made him resemble the porter of an English hotel. His enormous mustache, of long straight hairs, growing gradually thin at each side and terminating in a single blond thread so fine that one could not perceive where it ended, seemed to weigh heavily on the corners of his mouth and, drawing down the cheeks, left a decided wrinkle about the lips.

In Alsatian French, he invited the travelers to come in, saying in a suave tone: "Will you descend, gentlemen and ladies?"

The two good sisters were the first to obey, with the docility of saints accustomed ever to submission. The Count and Countess then appeared, followed by the manufacturer and his wife; then Loiseau, pushing ahead of him his larger half. The last-named, as he set foot on the earth, said to the officer: "Good evening, sir," more as a measure of prudence than politeness. The officer, insolent as all-powerful people usually are, looked at him without a word.

Ball-of-Fat and Cornudet, although nearest the door, were the last to descend, grave and haughty before the enemy. The fat girl tried to control herself and be calm. The democrat waved a tragic hand and his long beard seemed to tremble a little and grow redder. They wished to preserve their dignity, comprehending that in such meetings as these they represented in some degree their great country, and somewhat disgusted with the docility of her companions, the fat girl tried to show more pride than her neighbors, the honest women, and, as she felt that some one should set an example, she continued her attitude of resistance assumed at the beginning of the journey.

They entered the vast kitchen of the inn, and the German, having demanded their traveling papers signed by the General-in-chief (in which the name, the description, and profession of each traveler was mentioned), and having examined them all critically, comparing the people and their signatures, said: "It is quite right," and went out.

Then they breathed. They were still hungry and supper was ordered. A half hour was necessary to prepare it, and while two servants were attending to this they went to their rooms. They found them along a corridor which terminated in a large glazed door.

Finally, they sat down at table, when the proprietor of the inn himself appeared. He was a former horse merchant, a large, asthmatic man, with a constant wheezing and rattling in his throat. His father had left him the name of Follenvie. He asked:

"Is Miss Elizabeth Rousset here?"

Ball-of-Fat started as she answered: "It is I."

"The Prussian officer wishes to speak with you immediately."

"With me?"

"Yes, that is, if you are Miss Elizabeth Rousset."

She was disturbed, and reflecting for an instant, declared flatly:

"That is my name, but I shall not go."

A stir was felt around her; each discussed and tried to think of the cause of this order. The Count approached her, saying:

"You are wrong, Madame, for your refusal may lead to considerable difficulty, not only for yourself, but for all your companions. It is never worth while to resist those in power. This request cannot assuredly bring any danger; it is, without doubt, about some forgotten formality."

Everybody agreed with him, asking, begging, beseeching her to go, and at last they convinced her that it was best; they all feared the complications that might result from disobedience. She finally said:

"It is for you that I do this, you understand."

The Countess took her by the hand, saying: "And we are grateful to you for it."

She went out. They waited before sitting down at table.

Each one regretted not having been sent for in the place of this violent, irascible girl, and mentally prepared some platitudes, in case they should be called in their turn.

But at the end of ten minutes she reappeared, out of breath, red to suffocation, and exasperated. She stammered: "Oh! the rascal! the rascal!"

All gathered around to learn something, but she said nothing; and when the Count insisted, she responded with great dignity: "No, it does not concern you; I can say nothing."

Then they all seated themselves around a high soup tureen whence came the odor of cabbage. In spite of alarm, the supper was gay. The cider was good, the beverage Loiseau and the good sisters took as a means of economy. The others called for wine; Cornudet demanded beer. He had a special fashion of uncorking the bottle, making froth on the liquid, carefully filling the glass and then holding it before the light to better appreciate the color. When he drank, his great beard, which still kept some of the foam of his beloved beverage, seemed to tremble with tenderness; his eyes were squinted, in order not to lose sight of his tipple, and he had the unique air of fulfilling the function for which he was born. One would say that there was in his mind a meeting, like that of affinities, between the two great passions that occupied his life—Pale Ale and Revolutions; and assuredly he could not taste the one without thinking of the other.

Mr. and Mrs. Follenvie dined at the end of the table. The man, rattling like a cracked locomotive, had too much trouble in breathing to talk while eating, but his wife was never silent. She told all her impressions at the arrival of the Prussians, what they did, what they said, reviling them because they cost her some money, and because she had two sons in the army. She addressed herself especially to the Countess, flattered by being able to talk with a lady of quality.

When she lowered her voice to say some delicate thing, her husband would interrupt, from time to time, with: "You had better keep silent, Madame Follenvie." But she paid no attention, continuing in this fashion:

"Yes, Madame, those people there not only eat our potatoes and pork, but our pork and potatoes. And it must not be believed that they are at all proper—oh, no! such filthy things they do, saving the respect I owe to you! And if you could see them exercise for hours in the day! They are all there in the field, marching ahead, then marching back, turning here and turning there. They might be cultivating the land, or at least working on the roads of their own country! But no, Madame, these military men are profitable to no one. Poor people have to feed them, or perhaps be murdered! I am only an old woman without education, it is true, but when I see some endangering their constitutions by raging from morning to night, I say: When there are so many people found to be useless, how unnecessary it is for others to take so much trouble to be nuisances! Truly, is it not an abomination to kill people, whether they be Prussian, or English, or Polish, or French? If one man revenges himself upon another who has done him some injury, it is wicked and he is punished; but when they exterminate our boys, as if they were game, with guns, they give decorations, indeed, to the one who destroys the most! Now, you see, I can never understand that, never!"

Cornudet raised his voice: "War is a barbarity when one attacks a peaceable neighbor, but a sacred duty when one defends his country."

The old woman lowered her head:

"Yes, when one defends himself, it is another thing; but why not make it a duty to kill all the kings who make these wars for their pleasure?"

Cornudet's eyes flashed. "Bravo, my countrywoman!" said he.

Mr. Carré-Lamadon reflected profoundly. Although he was prejudiced as a Captain of Industry, the good sense of this peasant woman made him think of the opulence that would be brought into the country were the idle and consequently mischievous hands, and the troops which were now maintained in unproductiveness, employed in some great industrial work that it would require centuries to achieve.

Loiseau, leaving his place, went to speak with the innkeeper in a low tone of voice. The great man laughed, shook, and squeaked, his corpulence quivered with joy at the jokes of his neighbor, and he bought of him six cases of wine for spring, after the Prussians had gone.

As soon as supper was finished, as they were worn out with fatigue, they retired.

However, Loiseau, who had observed things, after getting his wife to bed, glued his eye and then his ear to a hole in the wall, to try and discover what are known as "the mysteries of the corridor."

At the end of about an hour, he heard a groping, and, looking quickly, he perceived Ball-of-Fat, who appeared still more plump in a blue cashmere negligée trimmed with white lace. She had a candle in her hand and was directing her steps toward the great door at the end of the corridor. But a door at the side opened, and when she returned at the end of some minutes Cornudet, in his suspenders, followed her. They spoke low, then they stopped. Ball-of-Fat seemed to be defending the entrance to her room with energy. Loiseau, unfortunately, could not hear all their words, but, finally, as they raised their voices, he was able to catch a few. Cornudet insisted with vivacity. He said:

"Come, now, you are a silly woman; what harm can be done?"

She had an indignant air in responding: "No, my dear, there are moments when such things are out of place. Here it would be a shame."

He doubtless did not comprehend and asked why. Then she cried out, raising her voice still more:

"Why? you do not see why? When there are Prussians in the house, in the very next room, perhaps?"

He was silent. This patriotic shame of the harlot, who would not suffer his caress so near the enemy, must have awakened the latent dignity in his heart, for after simply kissing her, he went back to his own door with a bound.

Loiseau, much excited, left the aperture, cut a caper in his room, put on his pajamas, turned back the clothes that covered the bony carcass of his companion, whom he awakened with a kiss, murmuring: "Do you love me, dearie?"

Then all the house was still. And immediately there arose somewhere, from an uncertain quarter, which might be the cellar but was quite as likely to be the garret, a powerful snoring, monotonous and regular, a heavy, prolonged sound, like a great kettle under pressure. Mr. Follenvie was asleep.

As they had decided that they would set out at eight o'clock the next morning, they all collected in the kitchen. But the carriage, the roof of which was covered with snow, stood undisturbed in the courtyard, without horses and without a conductor. They sought him in vain in the stables, in the hay, and in the coach-house. Then they resolved to scour the town, and started out. They found themselves in a square, with a church at one end and some low houses on either side, where they perceived some Prussian soldiers. The first one they saw was paring potatoes. The second, further off, was cleaning the hairdresser's shop. Another, bearded to the eyes, was tending a troublesome brat, cradling it and trying to appease it; and the great peasant women, whose husbands were "away in the army," indicated by signs to their obedient conquerors the work they wished to have done: cutting wood, cooking the soup, grinding the coffee, or what not. One of them even washed the linen of his hostess, an impotent old grandmother.

The Count, astonished, asked questions of the beadle who came out of the rectory. The old man responded:

"Oh! those men are not wicked; they are not the Prussians we hear about. They are from far off, I know not where; and they have left wives and children in their country; it is not amusing to them, this war, I can tell you! I am sure they also weep for their homes, and that it makes as much sorrow among them as it does among us. Here, now, there is not so much unhappiness for the moment, because the soldiers do no harm and they work as if they were in their own homes. You see, sir, among poor people it is necessary that they aid one another. These are the great traits which war develops."

Cornudet, indignant at the cordial relations between the conquerors and the conquered, preferred to shut himself up in the inn. Loiseau had a joke for the occasion: "They will repeople the land."

Mr. Carré-Lamadon had a serious word: "They try to make amends."

But they did not find the driver. Finally, they discovered him in a *café* of the village, sitting at table fraternally with the officer of ordnance. The Count called out to him:

"Were you not ordered to be ready at eight o'clock?"

"Well, yes; but another order has been given me since."

"By whom?"

"Faith! the Prussian commander."

"What was it?"

"Not to harness at all."

"Why?"

"I know nothing about it. Go and ask him. They tell me not to harness, and I don't harness. That's all."

"Did he give you the order himself?"

"No, sir, the innkeeper gave the order for him."

"When was that?"

"Last evening, as I was going to bed."

The three men returned, much disturbed. They asked for Mr. Follenvie, but the servant answered that that gentleman, because of his asthma, never rose before ten o'clock. And he had given strict orders not to be wakened before that, except in case of fire.

They wished to see the officer, but that was absolutely impossible, since, while he lodged at the inn, Mr. Follenvie alone was authorized to speak to him upon civil affairs. So they waited. The women went up to their rooms again and occupied themselves with futile tasks.

Cornudet installed himself near the great chimney in the kitchen, where there was a good fire burning. He ordered one of the little tables to be brought from the *café*, then a can of beer, he then drew out his pipe, which plays among democrats a part almost equal to his own, because in serving Cornudet it was serving its country. It was a superb pipe, an admirably colored meerschaum, as black as the teeth of its master, but perfumed, curved, glistening, easy to the hand, completing his physiognomy. And he remained motionless, his eyes as much fixed upon the flame of the fire as upon his favorite tipple and its frothy crown; and each time that he drank, he passed his long, thin fingers through his scanty, gray hair, with an air of satisfaction, after which he sucked in his mustache fringed with foam.

Loiseau, under the pretext of stretching his legs, went to place some wine among the retailers of the country. The Count and the manufacturer began to talk politics. They could foresee the future of France. One of them believed in an Orléans, the other in some unknown savior for the country, a hero who would reveal himself when all were in despair: a Guesclin, or a Joan of Arc, perhaps, or would it be another Napoleon First?[4] Ah! if the Prince Imperial were not so young!

Cornudet listened to them and smiled like one who holds the word of destiny. His pipe perfumed the kitchen.

As ten o'clock struck, Mr. Follenvie appeared. They asked him hurried questions; but he could only repeat two or three times without variation, these words:

"The officer said to me: 'Mr. Follenvie, you see to it that the carriage is not harnessed for those travelers to-morrow. I do not wish them to leave without my order. That is sufficient.'"

Then they wished to see the officer. The Count sent him his card, on which Mr. Carré-Lamadon wrote his name and all his titles. The Prussian sent back word that he would meet the two gentlemen after he had breakfasted, that is to say, about one o'clock.

The ladies reappeared and ate a little something, despite their disquiet. Ball-of-Fat seemed ill and prodigiously troubled.

They were finishing their coffee when the word came that the officer was ready to meet the gentlemen. Loiseau joined them; but when they tried to enlist Cornudet, to give more solemnity to their proceedings, he declared proudly that he would have nothing to do with the Germans; and he betook himself to his chimney corner and ordered another liter of beer.

The three men mounted the staircase and were introduced to the best room of the inn, where the officer received them, stretched out in an armchair, his feet on the mantelpiece, smoking a long, porcelain pipe, and enveloped in a flamboyant dressing-gown, appropriated, without doubt, from some dwelling belonging to a common citizen of bad taste. He did not rise, nor greet them in any way, not even looking at them. It was a magnificent display of natural blackguardism transformed into the military victor.

At the expiration of some moments, he asked: "What is it you wish?"

The Count became spokesman: "We desire to go on our way, sir."

"No."

"May I ask the cause of this refusal?"

"Because I do not wish it."

"But, I would respectfully observe to you, sir, that your General-in-chief gave us permission to go to Dieppe; and I know of nothing we have done to merit your severity."

"I do not wish it—that is all; you can go."

All three having bowed, retired.

The afternoon was lamentable. They could not understand this caprice of the German; and the most singular ideas would come into their heads to trouble them. Everybody stayed in the kitchen and discussed the situation endlessly, imagining all sorts of unlikely things. Perhaps they would be retained as hostages—but to what end?—or taken prisoners—or rather a considerable ransom might be demanded. At this thought a panic prevailed. The richest were the most frightened, already seeing themselves constrained to pay for their lives with sacks of gold poured into the hands of this insolent soldier. They racked their brains to think of some acceptable falsehoods to conceal their riches and make them pass themselves off for poor people, very poor people. Loiseau took off the chain to his watch and hid it away in his pocket. The falling night increased their apprehensions. The lamp was lighted, and as there was still two hours before dinner, Madame Loiseau proposed a game of Thirty-one. It would be a diversion. They accepted. Cornudet himself, having smoked out his pipe, took part for politeness.

The Count shuffled the cards, dealt, and Ball-of-Fat had thirty-one at the outset; and immediately the interest was great enough to appease the fear that haunted their minds. Then Cornudet perceived that the house of Loiseau was given to tricks.

As they were going to the dinner table, Mr. Follenvie again appeared, and, in wheezing, rattling voice, announced:

"The Prussian officer orders me to ask Miss Elizabeth Rousset if she has yet changed her mind."

Ball-of-Fat remained standing and was pale; then suddenly becoming crimson, such a stifling anger took possession of her that she could not speak. But finally she flashed out: "You may say to the dirty beast, that idiot, that carrion of a Prussian, that I shall never change it; you understand, never, never, never!"

The great innkeeper went out. Then Ball-of-Fat was immediately surrounded, questioned, and solicited by all to disclose the mystery of his visit. She resisted, at first, but soon becoming exasperated, she said: "What does he want? You really want to know what he wants? He wants to sleep with me."

Everybody was choked for words, and indignation was rife. Cornudet broke his glass, so violently did he bring his fist down upon the table. There was a clamor of censure against this ignoble soldier, a blast of anger, a union of all for resistance, as if a demand had been made on each one of the party for the sacrifice exacted of her. The Count declared with disgust that those people conducted themselves after the fashion of the ancient barbarians. The women, especially, showed to Ball-of-Fat a most energetic and tender commiseration. The good sisters who only showed themselves at mealtime, lowered their heads and said nothing.

They all dined, nevertheless, when the first *furore* had abated. But there was little conversation; they were thinking.

The ladies retired early, and the men, all smoking, organized a game at cards to which Mr. Follenvie was invited, as they intended to put a few casual questions to him on the subject of conquering the resistance of this officer. But he thought of nothing but the cards and, without listening or answering, would keep repeating: "To the game, sirs, to the game." His attention was so taken that he even forgot to expectorate, which must have put him some points to the good with the organ in his breast. His whistling lungs ran the whole asthmatic scale, from deep, profound tones to the sharp rustiness of a young cock essaying to crow.

He even refused to retire when his wife, who had fallen asleep previously, came to look for him. She went away alone, for she was an "early bird," always up with the sun, while her husband was a "night owl," always ready to pass the night with his friends. He cried out to her: "Leave my creamed chicken before the fire!" and then went on with his game. When they saw that they could get nothing from him, they declared that it was time to stop, and each sought his bed.

They all rose rather early the next day, with an undefined hope of getting away, which desire the terror of passing another day in that horrible inn greatly increased.

Alas! the horses remained in the stable and the driver was invisible. For want of better employment, they went out and walked around the carriage.

The breakfast was very doleful; and it became apparent that a coldness had arisen toward Ball-of-Fat, and that the night, which brings counsel, had slightly modified their judgments. They almost wished now that the Prussian had secretly found this girl, in order to give her companions a pleasant surprise in the morning. What could be more simple? Besides, who would know anything about it? She could save appearances by telling the officer that she took pity on their distress. To her, it would make so little difference!

No one had avowed these thoughts yet.

In the afternoon, as they were almost perishing from *ennui*,* the Count proposed that they take a walk around the village. Each wrapped up warmly and the little party set out, with the exception of Cornudet, who preferred to remain near the fire, and the good sisters, who passed their time in the church or at the curate's.

The cold, growing more intense every day, cruelly pinched their noses and ears; their feet became so numb that each step was torture; and when they came to a field it seemed to them frightfully sad under this limitless white, so that everybody returned immediately, with hearts hard pressed and souls congealed.

The four women walked ahead, the three gentlemen followed just behind. Loiseau, who understood the situation, asked suddenly if they thought that girl there was going to keep them long in such a place as this. The Count, always courteous, said that they could not exact from a woman a sacrifice so hard, unless it should come

---

* Boredom.

of her own will. Mr. Carré-Lamadon remarked that if the French made their return through Dieppe, as they were likely to, a battle would surely take place at Tôtes. This reflection made the two others anxious.

"If we could only get away on foot," said Loiseau.

The Count shrugged his shoulders: "How can we think of it in this snow? and with our wives?" he said. "And then, we should be pursued and caught in ten minutes and led back prisoners at the mercy of these soldiers."

It was true, and they were silent.

The ladies talked of their clothes, but a certain constraint seemed to disunite them. Suddenly at the end of the street, the officer appeared. His tall, wasp-like figure in uniform was outlined upon the horizon formed by the snow, and he was marching with knees apart, a gait particularly military, which is affected that they may not spot their carefully blackened boots.

He bowed in passing near the ladies and looked disdainfully at the men, who preserved their dignity by not seeing him, except Loiseau, who made a motion toward raising his hat.

Ball-of-Fat reddened to the ears, and the three married women resented the great humiliation of being thus met by this soldier in the company of this girl whom he had treated so cavalierly.

But they spoke of him, of his figure and his face. Madame Carré-Lamadon, who had known many officers and considered herself a connoisseur of them, found this one not at all bad; she regretted even that he was not French, because he would make such a pretty hussar, one all the women would rave over.

Again in the house, no one knew what to do. Some sharp words, even, were said about things very insignificant. The dinner was silent, and almost immediately after it, each one went to his room to kill time in sleep.

They descended the next morning with weary faces and exasperated hearts. The women scarcely spoke to Ball-of-Fat.

A bell began to ring. It was for a baptism. The fat girl had a child being brought up among the peasants of Yvetot. She had not seen it for a year, or thought of it; but now the idea of a child being baptized threw into her heart a sudden and violent tenderness for her own, and she strongly wished to be present at the ceremony.

As soon as she was gone, everybody looked at each other, then pulled their chairs together, for they thought that finally something should be decided upon. Loiseau had an inspiration: it was to hold Ball-of-Fat alone and let the others go.

Mr. Follenvie was charged with the commission, but he returned almost immediately, for the German, who understood human nature, had put him out. He pretended that he would retain everybody so long as his desire was not satisfied.

Then the commonplace nature of Mrs. Loiseau burst out with:

"Well, we are not going to stay here to die of old age. Since it is the trade of this creature to accommodate herself to all kinds, I fail to see how she has the right to refuse one more than another. I can tell you she has received all she could find in Rouen, even the coachmen! Yes, Madame, the prefect's coachman! I know him very well, for he bought his wine at our house. And to think that to-day we should be drawn into this embarrassment by this affected woman, this minx! For my part, I find that this officer conducts himself very well. He has perhaps suffered privations for a long time; and doubtless he would have preferred us three; but no, he is contented with common property. He respects married women. And we must remember too that he is master. He has only to say 'I wish,' and he could take us by force with his soldiers."

The two women had a cold shiver. Pretty Mrs. Carré-Lamadon's eyes grew brilliant and she became a little pale, as if she saw herself already taken by force by the officer.

The men met and discussed the situation. Loiseau, furious, was for delivering "the wretch" bound hand and foot to the enemy. But the Count, descended through three generations of ambassadors, and endowed with the temperament of a diplomatist, was the advocate of ingenuity.

"It is best to decide upon something," said he. Then they conspired.

The women kept together, the tone of their voices was lowered, each gave advice and the discussion was general. Everything was very harmonious. The ladies especially found delicate shades and charming subtleties of expression for saying the most unusual things. A stranger would have understood nothing, so great was the precaution of language observed. But the light edge of modesty, with which every woman of the world is barbed, only covers the surface; they blossom out in a scandalous adventure of this kind, being deeply amused and feeling themselves in their element, mixing love with sensuality as a greedy cook prepares supper for his master.

Even gaiety returned, so funny did the whole story seem to them at last. The Count found some of the jokes a little off color, but they were so well told that he was forced to smile. In his turn, Loiseau came out with some still bolder tales, and yet nobody was wounded. The brutal thought, expressed by his wife, dominated all minds: "Since it is her trade, why should she refuse this one more than another?" The genteel Mrs. Carré-Lamadon seemed to think that in her place, she would refuse this one less than some others.

They prepared the blockade at length, as if they were about to surround a fortress. Each took some rôle to play, some arguments he would bring to bear, some maneuvers that he would endeavor to put into execution. They decided on the plan of attack, the ruse to employ, the surprise of assault, that should force this living citadel to receive the enemy in her room.

Cornudet remained apart from the rest, and was a stranger to the whole affair.

So entirely were their minds distracted that they did not hear Ball-of-Fat enter. The Count uttered a light "Ssh!" which turned all eyes in her direction. There she was. The abrupt silence and a certain embarrassment hindered them from speaking to her at first. The Countess, more accustomed to the duplicity of society than the others, finally inquired:

"Was it very amusing, that baptism?"

The fat girl, filled with emotion, told them all about it, the faces, the attitudes, and even the appearance of the church. She added: "It is good to pray sometimes."

And up to the time for luncheon these ladies continued to be amiable toward her, in order to increase her docility and her confidence in their counsel. At the table they commenced the approach. This was in the shape of a vague conversation upon devotion. They cited ancient examples: Judith and Holophernes, then, without reason, Lucrece and Sextus, and Cleopatra obliging all the generals of the enemy to pass by her couch and reducing them in servility to slaves.[5] Then they brought out a fantastic story, hatched in the imagination of these ignorant millionaires, where the women of Rome went to Capua for the purpose of lulling Hannibal to sleep in their arms, and his lieutenants and phalanxes of mercenaries as well. They cited all the women who have been taken by conquering armies, making a battlefield of their bodies, making them also a weapon, and a means of success; and all those hideous and detestable beings who have conquered by their heroic caresses, and sacrificed their chastity to vengeance or a beloved cause. They even spoke in veiled terms of that great English family which allowed one of its women to be inoculated with a horrible and contagious disease in order to transmit it to Bonaparte, who was miraculously saved by a sudden illness at the hour of the fatal rendezvous.

And all this was related in an agreeable, temperate fashion, except as it was enlivened by the enthusiasm deemed proper to excite emulation.

One might finally have believed that the sole duty of woman here below was a sacrifice of her person, and a continual abandonment to soldierly caprices.

The two good sisters seemed not to hear, lost as they were in profound thought. Ball-of-Fat said nothing.

During the whole afternoon they let her reflect. But, in the place of calling her "Madame" as they had up to this time, they simply called her "Mademoiselle" without knowing exactly why, as if they had a desire to put her down a degree in their esteem, which she had taken by storm, and make her feel her shameful situation.

The moment supper was served, Mr. Follenvie appeared with his old phrase: "The Prussian officer orders me to ask if Miss Elizabeth Rousset has yet changed her mind."

Ball-of-Fat responded dryly: "No, sir."

But at dinner the coalition weakened. Loiseau made three unhappy remarks. Each one beat his wits for new examples but found nothing; when the Countess, without premeditation, perhaps feeling some vague need of rendering homage to religion, asked the elder of the good sisters to tell them some great deeds in the lives of the saints. It appeared that many of their acts would have been considered crimes in our eyes; but the Church gave absolution of them readily, since they were done for the glory of God, or for the good of all. It was a powerful argument; the Countess made the most of it.

Thus it may be by one of those tacit understandings, or the veiled complacency in which anyone who wears the ecclesiastical garb excels, it may be simply from the effect of a happy unintelligence, a helpful stupidity, but in fact the religious sister lent a formidable support to the conspiracy. They had thought her timid, but she showed herself courageous, verbose, even violent. She was not troubled by the chatter of the casuist; her doctrine seemed a bar of iron; her faith never hesitated; her conscience had no scruples. She found the sacrifice of Abraham perfectly simple, for she would immediately kill father or mother on an order from on high. And nothing, in her opinion, could displease the Lord, if the intention was laudable. The Countess put to use the authority of her unwitting accomplice, and added to it the edifying paraphrase and axiom of Jesuit morals: "The end justifies the means."

Then she asked her: "Then, my sister, do you think that God accepts intentions, and pardons the deed when the motive is pure?"

"Who could doubt it, Madame? An action blamable in itself often becomes meritorious by the thought it springs from."

And they continued thus, unraveling the will of God, foreseeing his decisions, making themselves interested in things that, in truth, they would never think of noticing. All this was guarded, skillful, discreet. But each word of the saintly sister in a cap helped to break down the resistance of the unworthy courtesan. Then the conversation changed a little, the woman of the chaplet speaking of the houses of her order, of her Superior, of herself, of her dainty neighbor, the dear sister Saint-Nicephore. They had been called to the hospitals of Havre to care for the hundreds of soldiers stricken with smallpox. They depicted these miserable creatures, giving details of the malady. And while they were stopped, *en route,* by the caprice of this Prussian officer, a great number of Frenchmen might die, whom perhaps they could have saved! It was a specialty with her, caring for soldiers. She had been in Crimea, in Italy, in Austria, and, in telling of her campaigns, she revealed herself as one of those religious aids to drums and trumpets, who seem made to follow camps, pick up the wounded in the thick of battle, and, better than an officer, subdue with a word great bands of undisciplined recruits. A true, good sister of the rataplan, whose ravaged face, marked with innumerable scars, appeared the image of the devastation of war.

No one could speak after her, so excellent seemed the effect of her words.

As soon as the repast was ended they quickly went up to their rooms, with the purpose of not coming down the next day until late in the morning.

The luncheon was quiet. They had given the grain of seed time to germinate and bear fruit. The Countess proposed that they take a walk in the afternoon. The Count, being agreeably inclined, gave an arm to Ball-of-Fat and walked behind the others with her. He talked to her in a familiar, paternal tone, a little disdainful, after the manner of men having girls in their employ, calling her "my dear child," from the height of his social position, of his undisputed honor. He reached the vital part of the question at once:

"Then you prefer to leave us here, exposed to the violences which follow a defeat, rather than consent to a favor which you have so often given in your life?"

Ball-of-Fat answered nothing.

Then he tried to reach her through gentleness, reason, and then the sentiments. He knew how to remain "The Count," even while showing himself gallant or complimentary, or very amiable if it became necessary. He exalted the service that she would render them, and spoke of their appreciation; then suddenly became gaily familiar, and said:

"And you know, my dear, it would be something for him to boast of that he had known a pretty girl; something it is difficult to find in his country."

Ball-of-Fat did not answer but joined the rest of the party. As soon as they entered the house she went to her room and did not appear again. The disquiet was extreme. What were they to do? If she continued to resist, what an embarrassment!

The dinner hour struck. They waited in vain. Mr. Follenvie finally entered and said that Miss Rousset was indisposed, and would not be at the table. Everybody pricked up his ears. The Count went to the innkeeper and said in a low voice:

"Is he in there?"

"Yes."

For convenience, he said nothing to his companions, but made a slight sign with his head. Immediately a great sigh of relief went up from every breast and a light appeared in their faces. Loiseau cried out:

"Holy Christopher! I pay for the champagne, if there is any to be found in the establishment." And Mrs. Loiseau was pained to see the proprietor return with four quart bottles in his hands.

Each one had suddenly become communicative and buoyant. A wanton joy filled their hearts. The Count suddenly perceived that Mrs. Carré-Lamadon was charming, the manufacturer paid compliments to the Countess. The conversation was lively, gay, full of touches.

Suddenly Loiseau, with anxious face and hand upraised, called out: "Silence!" Everybody was silent, surprised, already frightened. Then he listened intently and said: "S-s-sh!" his two eyes and his hands raised toward the ceiling, listening, and then continuing, in his natural voice: "All right! All goes well!"

They failed to comprehend at first, but soon all laughed. At the end of a quarter of an hour he began the same farce again, renewing it occasionally during the whole afternoon. And he pretended to call to some one in the story above, giving him advice in a double meaning, drawn from the fountainhead—the mind of a commercial traveler. For some moments he would assume a sad air, breathing in a whisper: "Poor girl!" Then he would murmur between his teeth, with an appearance of rage: "Ugh! That scamp of a Prussian." Sometimes, at a moment when no more was thought about it, he would say, in an affected voice, many times over: "Enough! enough!" and add, as if speaking to himself: "If we could only see her again, it isn't necessary that he should kill her, the wretch!"

Although these jokes were in deplorable taste, they amused all and wounded no one, for indignation, like other things, depends upon its surroundings, and the atmosphere which had been gradually created around them was charged with sensual thoughts.

At the dessert the women themselves made some delicate and discreet allusions. Their eyes glistened; they had drunk much. The Count, who preserved, even in his flights, his grand appearance of gravity, made a comparison, much relished, upon the subject of those wintering at the pole, and the joy of shipwrecked sailors who saw an opening toward the south.

Loiseau suddenly arose, a glass of champagne in his hand, and said: "I drink to our deliverance." Everybody was on his feet; they shouted in agreement. Even the two good sisters consented to touch their lips to the froth of the wine which they had never before tasted. They declared that it tasted like charged lemonade, only much nicer.

Loiseau resumed: "It is unfortunate that we have no piano, for we might make up a quadrille."

Cornudet had not said a word, nor made a gesture; he appeared plunged in very grave thoughts, and made sometimes a furious motion, so that his great beard seemed to wish to free itself. Finally, toward midnight, as they were separating, Loiseau, who was staggering, touched him suddenly on the stomach and said to him in a stammer: "You are not very funny, this evening; you have said nothing, citizen!" Then Cornudet raised his head brusquely and, casting a brilliant, terrible glance around the company, said: "I tell you all that you have been guilty of infamy!" He rose, went to the door, and again repeated: "Infamy, I say!" and disappeared.

This made a coldness at first. Loiseau, interlocutor, was stupefied;

but he recovered immediately and laughed heartily as he said: "He is very green, my friends. He is very green." And then, as they did not comprehend, he told them about the "mysteries of the corridor." Then there was a return of gaiety. The women behaved like lunatics. The Count and Mr. Carré-Lamadon wept from the force of their laughter. They could not believe it.

"How is that? Are you sure?"

"I tell you I saw it."

"And she refused——"

"Yes, because the Prussian officer was in the next room."

"Impossible!"

"I swear it!"

The Count was stifled with laughter. The industrial gentleman held his sides with both hands. Loiseau continued:

"And now you understand why he saw nothing funny this evening! No, nothing at all!" And the three started out half ill, suffocated.

They separated. But Mrs. Loiseau, who was of a spiteful nature, remarked to her husband as they were getting into bed, that "that *grisette*"* of a little Carré-Lamadon was yellow with envy all the evening. "You know," she continued, "how some women will take to a uniform, whether it be French or Prussian! It is all the same to them! Oh! what a pity!"

And all night, in the darkness of the corridor, there were to be heard light noises, like whisperings and walking in bare feet, and imperceptible creakings. They did not go to sleep until late, that is sure, for there were threads of light shining under the doors for a long time. The champagne had its effect; they say it troubles sleep.

The next day a clear winter's sun made the snow very brilliant. The diligence, already harnessed, waited before the door, while an army of white pigeons, in their thick plumage, with rose-colored eyes, with a black spot in the center, walked up and down gravely among the legs of the six horses, seeking their livelihood in the manure there scattered.

---

* Derisive French term for a working-class girl.

The driver, enveloped in his sheepskin, had a lighted pipe under the seat, and all the travelers, radiant, were rapidly packing some provisions for the rest of the journey. They were only waiting for Ball-of-Fat. Finally she appeared.

She seemed a little troubled, ashamed. And she advanced timidly toward her companions, who all, with one motion, turned as if they had not seen her. The Count, with dignity, took the arm of his wife and removed her from this impure contact.

The fat girl stopped, half stupefied; then, plucking up courage, she approached the manufacturer's wife with "Good morning, Madame," humbly murmured. The lady made a slight bow of the head which she accompanied with a look of outraged virtue. Everybody seemed busy, and kept themselves as far from her as if she had had some infectious disease in her skirts. Then they hurried into the carriage, where she came last, alone, and where she took the place she had occupied during the first part of the journey.

They seemed not to see her or know her; although Madame Loiseau, looking at her from afar, said to her husband in a half-tone: "Happily, I don't have to sit beside her."

The heavy carriage began to move and the remainder of the journey commenced. No one spoke at first. Ball-of-Fat dared not raise her eyes. She felt indignant toward all her neighbors, and at the same time humiliated at having yielded to the foul kisses of this Prussian, into whose arms they had hypocritically thrown her.

Then the Countess, turning toward Mrs. Carré-Lamadon, broke the difficult silence:

"I believe you know Madame d'Etrelles?"

"Yes, she is one of my friends."

"What a charming woman!"

"Delightful! A very gentle nature, and well educated, besides; then she is an artist to the tips of her fingers, sings beautifully, and draws to perfection."

The manufacturer chatted with the Count, and in the midst of the rattling of the glass, an occasional word escaped such as "coupon— premium—limit—expiration."

Loiseau, who had pilfered the old pack of cards from the inn, greasy through five years of contact with tables badly cleaned, began a game of bezique with his wife.

The good sisters took from their belt the long rosary which hung there, made together the sign of the cross, and suddenly began to move their lips in a lively manner, hurrying more and more, hastening their vague murmur, as if they were going through the whole of the "Ore-mus." And from time to time they kissed a medal, made the sign anew, then recommenced their muttering, which was rapid and continued.

Cornudet sat motionless, thinking.

At the end of three hours on the way, Loiseau put up the cards and said: "I am hungry."

His wife drew out a package from whence she brought a piece of cold veal. She cut it evenly in thin pieces and they both began to eat.

"Suppose we do the same," said the Countess.

They consented to it and she undid the provisions prepared for the two couples. It was in one of those dishes whose lid is decorated with a china hare, to signify that a *pâté* of hare is inside, a succulent dish of pork, where white rivers of lard cross the brown flesh of the game, mixed with some other viands hashed fine. A beautiful square of Gruyère cheese, wrapped in a piece of newspaper, preserved the im-print "divers things" upon the unctuous plate.

The two good sisters unrolled a big sausage which smelled of gar-lic; and Cornudet plunged his two hands into the vast pockets of his overcoat, at the same time, and drew out four hard eggs and a piece of bread. He removed the shells and threw them in the straw under his feet; then he began to eat the eggs, letting fall on his vast beard some bits of clear yellow, which looked like stars caught there.

Ball-of-Fat, in the haste and distraction of her rising, had not thought of anything; and she looked at them exasperated, suffocating with rage, at all of them eating so placidly. A tumultuous anger swept over her at first, and she opened her mouth to cry out at them, to hurl at them a flood of injury which mounted to her lips; but she could not speak, her exasperation strangled her.

No one looked at her or thought of her. She felt herself drowned in the scorn of these honest scoundrels, who had first sacrificed her and then rejected her, like some improper or useless article. She thought of her great basket full of good things which they had greedily devoured, of her two chickens shining with jelly, of her *pâtés*, her pears, and the four bottles of Bordeaux; and her fury suddenly falling, as a cord drawn too tightly breaks, she felt ready to weep. She made terrible efforts to prevent it, making ugly faces, swallowing her sobs as children do, but the tears came and glistened in the corners of her eyes, and then two great drops, detaching themselves from the rest, rolled slowly down her cheeks. Others followed rapidly, running down like little streams of water that filter through rock, and, falling regularly, rebounded upon her breast. She sits erect, her eyes fixed, her face rigid and pale, hoping that no one will notice her.

But the Countess perceives her and tells her husband by a sign. He shrugs his shoulders, as much as to say:

"What would you have me do, it is not my fault."

Mrs. Loiseau indulged in a mute laugh of triumph and murmured: "She weeps for shame."

The two good sisters began to pray again, after having wrapped in a paper the remainder of their sausage.

Then Cornudet, who was digesting his eggs, extended his legs to the seat opposite, crossed them, folded his arms, smiled like a man who is watching a good farce, and began to whistle the "Marseillaise."[6]

All faces grew dark. The popular song assuredly did not please his neighbors. They became nervous and agitated, having an appearance of wishing to howl, like dogs, when they hear a barbarous organ. He perceived this but did not stop. Sometimes he would hum the words:

> "Sacred love of country
> Help, sustain th' avenging arm;
> Liberty, sweet Liberty
> Ever fight, with no alarm."

They traveled fast, the snow being harder. But as far as Dieppe, during the long, sad hours of the journey, across the jolts in the road, through the falling night, in the profound darkness of the carriage, he continued his vengeful, monotonous whistling with a ferocious obstinacy, constraining his neighbors to follow the song from one end to the other, and to recall the words that belonged to each measure.

And Ball-of-Fat wept continually; and sometimes a sob, which she was not able to restrain, echoed between the two rows of people in the shadows.

PAUL'S MISTRESS

THE RESTAURANT GRILLON, A small commonwealth of boatmen, was slowly emptying. In front of the door all was tumult—cries and calls—and jolly rowers in white flannels gesticulated with oars on their shoulders.

The ladies in bright spring toilettes stepped aboard the skiffs with care, and seating themselves astern, arranged their dresses, while the landlord of the establishment, a mighty, red-bearded, self-possessed individual of renowned strength, offered his hand to the pretty creatures, and kept the frail crafts steady.

The rowers, bare-armed, with bulging chests, took their places in their turn, posing for their gallery as they did so—a gallery consisting of middle-class people dressed in their Sunday clothes, of workmen and soldiers leaning upon their elbows on the parapet of the bridge, all taking a great interest in the sight.

One by one the boats cast off from the landing stage. The oarsmen bent forward and then threw themselves backward with even swing, and under the impetus of the long curved oars, the swift skiffs glided along the river, grew smaller in the distance, and finally disappeared under the railway bridge, as they descended the stream toward La Grenouillère.[7] One couple only remained behind. The young man, still almost beardless, slender, with a pale countenance, held his mistress, a thin little brunette with the gait of a grasshopper, by the waist; and occasionally they gazed into each other's eyes. The landlord shouted:

"Come, Mr. Paul, make haste," and they drew near.

Of all the guests of the house, Mr. Paul was the most liked and most respected. He paid well and punctually, while the others hung back for a long time if indeed they did not vanish without paying. Besides which he was a sort of walking advertisement for the establishment, inasmuch as his father was a senator. When a stranger would inquire: "Who on earth is that little chap who thinks so much of himself because of his girl?" some *habitué** would reply, half-aloud, with a mysterious and important air: "Don't you know? That is Paul Baron, a senator's son."

And invariably the other would exclaim:

"Poor devil! He is not half-grown."

Mother Grillon, a good and worthy business woman, described the young man and his companion as "her two turtledoves," and appeared quite touched by this passion, which was profitable for her house.

The couple advanced at a slow pace. The skiff "Madeleine" was ready, and at the moment of embarking they kissed each other, which caused the public collected on the bridge to laugh. Mr. Paul took the oars, and rowed away for La Grenouillère.

When they arrived it was just upon three o'clock and the large floating *café* overflowed with people.

The immense raft, sheltered by a tarpaulin roof, is joined to the charming island of Croissy by two narrow footbridges, one of which leads into the center of the aquatic establishment, while the other unites with a tiny islet, planted with a tree and called "The Flower Pot," and thence leads to land near the bath office.

Mr. Paul made fast his boat alongside the establishment, climbed over the railing of the *café*, and then, grasping his mistress's hands, assisted her out of the boat. They both seated themselves at the end of a table opposite each other.

On the opposite side of the river along the market road, a long string of vehicles was drawn up. Cabs alternated with the fine carriages of the swells; the first, clumsy, with enormous bodies crushing the springs, drawn by broken-down hacks with hanging heads and broken knees; the second, slightly built on light wheels, with horses

---

* Regular customer.

slender and straight, their heads well up, their bits snowy with foam, and with coachmen solemn in livery, heads erect in high collars, waiting bolt upright, with whips resting on their knees.

The bank was covered with people who came off in families, or in parties, or in couples, or alone. They plucked at the blades of grass, went down to the water, ascended the path, and having reached the spot, stood still awaiting the ferryman. The clumsy punt plied incessantly from bank to bank, discharging its passengers upon the island. The arm of the river (called the Dead Arm) upon which this refreshment wharf lay, seemed asleep, so feeble was the current. Fleets of yawls, of skiffs, of canoes, of podoscaphs (a light boat propelled by wheels set in motion by a treadle), of gigs, of craft of all forms and of all kinds, crept about upon the motionless stream, crossing each other, intermingling, running foul of one another, stopping abruptly under a jerk of the arms only to shoot off afresh under a sudden strain of the muscles and gliding swiftly along like great yellow or red fishes.

Others arrived continually; some from Chaton up the stream; others from Bougival down it; laughter crossed the water from one boat to another, calls, admonitions, or imprecations. The boatmen exposed the bronzed and knotted muscles of their biceps to the heat of the day; and like strange floating flowers, the silk parasols, red, green, blue, or yellow, of the ladies bloomed in the sterns of the boats.

A July sun flamed high in the heavens; the atmosphere seemed full of burning merriment; not a breath of air stirred the leaves of the willows or poplars.

Down there Mont-Valérien reared its fortified ramparts, tier above tier, in the intense light; while on the right the divine slopes of Louviennes, following the bend of the river, disposed themselves in a semicircle, displaying in turn across the rich and shady lawns of large gardens the white walls of country seats.

Upon the outskirts of La Grenouillère a crowd of promenaders moved about beneath the giant trees which make this corner of the island one of the most delightful parks in the world.

Women and girls with breasts developed beyond all measurement, with exaggerated bustles, their complexions plastered with rouge, their eyes daubed with charcoal, their lips blood-red, laced up, rigged out in outrageous dresses, trailed the crying bad taste of their toilettes over the fresh green sward; while beside them young men posed in their fashion-plate garments with light gloves, varnished boots, canes the size of a thread, and single eyeglasses emphasizing the insipidity of their smiles.

Opposite La Grenouillère the island is narrow, and on its other side, where also a ferryboat plies, bringing people unceasingly across from Croissy, the rapid branch of the river, full of whirlpools and eddies and foam, rushes along with the strength of a torrent.

A detachment of pontoon-builders, in the uniform of artillerymen, was encamped upon this bank, and the soldiers seated in a row on a long beam watched the water flowing.

In the floating establishment there was a boisterous and uproarious crowd. The wooden tables upon which the spilt refreshments made little sticky streams were covered with half-empty glasses and surrounded by half-tipsy individuals. The crowd shouted, sang, and brawled. The men, their hats at the backs of their heads, their faces red, with the shining eyes of drunkards, moved about vociferating and evidently looking for the quarrels natural to brutes. The women, seeking their prey for the night, sought for free liquor in the meantime; and in the unoccupied space between the tables, the ordinary local public outnumbered a whole regiment of boatmen, *Rowkickers-up,* with their companions in short flannel petticoats.

One of them performed on the piano and appeared to play with his feet as well as his hands; four couples glided through a quadrille, and some young men watched them, polished and correct, men who would have looked demure even if vice itself had appeared.

For there you see in full the pomp and vanity of the world, all its well-bred debauchery, all the seamy side of Parisian society—a mixture of counter-jumpers, of strolling players, of low journalists, of gentlemen in tutelage, of rotten stock-jobbers, of ill-famed debauchees, of old, used-up fast men; a doubtful crowd of suspicious characters, half-known, half-sunk, half-recognized, half-criminal, pickpockets, rogues, procurers of women, sharpers with dignified manners, and a bragging air which seems to say: "I shall kill the first who treats me as a scoundrel."

The place reeks of folly, and stinks of the scum and the gallantry of the shops. Male and female there give themselves airs. There dwells an odor of so-called love, and there one fights for a yes, or for a no, in order to sustain a worm-eaten reputation, which a thrust of the sword or a pistol bullet would destroy further.

Some of the neighboring inhabitants looked in out of curiosity every Sunday; some young men, very young, appeared there every year to learn how to live, some promenaders lounging about showed themselves there; some greenhorns wandered thither. With good reason is it named La Grenouillère. At the side of the covered wharf where they drank, and quite close to the Flower Pot, people bathed. Those among the women who possessed the requisite roundness of form came there to display their wares and to make clients. The rest, scornful, although well filled out with wadding, shored up with springs, corrected here and altered there, watched their dabbling sisters with disdain.

The swimmers crowded on to a little platform to dive thence headforemost. Straight like vine poles, or round like pumpkins, gnarled like olive branches, bowed over in front, or thrown backward by the size of their stomachs, and invariably ugly, they leaped into the water splashing it almost over the drinkers in the *café*.

Notwithstanding the great trees which overhang the floating-house, and notwithstanding the vicinity of the water a suffocating heat filled the place. The fumes of the spilt liquors mingled with the effluvia of the bodies and with the strong perfumes with which the skin of the trader in love is saturated and which evaporate in this furnace. But beneath all these diverse scents a slight aroma of rice-powder lingered, disappearing and reappearing, and perpetually encountered as though some concealed hand had shaken an invisible powder-puff in the air. The show was upon the river, whither the perpetual coming and going of the boats attracted the eyes. The boatwomen sprawled upon their seats opposite their strong-wristed males, and scornfully contemplated the dinner hunters prowling about the island.

Sometimes when a succession of boats, just started, passed at full speed, the friends who stayed ashore gave vent to shouts, and all the people as if suddenly seized with madness set to work yelling.

At the bend of the river toward Chaton fresh boats continually appeared. They came nearer and grew larger, and if only faces were recognized, the vociferations broke out anew.

A canoe covered with an awning and manned by four women came slowly down the current. She who rowed was petite, thin, faded, in a cabin-boy's costume, her hair drawn up under an oilskin cap. Opposite her, a lusty blonde, dressed as a man, with a white flannel jacket, lay upon her back at the bottom of the boat, her legs in the air, resting on the seat at each side of the rower. She smoked a cigarette, while at each stroke of the oars, her chest and her stomach quivered, shaken by the stroke. At the back, under the awning, two handsome girls, tall and slender, one dark and the other fair, held each other by the waist as they watched their companions.

A cry arose from La Grenouillère, "There is Lesbos,"* and all at once a furious clamor, a terrifying scramble, took place; the glasses were knocked down; people clambered on to the tables; all in a frenzy of noise bawled: "Lesbos! Lesbos! Lesbos!" The shout rolled along, became indistinct, was no longer more than a kind of deafening howl, and then suddenly it seemed to start anew, to rise into space, to cover the plain, to fill the foliage of the great trees, to extend to the distant slopes, and reach even to the sun.

The rower, in the face of this ovation, had quietly stopped. The handsome blonde, stretched out upon the bottom of the boat, turned her head with a careless air, as she raised herself upon her elbows; and the two girls at the back commenced laughing as they saluted the crowd.

Then the hullabaloo was doubled, making the floating establish-

---

* Derisive euphemism for a lesbian.

ment tremble. The men took off their hats, the women waved their handkerchiefs, and all voices, shrill or deep, together cried:

"Lesbos."

It was as if these people, this collection of the corrupt, saluted their chiefs like the war-ships which fire guns when an admiral passes along the line.

The numerous fleet of boats also saluted the women's boat, which pushed along more quickly to land farther off.

Mr. Paul, contrary to the others, had drawn a key from his pocket and whistled with all his might. His nervous mistress grew paler, caught him by the arm to make him be quiet, and upon this occasion she looked at him with fury in her eyes. But he appeared exasperated, as though borne away by jealousy of some man or by deep anger, instinctive and ungovernable. He stammered, his lips quivering with indignation:

"It is shameful! They ought to be drowned like puppies with a stone about the neck."

But Madeleine instantly flew into a rage; her small and shrill voice became a hiss, and she spoke volubly, as though pleading her own cause:

"And what has it to do with you—you indeed? Are they not at liberty to do what they wish since they owe nobody anything? A truce to your airs, and mind your own business."

But he cut her speech short:

"It is the police whom it concerns, and I will have them marched off to St. Lazare; indeed I will."

She gave a start:

"You?"

"Yes, I! And in the meantime I forbid you to speak to them—you understand, I forbid you to do so."

Then she shrugged her shoulders and grew calm in a moment:

"My friend, I shall do as I please; if you are not satisfied, be off, and instantly. I am not your wife, am I? Very well then, hold your tongue."

He made no reply and they stood face to face, their lips tightly closed and their breathing rapid.

At the other end of the great wooden *café* the four women made their entry. The two in men's costumes marched in front: the one thin like an oldish tomboy, with yellow lines on her temples; the other filling out her white flannel garments with her fat, swelling out her big trousers with her buttocks and swaying about like a fat goose with enormous legs and yielding knees. Their two friends followed them, and the crowd of boatmen thronged about to shake their hands.

The four had hired a small cottage close to the water's edge, and lived there as two households would have lived.

Their vice was public, recognized, patent to all. People talked of it as a natural thing, which almost excited their sympathy, and whispered in very low tones strange stories of dramas begotten of furious feminine jealousies, of the stealthy visit of well-known women and of actresses to the little house close to the water's edge.

A neighbor, horrified by these scandalous rumors, apprised the police, and the inspector, accompanied by a man, had come to make inquiry. The mission was a delicate one; it was impossible, in short, to accuse these women, who did not abandon themselves to prostitution, of any tangible crime. The inspector, very much puzzled, and, indeed, ignorant of the nature of the offenses suspected, had asked questions at random, and made a lofty report conclusive of their innocence.

They laughed about it all the way to St. Germain. They walked about the Grenouillère establishment with stately steps like queens; and seemed to glory in their fame, rejoicing in the gaze that was fixed on them, so superior to this crowd, to this mob, to these plebeians.

Madeleine and her lover watched them approach, and the girl's eyes lightened.

When the first two had reached the end of the table, Madeleine cried:

"Pauline!"

The large woman turned and stopped, continuing all the time to hold the arm of her feminine cabin-boy:

"Good gracious, Madeleine! Do come and talk to me, my dear."

Paul squeezed his fingers upon his mistress's wrist; but she said to him, with such an air: "You know, my fine fellow, you can be off," that he said nothing and remained alone.

Then they chatted in low voices, all three of them standing. Many pleasant jests passed their lips, they spoke quickly; and Pauline now and then looked at Paul, by stealth, with a shrewd and malicious smile.

At last, putting up with it no longer, he suddenly rose and in a single bound was at their side, trembling in every limb. He seized Madeleine by the shoulders.

"Come, I wish it," said he; "I have forbidden you to speak to these scoundrels."

Whereupon Pauline raised her voice and set to work blackguarding him with her Billingsgate vocabulary. All the bystanders laughed; they drew near him; they raised themselves on tiptoe in order the better to see him. He remained dumb under this downpour of filthy abuse. It appeared to him that the words which came from that mouth and fell upon him defiled him like dirt, and, in presence of the row which was beginning, he fell back, retraced his steps, and rested his elbows on the railing toward the river, turning his back upon the victorious women.

There he stayed watching the water, and sometimes with rapid gesture as though he could pluck it out, he removed with his sinewy fingers the tear formed in his eye.

The fact was that he was hopelessly in love, without knowing why, notwithstanding his refined instincts, in spite of his reason, in spite, indeed, of his will. He had fallen into this love as one falls into a sloughy hole. Of a tender and delicate disposition, he had dreamed of liaisons, exquisite, ideal, and impassioned, and there that little bit of a woman, stupid, like all girls, with an exasperating stupidity, not even pretty, but thin and a spitfire, had taken him prisoner, possessing him from head to foot, body and soul. He had submitted to this feminine witchery, mysterious and all powerful, this unknown power, this prodigious domination—arising no one knows whence, but from the demon of the flesh—which casts the most sensible man at the feet of some girl or other without there being anything in her to explain her fatal and sovereign power.

And there at his back he felt that some infamous thing was brewing. Shouts of laughter cut him to the heart. What should he do? He knew well, but he could not do it.

He steadily watched an angler upon the bank opposite him, and his motionless line.

Suddenly, the worthy man jerked a little silver fish, which wriggled at the end of his line, out of the river. Then he endeavored to extract his hook, pulled and turned it, but in vain. At last, losing patience, he commenced to tear it out, and all the bleeding gullet of the fish, with a portion of its intestines came out. Paul shuddered, rent to his heartstrings. It seemed to him that the hook was his love, and that if he should pluck it out, all that he had in his breast would come out in the same way at the end of a curved iron, fixed in the depths of his being, to which Madeleine held the line.

A hand was placed upon his shoulder; he started and turned; his mistress was at his side. They did not speak to each other; and like him she rested her elbows upon the railing, and fixed her eyes upon the river.

He sought for what he ought to say to her and could find nothing. He could not even disentangle his own emotions; all that he was sensible of was joy at feeling her there close to him, come back again, as well as shameful cowardice, a craving to pardon everything, to permit everything, provided she never left him.

At last, at the end of some minutes, he asked her in a very gentle voice:

"Do you wish that we should leave? It will be nicer in the boat."

She answered: "Yes, my dear."

And he assisted her into the skiff, pressing her hands, all softened, with some tears still in his eyes. Then she looked at him with a smile and they kissed each other anew.

They reascended the river very slowly, skirting the willow-bordered, grass-covered bank, bathed and still in the afternoon warmth. When they had returned to the Restaurant Grillon, it was barely six o'clock. Then leaving their boat they set off on foot toward Bezons, across the fields and along the high poplars which bordered the river. The long grass ready to be mowed was full of flowers. The sinking sun glowed from beneath a sheet of red light, and in the tempered heat of the closing day the floating exhalations from the grass, mingled with the damp scents from the river, filled the air with a soft languor, with a happy light, with an atmosphere of blessing.

A soft weakness overtook his heart, a species of communion with this splendid calm of evening, with this vague and mysterious chilliness of unhidden life, with the keen and melancholy poetry which seems to arise from flowers and things, and reveals itself to the senses at this sweet and pensive time.

Paul felt all that; but for her part she did not understand anything of it. They walked side by side; and, suddenly, tired of being silent, she sang. She sang in her shrill and false voice some street song, some catchy air, which jarred upon the profound and serene harmony of the evening.

Then he looked at her and felt an impassable abyss between them. She beat the grass with her parasol, her head slightly inclined, admiring her feet and singing, spinning out the notes, attempting trills, and venturing on shakes. Her smooth little brow, of which he was so fond, was at that time absolutely empty! empty! There was nothing therein but this music of a bird-organ; and the ideas which formed there by chance were like this music. She did not understand anything of him; they were now as separated as if they did not live together. Did his kisses never go any further than her lips?

Then she raised her eyes to him and laughed again. He was moved to the quick and, extending his arms in a paroxysm of love, he embraced her passionately.

As he was rumpling her dress she ended by disengaging herself, murmuring by way of compensation as she did so:

"That's enough. You know I love you!"

But he clasped her round the waist and seized by madness, carried her rapidly away. He kissed her on the cheek, on the temple, on the neck, all the while dancing with joy. They threw themselves down panting at the edge of a thicket, lit up by the rays of the setting sun, and before they had recovered breath they were friends again without her understanding his transport.

They returned, holding each other by the hand, when, suddenly, through the trees, they perceived on the river the skiff manned by the four women. Fat Pauline also saw them, for she drew herself up and blew kisses to Madeleine. And then she cried:

"Until to-night!"

Madeleine replied: "Until to-night!"

Paul felt as if his heart had suddenly been frozen.

They re-entered the house for dinner and installed themselves in one of the arbors, close to the water. They set about eating in silence. When night arrived, the waiter brought a candle inclosed in a glass globe, which gave a feeble and glimmering light; and they heard every moment the bursting out of the shouts of the boatmen in the great saloon on the first floor.

Toward dessert, Paul, taking Madeleine's hand, tenderly said to her:

"I feel very tired, my darling; unless you have any objection, we will go to bed early."

She, however, understood the ruse, and shot an enigmatical glance at him—that glance of treachery which so readily appears in the depth of a woman's eyes. Having reflected she answered:

"You can go to bed if you wish, but I have promised to go to the ball at La Grenouillère."

He smiled in a piteous manner, one of those smiles with which one veils the most horrible suffering, and replied in a coaxing but agonized tone:

"If you were very kind, we should remain here, both of us."

She indicated no with her head, without opening her mouth.

He insisted:

"I beg of you, my darling."

Then she roughly broke out:

"You know what I said to you. If you are not satisfied, the door is open. No one wishes to keep you. As for myself, I have promised; I shall go."

He placed his two elbows upon the table, covered his face with his hands and remained there pondering sorrowfully.

The boat people came down again, shouting as usual, and set off in their vessels for the ball at La Grenouillère.

Madeleine said to Paul:

"If you are not coming, say so, and I will ask one of these gentlemen to take me."

Paul rose:

"Let us go!" murmured he.

And they left.

The night was black, the sky full of stars, but the air was heat-laden by oppressive breaths of wind, burdened with emanations, and with living germs, which destroyed the freshness of the night. It offered a heated caress, made one breathe more quickly, gasp a little, so thick and heavy did it seem. The boats started on their way, bearing Venetian lanterns at the prow. It was not possible to distinguish the craft, but only the little colored lights, swift and dancing up and down like glowworms in a fit, while voices sounded from all sides in the shade. The young people's skiff glided gently along. Now and then, when a fast boat passed near them, they could, for a moment, see the white back of the rower, lit up by his lantern.

When they turned the elbow of the river, La Grenouillère appeared to them in the distance. The establishment, *en fête,* * was decorated with sconces and with colored garlands draped with clusters of lights. On the Seine some great barges moved about slowly, representing domes, pyramids, and elaborate erections in fires of all colors. Illuminated festoons hung right down to the water, and sometimes a red or blue lantern, at the end of an immense invisible fishing-rod, seemed like a great swinging star.

All this illumination spread a light around the *café*, lit up the great trees on the bank, from top to bottom, the trunks standing out in pale gray and the leaves in milky green upon the deep black of the fields and the heavens. The orchestra, composed of five suburban

* Festive.

artists, flung far its public-house dance-music, poor of its kind and jerky, inciting Madeleine to sing anew.

She desired to enter at once. Paul desired first to take a stroll on the island, but he was obliged to give way. The attendance was now more select. The boatmen, always alone, remained, with here and there some citizens, and some young men escorted by girls. The director and organizer of this majestic *cancan*, in a jaded black suit, walked about in every direction, baldheaded and worn by his old trade of purveyor of cheap public amusements.

Fat Pauline and her companions were not there; and Paul breathed again.

They danced; couples opposite each other capered in the maddest fashion, throwing their legs in the air, until they were upon a level with the noses of their partners.

The women, whose thighs seemed disjointed, kicked their feet up above their heads with astounding facility, balanced their bodies, wagged their backs and shook their sides, shedding around them the enticing scent of womanhood.

The men squatted like toads, some making signs; some twisted and distorted themselves, grimacing and hideous; some turned cartwheels on their hands, or, perhaps, trying to make themselves funny, sketched the manners of the day with exaggerated gracefulness.

A fat servant-maid and two waiters served refreshments.

The *café* boat being only covered with a roof and having no wall whatever to shut it in, this harebrained dance was open to the face of the peaceful night and of the firmament powdered with stars.

Suddenly, Mont-Valérien, opposite, appeared, illumined, as if some conflagration had arisen behind it. The radiance spread itself and deepened upon the sky, describing a large luminous circle of white, wan light. Then something or other red appeared, grew greater, shining with a burning crimson, like that of hot metal upon the anvil. It gradually developed into a round body rising from the earth; and the moon, freeing herself from the horizon, rose slowly into space. As she ascended, the purple tint faded and became yellow, a shining bright yellow, and the satellite grew smaller in proportion as her distance increased.

Paul watched the moon for some time, lost in contemplation, forgetting his mistress; when he returned to himself the latter had vanished.

He sought for her, but could not find her. He threw his anxious eye over table after table, going to and fro unceasingly, inquiring after her from this one and that one. No one had seen her. He was tormented with disquietude, when one of the waiters said to him:

"You are looking for Madame Madeleine, are you not? She left but a few moments ago, in company with Madame Pauline." And at the same instant, Paul perceived the cabin-boy and the two pretty girls standing at the other end of the *café*, all three holding each others' waists and lying in wait for him, whispering to one another. He understood, and, like a madman, dashed off into the island.

He first ran toward Chaton, but having reached the plain, retraced his steps. Then he began to search the dense coppices, occasionally roaming about distractedly, or halting to listen.

The toads all about him poured out their short metallic notes.

From the direction of Bougival, some unknown bird warbled a song which reached him from the distance.

Over the large lawns the moon shed a soft light, resembling powdered wool; it penetrated the foliage, silvered the bark of the poplars, and riddled with its brilliant rays the waving tops of the great trees. The entrancing poetry of this summer night had, in spite of himself, entered into Paul, athwart his infatuated anguish, stirring his heart with a ferocious irony, and increasing even to madness his craving for an ideal tenderness, for passionate outpourings on the bosom of an adored and faithful woman. He was compelled to stop, choked by hurried and rending sobs.

The convulsion over, he started anew.

Suddenly, he received what resembled the stab of a poniard. There, behind that bush, some people were kissing. He ran thither; and found an amorous couple whose faces were united in an endless kiss.

He dared not call, knowing well that she would not respond, and he had a frightful dread of discovering them all at once.

The flourishes of the quadrilles, with the earsplitting solos of the cornet, the false shriek of the flute, the shrill squeaking of the violin, irritated his feelings, and increased his suffering. Wild and limping music was floating under the trees, now feeble, now stronger, wafted hither and thither by the breeze.

Suddenly he thought that possibly she had returned. Yes, she had returned! Why not? He had stupidly lost his head, without cause, carried away by his fears, by the inordinate suspicions which had for some time overwhelmed him. Seized by one of those singular calms which will sometimes occur in cases of the greatest despair, he returned toward the ball-room.

With a single glance of the eye, he took in the whole room. He made the round of the tables, and abruptly again found himself face to face with the three women. He must have had a doleful and queer expression of countenance, for all three burst into laughter.

He made off, returned to the island, and threw himself into the coppice panting. He listened again, listened a long time, for his ears were singing. At last, however, he believed he heard farther off a little, sharp laugh, which he recognized at once; and he advanced very quietly, on his knees, removing the branches from his path, his heart beating so rapidly, that he could no longer breathe.

Two voices murmured some words, the meaning of which he did not understand, and then they were silent.

Next, he was possessed by a frightful longing to fly, to save himself, forever, from this furious passion which threatened his existence. He was about to return to Chaton and take the train, resolved never to come back again, never again to see her. But her likeness suddenly rushed in upon him, and he mentally pictured the moment in the morning when she would awake in their warm bed, and would press coaxingly against him, throwing her arms around his neck, her hair disheveled, and a little entangled on the forehead, her eyes still shut and her lips apart ready to receive the first kiss. The sudden recollection of this morning caress filled him with frantic recollections and the maddest desire.

The couple began to speak again; and he approached, stooping low. Then a faint cry rose from under the branches quite close to him. He advanced again, always in spite of himself, invincibly attracted, without being conscious of anything—and he saw them.

He stood there astounded and speechless, as if he had suddenly stumbled upon a corpse, dead and mutilated. Then, in an involuntary flash of thought, he remembered the little fish whose entrails he had felt being torn out! But Madeleine spoke to her companion in the same tone in which she had often called him by name, and he was seized by such a fit of anguish that he turned and fled.

He struck against two trees, fell over a root, set off again, and suddenly found himself near the rapid branch of the river, which was lit up by the moon. The torrent-like current made great eddies where the light played upon it. The high bank dominated the stream like a cliff, leaving a wide obscure zone at its foot where the eddies could be heard swirling in the darkness.

On the other bank, the country seats of Croissy could be plainly seen.

Paul saw all this as though in a dream; he thought of nothing, understood nothing, and all things, even his very existence, appeared vague, far-off, forgotten, done with.

The river was there. Did he know what he was doing? Did he wish to die? He was mad. He turned, however, toward the island, toward her, and in the still air of the night, in which the faint and persistent burden of the music was borne up and down, he uttered, in a voice frantic with despair, bitter beyond measure, and superhumanly low, a frightful cry:

"Madeleine!"

His heartrending call shot across the great silence of the sky, and sped around the horizon. Then with a tremendous leap, with the bound of a wild animal, he jumped into the river. The water rushed on, closed over him, and from the place where he had disappeared a series of great circles started, enlarging their brilliant undulations, until they finally reached the other bank. The two women had heard the noise of the plunge. Madeleine drew herself up and exclaimed:

"It is Paul,"—a suspicion having arisen in her soul,—"he has drowned himself"; and she rushed toward the bank, where Pauline rejoined her.

A clumsy punt, propelled by two men, turned and returned on the spot. One of the men rowed, the other plunged into the water a great pole and appeared to be looking for something. Pauline cried:

"What are you doing? What is the matter?"

An unknown voice answered:

"It is a man who has just drowned himself."

The two ghastly women, squeezing each other tightly, followed the maneuvers of the boat. The music of La Grenouillère continued to sound in the distance, seeming with its cadences to accompany the movements of the somber fishermen; and the river which now concealed a corpse, whirled round and round, illuminated. The search was prolonged. The horrible suspense made Madeleine shiver all over. At last, after at least half an hour, one of the men announced:

"I have got it."

And he pulled up his long pole very gently, very gently. Then something large appeared upon the surface.

The other mariner left his oars, and by uniting their strength and hauling upon the inert weight, they succeeded in getting it into their boat.

Then they made for land, seeking a place well lighted and low. At the moment they landed, the women also arrived. The moment she saw him, Madeleine fell back with horror. In the moonlight he already appeared green, with his mouth, his eyes, his nose, his clothes full of slime. His fingers, closed and stiff, were hideous. A kind of black and liquid plaster covered his whole body. The face appeared swollen, and from his hair, glued up by the ooze, there ran a stream of dirty water.

"Do you know him?" asked one.

The other, the Croissy ferryman, hesitated:

"Yes, it certainly seems to me that I have seen that head; but you know when a body is in that state one cannot recognize it easily." And then, suddenly:

"Why, it's Mr. Paul!"

"Who is Mr. Paul?" inquired his comrade.

The first answered:

"Why, Mr. Paul Baron, the son of the senator, the little chap who was so amorous."

The other added, philosophically:

"Well, his fun is ended now; it is a pity, all the same, when one is rich!"

Madeleine sobbed and fell fainting. Pauline approached the body and asked:

"Is he indeed quite dead?"

The men shrugged their shoulders.

"Oh! after that length of time, certainly."

Then one of them asked:

"Was it not at the Grillon that he lodged?"

"Yes," answered the other; "we had better take him back there, there will be something to be made of it."

They embarked again in their boat and set out, moving off slowly on account of the rapid current. For a long time after they were out of sight of the place where the women remained, the regular splash of the oars in the water could be heard.

Then Pauline took the poor weeping Madeleine in her arms, petted her, embraced her for a long while, and consoled her.

"What would you have; it is not your fault, is it? It is impossible to prevent men committing folly. He wished it; so much the worse for him, after all!"

And then lifting her up:

"Come, my dear, come and sleep at the house; it is impossible for you to go back to the Grillon tonight."

And she embraced her again, saying: "Come, we will cure you."

Madeleine arose, and weeping all the while but with fainter sobs, laid her head upon Pauline's shoulder, as though it had found a refuge in a closer and more certain affection, more familiar and more confiding, and set off with very slow steps.

MARROCA

You ASK ME, MY dear friend, to send you my impressions of Africa, and an account of my adventures, especially of my love affairs in this seductive land. You laughed a great deal beforehand at my dusky sweethearts, as you called them, and declared that you could see me returning to France followed by a tall, ebony-colored woman, with a yellow silk handkerchief round her head, and wearing voluminous bright-colored trousers.

No doubt the Moorish dames will have their turn, for I have seen several who made me feel very much inclined to fall in love with them. But by way of making a beginning, I came across something better, and very original.

In your last letter to me, you say: "When I know how people love in a country, I know that country well enough to describe it, although I may never have seen it." Let me tell you, then, that here they love furiously. From the very first moment one feels a sort of trembling ardor, of constant desire, to the very tips of the fingers, which overexcites the powers and faculties of physical sensation, from the simple contact of the hands down to that requirement which makes us commit so many follies.

Do not misunderstand me. I do not know whether you call love of the heart a love of the soul; whether sentimental idealism, Platonic love, in a word, can exist on this earth; I doubt it, myself. But that other love, sensual love, which has something good, a great deal of good about it, is really terrible in this climate. The heat, the burning atmosphere which makes you feverish, the suffocating blasts of wind from the south, waves of fire from the desert which is so near us, that oppressive sirocco which is more destructive and withering than fire, a perpetual conflagration of an entire continent, burned even to its stones by a fierce and devouring sun, inflame the blood, excite the flesh, and make brutes of us.

But to come to my story. I shall not dwell on the beginning of my stay in Africa. After visiting Bona, Constantine, Biskara, and Setif, I went to Bougie through the defiles of Chabet,[8] by an excellent road cut through a large forest, which follows the sea at a height of six hundred feet above it and leads to that wonderful bay of Bougie, which is as beautiful as that of Naples, of Ajaccio, or of Douarnenez, which are the most lovely that I know of.

Far away in the distance, before one rounds the large inlet where the water is perfectly calm, one sees Bougie. It is built on the steep sides of a high hill covered with trees, and forms a white spot on that green slope; it might almost be taken for the foam of a cascade falling into the sea.

I had no sooner set foot in that small, delightful town, than I knew that I should stay for a long time. In all directions the eye rests on rugged, strangely shaped hilltops, so close together that you can hardly see the open sea, so that the gulf looks like a lake. The blue water is wonderfully transparent, and the azure sky, a deep azure, as if it had received two coats of color, expands its wonderful beauty above it. They seem to be looking at themselves in a glass, a veritable reflection of each other.

Bougie is a town of ruins, and on the quay is such a magnificent ruin that you might imagine you were at the opera. It is the old Saracen Gate, overgrown with ivy, and there are ruins in all directions on the hills round the town, fragments of Roman walls, bits of Saracen monuments, and remains of Arabic buildings.

I had taken a small, Moorish house, in the upper town. You know those dwellings, which have been described so often. They have no windows on the outside; but they are lighted from top to bottom by an inner court. On the first floor, they have a large, cool room, in which one spends the days, and a terrace on the roof, on which one spends the nights.

I at once fell in with the custom of all hot countries, that is to say, of taking a *siesta* after lunch. That is the hottest time in Africa, the time when one can scarcely breathe; when the streets, the fields, and the long, dazzling, white roads are deserted, when everyone is asleep, or at any rate, trying to sleep, attired as scantily as possible.

In my drawing-room, which had columns of Arabic architecture, I had placed a large, soft couch, covered with a carpet from Djebel Amour. There, very nearly in the costume of Assan, I sought to rest, but I could not sleep, as I was tortured by continence. There are two forms of torture on this earth which I hope you will never know: the want of water, and the want of women, and I do not know which is the worst. In the desert, men would commit any infamy for the sake of a glass of clean, cold water, and what would one not do in some of the towns of the littoral for the companionship of a handsome woman? There is no lack of girls in Africa; on the contrary, they abound, but, to continue my comparison, they are as unwholesome as the muddy water in the pools of Sahara.

Well one day, when I was feeling more enervated than usual, I was trying in vain to close my eyes. My legs twitched as if they were being pricked, and I tossed about uneasily on my couch. At last, unable to bear it any longer, I got up and went out. It was a terribly hot day, in the middle of July, and the pavement was hot enough to bake bread on. My shirt, which was soaked with perspiration, clung to my body; on the horizon there was a slight, white vapor, which seemed to be palpable heat.

I went down to the sea, and circling the port, walked along the shore of the pretty bay where the baths are. There was nobody about, and nothing was stirring; not a sound of bird or of beast was to be heard, the very waves did not lap, and the sea appeared to be asleep in the sun.

Suddenly, behind one of the rocks, which were half covered by the silent water, I heard a slight movement. Turning round, I saw a tall, naked girl, sitting up to her bosom in the water, taking a bath; no doubt she reckoned on being alone at that hot period of the day. Her head was turned toward the sea, and she was moving gently up and down, without seeing me.

Nothing could be more surprising than that picture of a beautiful woman in the water, which was as clear as crystal, under a blaze of light. She was a marvelously beautiful woman, tall, and modeled like a statue. She turned round, uttered a cry, and half swimming, half walking, hid herself altogether behind her rock. I knew she must necessarily come out, so I sat down on the beach and waited. Presently, she just showed her head, which was covered with thick black plaits of hair. She had a rather large mouth, with full lips, large, bold eyes, and her skin, which was tanned by the climate, looked like a piece of old, hard, polished ivory.

She called out to me: "Go away!" and her full voice, which corresponded to her strong build, had a guttural accent. As I did not move, she added: "It is not right of you to stop there, Monsieur." I did not move, however, and her head disappeared. Ten minutes passed, and then her hair, then her forehead, and then her eyes reappeared, but slowly and prudently, as if she were playing at hide-and-seek, and were looking to see who was near. This time she was furious, and called out: "You will make me catch a chill, for I shall not come out as long as you are there." Thereupon, I got up and went away, but not without looking round several times. When she thought I was far enough off, she came out of the water. Bending down and turning her back to me, she disappeared in a cavity of the rock, behind a petticoat that was hanging up in front of it.

I went back the next day. She was bathing again, but she had a bathing costume and she began to laugh, and showed her white teeth. A week later we were friends, and in another week we were eager lovers. Her name was Marroca, and she pronounced it as if there were a dozen *rs* in it. She was the daughter of Spanish colonists, and had married a Frenchman, whose name was Pontabèze. He was in government employ, though I never exactly knew what his functions were. I found out that he was always very busy, and I did not care for anything else.

She then altered her time for having her bath, and came to my house every day, to take her *siesta* there. What a *siesta*! It could scarcely be called reposing! She was a splendid girl, of a somewhat animal but superb type. Her eyes were always glowing with passion;

her half-open mouth, her sharp teeth, and even her smiles, had some-thing ferociously loving about them; and her curious, long and coni-cal breasts gave her whole body something of the animal, made her a sort of inferior yet magnificent being, a creature destined for unbri-dled love, and roused in me the idea of those ancient deities who gave expression to their tenderness on the grass and under the trees.

And then, her mind was as simple as two and two are four, and a sonorous laugh served her instead of thought.

Instinctively proud of her beauty, she hated the slightest covering, and ran and frisked about my house with daring and unconscious im-modesty. When she was at last overcome and worn out by her cries and movements, she used to sleep soundly and peacefully, while the overwhelming heat brought out minute spots of perspiration on her brown skin.

Sometimes she returned in the evening, when her husband was on duty somewhere, and we used to lie on the terrace, scarcely covered by some fine, gauzy, Oriental fabric. When the full moon lit up the town and the gulf, with its surrounding frame of hills, we saw on all the other terraces a recumbent army of silent phantoms, who would occasionally get up, change their places, and lie down again, in the languorous warmth of the starry night.

In spite of the brightness of African nights, Marroca would insist upon stripping herself almost naked in the clear rays of the moon; she did not trouble herself much about anybody who might see us, and often, in spite of my fears and entreaties, she uttered long, resound-ing cries, which made the dogs in the distance howl.

One night, when I was sleeping under the starry sky, she came and kneeled down on my carpet, and putting her lips, which curled slightly, close to my face, she said:

"You must come and stay at my house."

I did not understand her, and asked:

"What do you mean?"

"Yes, when my husband has gone away you must come and be with me."

I could not help laughing, and said: "Why, as you come here?"

And she went on, almost talking into my mouth, sending her hot breath into my throat, and moistening my mustache with her lips:

"I want it as a remembrance."

Still I did not grasp her meaning. Then she put her arms round my neck and said: "When you are no longer here, I shall think of it."

I was touched and amused at the same time and replied: "You must be mad. I would much rather stop here."

As a matter of fact, I have no liking for assignations under the conjugal roof; they are mouse-traps, in which the unwary are always caught. But she begged and prayed, and even cried, and at last said: "You shall see how I will love you there."

Her wish seemed so strange that I could not explain it to myself; but on thinking it over, I thought I could discern a profound hatred for her husband, the secret vengeance of a woman who takes a pleasure in deceiving him, and who, moreover, wishes to deceive him in his own house.

"Is your husband very unkind to you?" I asked her. She looked vexed, and said:

"Oh, no, he is very kind."

"But you are not fond of him?"

She looked at me with astonishment in her large eyes. "Indeed, I am very fond of him, very; but not so fond as I am of you."

I could not understand it all, and while I was trying to get at her meaning, she pressed one of those kisses, whose power she knew so well, on to my lips, and whispered: "But you will come, will you not?"

I resisted, however, and so she got up immediately, and went away; nor did she come back for a week. On the eighth day she came back, stopped gravely at the door of my bode, and said: "Are you coming to my house to-night? If you refuse, I shall go away."

Eight days is a very long time, my friend, and in Africa those eight days are as good as a month. "Yes," I said, and opened my arms, and she threw herself into them.

At night she waited for me in a neighboring street, and took me to their house, which was very small, and near the harbor. I first of all went through the kitchen, where they had their meals, and then into a very tidy, whitewashed room, with photographs on the walls and paper flowers under a glass case. Marroca seemed beside herself with pleasure, and she jumped about and said: "There, you are at home, now." And I certainly acted as though I were, though I felt rather embarrassed and somewhat uneasy.

Suddenly a loud knocking at the door made us start, and a man's voice called out: "Marroca, it is I."

She started: "My husband! Here, hide under the bed, quickly."

I was distractedly looking for my coat, but she gave me a push, and panted out: "Come along, come along."

I lay down flat on my stomach, and crept under the bed without a word, while she went into the kitchen. I heard her open a cupboard and then shut it again, and she came back into the room carrying some object which I could not see, but which she quickly put down. Then, as her husband was getting impatient, she said, calmly: "I cannot find the matches." Suddenly she added: "Oh, here they are; I will come and let you in."

The man came in, and I could see nothing of him but his feet, which were enormous. If the rest of him was in proportion, he must have been a giant.

I heard kisses, a little pat on her naked flesh, and a laugh, and he said, in a strong Marseilles accent: "I forgot my purse, so I was obliged to come back; you were sound asleep, I suppose."

He went to the cupboard, and was a long time in finding what he wanted; and as Marroca had thrown herself on to the bed, as if she were tired out, he went up to her, and no doubt tried to caress her, for she flung a volley of angry *rs* at him. His feet were so close to me that I felt a stupid, inexplicable longing to catch hold of them, but I restrained myself. When he saw that he could not succeed in his wish, he got angry, and said: "You are not at all nice, to-night. Good-bye."

I heard another kiss, then the big feet turned, and I saw the nails in the soles of his shoes as he went into the next room, the front door was shut, and I was saved!

I came slowly out of my retreat, feeling rather humiliated, and while Marroca danced a jig round me, shouting with laughter, and clapping her hands, I threw myself heavily into a chair. But I jumped up with a bound, for I had sat down on something cold, and as I was no more dressed than my accomplice was, the contact made me start. I looked round. I had sat down on a small ax, used for cutting wood, and as sharp as a knife. How had it got there? I had certainly not seen it when I went in; but Marroca seeing me jump up, nearly choked with laughter, and coughed with both hands on her sides.

I thought her amusement rather out of place; we had risked our lives stupidly, I still felt a cold shiver down my back, and I was rather hurt at her foolish laughter.

"Supposing your husband had seen me?" I said.

"There was no danger of that," she replied.

"What do you mean? No danger? That is a good joke! If he had stooped down, he must have seen me."

She did not laugh any more, she only looked at me with her large eyes, which were bright with merriment.

"He would not have stooped."

"Why?" I persisted. "Just suppose that he had let his hat fall, he would have been sure to pick it up, and then—I was well prepared to defend myself, in this costume!"

She put her two strong, round arms about my neck, and, lowering her voice, as she did when she said "I *adorre* you," she whispered:

"Then he would *never* have got up again."

I did not understand her, and said: "What do you mean?"

She gave me a cunning wink, and put out her hand to the chair on which I had sat down, and her outstretched hands, her smile, her half-open lips, her white, sharp, and ferocious teeth, all drew my attention to the little ax which was used for cutting wood, the sharp blade of which was glistening in the candle-light. While she put out her hand as if she were going to take it, she put her left arm round me, and drawing me to her, and putting her lips against mine, with her right arm she made a motion as if she were cutting off the head of a kneeling man!

This, my friend, is the manner in which people here understand conjugal duties, love, and hospitality!

MOONLIGHT

THE ABBÉ* MARIGNAN, AS soldier of the Church, bore his fighting title well. He was a tall, thin priest, very fanatical, of an ecstatic but upright soul. All his beliefs were fixed, without ever a wavering. He thought that he understood God thoroughly, that he penetrated His designs, His wishes, His intentions.

When he promenaded with great strides in the garden walk of his little country parsonage, sometimes a question rose in his mind: "Why did God make that?" And in fancy taking the place of God, he searched obstinately, and nearly always he found the reason. It is not he who would have murmured in a transport of pious humility, "O Lord, thy ways are past finding out!" He said to himself, "I am the servant of God; I ought to know the reason of what He does, or to divine it if I do not."

Everything in nature seemed to him created with an absolute and admirable logic. The "wherefore" and the "because" were always balanced. The dawns were made to render glad your waking, the days to ripen the harvests, the rains to water them, the evenings to prepare for sleeping, and the nights dark for sleep.

The four seasons corresponded perfectly to all the needs of agriculture; and to him the suspicion could never have come that nature has no intentions, and that all which lives has bent itself, on the contrary, to the hard conditions of different periods, of climates, and of matter.

Only he did hate women; he hated them unconsciously, and he despised them by instinct. He often repeated the words of Christ, "Woman, what have I to do with thee?" and he added, "One would

---

* Father (that is, a Catholic priest).

almost say that God himself was ill-pleased with that particular work of his hands." Woman was indeed for him the "child twelve times unclean" of whom the poet speaks. She was the temptress who had ensnared the first man, and who still continued her work of damnation; she was the being who is feeble, dangerous, mysteriously troubling. And even more than her body of perdition, he hated her loving soul.

He had often felt women's tenderness attach itself to him, and though he knew himself to be unassailable, he grew exasperated at that need of loving which quivered always in their hearts.

God, to his mind, had only created woman to tempt man and to prove him. You should not approach her without those precautions for defence which you would take, and those fears which you would cherish, near a trap. She was, indeed, just like a trap, with her arms extended and her lips open towards a man.

He had indulgence only for nuns, rendered harmless by their vow; but he treated them harshly notwithstanding, because, ever living at the bottom of their chained-up hearts, of their chastened hearts, he perceived that eternal tenderness which constantly went out to him, although he was a priest.

He was conscious of it in their looks more moist with piety than the looks of monks, in their ecstasies, in their transports of love towards the Christ, which angered him because it was women's love; and he was also conscious of it, of that accursed tenderness, in their very docility, in the softness of their voices when they spoke to him, in their lowered eyes, and in the meekness of their tears when he reproved them roughly.

And he shook his cassock on issuing from the doors of the convent, and he went off with long strides, as though he had fled before some danger.

He had a niece who lived with her mother in a little house near by. He was bent on making her a sister of charity.

She was pretty, and hare-brained, and a great tease. When the abbé sermonized, she laughed; when he was angry at her, she kissed him vehemently, pressing him to her heart, while he would seek involuntarily to free himself from this embrace, which, notwithstanding, made him taste a certain sweet joy, awaking deep within him that sensation of fatherhood which slumbers in every man.

Often he talked to her of God, of his God, walking beside her along the foot-paths through the fields. She hardly listened, and looked at the sky, the grass, the flowers with a joy of living which could be seen in her eyes. Sometimes she rushed forward to catch some flying creature, and bringing it back, would cry: "Look, my uncle, how pretty it is; I should like to kiss it." And this necessity to "kiss flies," or lilac berries, worried, irritated, and revolted the priest, who saw, even in that, the ineradicable tenderness which ever springs at the hearts of women.

And now one day the sacristan's* wife, who kept house for the Abbé Marignan, told him, very cautiously, that his niece had a lover!

He experienced a dreadful emotion, and he stood choked, with the soap all over his face, being in the act of shaving.

When he found himself able to think and speak once more, he cried: "It is not true; you are lying, Mélanie!"

But the peasant woman put her hand on her heart: "May our Lord judge me if I am lying, Monsieur le Curé. I tell you she goes to him every evening as soon as your sister is in bed. They meet each other beside the river. You have only to go there between ten o'clock and midnight, and see for yourself."

He ceased scratching his chin, and he commenced to walk the room violently, as he always did in his hours of gravest thought. When he tried to begin his shaving again, he cut himself three times from nose to ear.

All day long, he remained silent, swollen with anger and with rage. To his priestly zeal against the mighty power of love was added the moral indignation of a father, of a teacher, of a keeper of souls, who has been deceived, robbed, played with by a child. He had that egotistical choking sensation such as parents feel when their daughter anounces that she has chosen a husband without them and in spite of their advice.

---

* A sacristan is an official responsible for maintaining a church's sacred vestments and vessels.

After his dinner, he tried to read a little, but he could not bring himself so far; and he grew angrier and angrier. When it struck ten, he took his cane, a formidable oaken club which he always carried when he had to go out at night to visit the sick. And he smilingly regarded the enormous cudgel, holding it in his solid, countryman's fist and cutting threatening circles with it in the air. Then, suddenly he raised it, and grinding his teeth, he brought it down upon a chair, the back of which, split in two, fell heavily to the ground.

He opened his door to go out; but he stopped upon the threshold, surprised by such a splendor of moonlight as you seldom see.

And since he was endowed with an exalted spirit, such a spirit as must have belonged to those dreamer-poets, the Fathers of the Church, he felt himself suddenly distracted, moved by the grand and serene beauty of the pale-faced night.

In his little garden, quite bathed with the soft brilliance, his fruit-trees, all arow, were outlining in shadow upon the walk, their slender limbs of wood scarce clothed by verdure; while the giant honeysuckle climbing on the house wall, exhaled delicious, sugared breaths, and seemed to cause to hover through the warm clear night a perfumed soul.

He began to breathe deep, drinking the air as drunkards drink their wine, and he walked slowly, being ravished, astounded, and almost oblivious of his niece.

As soon as he came into the open country he stopped to contemplate the whole plain, so inundated by this caressing radiance, so drowned in the tender and languishing charm of the serene nights. At every instant the frogs threw into space their short metallic notes, and the distant nightingales mingled with the seduction of the moonlight that fitful music of theirs which brings no thoughts but dreams, that light and vibrant melody of theirs which is composed for kisses.

The abbé continued his course, his courage failing, he knew not why. He felt, as it were, enfeebled, and suddenly exhausted; he had a great desire to sit down, to pause here, to praise God in all His works.

Down there, following the bends of the little river, wound a great line of poplars. On and about the banks, wrapping all the tortuous watercourse with a kind of light, transparent wadding, hung suspended a fine mist, a white vapor, which the moon-rays crossed, and silvered, and caused to gleam.

The priest paused yet again, penetrated to the bottom of his soul by a strong and growing emotion.

And a doubt, a vague uneasiness, seized on him; he perceived that one of those questions which he sometimes put to himself, was now being born.

Why had God done this? Since the night is destined for sleep, for unconsciousness, for repose, for forgetfulness of everything, why, then, make it more charming than the day, sweeter than the dawns and the sunsets? And this slow seductive star, more poetical than the sun, and so discreet that it seems designed to light up things too delicate, too mysterious, for the great luminary,—why was it come to brighten all the shades?

Why did not the cleverest of all songsters go to rest like the others? And why did he set himself to singing in the vaguely troubling dark?

Why this half-veil over the world? Why these quiverings of the heart, this emotion of the soul, this languor of the body?

Why this display of seductions which mankind never sees, being asleep in bed? For whom was intended this sublime spectacle, this flood of poetry poured from heaven to earth?

And the abbé did not understand at all.

But now, see, down there along the edge of the field appeared two shadows walking side by side under the arched roof of the trees all soaked in glittering mist.

The man was the taller, and had his arm about his mistress's neck, and from time to time he kissed her on the forehead. They animated suddenly the lifeless landscape, which enveloped them like a divine frame made expressly for this. They seemed, these two, like one being, the being for whom was destined this calm and silent night; and they came on towards the priest like a living answer, the answer vouchsafed by his Master to his question.

He stood stock-still, quite overwhelmed, and with a beating heart. And he thought to see here some Bible story, like the loves of Ruth and Boaz, the accomplishment of the will of the Lord in one of those great scenes talked of in the holy books. Through his head began to hum the versicles of the Song of Songs, the ardent cries, the calls of the body, all the passionate poetry of that poem which burns with tenderness and love.

And he said to himself, "God perhaps has made such nights as this to clothe with the ideal the loves of men."

He withdrew before this couple who went ever arm in arm. For all that, it was really his niece; but now he asked himself if he had not been about to disobey God. And does not God indeed permit love, since He surrounds it visibly with splendor such as this?

And he fled, in a maze, almost ashamed, as if he had penetrated into a temple where he had not the right to go.

THE WILL

I KNEW THAT TALL young fellow, René de Bourneval. He was an agreeable man, though of a rather melancholy turn of mind, and prejudiced against everything, very skeptical, and fond of tearing worldly hypocrisies to pieces. He often used to say:

"There are no honorable men, or, at any rate, they only appear so when compared to low people."

He had two brothers, whom he shunned, the Messieurs de Courcils. I thought they were by another father, on account of the difference in the name. I had frequently heard that something strange had happened in the family, but I did not know the details.

As I took a great liking to him, we soon became intimate, and one evening, when I had been dining with him alone, I asked him by chance: "Are you by your mother's first or second marriage?" He grew rather pale; then he flushed, and did not speak for a few moments; he was visibly embarrassed. Then he smiled in that melancholy and gentle manner peculiar to him, and said:

"My dear friend, if it will not weary you, I can give you some very strange particulars about my life. I know you to be a sensible man, so I do not fear that our friendship will suffer by my revelations, and should it suffer, I should not care about having you for my friend any longer.

"My mother, Madame de Courcils, was a poor, little, timid woman, whom her husband had married for the sake of her fortune. Her whole life was a continual martyrdom. Of a loving, delicate mind, she was constantly ill-treated by the man who ought to have been my father, one of those boors called country gentlemen. A month after their marriage he was living with a servant, and besides

76

that, the wives and daughters of his tenants were his mistresses, which did not prevent him from having three children by his wife, that is, if you count me in. My mother said nothing, and lived in that noisy house like a little mouse. Set aside, disparaged, nervous, she looked at people with bright, uneasy, restless eyes, the eyes of some terrified creature which can never shake off its fear. And yet she was pretty, very pretty and fair, a gray blonde, as if her hair had lost its color through her constant fears.

"Among Monsieur de Courcils's friends who constantly came to the château there was an ex-cavalry officer, a widower, a man to be feared, a man at the same time tender and violent, and capable of the most energetic resolution, Monsieur de Bourneval, whose name I bear. He was a tall, thin man, with a heavy black mustache, and I am very like him. He was a man who had read a great deal, and whose ideas were not like those of most of his class. His great-grandmother had been a friend of J. J. Rousseau, and you might have said that he had inherited something of this ancestral connection. He knew the "Contrat Social" and the "Nouvelle Héloïse" by heart, and, indeed, all those philosophical books which led the way to the overthrow of our old usages, prejudices, superannuated laws, and imbecile morality.

"It seems that he loved my mother, and she loved him, but their intrigue was carried on so secretly that no one guessed it. The poor, neglected, unhappy woman must have clung to him in a despairing manner, and in her intimacy with him must have imbibed all his ways of thinking, theories of free thought, audacious ideas of independent love. But as she was so timid that she never ventured to speak aloud, it was all driven back, condensed, and expressed in her heart, which never opened itself.

"My two brothers were very cruel to her, like their father, and never gave her a caress. Used to seeing her count for nothing in the house, they treated her rather like a servant, and so I was the only one of her sons who really loved her, and whom she loved.

"When she died I was seventeen, and I must add, in order that you may understand what follows, that there had been a lawsuit between my father and my mother. Their property had been separated, to my mother's advantage, as, thanks to the workings of the law and the intelligent devotion of a lawyer to her interests, she had preserved the right to make her will in favor of anyone she pleased.

"We were told that there was a will lying at the lawyer's, and were invited to be present at the reading of it. I can remember it, as if it were yesterday. It was a grand, dramatic, yet burlesque and surprising scene, brought about by the posthumous revolt of a dead woman, by a cry for liberty from the depths of her tomb, on the part of a martyred woman who had been crushed by a man's habits during her life, and, who, from her grave, uttered a despairing appeal for independence.

"The man who thought that he was my father, a stout, ruddy-faced man, who gave you the idea of a butcher, and my brothers, two great fellows of twenty and twenty-two, were waiting quietly in their chairs. Monsieur de Bourneval, who had been invited to be present, came in and stood behind me. He was very pale, and bit his mustache, which was turning gray. No doubt he was prepared for what was going to happen. The lawyer, after opening the envelope in our presence, double-locked the door and began to read the will, which was sealed with red wax, and the contents of which he knew not."

My friend stopped suddenly and got up, and from his writing-table took an old paper, unfolded it, kissed it and then continued:

"This is the will of my beloved mother:

"I, the undersigned, Anne-Catherine-Geneviève-Mathilde de Croixluce, the legitimate wife of Léopold-Joseph Gontran de Courcils, sound in body and mind, here express my last wishes:

"I first of all ask God, and then my dear son René, to pardon me for the act I am about to commit. I believe that my child's heart is great enough to understand me, and to forgive me. I have suffered my whole life long. I was married out of calculation, then despised, misunderstood, oppressed, and constantly deceived by my husband.

"I forgive him, but I owe him nothing.

"My eldest sons never loved me, never caressed me, scarcely treated me as a mother, but during my whole life I was everything that I ought to have been, and I owe them nothing more after my death. The ties of blood cannot exist without daily and constant affection. An ungrateful son is less than a stranger; he is a culprit, for he has no right to be indifferent toward his mother.

"I have always trembled before men, before their unjust laws, their inhuman customs, their shameful prejudices. Before God, I have no longer any fear. Dead, I fling aside disgraceful hypocrisy; I dare to speak my thoughts, and to avow and to sign the secret of my heart.

"I therefore leave that part of my fortune of which the law allows me to dispose, as a deposit with my dear lover Pierre-Gennes-Simon de Bourneval, to revert afterward to our dear son René.

"(This wish is, moreover, formulated more precisely in a notarial deed.)

"And I declare before the Supreme Judge who hears me, that I should have cursed Heaven and my own existence, if I had not met my lover's deep, devoted, tender, unshaken affection, if I had not felt in his arms that the Creator made His creatures to love, sustain, and console each other, and to weep together in the hours of sadness.

"Monsieur de Courcils is the father of my two eldest sons; René alone owes his life to Monsieur de Bourneval. I pray to the Master of men and of their destinies to place father and son above social prejudices, to make them love each other until they die, and to love me also in my coffin.

"These are my last thoughts, and my last wish.

"Mathilde de Croixluce.

"Monsieur de Courcils had risen, and he cried:

" 'It is the will of a mad woman.'

"Then Monsieur de Bourneval stepped forward and said in a loud and penetrating voice: 'I, Simon de Bourneval, solemnly declare that this writing contains nothing but the strict truth, and I am ready to prove it by letters which I possess.'

"On hearing that, Monsieur de Courcils went up to him, and I thought that they were going to collar each other. There they stood, both of them tall, one stout and the other thin, both trembling. My mother's husband stammered out:

" 'You are a worthless wretch!'

"And the other replied in a loud, dry voice:

" 'We will meet somewhere else, Monsieur. I should have already slapped your ugly face, and challenged you a long time ago, if I had not, before all else, thought of the peace of mind of that poor woman whom you made to suffer so much during her lifetime.'

"Then, turning to me, he said:

" 'You are my son; will you come with me? I have no right to take you away, but I shall assume it, if you will allow me.' I shook his hand without replying, and we went out together; I was certainly three parts mad.

"Two days later Monsieur de Bourneval killed Monsieur de Courcils in a duel. My brothers, fearing some terrible scandal, held their tongues. I offered them, and they accepted, half the fortune which my mother had left me. I took my real father's name, renouncing that which the law gave me, but which was not really mine. Monsieur de Bourneval died three years afterward, and I have not consoled myself yet."

He rose from his chair, walked up and down the room, and, standing in front of me, said:

"I maintain that my mother's will was one of the most beautiful and loyal, as well as one of the grandest, acts that a woman could perform. Do you not think so?"

I gave him both my hands:

"Most certainly I do, my friend."

THE AWAKENING

During the three years that she had been married, she had not left the Val de Ciré, where her husband possessed two cotton-mills. She led a quiet life, and, although without children, she was quite happy in her house among the trees, which the work-people called the "château."

Although Monsieur Vasseur was considerably older than she was, he was very kind. She loved him, and no guilty thought had ever entered her mind.

Her mother came and spent every summer at Ciré, and then returned to Paris for the winter, as soon as the leaves began to fall.

Jeanne coughed a little every autumn, for the narrow valley through which the river wound was very foggy for five months in the year. First of all, slight mists hung over the meadows, making all the low-lying ground look like a large pond, out of which the roofs of the houses rose. Then a white vapor, which rose like a tide, enveloped everything, turning the valley into a phantom land, through which men moved like ghosts, without recognizing each other ten yards off, and the trees, wreathed in mist and dripping with moisture, rose up through it.

But the people who went along the neighboring hills, and looked down upon the deep, white depression of the valley, saw the two huge chimneys of Monsieur Vasseur's factories rising above the mist below. Day and night they vomited forth two long trails of black smoke, the sole indication that people were living in the hollow, which looked as if it were filled with a cloud of cotton.

That year, when October came, the medical men advised the young woman to go and spend the winter in Paris with her mother, as the air of the valley was dangerous for her weak chest, and she went. For a month or so, she thought continually of the house which she had left, the home to which she seemed rooted, the well-known furniture and quiet ways of which she loved so much. But by degrees she grew accustomed to her new life, and got to like entertainments, dinner and evening parties, and balls.

Till then she had retained her girlish manners, had been undecided and rather sluggish, walked languidly, and had a tired smile, but now she became animated and merry, and was always ready for pleasure. Men paid her marked attentions, and she was amused at their talk and made fun of their gallantries, as she felt sure that she could resist them, for she was rather disgusted with love from what she had learned of it in marriage.

The idea of giving up her body to the coarse caresses of such bearded creatures made her laugh with pity and shudder a little with ignorance.

She asked herself how women could consent to degrading contacts with strangers, the more so as they were already obliged to endure them with their legitimate husbands. She would have loved her husband much more if they had lived together like two friends, and had restricted themselves to chaste kisses, which are the caresses of the soul.

But she was much amused by their compliments, by the desire which showed itself in their eyes, a desire she did not share, by declarations of love whispered into her ear as they were returning to the drawing-room after some grand dinner, by words murmured so low that she almost had to guess them, words which left her blood quite cool, and her heart untouched, while gratifying her unconscious coquetry, kindling a flame of pleasure within her, making her lips open, her eyes grow bright, and her woman's heart, to which homage was due, quiver with delight.

She was fond of those *tête-à-têtes** in the dusk, when a man grows pressing, hesitates, trembles and falls on his knees. It was a delicious

---

* Private conversations between two people.

and new pleasure to her to know that they felt a passion which left her quite unmoved, able to say *no* by a shake of the head and by pursing her lips, able to withdraw her hands, to get up and calmly ring for lights, and to see the man who had been trembling at her feet get up, confused and furious when he heard the footman coming.

She often uttered a hard laugh, which froze the most burning words, and said harsh things, which fell like a jet of icy water on the most ardent protestations, while the intonations of her voice were enough to make any man who really loved her kill himself. There were two especially who made obstinate love to her, although they did not at all resemble one another.

One of them, Paul Péronel, was a tall man of the world, gallant and enterprising, a man who was accustomed to successful love affairs, one who knew how to wait, and when to seize his opportunity.

The other, Monsieur d'Avancelle, quivered when he came near her, scarcely ventured to express his love, but followed her like a shadow, and gave utterance to his hopeless desire by distracted looks, and the assiduity of his attentions to her. She made him a kind of servant and treated him as if he had been her slave.

She would have been much amused if anybody had told her that she would love him, and yet she did love him, after a singular fashion. As she saw him continually, she had grown accustomed to his voice, to his gestures, and to his manner, just as one grows accustomed to those with whom one meets continually. Often his face haunted her in her dreams, and she saw him as he really was; gentle, delicate in all his actions, humble, but passionately in love. She would awake full of these dreams, fancying that she still heard him and felt him near her, until one night (most likely she was feverish) she saw herself alone with him in a small wood, where they were both sitting on the grass. He was saying charming things to her, while he pressed and kissed her hands. She could feel the warmth of his skin and of his breath and she was stroking his hair in a very natural manner.

We are quite different in our dreams to what we are in real life. She felt full of love for him, full of calm and deep love, and was happy in stroking his forehead and in holding him against her. Gradually he put his arms round her, kissed her eyes and her cheeks without her attempting to get away from him; their lips met, and she yielded.

When she saw him again, unconscious of the agitation that he had caused her, she felt that she grew red, and while he was telling her of his love, she was continually recalling to mind their previous meeting, without being able to get rid of the recollection.

She loved him, loved him with refined tenderness, chiefly from the remembrance of her dream, although she dreaded the accomplishment of the desires which had arisen in her mind.

At last he perceived it, and then she told him everything, even to the dread of his kisses, and she made him swear that he would respect her, and he did so. They spent long hours of transcendental love together, during which their souls alone embraced, and when they separated, they were enervated, weak, and feverish.

Sometimes their lips met, and with closed eyes they reveled in that long, yet chaste caress. She felt, however, that he could not resist much longer, and as she did not wish to yield, she wrote and told her husband that she wanted to come to him, and to return to her tranquil, solitary life. But in reply, he wrote her a very kind letter, and strongly advised her not to return in the middle of the winter, and so expose herself to the sudden change of climate, and to the icy mists of the valley, and she was thunderstruck and angry with that confiding man, who did not guess, who did not understand, the struggles of her heart.

February was a warm, bright month, and although she now avoided being alone with Monsieur Avancelle, she sometimes accepted his invitation to drive round the lake in the Bois de Boulogne with him, when it was dusk.

On one of those evenings, it was so warm that it seemed as if the sap in every tree and plant were rising. Their cab was going at a walk; it was growing dusk, and they were sitting close together, holding each other's hands, and she said to herself:

"It is all over, I am lost!" for she felt her desires rising in her again, the imperious demand for that supreme embrace which she had undergone in her dream. Every moment their lips sought each other, clung together, and separated, only to meet again immediately.

He did not venture to go into the house with her, but left her at her door, more in love with him than ever, and half fainting.

Monsieur Paul Péronel was waiting for her in the little drawing-room, without a light, and when he shook hands with her, he felt how feverish she was. He began to talk in a low, tender voice, lulling her tired mind with the charm of amorous words.

She listened to him without replying, for she was thinking of the other; she thought she was listening to the other, and thought she felt him leaning against her, in a kind of hallucination. She saw only him, and did not remember that any other man existed on earth, and when her ears trembled at those three syllables: "I love you," it was he, the other man, who uttered them, who kissed her hands, who strained her to his breast, like the other had done shortly before in the cab. It was he who pressed victorious kisses on her lips, it was he whom she held in her arms and embraced, to whom she was calling, with all the longings of her heart, with all the overwrought ardor of her body.

When she awoke from her dream, she uttered a terrible cry. Paul Péronel was kneeling by her and was thanking her passionately, while he covered her disheveled hair with kisses, and she almost screamed out: "Go away! go away! go away!"

And as he did not understand what she meant, and tried to put his arm round her waist again, she writhed, as she stammered out:

"You are a wretch, and I hate you! Go away! go away!" And he got up in great surprise, took up his hat, and went.

The next day she returned to Val de Ciré, and her husband, who had not expected her for some time, blamed her for her freak.

"I could not live away from you any longer," she said.

He found her altered in character and sadder than formerly, but when he said to her: "What is the matter with you? You seem unhappy. What do you want?" she replied:

"Nothing. Happiness exists only in our dreams in this world."

Avancelle came to see her the next summer, and she received him without any emotion and without regret, for she suddenly perceived that she had never loved him, except in a dream, from which Paul Péronel had brutally roused her.

But the young man, who still adored her, thought as he returned to Paris:

"Women are really very strange, complicated, and inexplicable beings."

THE FALSE GEMS

M. LANTIN HAD MET the young woman at a *soirée*,* at the home of the assistant chief of his bureau, and at first sight had fallen madly in love with her.

She was the daughter of a country physician who had died some months previously. She had come to live in Paris, with her mother, who visited much among her acquaintances, in the hope of making a favorable marriage for her daughter. They were poor and honest, quiet and unaffected.

The young girl was a perfect type of the virtuous woman whom every sensible young man dreams of one day winning for life. Her simple beauty had the charm of angelic modesty, and the imperceptible smile which constantly hovered about her lips seemed to be the reflection of a pure and lovely soul. Her praises resounded on every side. People were never tired of saying: "Happy the man who wins her love! He could not find a better wife."

Now M. Lantin enjoyed a snug little income of $700, and, thinking he could safely assume the responsibilities of matrimony, proposed to this model young girl and was accepted.

He was unspeakably happy with her; she governed his household so cleverly and economically that they seemed to live in luxury. She lavished the most delicate attentions on her husband, coaxed and fondled him, and the charm of her presence was so great that six years after their marriage M. Lantin discovered that he loved his wife even more than during the first days of their honeymoon.

---

* Party.

He only felt inclined to blame her for two things: her love of the theater, and a taste for false jewelry. Her friends (she was acquainted with some officers' wives) frequently procured for her a box at the theater, often for the first representations of the new plays; and her husband was obliged to accompany her, whether he willed or not, to these amusements, though they bored him excessively after a day's labor at the office.

After a time, M. Lantin begged his wife to get some lady of her acquaintance to accompany her. She was at first opposed to such an arrangement; but, after much persuasion on his part, she finally consented—to the infinite delight of her husband.

Now, with her love for the theater came also the desire to adorn her person. True, her costumes remained as before, simple, and in the most correct taste; but she soon began to ornament her ears with huge rhinestones which glittered and sparkled like real diamonds. Around her neck she wore strings of false pearls, and on her arms bracelets of imitation gold.

Her husband frequently remonstrated with her, saying:

"My dear, as you cannot afford to buy real diamonds, you ought to appear adorned with your beauty and modesty alone, which are the rarest ornaments of your sex."

But she would smile sweetly, and say:

"What can I do? I am so fond of jewelry. It is my only weakness. We cannot change our natures."

Then she would roll the pearl necklaces around her fingers, and hold up the bright gems for her husband's admiration, gently coaxing him:

"Look! are they not lovely? One would swear they were real."

M. Lantin would then answer, smilingly:

"You have Bohemian tastes, my dear."

Often of an evening, when they were enjoying a tête-à-tête by the fireside, she would place on the tea table the leather box containing the "trash," as M. Lantin called it. She would examine the false gems with a passionate attention as though they were in some way connected with a deep and secret joy; and she often insisted on passing a necklace around her husband's neck, and laughing heartily would exclaim: "How droll you look!" Then she would throw herself into his arms and kiss him affectionately.

One evening in winter she attended the opera, and on her return was chilled through and through. The next morning she coughed, and eight days later she died of inflammation of the lungs.

M. Lantin's despair was so great that his hair became white in one month. He wept unceasingly; his heart was torn with grief, and his mind was haunted by the remembrance, the smile, the voice—by every charm of his beautiful, dead wife.

Time, the healer, did not assuage his grief. Often during office hours, while his colleagues were discussing the topics of the day, his eyes would suddenly fill with tears, and he would give vent to his grief in heartrending sobs. Everything in his wife's room remained as before her decease; and here he was wont to seclude himself daily and think of her who had been his treasure—the joy of his existence.

But life soon became a struggle. His income, which in the hands of his wife had covered all household expenses, was now no longer sufficient for his own immediate wants; and he wondered how she could have managed to buy such excellent wines, and such rare delicacies, things which he could no longer procure with his modest resources.

He incurred some debts and was soon reduced to absolute poverty. One morning, finding himself without a cent in his pocket, he resolved to sell something, and, immediately, the thought occurred to him of disposing of his wife's paste jewels. He cherished in his heart a sort of rancor against the false gems. They had always irritated him in the past, and the very sight of them spoiled somewhat the memory of his lost darling.

To the last days of her life, she had continued to make purchases; bringing home new gems almost every evening. He decided to sell the heavy necklace which she seemed to prefer, and which, he thought, ought to be worth about six or seven francs;[9] for although paste it was, nevertheless, of very fine workmanship.

He put it in his pocket and started out in search of a jeweler's shop. He entered the first one he saw; feeling a little ashamed to expose his misery, and also to offer such a worthless article for sale.

"Sir," said he to the merchant, "I would like to know what this is worth."

The man took the necklace, examined it, called his clerk and made some remarks in an undertone; then he put the ornament back on the counter, and looked at it from a distance to judge of the effect.

M. Lantin was annoyed by all this detail and was on the point of saying: "Oh! I know well enough it is not worth anything," when the jeweler said: "Sir, that necklace is worth from twelve to fifteen thousand francs; but I could not buy it unless you tell me now whence it comes."

The widower opened his eyes wide and remained gaping, not comprehending the merchant's meaning. Finally he stammered: "You say—are you sure?" The other replied dryly: "You can search elsewhere and see if anyone will offer you more. I consider it worth fifteen thousand at the most. Come back here if you cannot do better."

M. Lantin, beside himself with astonishment, took up the necklace and left the store. He wished time for reflection.

Once outside, he felt inclined to laugh, and said to himself: "The fool! Had I only taken him at his word! That jeweler cannot distinguish real diamonds from paste."

A few minutes after, he entered another store in the Rue de la Paix. As soon as the proprietor glanced at the necklace, he cried out:

"Ah, *parbleu!** I know it well; it was bought here."

M. Lantin was disturbed, and asked:

"How much is it worth?"

"Well, I sold it for twenty thousand francs. I am willing to take it back for eighteen thousand when you inform me, according to our legal formality, how it comes to be in your possession."

This time M. Lantin was dumfounded. He replied:

"But—but—examine it well. Until this moment I was under the impression that it was paste."

---

* Of course!

Said the jeweler:

"What is your name, sir?"

"Lantin—I am in the employ of the Minister of the Interior. I live at No. 16 Rue des Martyrs."

The merchant looked through his books, found the entry, and said: "That necklace was sent to Mme. Lantin's address, 16 Rue des Martyrs, July 20, 1876."

The two men looked into each other's eyes—the widower speechless with astonishment, the jeweler scenting a thief. The latter broke the silence by saying:

"Will you leave this necklace here for twenty-four hours? I will give you a receipt."

"Certainly," answered M. Lantin, hastily. Then, putting the ticket in his pocket, he left the store.

He wandered aimlessly through the streets, his mind in a state of dreadful confusion. He tried to reason, to understand. His wife could not afford to purchase such a costly ornament. Certainly not. But, then, it must have been a present!—a present!—a present from whom? Why was it given her?

He stopped and remained standing in the middle of the street. A horrible doubt entered his mind—she? Then all the other gems must have been presents, too! The earth seemed to tremble beneath him,—the tree before him was falling—throwing up his arms, he fell to the ground, unconscious. He recovered his senses in a pharmacy into which the passers-by had taken him, and was then taken to his home. When he arrived he shut himself up in his room and wept until nightfall. Finally, overcome with fatigue, he threw himself on the bed, where he passed an uneasy, restless night.

The following morning he arose and prepared to go to the office. It was hard to work after such a shock. He sent a letter to his employer requesting to be excused. Then he remembered that he had to return to the jeweler's. He did not like the idea; but he could not leave the necklace with that man. So he dressed and went out.

It was a lovely day; a clear blue sky smiled on the busy city below, and men of leisure were strolling about with their hands in their pockets.

Observing them, M. Lantin said to himself: "The rich, indeed, are happy. With money it is possible to forget even the deepest sorrow. One can go where one pleases, and in travel find that distraction which is the surest cure for grief. Oh! if I were only rich!"

He began to feel hungry, but his pocket was empty. He again remembered the necklace. Eighteen thousand francs! Eighteen thousand francs! What a sum!

He soon arrived in the Rue de la Paix, opposite the jeweler's. Eighteen thousand francs! Twenty times he resolved to go in, but shame kept him back. He was hungry, however,—very hungry, and had not a cent in his pocket. He decided quickly, ran across the street in order not to have time for reflection, and entered the store.

The proprietor immediately came forward, and politely offered him a chair; the clerks glanced at him knowingly.

"I have made inquiries, M. Lantin," said the jeweler, "and if you are still resolved to dispose of the gems, I am ready to pay you the price I offered."

"Certainly, sir," stammered M. Lantin.

Whereupon the proprietor took from a drawer eighteen large bills, counted and handed them to M. Lantin, who signed a receipt and with a trembling hand put the money into his pocket.

As he was about to leave the store, he turned toward the merchant, who still wore the same knowing smile, and lowering his eyes, said:

"I have—I have other gems which I have received from the same source. Will you buy them also?"

The merchant bowed: "Certainly, sir."

M. Lantin said gravely: "I will bring them to you." An hour later he returned with the gems.

The large diamond earrings were worth twenty thousand francs; the bracelets thirty-five thousand; the rings, sixteen thousand; a set of emeralds and sapphires, fourteen thousand; a gold chain with solitaire pendant, forty thousand—making the sum of one hundred and forty-three thousand francs.

The jeweler remarked, jokingly:

"There was a person who invested all her earnings in precious stones."

M. Lantin replied, seriously:

"It is only another way of investing one's money."

That day he lunched at Voisin's and drank wine worth twenty francs a bottle. Then he hired a carriage and made a tour of the Bois, and as he scanned the various turn-outs with a contemptuous air he could hardly refrain from crying out to the occupants:

"I, too, am rich!—I am worth two hundred thousand francs."

Suddenly he thought of his employer. He drove up to the office, and entered gaily, saying:

"Sir, I have come to resign my position. I have just inherited three hundred thousand francs."

He shook hands with his former colleagues and confided to them some of his projects for the future; then he went off to dine at the Café Anglais.

He seated himself beside a gentleman of aristocratic bearing, and during the meal informed the latter confidentially that he had just inherited a fortune of four hundred thousand francs.

For the first time in his life he was not bored at the theater, and spent the remainder of the night in a gay frolic.

Six months afterward he married again. His second wife was a very virtuous woman, with a violent temper. She caused him much sorrow.

THE CONFESSION

MARGUÉRITE DE THÉRELLES WAS dying. Although but fifty-six, she seemed like seventy-five at least. She panted, paler than the sheets, shaken by dreadful shiverings, her face convulsed, her eyes haggard, as if she had seen some horrible thing.

Her eldest sister, Suzanne, six years older, sobbed on her knees beside the bed. A little table drawn close to the couch of the dying woman, and covered with a napkin, bore two lighted candles, the priest being momentarily expected to give extreme unction and the communion, which should be the last.

The apartment had that sinister aspect, that air of hopeless farewells, which belongs to the chambers of the dying. Medicine bottles stood about on the furniture, linen lay in the corners, pushed aside by foot or broom. The disordered chairs themselves seemed affrighted, as if they had run, in all the senses of the word. Death, the formidable, was there, hidden, waiting.

The story of the two sisters was very touching. It was quoted far and wide; it had made many eyes to weep.

Suzanne, the elder, had once been madly in love with a young man, who had also been in love with her. They were engaged, and were only waiting the day fixed for the contract, when Henry de Lampierre suddenly died.

The despair of the young girl was dreadful, and she vowed that she would never marry. She kept her word. She put on widow's weeds, which she never took off.

Then her sister, her little sister Marguérite, who was only twelve years old, came one morning to throw herself into the arms of the elder, and said: "Big Sister, I do not want thee to be unhappy. I do not

94

want thee to cry all thy life. I will never leave thee, never, never! I—
I, too, shall never marry. I shall stay with thee always, always, always!"

Suzanne, touched by the devotion of the child, kissed her, but did
not believe.

Yet the little one, also, kept her word, and despite the entreaties
of her parents, despite the supplications of the elder, she never married. She was pretty, very pretty; she refused many a young man who
seemed to love her truly; and she never left her sister more.

They lived together all the days of their life, without ever being separated a single time. They went side by side, inseparably united. But
Marguérite seemed always sad, oppressed, more melancholy than the
elder, as though perhaps her sublime sacrifice had broken her spirit.
She aged more quickly, had white hair from the age of thirty, and often
suffering, seemed afflicted by some secret, gnawing trouble.

Now she was to be the first to die.

Since yesterday she was no longer able to speak. She had only said,
at the first glimmers of day-dawn:

"Go fetch Monsieur le Curé, the moment has come."

And she had remained since then upon her back, shaken with
spasms, her lips agitated as though dreadful words were mounting
from her heart without power of issue, her look mad with fear, terrible to see.

Her sister, torn by sorrow, wept wildly, her forehead resting on
the edge of the bed, and kept repeating:

"Margot, my poor Margot, my little one!"

She had always called her, "Little One," just as the younger had always called her "Big Sister."

Steps were heard on the stairs. The door opened. A choir-boy appeared, followed by an old priest in a surplice. As soon as she perceived him, the dying woman, with one shudder, sat up, opened her
lips, stammered two or three words, and began to scratch the sheet
with her nails as if she had wished to make a hole.

The Abbé Simon approached, took her hand, kissed her brow, and
with a soft voice:

"God pardon thee, my child; have courage, the moment is now come, speak."

Then Marguérite, shivering from head to foot, shaking her whole couch with nervous movements, stammered:

"Sit down, Big Sister . . . listen."

The priest bent down towards Suzanne, who was still flung upon the bed's foot. He raised her, placed her in an arm-chair, and taking a hand of each of the sisters in one of his own, he pronounced:

"Lord, my God! Endue them with strength, cast Thy mercy upon them."

And Marguérite began to speak. The words issued from her throat one by one, raucous, with sharp pauses, as though very feeble.

"Pardon, pardon, Big Sister; oh, forgive! If thou knewest how I have had fear of this moment all my life . . ."

Suzanne stammered through her tears:

"Forgive thee what, Little One? Thou hast given all to me, sacrificed everything; thou art an angel . . ."

But Marguérite interrupted her:

"Hush, hush! Let me speak . . . do not stop me. It is dreadful . . . let me tell all . . . to the very end, without flinching. Listen. Thou rememberest . . . thou rememberest . . . Henry . . ."

Suzanne trembled and looked at her sister. The younger continued:

"Thou must hear all, to understand. I was twelve years old, only twelve years old; thou rememberest well, is it not so? And I was spoiled, I did everything that I liked! Thou rememberest, surely, how they spoiled me? Listen. The first time that he came he had varnished boots. He got down from his horse at the great steps, and he begged pardon for his costume, but he came to bring some news to papa. Thou rememberest, is it not so? Don't speak—listen. When I saw him I was completely carried away, I found him so very beautiful; and I remained standing in a corner of the *salon** all the time that he was

---

* Living room.

talking. Children are strange . . . and terrible. Oh yes . . . I have dreamed of all that.

"He came back again . . . several times . . . I looked at him with all my eyes, with all my soul . . . I was large of my age . . . and very much more knowing than any one thought. He came back often . . . I thought only of him. I said, very low:

" 'Henry . . . Henry de Lampierre!'

"Then they said that he was going to marry thee. It was a sorrow; oh, Big Sister, a sorrow . . . a sorrow! I cried for three nights without sleeping. He came back every day, in the afternoon, after his lunch . . . thou rememberest, is it not so? Say nothing . . . listen. Thou madest him cakes which he liked . . . with meal, with butter and milk. Oh, I know well how. I could make them yet if it were needed. He ate them at one mouthful, and . . . and then he drank a glass of wine, and then he said, 'It is delicious.' Thou rememberest how he would say that?

"I was jealous, jealous! The moment of thy marriage approached. There were only two weeks more. I became crazy. I said to myself: 'He shall not marry Suzanne, no, I will not have it! It is I whom he will marry when I am grown up. I shall never find any one whom I love so much.' But one night, ten days before the contract, thou tookest a walk with him in front of the château by moonlight . . . and there . . . under the fir, under the great fir . . . he kissed thee . . . kissed . . . holding thee in his two arms . . . so long. Thou rememberest, is it not so? It was probably the first time . . . yes . . . Thou wast so pale when thou camest back to the *salon*.

"I had seen you two; I was there, in the shrubbery. I was angry! If I could I should have killed you both!

"I said to myself: 'He shall not marry Suzanne, never! He shall marry no one. I should be too unhappy.' And all of a sudden I began to hate him dreadfully.

"Then, dost thou know what I did? Listen. I had seen the gardener making little balls to kill strange dogs. He pounded up a bottle with a stone and put the powdered glass in a little ball of meat.

"I took a little medicine bottle that mamma had; I broke it small with a hammer, and I hid the glass in my pocket. It was a shining powder . . . The next day, as soon as you had made the little cakes . . . I split them with a knife and I put in the glass . . . He ate three of them . . . I too, I ate one . . . I threw the other six into the pond. The two swans died three days after . . . Dost thou remember? Oh, say nothing . . . listen, listen. I, I alone did not die . . . but I have always been sick. Listen . . . He died—thou knowest well . . . listen . . . that, that is nothing. It is afterwards, later . . . always . . . the worst . . . listen.

"My life, all my life . . . what torture! I said to myself: 'I will never leave my sister. And at the hour of death I will tell her all . . .' There! And ever since, I have always thought of that moment when I should tell thee all. Now it is come. It is terrible. Oh . . . Big Sister!

"I have always thought, morning and evening, by night and by day, 'Some time I must tell her that . . .' I waited . . . What agony! . . . It is done. Say nothing. Now I am afraid . . . am afraid . . . oh, I am afraid. If I am going to see him again, soon, when I am dead. See him again . . . think of it! The first! Before thou! I shall not dare. I must . . . I am going to die . . . I want you to forgive me. I want it . . . I cannot go off to meet him without that. Oh, tell her to forgive me, Monsieur le Curé, tell her . . . I implore you to do it. I cannot die without that . . ."

She was silent, and remained panting, always scratching the sheet with her withered nails.

Suzanne had hidden her face in her hands, and did not move. She was thinking of him whom she might have loved so long! What a good life they should have lived together! She saw him once again in that vanished by-gone time, in that old past which was put out forever. The beloved dead—how they tear your hearts! Oh, that kiss, his only kiss! She had hidden it in her soul. And after it nothing, nothing more her whole life long!

All of a sudden the priest stood straight, and, with strong vibrant voice, he cried:

"Mademoiselle Suzanne, your sister is dying!"

Then Suzanne, opening her hands, showed her face soaked with tears, and throwing herself upon her sister, she kissed her with all her might, stammering:

"I forgive thee, I forgive thee, Little One."

REGRET

MONSIEUR SAVEL, WHO WAS called in Mantes "Father Savel," had just risen from bed. He wept. It was a dull autumn day; the leaves were falling. They fell slowly in the rain, resembling another rain, but heavier and slower. M. Savel was not in good spirit. He walked from the fireplace to the window, and from the window to the fireplace. Life has its somber days. It will no longer have any but somber days for him now, for he has reached the age of sixty-two. He is alone, an old bachelor, with nobody about him. How sad it is to die alone, all alone, without the disinterested affection of anyone!

He pondered over his life, so barren, so void. He recalled the days gone by, the days of his infancy, the house, the house of his parents; his college days, his follies, the time of his probation in Paris, the illness of his father, his death. He then returned to live with his mother. They lived together, the young man and the old woman, very quietly, and desired nothing more. At last the mother died. How sad a thing is life! He has lived always alone, and now, in his turn, he too, will soon be dead. He will disappear, and that will be the finish. There will be no more of Savel upon the earth. What a frightful thing! Other people will live, they will live, they will laugh. Yes, people will go on amusing themselves, and he will no longer exist! Is it not strange that people can laugh, amuse themselves, be joyful under that eternal certainty of death! If this death were only probable, one could then have hope; but no, it is inevitable, as inevitable as that night follows the day.

If, however, his life had been complete! If he had done something; if he had had adventures, grand pleasures, successes, satisfaction of some kind or another. But now, nothing. He had done nothing, never anything but rise from bed, eat, at the same hours, and go to bed again. And he has gone on like that to the age of sixty-two years. He had not even taken unto himself a wife, as other men do. Why? Yes, why was it that he was not married? He might have been, for he possessed considerable means. Was it an opportunity which had failed him? Perhaps! But one can create opportunities. He was indifferent; that was all. Indifference had been his greatest drawback, his defect, his vice. How some men miss their lives through indifference! To certain natures, it is so difficult to get out of bed, to move about, to take long walks, to speak, to study any question.

He had not even been in love. No woman had reposed on his bosom, in a complete abandon of love. He knew nothing of this delicious anguish of expectation, of the divine quivering of the pressed hand, of the ecstasy of triumphant passion.

What superhuman happiness must inundate your heart when lips encounter lips for the first time, when the grasp of four arms makes one being of you, a being unutterably happy, two beings infatuated with each other.

M. Savel was sitting down, his feet on the fender, in his dressing gown. Assuredly his life had been spoiled, completely spoiled. He had however, loved. He had loved secretly, dolorously, and indifferently, just as was characteristic of him in everything. Yes, he had loved his old friend, Madame Saudres, the wife of his old companion, Saudres. Ah! if he had known her as a young girl! But he had encountered her too late; she was already married. Unquestionably he would have asked her hand; that he would! How he had loved her, nevertheless, without respite, since the first day he had set eyes on her!

He recalled, without emotion, all the times he had seen her, his grief on leaving her, the many nights that he could not sleep because of his thinking of her.

In the mornings he always got up somewhat less amorous than in the evening.

Why? Seeing that she was formerly pretty and plump, blond and joyous. Saudres was not the man she would have selected. She was now fifty-two years of age. She seemed happy. Ah! if she had only loved him in days gone by; yes, if she had only loved him! And why should she not have loved him, he, Savel, seeing that he loved her so much, yes, her, Madame Saudres!

If only she could have divined something— Had she not divined anything, had she not seen anything, never comprehended anything? But then, what would she have thought? If he had spoken what would she have answered?

And Savel asked himself a thousand other things. He reviewed his whole life, seeking to grasp again a multitude of details.

He recalled all the long evenings spent at the house of Saudres, when the latter's wife was young and so charming.

He recalled many things that she had said to him, the sweet intonations of her voice, the little significant smiles that meant so much.

He recalled the walks that the three of them had had, along the banks of the Seine, their lunches on the grass on the Sundays, for Saudres was employed at the subprefecture. And all at once the distinct recollection came to him of an afternoon spent with her in a little plantation on the banks of the river.

They had set out in the morning, carrying their provisions in baskets. It was a bright spring morning, one of those days which inebriate one. Everything smelled fresh, everything seemed happy. The voices of the birds sounded more joyous, and the flapping of their wings more rapid. They had lunch on the grass, under the willow-trees, quite close to the water, which glittered in the sun's rays. The air was balmy, charged with the odors of fresh vegetation; they had drunk the most delicious wines. How pleasant everything was on that day!

After lunch, Saudres went to sleep on the broad of his back, "The best nap he had in his life," said he, when he woke up.

Madame Saudres had taken the arm of Savel, and they had started to walk along the river's bank.

She leaned tenderly on his arm. She laughed and said to him: "I am intoxicated, my friend, I am quite intoxicated." He looked at her, his heart beating rapidly. He felt himself grow pale, hoping that he had not looked too boldly at her, and that the trembling of his hands had not revealed his passion.

She had decked her head with wild flowers and water-lilies, and she had asked him: "Do you not like to see me appear thus?"

As he did not answer—for he could find nothing to say, he should rather have gone down on his knees—she burst out laughing, a sort of discontented laughter which she threw straight in his face, saying: "Great goose, what ails you? You might at least speak!"

He felt like crying, and could not even yet find a word to say.

All these things came back to him now, as vividly as on the day when they took place. Why had she said this to him, "Great goose, what ails you? You might at least speak!"

And he recalled how tenderly she had leaned on his arm. And in passing under a shady tree he had felt her ear leaning against his cheek, and he had tilted his head abruptly, for fear that she had not meant to bring their flesh into contact.

When he had said to her: "Is it not time to return?" she darted at him a singular look. "Certainly," she said, "certainly," regarding him at the same time, in a curious manner. He had not thought of anything then; and now the whole thing appeared to him quite plain.

"Just as you like, my friend. If you are tired let us go back."

And he had answered: "It is not that I am fatigued; but Saudres has perhaps waked up now."

And she had said: "If you are afraid of my husband's being awake, that is another thing. Let us return."

In returning she remained silent and leaned no longer on his arm. Why?

At that time it had never occurred to him to ask himself, "Why." Now he seemed to apprehend something that he had not then understood.

What was it?

M. Savel felt himself blush, and he got up at a bound, feeling thirty years younger, believing that he now understood Madame Saudres then to say, "I love you."

Was it possible? That suspicion which had just entered into his soul, tortured him. Was it possible that he could not have seen, not have dreamed?

Oh! if that could be true, if he had rubbed against such good fortune without laying hold of it!

He said to himself: "I wish to know. I cannot remain in this state of doubt. I wish to know!" He put on his clothes quickly, dressed in hot haste. He thought: "I am sixty-two years of age, she is fifty-eight; I may ask her that now without giving offense."

He started out.

The Saudres' house was situated on the other side of the street, almost directly opposite his own. He went up to it, knocked, and a little servant came to open the door.

"You there at this hour, M. Savel? Has some accident happened to you?"

M. Savel responded:

"No, my girl; but go and tell your mistress that I want to speak to her at once."

"The fact is, Madame is preparing her stock of pear-jams for the winter, and she is standing in front of the fire. She is not dressed, as you may well understand."

"Yes, but go and tell her that I wish to see her on an important matter."

The little servant went away and Savel began to walk, with long, nervous strides, up and down the drawing-room. He did not feel himself the least embarrassed, however. Oh! he was merely going to ask her something, as he would have asked her about some cooking receipt, and that was: "Do you know that I am sixty-two years of age?"

The door opened and Madame appeared. She was now a gross woman, fat and round, with full cheeks, and a sonorous laugh. She walked with her arms away from her body, and her sleeves tucked up to the shoulders, her bare arms all smeared with sugar juice. She asked, anxiously:

"What is the matter with you, my friend; you are not ill, are you?"

"No, my dear friend; but I wish to ask you one thing, which to me is of the first importance, something which is torturing my heart, and I want you to promise that you will answer me candidly."

She laughed, "I am always candid. Say on."

"Well, then. I have loved you from the first day I ever saw you. Can you have any doubt of this?"

She responded laughing, with something of her former tone of voice:

"Great goose! what ails you? I knew it well from the very first day!"

Savel began to tremble. He stammered out: "You knew it? Then—"

He stopped.

She asked:

"Then? What?"

He answered:

"Then—what would you think?—what—what—what would you have answered?"

She broke forth into a peal of laughter, which made the sugar juice run off the tips of her fingers on to the carpet.

"I? But you did not ask me anything. It was not for me to make a declaration."

He then advanced a step toward her.

"Tell me—tell me— You remember the day when Saudres went to sleep on the grass after lunch—when we had walked together as far as the bend of the river, below—"

He waited, expectantly. She had ceased to laugh, and looked at him, straight in the eyes.

"Yes, certainly, I remember it."

He answered, shivering all over.

"Well,—that day—if I had been—if I had been—enterprising— what would you have done?"

She began to laugh as only a happy woman can laugh, who has nothing to regret, and responded frankly, in a voice tinged with irony:

"I would have yielded, my friend."

She then turned on her heels and went back to her jam-making.

Savel rushed into the street, cast down, as though he had encountered some great disaster. He walked with giant strides, through the rain, straight on, until he reached the river, without thinking where he was going. When he reached the bank he turned to the right and followed it. He walked a long time, as if urged on by some instinct. His clothes were running with water, his hat was crushed in, as soft as a piece of rag and dripping like a thatched roof. He walked on, straight in front of him. At last, he came to the place where they had lunched so long, long ago, the recollection of which had tortured his heart. He sat down under the leafless trees, and he wept.

THE AVENGER

WHEN M. ANTOINE LEUILLET married the Widow Mathilde Souris, he had been in love with her for nearly ten years.

M. Souris had been his friend, his old college chum. Leuillet was very fond of him, but found him rather a muff.* He often used to say: "That poor Souris will never set the Seine on fire."

When Souris married Mlle. Mathilde Duval, Leuillet was surprised and somewhat vexed, for he had a slight weakness for her. She was the daughter of a neighbor of his, a retired haberdasher with a good deal of money. She was pretty, well-mannered, and intelligent. She accepted Souris on account of his money.

Then Leuillet cherished hopes of another sort. He began paying attentions to his friend's wife. He was a handsome man, not at all stupid, and also well off. He was confident that he would succeed; he failed. Then he fell really in love with her, and he was the sort of lover who is rendered timid, prudent, and embarrassed by intimacy with the husband. Mme. Souris fancied that he no longer meant anything serious by his attentions to her, and she became simply his friend. This state of affairs lasted nine years.

Now, one morning, Leuillet received a startling communication from the poor woman. Souris had died suddenly of aneurism of the heart.

He got a terrible shock, for they were of the same age; but, the very next moment, a sensation of profound joy, of infinite relief, of deliverance, penetrated his body and soul. Mme. Souris was free.

* Oaf.

He had the tact, however, to make such a display of grief as the occasion required; he waited for the proper time to elapse, and attended to all the conventional usages. At the end of fifteen months, he married the widow.

His conduct was regarded as not only natural but generous. He had acted like a good friend and an honest man. In short, he was happy, quite happy.

They lived on terms of the closest confidence, having from the first understood and appreciated each other. One kept nothing secret from the other, and they told each other their inmost thoughts. Leuillet now loved his wife with a calm, trustful affection; he loved her as a tender, devoted partner, who is an equal and a confidant. But there still lingered in his soul a singular and unaccountable grudge against the deceased Souris, who had been the first to possess this woman, who had had the flower of her youth and of her soul, and who had even robbed her of her poetic attributes. The memory of the dead husband spoiled the happiness of the living husband; and this posthumous jealousy now began to torment Leuillet's heart day and night.

The result was that he was incessantly talking about Souris, asking a thousand minute and intimate questions about him, and seeking for information as to all his habits and personal characteristics. And he pursued him with railleries even into the depths of the tomb, recalling with self-satisfaction his oddities, emphasizing his absurdities, and pointing out his defects.

Constantly he would call out to his wife from one end to the other of the house:

"Hallo, Mathilde!"

"Here I am, dear."

"Come and let us have a chat."

She always came over to him, smiling, well aware that Souris was to be the subject of the chat, and anxious to gratify her second husband's harmless fad.

"I say! do you remember how Souris wanted one day to prove to me that small men are always better loved than big men?"

And he launched out into reflections unfavorable to the defunct husband, who was small, and discreetly complimentary to himself, as he happened to be tall.

And Mme. Leuillet let him think that he was quite right; and she laughed very heartily, turned the first husband into ridicule in a playful fashion for the amusement of his successor, who always ended by remarking:

"Never mind! Souris was a muff!"

They were happy, quite happy. And Leuillet never ceased to testify his unabated attachment to his wife by all the usual manifestations.

Now, one night, when they happened to be both kept awake by a renewal of youthful ardor, Leuillet, who held his wife clasped tightly in his arms and had his lips glued to hers, said:

"Tell me this, darling."

"What?"

"Souris—'tisn't easy to put the question—was he very—very loving?"

She gave him a warm kiss, as she murmured:

"Not as much as you, my sweet."

His male vanity was flattered, and he went on:

"He must have been—rather a flat—eh?"

She did not answer. There was merely a sly little laugh on her face, which she pressed close to her husband's neck.

He persisted in his questions:

"Come now! Don't deny that he was a flat—well, I mean, rather an awkward sort of fellow?"

She nodded slightly.

"Well, yes, rather awkward."

He went on:

"I'm sure he used to weary you many a night—isn't that so?"

This time she had an access of frankness, and she replied:

"Oh! yes."

He embraced her once more when she made this acknowledgment, and murmured:

"What an ass he was! You were not happy with him?"

She answered:

"No. He was not always jolly."

Leuillet felt quite delighted, making a comparison in his own mind between his wife's former situation and her present one.

He remained silent for some time; then, with a fresh outburst of curiosity, he said:

"Tell me this!"

"What?"

"Will you be quite candid—quite candid with me?"

"Certainly, dear."

"Well, look here! Were you never tempted to—to deceive this imbecile, Souris?"

Mme. Leuillet uttered a little "Oh!" in a shamefaced way, and again cuddled her face closer to her husband's chest. But he could see that she was laughing.

He persisted:

"Come now, confess it! He had a head just suited for a cuckold, this blockhead! It would be so funny! The good Souris! Oh! I say, darling, you might tell it to me—only to me!"

He emphasized the words "to me," feeling certain that if she wanted to show any taste when she deceived her husband, he, Leuillet, would have been the man; and he quivered with joy at the expectation of this avowal, sure that if she had not been the virtuous woman she was he could have won her then.

But she did not reply, laughing incessantly as if at the recollection of something infinitely comic.

Leuillet, in his turn, burst out laughing at the notion that he might have made a cuckold of Souris. What a good joke! What a capital lot of fun, to be sure!

He exclaimed in a voice broken by convulsions of laughter:

"Oh! poor Souris! poor Souris! Ah! yes, he had that sort of head—oh, certainly he had!"

And Mme. Leuillet now twisted herself under the sheets, laughing till the tears almost came into her eyes.

And Leuillet repeated: "Come, confess it! confess it! Be candid.

You must know that it cannot be unpleasant to me to hear such a thing."

Then she stammered, still choking with laughter:

"Yes, yes."

Her husband pressed her for an answer:

"Yes, what? Look here! tell me everything."

She was now laughing in a more subdued fashion, and, raising her mouth up to Leuillet's ear, which was held toward her in anticipation of some pleasant piece of confidence she whispered: "Yes—I did deceive him!"

He felt a cold shiver down his back, and utterly dumfounded, he gasped:

"You—you—did—really—deceive him?"

She was still under the impression that he thought the thing infinitely pleasant, and replied:

"Yes—really—really."

He was obliged to sit up in bed so great was the shock he received, holding his breath, just as overwhelmed as if he had just been told that he was a cuckold himself. At first he was unable to articulate properly; then after the lapse of a minute or so, he merely ejaculated:

"Ah!"

She, too, had stopped laughing now, realizing her mistake too late. Leuillet, at length asked:

"And with whom?"

She kept silent, cudgeling her brain to find some excuse.

He repeated his question:

"With whom?"

At last, she said:

"With a young man."

He turned toward her abruptly, and in a dry tone, said:

"Well, I suppose it wasn't with some kitchen-slut. I ask you who was the young man—do you understand?"

She did not answer. He tore away the sheet which she had drawn over her head and pushed her into the middle of the bed, repeating:

"I want to know with what young man—do you understand?"

Then, she replied, having some difficulty in uttering the words:

"I only wanted to laugh." But he fairly shook with rage:

"What? How is that? You only wanted to laugh? So then you were making game of me? I'm not going to be satisfied with these evasions, let me tell you! I ask you what was the young man's name?"

She did not reply, but lay motionless on her back.

He caught hold of her arm and pressed it tightly:

"Do you hear me, I say? I want you to give me an answer when I speak to you."

Then she said, in nervous tones:

"I think you must be going mad! Let me alone!"

He trembled with fury, so exasperated that he scarcely knew what he was saying, and, shaking her with all his strength, he repeated:

"Do you hear me? do you hear me?"

She wrenched herself out of his grasp with a sudden movement and with the tips of her fingers slapped her husband on the nose. He entirely lost his temper, feeling that he had been struck, and angrily pounced down on her.

He now held her under him, boxing her ears in a most violent manner, and exclaiming:

"Take that—and that—and that—there you are, you trollop, you strumpet—you strumpet!"

Then when he was out of breath, exhausted from beating her, he got up and went over to the bureau to get himself a glass of sugared orange-water, almost ready to faint after his exertion.

And she lay huddled up in bed, crying and heaving great sobs, feeling that there was an end of her happiness, and that it was all her own fault.

Then in the midst of her tears, she faltered:

"Listen, Antoine, come here! I told you a lie—listen! I'll explain it to you."

And now, prepared to defend herself, armed with excuses and subterfuges, she slightly raised her head all disheveled under her crumpled nightcap.

And he turning toward her, drew close to her, ashamed at having whacked her, but feeling still in his heart's core as a husband an inexhaustible hatred against the woman who had deceived his predecessor, Souris.

THE ARTIST'S WIFE

CURVED LIKE A CRESCENT moon, the little town of Étretat, with its white cliffs and its blue sea, is reposing under the sun of a grand July day. At the two points of the crescent are the two gates, the little one at the right, and the large one at the left, as if it were gradually advancing to the water—on one side a dwarfed foot, on the other, a leg of giant proportions; and the spire, nearly as high as the cliff, large at the base and fine at the summit, points its slim head toward the heavens.

Along the beach, upon the float, a crowd is seated watching the bathers. Upon the terrace of the Casino, another crowd, seated or walking, parades under the full light of day, a garden of pretty costumes, shaded by red and blue umbrellas embroidered in great flowers of silk. At the end of the promenade, on the terrace, there are other people, calm, quiet, walking slowly along up and down, as far as possible from the elegant multitude.

A young man, well-known, and celebrated as a painter, John Summer, was walking along with a listless air beside an invalid chair in which reposed a young woman, his wife. A domestic rolled the little carriage along, gently, while the crippled woman looked with sad eyes upon the joy of the heavens, the joy of the day, and the joy of other people.

They were not talking, they were not looking at each other. The woman said: "Let us stop a little."

They stopped, and the painter seated himself upon a folding chair arranged for him by the valet. Those who passed behind the couple, sitting there mute and motionless, regarded him with pitying looks. A complete legend of devotion had found its way about. He had married her in spite of her infirmity, moved by his love, they said.

Not far from there, two young men were seated on a capstan, chatting and looking off toward the horizon.

"No, it is not true," said one of them, "I tell you I know much of John Summer's life."

"Then why did he marry her? For she was really an invalid at that time, was she not?"

"Just as you see her now. He married her—he married her—as one marries—well, because he was a fool!"

"How is that?"

"How is that? That is how, my friend. That is the whole of it. One is a goose because he is a goose. And then you know, painters make a specialty of ridiculous marriages; they nearly always marry their models, or some old mistress, or some one of the women among the varied assortment they run up against. Why is it? Does anyone know? It would seem, on the contrary, that constant association with this race that we call models would be enough to disgust them forever with that kind of female. Not at all. After having made them pose, they marry them. Read that little book of Alphonse Daudet, 'Artists' Wives,' so true, so cruel, and so beautiful.

"As for the couple you see there, the accident that brought about that marriage was of a unique and terrible kind. The little woman played a comedy, or rather a frightful drama. In fact, she risked all for all. Was she sincere? Does she really love John? Can one ever know that? Who can determine, with any precision, the real from the make-believe, in the acts of women? They are always sincere in an eternal change of impressions. They are passionate, criminal, devoted, admirable, and ignoble, ready to obey un-seizable emotions. They lie without ceasing, without wishing to, without knowing it, without comprehension, and they have with this, in spite of this, an absolute freedom from sensation and sentiment, which they evince in violent resolutions, unexpected, incomprehensible folly, putting to rout all our reason, all our custom of deliberation, and all our combination of egotism. The unforeseen bluntness of their determinations make them, to us, indecipherable enigmas. We are always asking: 'Are they sincere? Are they false?'

"But, my friend, they are sincere and false at the same time, because it is in their nature to be the two extremes and neither the one nor the other. Look at the means the most honest employ for obtaining what they wish. They are both complicated and simple, these means are. So complicated that we never guess them in advance, so simple that after we have been the victims of them, we cannot help being astonished and saying to ourselves: 'My! Did she play me as easily as that?' And they succeed always, my good friend, especially when it is a question of making us marry them.

"But here is John Summer's story:

"The little wife was a model, as the term is usually understood. She posed for him. She was pretty, particularly elegant, and possessed, it appears, a divine figure. He became her lover, as one becomes the lover of any seductive woman he sees often. He imagines he loves her with his whole soul. It is a singular phenomenon. As soon as one desires a woman, he believes sincerely that he can no longer live without her. They know very well that their time has arrived. They know that disgust always follows possession; that, in order to pass one's existence by the side of another being, not brutal, physical appetite, so quickly extinguished, is the need, but an accordance of soul, of temperament, of humor. In a seduction that one undertakes, in bodily form, it is necessary to mingle a certain sensual intoxication with a charming depth of mind.

"Well, he believed that he loved her; he made her a heap of promises of fidelity and lived completely with her. She was gentle and endowed with that undeniable elegance which the Parisian woman acquires so easily. She tippled and babbled and said silly things, which seemed *spirituelle*, from the droll way in which she put them. She had each moment some little trick or pretty gesture to charm the eye of the painter. When she raised an arm, or stooped down, or got into a carriage, and when she took your hand, her movements were always perfect, exactly as they should be.

"For three months John did not perceive that, in reality, she was like all models. They rented for the summer a little house at Andressy. I was there one evening, when the first disquiet germinated in the mind of my friend.

"As the night was radiant, we wished to take a turn along the bank of the river. The moon threw in the water a glittering shower of light, crumbling its yellow reflections in the eddy, in the current, in the whole of the large river, flowing slowly along.

"We were going along the bank, a little quiet from the vague exaltation which the dreaminess of the evening threw about us. We were wishing we might accomplish superhuman things, might love some unknown beings, deliciously poetic. Strange ecstasies, desires, and aspirations were trembling in us.

"And we kept silent, penetrated by the serene and living freshness of the charming night, by that freshness of the moon which seems to go through the body, penetrate it, bathe the mind, perfume it and steep it in happiness.

"Suddenly Josephine (she called herself Josephine) cried out:

" 'Oh! did you see the great fish that jumped down there?'

"He replied, without looking or knowing: 'Yes, dearie.'

"She was angry. 'No, you have not seen it since your back was turned to it.'

"He laughed. 'Yes, it is true. It is so fine here that I was thinking of nothing.'

"She was silent; but at the end of a minute, the need of speaking seized her, and she asked:

" 'Are you going to Paris to-morrow?'

"He answered: 'I don't know.'

"Again she was irritated:

" 'Perhaps you think it is amusing to walk out without saying anything,' she said; 'one usually talks if he is not too stupid.'

"He said nothing. Then, knowing well, thanks to her wicked,

womanly instinct, that he would be exasperated, she began to sing that irritating air with which our ears and minds had been wearied for the past two years:

"'I was looking in the air.'"

"He murmured: 'I beg you be quiet.'"
"She answered furiously: 'Why should I keep quiet?'"
"He replied: 'You will arouse the neighborhood.'"
"Then the scene took place, the odious scene, with unexpected reproaches, tempestuous recriminations, then tears. All was over. They went back to the house. He allowed her to go on without reply, calmed by the divine evening and overwhelmed by the whirlwind of foolishness.

"Three months later, he was struggling desperately in the invincible, invisible bonds with which habit enlaces our life. She held him, oppressed him, martyrized him. They quarreled from morning until evening, insulting and combating each other.

"Finally, he wished to end it, to break, at any price. He sold all his work, realizing some twenty thousand francs (he was then little known) and, borrowing some money from friends, he left it all on the chimney-piece with a letter of adieu.

"He came to my house as a refuge. Toward three o'clock in the afternoon, the bell rang. I opened the door. A woman jumped into my face, brushed me aside, and rushed into my studio; it was she.

"He stood up on seeing her enter. She threw at his feet the envelope containing the bank-notes, with a truly noble gesture and said, with short breath:

"'Here is your money. I do not care for it.'"

"She was very pale and trembling, ready, apparently for any folly. He, too, grew pale, pale from anger and vexation, ready, perhaps, for any violence.

"He asked: 'What do you want, then?'"

"She replied: 'I do not wish to be treated like a child. You have implored me and taken me. I ask you for nothing—only protect me.'"

"He stamped his foot, saying: 'No, it is too much! And if you believe that you are going—'

"I took hold of his arm. 'Wait, John,' said I, 'let me attend to it.'

"I went toward her, and gently, little by little, I reasoned with her, emptying the sack of arguments that are usually employed in such cases. She listened to me motionless, with eyes fixed, obstinate and dumb. Finally, thinking of nothing more to say, and seeing that the affair would not end pleasantly, I struck one more last note. I said:

" 'He will always love you, little one, but his family wishes him to marry, and you know—'

"This was a surprise for her! 'Ah!—Ah!—now I comprehend—' she began.

"And turning toward him she continued: 'And so—you are going to marry!'

"He answered carelessly: 'Yes.'

"Then she took a step forward: 'If you marry, I will kill myself—you understand.'

" 'Well, then, kill yourself,' he hissed over his shoulder.

"She choked two or three times, her throat seeming bound by a frightful anguish. 'You say—you say— Repeat it!'

"He repeated: 'Well, kill yourself, if that pleases you!'

"She replied, very pale with fright: 'It is not necessary to dare me. I will throw myself from that window.'

"He began to laugh, advanced to the window, opened it, bowed like a person allowing some one to precede him, saying:

" 'Here is the way; after you!'

"She looked at him a second with fixed eyes, terribly excited; then, taking a leap, as one does in jumping a hedge in the field, she passed before him, before me, leaped over the sill and disappeared.

"I shall never forget the effect that this open window made upon me, after having seen it traversed by that falling body; it appeared to me in a second, great as the sky and as empty as space. And I recoiled instinctively, not daring to look, as if I had fallen myself.

"John, dismayed, made no motion.

"They took up the poor girl with both legs broken. She could never walk again.

"Her lover, foolish with remorse, and perhaps touched by re-membrance, took her and married her. There you have it, my dear."

The evening was come. The young woman, being cold, wished to go in; and the domestic began to roll the invalid's little carriage toward the village. The painter walked along beside his wife, without having exchanged a word with her for an hour.

A COWARD

IN SOCIETY THEY CALLED him "the handsome Signoles." His name was
Viscount Gontran Joseph de Signoles.

An orphan and the possessor of a sufficient fortune, as the saying
goes, he cut a dash. He had a fine figure and bearing, enough conversation to make people credit him with cleverness, a certain natural grace, an air of nobility and of pride, a gallant mustache, and a
gentle eye—a thing which pleases women.

In the drawing-rooms he was in great request, much sought after
as a partner for the waltz; and he inspired among men that smiling
hatred which they always cherish for others of an energetic figure.
He passed a happy and tranquil life, in a comfort of mind which was
most complete. It was known that he was a good fencer, and as a
pistol-shot even better.

"If ever I fight a duel," said he, "I shall choose pistols. With that
weapon I am sure of killing my man."

Now, one night, having accompanied two young ladies, his friends,
escorted by their husbands, to the theatre, he invited them all after the
play to take an ice at Tortoni's. They had been there for several minutes, when he perceived that a gentleman seated at a neighboring table
was staring obstinately at one of his companions. She seemed put out,
uneasy, lowered her head. At last she said to her husband:

"There is a man who is looking me out of countenance. I do not
know him; do you?"

The husband, who had seen nothing, raised his eyes, but declared:
"No, not at all."

The young lady continued, half smiling, half vexed.

"It is very unpleasant; that man is spoiling my ice."

Her husband shrugged his shoulders:

"Bast! don't pay any attention to it. If we had to occupy ourselves about every insolent fellow that we meet we should never have done."

But the viscount had risen brusquely. He could not allow that this stranger should spoil an ice which he had offered. It was to him that this insult was addressed, because it was through him and on his account that his friends had entered this café. So the matter concerned him only.

He advanced towards the man and said to him:

"You have, sir, a manner of looking at those ladies which I cannot tolerate. I beg of you to be so kind as to cease from this insistence."

The other answered:

"You are going to mind your own business, curse you."

The viscount said, with close-pressed teeth:

"Take care, sir, you will force me to pass bounds."

The gentleman answered but one word, a foul word, which rang from one end of the café to the other, and, like a metal spring, caused every guest to execute a sudden movement. All those whose backs were turned wheeled round; all the others raised their heads; three waiters pivoted upon their heels like tops; the two ladies at the desk gave a jump, then turned round their whole bodies from the waists up, as if they had been two automata obedient to the same crank.

A great silence made itself felt. Then, on a sudden, a dry sound cracked in the air. The viscount had slapped his adversary's face. Every one rose to interfere. Cards were exchanged between the two.

When the viscount had reached home he paced his room for several minutes with great, quick strides. He was too much agitated to reflect at all. One single idea was hovering over his mind—"a duel"—without arousing in him as yet an emotion of any sort. He had done that which he ought to have done; he had shown himself to be that which he ought to be. People would talk about it, they would praise him, they would congratulate him. He repeated in a loud voice, speaking as one speaks when one's thoughts are very much troubled:

"What a brute the fellow was!"

Then he sat down and began to reflect. He must find seconds, the first thing in the morning. Whom should he choose? He thought over those men of his acquaintance who had the best positions, who were the most celebrated. He finally selected the Marquis de la Tour-Noire, and the Colonel Bourdin, a nobleman and a soldier. Very good indeed! Their names would sound well in the papers. He perceived that he was thirsty, and he drank, one after another, three glasses of water; then he began again to walk up and down the room. He felt himself full of energy. If he blustered a little, if he showed himself resolute at all points, if he demanded rigorous and dangerous conditions, if he insisted on a serious duel, very serious, terrible, his opponent would probably withdraw and make apologies.

He picked up the card which he had pulled out of his pocket and thrown on the table, and he reread it with a single glance. He had already done so at the café and in the cab, by the glimmer of every street lamp, on his way home. "Georges Lamil, 51 Rue Moncey." Nothing more.

He examined these assembled letters, which seemed to him mysterious, and full of a confused meaning. Georges Lamil? Who was this man? What had he been about? Why had he stared at that woman in such a way? Was it not revolting that a stranger, an unknown, should so come and trouble your life, all on a sudden, simply because he had been pleased to fix his eyes insolently upon a woman that you knew? And the viscount repeated yet again, in a loud voice:

"What a brute!"

Then he remained motionless, upright, thinking, his look ever planted on the card. A rage awoke in him against this piece of paper, an anger full of hate in which was mixed a strange, uneasy feeling. It was stupid, this whole affair! He took a little penknife which lay open to his hand, and pricked it into the middle of the printed name, as if he had poniarded some one.

However, they must fight! He considered himself as indeed the insulted party. And, having thus the right, should he choose the pistol or the sword? With the sword he risked less; but with the pistol he had the chance of making his adversary withdraw. It is very rare that a duel with swords proves mortal, a mutual prudence preventing the combatants from engaging near enough for the point of a rapier to enter very deep. With the pistol he risked his life seriously; but he might also come out of the affair with all the honors of the situation, and without going so far as an actual meeting.

He said:

"I must be firm. He will be afraid."

The sound of his voice made him tremble and he looked about him. He felt himself very nervous. He drank another glass of water, then began to undress himself to go to bed.

As soon as he was in bed, he blew out the light and shut his eyes.

He thought:

"I've got all day to-morrow to attend to my affairs. I'd better sleep first so as to be calm."

He was very warm under the bedclothes, but he could not manage to doze off. He turned and twisted, remained five minutes on his back, then placed himself on his left side, then rolled over to his right.

He was still thirsty. He got up again to drink. Then an anxiety seized him:

"Shall I be afraid?"

Why did his heart fall to beating so madly at each of the well-known noises of his chamber? When the clock was about to strike, the little grinding sound of the spring which stands erect, caused him to give a start; and for several seconds after that he was obliged to open his mouth to breathe, he remained so much oppressed.

He set himself to reasoning with himself upon the possibility of this thing:

"Shall I be afraid?"

No, certainly not, he would not be afraid, because he was resolute to go to the end, because he had his will firmly fixed to fight and not to tremble. But he felt so deeply troubled that he asked himself:

"Can a man be afraid in spite of him?"

And this doubt invaded him, this uneasiness, this dread. If some force stronger than his will, if some commanding, and irresistible power should conquer him; what would happen? Yes, what could happen? He should certainly appear upon the field, since he willed to do it. But if he trembled? But if he fainted? And he thought of his situation, of his reputation, of his name.

And a curious necessity seized him on a sudden to get up again and look at himself in the mirror. He relit his candle. When he perceived his face reflected in the polished glass he hardly recognized himself, and it seemed to him that he had never seen this man before. His eyes appeared enormous; and he was pale, surely he was pale, very pale.

He remained upright before the mirror. He put out his tongue as if to test the state of his health, and all on a sudden this thought entered into him after the fashion of a bullet:

"The day after to-morrow, at this time, I shall perhaps be dead."

And his heart began again to beat furiously.

"The day after to-morrow, at this time, I shall perhaps be dead. This person before me, this 'I' which I see in this glass, will exist no longer. What! here I am, I am looking at myself, I feel myself to live, and in twenty-four hours I shall be laid to rest upon this couch, dead, my eyes shut, cold, inanimate, gone."

He turned towards his bed and he distinctly saw himself extended on the back in the same sheets which he had just left. He had the hollow face which dead men have, and that slackness to the hands which will never stir more.

So he grew afraid of his bed, and, in order not to look at it again, he passed into his smoking-room. He took a cigar mechanically, lit it, and again began to walk the room. He was cold; he went towards the bell to wake his valet; but he stopped, his hand lifted towards the bell-rope:

"That fellow will see that I am afraid."

And he did not ring, he made the fire himself. When his hands touched anything they trembled slightly, with a nervous shaking. His head wandered; his troubled thoughts became fugitive, sudden, melancholy; an intoxication seized on his spirit as if he had been drunk.

And ceaselessly he asked himself:

"What shall I do? What will become of me?"

His whole body vibrated, jerky tremblings ran over it; he got up, and approaching the window, he opened the curtains.

The day was coming, a day of summer. The rosy sky made rosy the city, the roofs, and the walls. A great fall of tenuous light, like a caress from the rising sun, enveloped the awakened world; and, with this glimmer, a hope gay, rapid, brutal, seized on the heart of the viscount! Was he mad to let himself be so struck down by fear, before anything had even been decided, before his seconds had seen those of this Georges Lamil, before he yet knew if he was going to fight at all?

He made his toilet, dressed himself, and left the house with a firm step.

He repeated to himself, while walking:

"I must be decided, very decided. I must prove that I am not afraid."

His seconds, the marquis and the colonel, put themselves at his disposition, and after having pressed his hands energetically, discussed the conditions of the meeting.

The colonel asked:

"You want a serious duel?"

The viscount answered:

"Very serious."

The marquis took up the word.

"You insist on pistols?"

"Yes."

"Do you leave us free to settle the rest?"

The viscount articulated with a dry, jerky voice:

"Twenty paces, firing at the word, lifting the arm instead of lowering it. Exchange of shots until some one is badly wounded."

The colonel declared, in a satisfied tone:

"Those are excellent conditions. You are a good shot; the chances are all in your favor."

And they separated. The viscount returned home to wait for them. His agitation, which had been temporarily calmed, was now increasing with every moment. He felt along his arms, along his legs, in his chest, a kind of quivering, a kind of continuous vibration; he could not stay in one place, neither sitting down nor standing up. He had no longer a trace of moisture in his mouth, and he made at every instant a noisy movement of the tongue as if to unglue it from his palate.

He tried to take his breakfast, but he could not eat. Then he thought of drinking in order to give himself courage, and had a decanter of rum brought him, from which he gulped down, one after the other, six little glasses.

A warmth, like a burn, seized on him. It was followed as soon by a giddiness of the soul. He thought:

"I know the way. Now it will go all right."

But at the end of an hour he had emptied the decanter, and his state of agitation was become again intolerable. He felt a wild necessity to roll upon the ground, to cry, to bite. Evening fell.

The sound of the door-bell caused him such a feeling of suffocation that he had not the strength to rise to meet his seconds.

He did not even dare to talk to them any longer—to say "How do you do?" to pronounce a single word, for fear lest they divine all from the alteration in his voice.

The colonel said:

"Everything is settled according to the conditions which you fixed. Your opponent at first insisted on the privileges of the offended party, but he yielded almost immediately, and has agreed to everything. His seconds are two officers.

The viscount said:

"Thank you."

The marquis resumed:

"Excuse us if we only just run in and out, but we've still a thousand things to do. We must have a good doctor, because the duel is not to stop till after some one is badly hit, and you know there's no trifling with bullets. A place must be appointed near some house where we can carry the wounded one of the two, if it is necessary, etc.; it will take us quite two or three hours more."

The viscount articulated a second time:

"Thank you."

The colonel asked:

"You're all right? You're calm?"

"Yes, quite calm, thanks."

The two men retired.

When he felt himself alone again, it seemed to him that he was going mad. His servant having lit the lamps, he sat down before his table to write some letters. After tracing at the top of a page, "This is my Will," he got up again and drew off, feeling incapable of putting two ideas together, of taking a single resolution, of deciding anything at all.

And so he was going to fight a duel! He could no longer escape that. What could be passing within him? He wanted to fight, he had that intention and that resolution firmly fixed; and he felt very plainly that, notwithstanding all the effort of his mind and all the tension of his will, he would not be able to retain strength enough to go as far as the place of the encounter. He tried to fancy the combat, his own attitude, and the bearing of his adversary.

From time to time, his teeth struck against one another in his mouth with a little dry noise. He tried to read, and took up de Châteauvillard's duelling code.[10] Then he asked himself:

"My adversary, has he frequented the shooting-galleries? Is he well known? What's his class? How can I find out?"

He remembered the book by Baron de Vaux upon pistol-shooters, and he searched through it from one end to the other. Georges Lamil was not mentioned. But, however, if the man had not been a good shot, he would not have accepted immediately that dangerous weapon and those conditions, which were mortal.

His pistol-case by Gastinne Renette lay on a little round table. As he passed he opened it and took out one of the pistols, then placed himself as if to shoot, and raised his arm; but he trembled from head to foot, and the barrel shook in all directions.

Then he said:

"It is impossible. I cannot fight like this."

At the end of the barrel he regarded that little hole, black and deep, which spits out death; he thought of dishonor, of the whispers in the clubs, of the laughter in the drawing-rooms, of the disdain of women, of the allusions in the papers, of the insults which would be thrown at him by cowards.

He went on staring at the pistol, and raising the hammer, he suddenly saw a priming glitter beneath it like a little red flame. The pistol had been left loaded, by chance, by oversight. And he experienced from that a confused inexplicable joy.

If in the presence of the other he had not the calm and noble bearing which is fit, he would be lost forever. He would be spotted, marked with a sign of infamy, hunted from society. And he should not have that calm and bold bearing; he knew it, he felt it. And yet he was really brave, because he wanted to fight! He was brave, because——. The thought which just grazed him did not even complete itself in his spirit, but, opening his mouth wide, he brusquely thrust the pistol-barrel into the very bottom of his throat and pressed upon the trigger. . . .

When his valet ran in, attracted by the report, he found him dead, on his back. A jet of blood had spattered the white paper on the table and made a great red stain below the four words:

"This is my Will."

THE NECKLACE

SHE WAS ONE OF those pretty and charming girls who are sometimes, as if by a mistake of destiny, born in a family of clerks. She had no dowry, no expectations, no means of being known, understood, loved, wedded, by any rich and distinguished man; and she let herself be married to a little clerk at the Ministry of Public Instruction.

She dressed plainly because she could not dress well, but she was as unhappy as though she had really fallen from her proper station; since with women there is neither caste nor rank; and beauty, grace, and charm act instead of family and birth. Natural fineness, instinct for what is elegant, suppleness of wit, are the sole hierarchy, and make from women of the people the equals of the very greatest ladies.

She suffered ceaselessly, feeling herself born for all the delicacies and all the luxuries. She suffered from the poverty of her dwelling, from the wretched look of the walls, from the worn-out chairs, from the ugliness of the curtains. All those things, of which another woman of her rank would never even have been conscious, tortured her and made her angry. The sight of the little Breton peasant who did her humble house-work aroused in her regrets which were despairing, and distracted dreams. She thought of the silent antechambers hung with Oriental tapestry, lit by tall bronze candelabra, and of the two great footmen in knee-breeches who sleep in the big arm-chairs, made drowsy by the heavy warmth of the hot-air stove. She thought of the long *salons* fitted up with ancient silk, of the delicate furniture carrying priceless curiosities, and of the coquettish perfumed boudoirs made for talks at five o'clock with intimate friends, with men famous and sought after, whom all women envy and whose attention they all desire.

When she sat down to dinner, before the round table covered with a table-cloth three days old, opposite her husband, who uncovered the soup-tureen and declared with an enchanted air, "Ah, the good *pot-au-feu!** I don't know anything better than that," she thought of dainty dinners, of shining silverware, of tapestry which peopled the walls with ancient personages and with strange birds flying in the midst of a fairy forest; and she thought of delicious dishes served on marvellous plates, and of the whispered gallantries which you listen to with a sphinx-like smile, while you are eating the pink flesh of a trout or the wings of a quail.

She had no dresses, no jewels, nothing. And she loved nothing but that; she felt made for that. She would so have liked to please, to be envied, to be charming, to be sought after.

She had a friend, a former school-mate at the convent, who was rich, and whom she did not like to go and see any more, because she suffered so much when she came back.

But, one evening, her husband returned home with a triumphant air, and holding a large envelope in his hand.

"There," said he, "here is something for you."

She tore the paper sharply, and drew out a printed card which bore these words:

"The Minister of Public Instruction and Mme. Georges Ramponneau request the honor of M. and Mme. Loisel's company at the palace of the Ministry on Monday evening, January 18th."

Instead of being delighted, as her husband hoped, she threw the invitation on the table with disdain, murmuring:

"What do you want me to do with that?"

"But, my dear, I thought you would be glad. You never go out, and this is such a fine opportunity. I had awful trouble to get it. Every one wants to go; it is very select, and they are not giving many invitations to clerks. The whole official world will be there."

---

* French stew of beef and vegetables.

She looked at him with an irritated eye and she said, impatiently:

"And what do you want me to put on my back?"

He had not thought of that; he stammered:

"Why, the dress you go to the theatre in. It looks very well, to me."

He stopped, distracted, seeing that his wife was crying. Two great tears descended slowly from the corners of her eyes towards the corners of her mouth. He stuttered:

"What's the matter? What's the matter?"

But, by a violent effort, she had conquered her grief, and she replied, with a calm voice, while she wiped her wet cheeks:

"Nothing. Only I have no dress, and therefore I can't go to this ball. Give your card to some colleague whose wife is better equipped than I."

He was in despair. He resumed:

"Come, let us see, Mathilde. How much would it cost, a suitable dress, which you could use on other occasions, something very simple?"

She reflected several seconds, making her calculations and wondering also what sum she could ask without drawing on herself an immediate refusal and a frightened exclamation from the economical clerk.

Finally, she replied, hesitatingly:

"I don't know exactly, but I think I could manage it with four hundred francs."

He had grown a little pale, because he was laying aside just that amount to buy a gun and treat himself to a little shooting next summer on the plain of Nanterre, with several friends who went to shoot larks down there, of a Sunday.

But he said:

"All right. I will give you four hundred francs. And try to have a pretty dress."

The day of the ball drew near, and Mme. Loisel seemed sad, uneasy, anxious. Her dress was ready, however. Her husband said to her one evening:

"What is the matter? Come, you've been so queer these last three days."

And she answered:

"It annoys me not to have a single jewel, not a single stone, nothing to put on. I shall look like distress. I should almost rather not go at all."

He resumed:

"You might wear natural flowers. It's very stylish at this time of the year. For ten francs you can get two or three magnificent roses."

She was not convinced.

"No; there's nothing more humiliating than to look poor among other women who are rich."

But her husband cried:

"How stupid you are! Go look up your friend Mme. Forestier, and ask her to lend you some jewels. You're quite thick enough with her to do that."

She uttered a cry of joy:

"It's true. I never thought of it."

The next day she went to her friend and told of her distress.

Mme. Forestier went to a wardrobe with a glass door, took out a large jewel-box, brought it back, opened it, and said to Mme. Loisel:

"Choose, my dear."

She saw first of all some bracelets, then a pearl necklace, then a Venetian cross, gold and precious stones of admirable workmanship. She tried on the ornaments before the glass, hesitated, could not make up her mind to part with them, to give them back. She kept asking:

"Haven't you any more?"

"Why, yes. Look. I don't know what you like."

All of a sudden she discovered, in a black satin box, a superb necklace of diamonds and her heart began to beat with an immoderate desire. Her hands trembled as she took it. She fastened it around her throat, outside her high-necked dress, and remained lost in ecstasy at the sight of herself.

Then she asked, hesitating, filled with anguish:

"Can you lend me that, only that?"

"Why, yes, certainly."

She sprang upon the neck of her friend, kissed her passionately, then fled with her treasure.

The day of the ball arrived. Mme. Loisel made a great success. She was prettier than them all, elegant, gracious, smiling, and crazy with joy. All the men looked at her, asked her name, endeavored to be introduced. All the attachés of the Cabinet wanted to waltz with her. She was remarked by the minister himself.

She danced with intoxication, with passion, made drunk by pleasure, forgetting all, in the triumph of her beauty, in the glory of her success, in a sort of cloud of happiness composed of all this homage, of all this admiration, of all these awakened desires, and of that sense of complete victory which is so sweet to woman's heart.

She went away about four o'clock in the morning. Her husband had been sleeping since midnight, in a little deserted anteroom, with three other gentlemen whose wives were having a very good time.

He threw over her shoulders the wraps which he had brought, modest wraps of common life, whose poverty contrasted with the elegance of the ball dress. She felt this and wanted to escape so as not to be remarked by the other women, who were enveloping themselves in costly furs.

Loisel held her back.

"Wait a bit. You will catch cold outside. I will go and call a cab."

But she did not listen to him, and rapidly descended the stairs. When they were in the street they did not find a carriage; and they began to look for one, shouting after the cabmen whom they saw passing by at a distance.

They went down towards the Seine, in despair, shivering with cold. At last they found on the quay one of those ancient noctambulant coupés which, exactly as if they were ashamed to show their misery during the day, are never seen round Paris until after nightfall.

It took them to their door in the Rue des Martyrs, and once more, sadly, they climbed up homeward. All was ended, for her. And as to him, he reflected that he must be at the Ministry at ten o'clock.

She removed the wraps, which covered her shoulders, before the glass, so as once more to see herself in all her glory. But suddenly she uttered a cry. She had no longer the necklace around her neck!

Her husband, already half-undressed, demanded:

"What is the matter with you?"

She turned madly towards him:

"I have—I have—I've lost Mme. Forestier's necklace."

He stood up, distracted.

"What!—how?—Impossible!"

And they looked in the folds of her dress, in the folds of her cloak, in her pockets, everywhere. They did not find it.

He asked:

"You're sure you had it on when you left the ball?"

"Yes, I felt it in the vestibule of the palace."

"But if you had lost it in the street we should have heard it fall. It must be in the cab."

"Yes. Probably. Did you take his number?"

"No. And you, didn't you notice it?"

"No."

They looked, thunderstruck, at one another. At last Loisel put on his clothes.

"I shall go back on foot," said he, "over the whole route which we have taken, to see if I can't find it."

And he went out. She sat waiting on a chair in her ball dress, without strength to go to bed, overwhelmed, without fire, without a thought.

Her husband came back about seven o'clock. He had found nothing.

He went to Police Headquarters, to the newspaper offices, to offer a reward; he went to the cab companies—everywhere, in fact, whither he was urged by the least suspicion of hope.

She waited all day, in the same condition of mad fear before this terrible calamity.

Loisel returned at night with a hollow, pale face; he had discovered nothing.

"You must write to your friend," said he, "that you have broken the clasp of her necklace and that you are having it mended. That will give us time to turn round."

She wrote at his dictation.

At the end of a week they had lost all hope.

And Loisel, who had aged five years, declared:

"We must consider how to replace that ornament."

The next day they took the box which had contained it, and they went to the jeweller whose name was found within. He consulted his books.

"It was not I, madame, who sold that necklace; I must simply have furnished the case."

Then they went from jeweller to jeweller, searching for a necklace like the other, consulting their memories, sick both of them with chagrin and with anguish.

They found, in a shop at the Palais Royal, a string of diamonds which seemed to them exactly like the one they looked for. It was worth forty thousand francs. They could have it for thirty-six.

So they begged the jeweller not to sell it for three days yet. And they made a bargain that he should buy it back for thirty-four thousand francs, in case they found the other one before the end of February.

Loisel possessed eighteen thousand francs which his father had left him. He would borrow the rest.

He did borrow, asking a thousand francs* of one, five hundred of another, five louis† here, three louis there. He gave notes, took up ruinous obligations, dealt with usurers, and all the race of lenders. He compromised all the rest of his life, risked his signature without even knowing if he could meet it; and, frightened by the pains yet to come, by the black misery which was about to fall upon him, by the prospect of all the physical privations and of all the moral tortures

---

* The franc was the primary unit of currency in France before the euro.
† A louis was a French coin worth 20 francs.

which he was to suffer, he went to get the new necklace, putting down upon the merchant's counter thirty-six thousand francs.

When Mme. Loisel took back the necklace, Mme. Forestier said to her, with a chilly manner:

"You should have returned it sooner, I might have needed it."

She did not open the case, as her friend had so much feared. If she had detected the substitution, what would she have thought, what would she have said? Would she not have taken Mme. Loisel for a thief?

Mme. Loisel now knew the horrible existence of the needy. She took her part, moreover, all on a sudden, with heroism. That dreadful debt must be paid. She would pay it. They dismissed their servant; they changed their lodgings; they rented a garret under the roof.

She came to know what heavy housework meant and the odious cares of the kitchen. She washed the dishes, using her rosy nails on the greasy pots and pans. She washed the dirty linen, the shirts, and the dish-cloths, which she dried upon a line; she carried the slops down to the street every morning, and carried up the water, stopping for breath at every landing. And, dressed like a woman of the people, she went to the fruiterer, the grocer, the butcher, her basket on her arm, bargaining, insulted, defending her miserable money sou by sou.

Each month they had to meet some notes, renew others, obtain more time.

Her husband worked in the evening making a fair copy of some tradesman's accounts, and late at night he often copied manuscript for five sous a page.

And this life lasted ten years.

At the end of ten years they had paid everything, everything, with the rates of usury, and the accumulations of the compound interest.

Mme. Loisel looked old now. She had become the woman of impoverished households—strong and hard and rough. With frowsy hair, skirts askew, and red hands, she talked loud while washing the floor with great swishes of water. But sometimes, when her husband was at the office, she sat down near the window, and she thought of that gay evening of long ago, of that ball where she had been so beautiful and so fêted.

What would have happened if she had not lost that necklace? Who knows? who knows? How life is strange and changeful! How little a thing is needed for us to be lost or to be saved!

But, one Sunday, having gone to take a walk in the Champs Élysées to refresh herself from the labors of the week, she suddenly perceived a woman who was leading a child. It was Mme. Forestier, still young, still beautiful, still charming.

Mme. Loisel felt moved. Was she going to speak to her? Yes, certainly. And now that she had paid, she was going to tell her all about it. Why not?

She went up.

"Good-day, Jeanne."

The other, astonished to be familiarly addressed by this plain good-wife, did not recognize her at all, and stammered:

"But—madame!—I do not know— You must have mistaken."

"No. I am Mathilde Loisel."

Her friend uttered a cry.

"Oh, my poor Mathilde! How you are changed!"

"Yes, I have had days hard enough, since I have seen you, days wretched enough—and that because of you!"

"Of me! How so?"

"Do you remember that diamond necklace which you lent me to wear at the ministerial ball?"

"Yes. Well?"

"Well, I lost it."

"What do you mean? You brought it back."

"I brought you back another just like it. And for this we have been ten years paying. You can understand that it was not easy for us, us who had nothing. At last it is ended, and I am very glad."

Mme. Forestier had stopped.

"You say that you bought a necklace of diamonds to replace mine?"

"Yes. You never noticed it, then! They were very like."

And she smiled with a joy which was proud and naïve at once.

Mme. Forestier, strongly moved, took her two hands.

"Oh, my poor Mathilde! Why, my necklace was paste. It was worth at most five hundred francs!"

A MEETING

IT WAS ALL AN accident, a pure accident. Tired of standing, Baron d'Etraille went—as all the Princess's rooms were open on that particular evening—into an empty bedroom, which appeared almost dark after coming out of the brilliantly-lighted drawing-rooms.

He looked round for a chair in which to have a doze, as he was sure his wife would not go away before daylight. As soon as he got inside the door he saw the big bed with its azure-and-gold hangings, in the middle of the great room, looking like a catafalque in which love was buried, for the Princess was no longer young. Behind it, a large bright spot looked like a lake seen at a distance from a window. It was a big looking-glass, which, discreetly covered with dark drapery very rarely let down, seemed to look at the bed, which was its accomplice. One might almost fancy that it felt regrets, and that one was going to see in it charming shapes of nude women and the gentle movement of arms about to embrace them.

The Baron stood still for a moment, smiling and rather moved, on the threshold of this chamber dedicated to love. But suddenly something appeared in the looking-glass, as if the phantoms which he had evoked had come up before him. A man and a woman who had been sitting on a low couch hidden in the shade had risen, and the polished surface, reflecting their figures, showed that they were kissing each other before separating.

The Baron recognized his wife and the Marquis de Cervigné. He turned and went away like a man fully master of himself, and waited till it was day before taking away the Baroness. But he had no longer any thoughts of sleeping.

As soon as they were alone, he said:

"Madame, I saw you just now in the Princess de Raynes's room. I need say no more, for I am not fond either of reproaches, acts of violence, or of ridicule. As I wish to avoid all such things, we shall separate without any scandal. Our lawyers will settle your position according to my orders. You will be free to live as you please when you are no longer under my roof; but, as you will continue to bear my name, I must warn you that should any scandal arise, I shall show myself inflexible."

She tried to speak, but he stopped her, bowed, and left the room.

He was more astonished and sad than unhappy. He had loved her dearly during the first period of their married life; but his ardor had cooled, and now he often had a caprice, either in a theater or in society, though he always preserved a certain liking for the Baroness.

She was very young, hardly four-and-twenty, small, slight,—too slight,—and very fair. She was a true Parisian doll: clever, spoiled, elegant, coquettish, witty, with more charm than real beauty. He used to say familiarly to his brother, when speaking of her:

"My wife is charming, attractive, but—there is nothing to lay hold of. She is like a glass of champagne that is all froth—when you have got to the wine it is very good, but there is too little of it, unfortunately."

He walked up and down the room in great agitation, thinking of a thousand things. At one moment he felt in a great rage, and felt inclined to give the Marquis a good thrashing, to horsewhip him publicly, in the club. But he thought that would not do, it would not be the thing; *he* would be laughed at, and not the other, and he felt that his anger proceeded more from wounded vanity than from a broken heart. So he went to bed, but could not get to sleep.

A few days afterward it was known in Paris that the Baron and Baroness d'Etraille had agreed to an amicable separation on account of incompatibility of temper. Nobody suspected anything, nobody laughed, and nobody was astonished.

The Baron, however, to avoid meeting her, traveled for a year; then he spent the summer at the seaside, and the autumn in shooting, returning to Paris for the winter. He did not meet his wife once.

He did not even know what people said about her. At any rate, she took care to save appearances, and that was all he asked for.

He got dreadfully bored, traveled again, restored his old castle of Villebosc—which took him two years; then for over a year he received relays of friends there, till at last, tired of all these commonplace, so-called pleasures, he returned to his mansion in the Rue de Lills, just six years after their separation.

He was then forty-five, with a good crop of gray hair, rather stout, and with that melancholy look of people who have been handsome, sought after, much liked, and are deteriorating daily.

A month after his return to Paris he took cold on coming out of his club, and had a bad cough, so his medical man ordered him to Nice for the rest of the winter.

He started by the express on Monday evening. He was late, got to the station only a very short time before the departure of the train, and had barely time to get into a carriage, with only one other occupant, who was sitting in a corner so wrapped in furs and cloaks that he could not even make out whether it were a man or a woman, as nothing of the figure could be seen. When he perceived that he could not find out, he put on his traveling-cap, rolled himself up in his rugs, and stretched himself out comfortably to sleep.

He did not wake up till the day was breaking, and looked immediately at his fellow-traveler. He had not stirred all night, and seemed still to be sound asleep.

M. d'Etraille made use of the opportunity to brush his hair and his beard, and to try and freshen himself up a little generally, for a night's traveling changes one's looks very much when one has attained a certain age.

A great poet has said:

"When we are young, our mornings are triumphant!"

Then we wake up with a cool skin, a bright eye, and glossy hair. When one grows older one wakes up in a very different state. Dull eyes, red, swollen cheeks, dry lips, the hair and beard all disarranged, impart an old, fatigued, worn-out look to the face.

The Baron opened his traveling dressing-case, made himself as tidy as he could, and then waited.

The engine whistled and the train stopped, and his neighbor moved. No doubt he was awake. They started off again, and then an oblique ray of the sun shone into the carriage just on to the sleeper, who moved again, shook himself, and then calmly showed his face.

It was a young, fair, pretty, stout woman, and the Baron looked at her in amazement. He did not know what to believe. He could really have sworn that it was his wife—but wonderfully changed for the better: stouter—why, she had grown as stout as he was—only it suited her much better than it did him.

She looked at him quietly, did not seem to recognize him, and then slowly laid aside her wraps. She had that calm assurance of a woman who is sure of herself, the insolent audacity of a first awaking, knowing and feeling that she was in her full beauty and freshness.

The Baron really lost his head. Was it his wife, or somebody else who was as like her as any sister could be? As he had not seen her for six years he might be mistaken.

She yawned, and he knew her by the gesture. She turned and looked at him again, calmly, indifferently, as if she scarcely saw him, and then looked out at the country again.

He was upset and dreadfully perplexed, and waited, looking at her sideways, steadfastly.

Yes; it was certainly his wife. How could he possibly have doubted? There could certainly not be two noses like that, and a thousand recollections flashed through him, slight details of her body, a beauty-spot on one of her limbs and another on her back. How often he had kissed them! He felt the old feeling of the intoxication of love stealing over him, and he called to mind the sweet odor of her skin, her smile when she put her arms on to his shoulders, the soft intonations of her voice, all her graceful, coaxing ways.

But how she had changed and improved! It was she and yet not she. He thought her riper, more developed, more of a woman, more seductive, more desirable, adorably desirable.

And this strange, unknown woman, whom he had accidentally met in a railway-carriage belonged to him; he had only to say to her:

"I insist upon it."

He had formerly slept in her arms, existed only in her love, and now he had found her again certainly, but so changed that he scarcely knew her. It was another, and yet she at the same time. It was another who had been born, formed, and grown since he had left her. It was she, indeed; she whom he had possessed but who was now altered, with a more assured smile and greater self-possession. There were two women in one, mingling a great deal of what was new and unknown with many sweet recollections of the past. There was something singular, disturbing, exciting about it—a kind of mystery of love in which there floated a delicious confusion. It was his wife in a new body and in new flesh which his lips had never pressed.

And he remembered that in six or seven years everything changes in us, only outlines can be recognized, and sometimes even they disappear.

The blood, the hair, the skin, all change, and are reconstituted, and when people have not seen each other for a long time they find, when they meet, another totally different being, although it be the same and bear the same name.

And the heart also can change. Ideas may be modified and renewed, so that in forty years of life we may, by gradual and constant transformations, become four or five totally new and different beings.

He dwelt on this thought till it troubled him; it had first taken possession of him when he surprised her in the Princess's room. He was not the least angry; it was not the same woman that he was looking at—that thin, excitable little doll of those days.

What was he to do? How should he address her? and what could he say to her? Had she recognized him?

The train stopped again. He got up, bowed, and said: "Bertha, do you want anything I can bring you?"

She looked at him from head to foot, and answered, without

showing the slightest surprise or confusion or anger, but with the most perfect indifference:

"I do not want anything—thank you."

He got out and walked up and down the platform a little in order to think, and, as it were, to recover his senses after a fall. What should he do now? If he got into another carriage it would look as if he were running away. Should he be polite or importunate? That would look as if he were asking for forgiveness. Should he speak as if he were her master? He would look like a fool, and besides, he really had no right to do so.

He got in again and took his place.

During his absence she had hastily arranged her dress and hair, and was now lying stretched out on the seat, radiant, but without showing any emotion.

He turned to her, and said: "My dear Bertha, since this singular chance has brought us together after a separation of six years—a quite friendly separation—are we to continue to look upon each other as irreconcilable enemies? We are shut up together, *tête-à-tête*, which is so much the better or so much the worse. I am not going to get into another carriage, so don't you think it is preferable to talk as friends till the end of our journey?"

She answered quite calmly again:

"Just as you please."

Then he suddenly stopped, really not knowing what to say; but as he had plenty of assurance, he sat down on the middle seat, and said:

"Well, I see I must pay my court to you; so much the better. It is, however, really a pleasure, for you are charming. You cannot imagine how you have improved in the last six years. I do not know any woman who could give me that delightful sensation which I experienced just now when you emerged from your wraps. I could really have thought such a change impossible."

Without moving her head or looking at him, she said: "I cannot say the same with regard to you; you have certainly deteriorated a great deal."

He got red and confused, and then, with a smile of resignation, he said:

"You are rather hard."

"Why?" was her reply. "I am only stating facts. I don't suppose you intend to offer me your love? It must, therefore, be a matter of perfect indifference to you what I think about you. But I see it is a painful subject, so let us talk of something else. What have you been doing since I last saw you?"

He felt rather out of countenance, and stammered:

"I? I have traveled, shot, and grown old, as you see. And you?"

She said, quite calmly: "I have taken care of appearances, as you ordered me."

He was very nearly saying something brutal, but he checked himself, and kissed his wife's hand:

"And I thank you," he said.

She was surprised. He was indeed strong and always master of himself.

He went on: "As you have acceded to my first request, shall we now talk without any bitterness?"

She made a little movement of surprise.

"Bitterness! I don't feel any; you are a complete stranger to me; I am only trying to keep up a difficult conversation."

He was still looking at her, carried away in spite of her harshness, and he felt seized with a brutal desire, the desire of the master.

Perceiving that she had hurt his feelings, she said:

"How old are you now? I thought you were younger than you look."

He grew rather pale:

"I am forty-five"; and then he added: "I forgot to ask after Princess de Raynes. Are you still intimate with her?"

She looked at him as if she hated him:

"Yes, certainly I am. She is very well, thank you."

They remained sitting side by side, agitated and irritated. Suddenly he said:

"My dear Bertha, I have changed my mind. You are my wife, and I expect you to come with me today. You have, I think, improved both morally and physically, and I am going to take you back again. I am your husband and it is my right to do so."

She was stupefied, and looked at him, trying to divine his thoughts; but his face was resolute and impenetrable.

"I am very sorry," she said, "but I have made other engagements."

"So much the worse for you," was his reply. "The law gives me the power, and I mean to use it."

They were getting to Marseilles, and the train whistled and slackened speed. The Baroness got up, carefully rolled up her wraps, and then turning to her husband, she said:

"My dear Raymond, do not make a bad use of the *tête-à-tête* which I had carefully prepared. I wished to take precautions, according to your advice, so that I might have nothing to fear from you or from other people, whatever might happen. You are going to Nice, are you not?"

"I shall go wherever you go."

"Not at all; just listen to me, and I am sure that you will leave me in peace. In a few moments, when we get to the station, you will see the Princess de Raynes and Countess Hermit waiting for me with their husbands. I wished them to see us, and to know that we had spent the night together in the railway-carriage. Don't be alarmed; they will tell it everywhere as a most surprising fact.

"I told you just now that I had most carefully followed your advice and saved appearances. Anything else does not matter, does it? Well, in order to do so, I wished to be seen with you. You told me carefully to avoid any scandal, and I am avoiding it, for, I am afraid—I am afraid—"

She waited till the train had quite stopped, and as her friends ran up to open the carriage door, she said:

"I am afraid that I am *enceinte*."*

The Princess stretched out her arms to embrace her, and the Baroness said, pointing to the Baron, who was dumb with astonishment, and trying to get at the truth:

---

* Pregnant.

"You do not recognize Raymond? He has certainly changed a good deal, and he agreed to come with me so that I might not travel alone. We take little trips like this occasionally, like good friends who cannot live together. We are going to separate here; he has had enough of me already."

She put out her hand, which he took mechanically, and then she jumped out on to the platform among her friends, who were waiting for her.

The Baron hastily shut the carriage door, for he was too much disturbed to say a word or come to any determination. He heard his wife's voice, and their merry laughter as they went away.

He never saw her again, nor did he ever discover whether she had told him a lie or was speaking the truth.

BED NO. 29

When Captain Epivent passed in the street all the ladies turned to look at him. He was the true type of a handsome officer of hussars. He was always on parade, always strutted a little and seemed preoccupied and proud of his leg, his figure, and his mustache. He had superb ones, it is true, a superb leg, figure, and mustache. The last-named was blond, very heavy, falling martially from his lip in a beautiful sweep the color of ripe wheat, carefully turned at the ends, and falling over both sides of his mouth in two powerful sprigs of hair cut square across. His waist was thin as if he wore a corset, while a vigorous masculine chest, bulged and arched, spread itself above his waist. His leg was admirable, a gymnastic leg, the leg of a dancer, whose muscular flesh outlined each movement under the clinging cloth of the red pantaloon.

He walked with muscles taut, with feet and arms apart, and with the slightly balanced step of the cavalier, who knows how to make the most of his limbs and his carriage, and who seems a conqueror in a uniform, but looks commonplace in a mufti.

Like many other officers, Captain Epivent carried a civil costume badly. He had no air of elegance as soon as he was clothed in the gray or black of the shop clerk. But in his proper setting he was a triumph. He had besides a handsome face, the nose thin and curved, blue eyes, and a good forehead. He was bald, without ever being able to comprehend why his hair had fallen off. He consoled himself with thinking that, with a heavy mustache, a head a little bald was not so bad.

He scorned everybody in general, with a difference in the degrees of his scorn.

In the first place, for him the middle class did not exist. He looked at them as he would look at animals, without according them more of his attention than he would give to sparrows or chickens. Officers, alone, counted in his world; but he did not have the same esteem for all officers. He only respected handsome men; an imposing presence, the true, military quality being first. A soldier was a merry fellow, a devil, created for love and war, a man of brawn, muscle, and hair, nothing more. He classed the generals of the French army according to their figure, their bearing, and the stern look of their faces. Bourbaki appeared to him the greatest warrior of modern times.

He often laughed at the officers of the line who were short and fat, and puffed while marching. And he had a special scorn for the poor recruits from the polytechnic schools, those thin, little men with spectacles, awkward and unskillful, who seemed as much made for a uniform as a wolf for saying mass, as he often asserted. He was indignant that they should be tolerated in the army, those abortions with the lank limbs, who marched like crabs, did not drink, ate little, and seemed to love equations better than pretty girls.

Captain Epivent himself had constant successes and triumphs with the fair sex.

Every time he took supper in company with a woman, he thought himself certain of finishing the night with her upon the same mattress, and, if unsurmountable obstacles hindered that evening, his victory was sure at least the following day. His comrades did not like him to meet their mistresses, and the merchants in the shops, who had their pretty wives at the counter, knew him, feared him, and hated him desperately. When he passed, the merchants' wives in spite of themselves exchanged a look with him through the glass of the front windows; one of those looks that avail more than tender words, which contain an appeal and a response, a desire and an avowal. And the husbands, who turned away with a sort of instinct, returned brusquely, casting a furious look at the proud, arched silhouette of the officer. And, when the captain has passed, smiling and content with his impression, the merchants, handling with nervous hands the objects spread out before them, declared:

"There's a great dandy. When shall we stop feeding all these good-for-nothings who go dragging their tinware through the streets? For my part, I would rather be a butcher than a soldier. Then if there's blood on my table, it is the blood of beasts, at least. And he is useful, the butcher; and the knife he carries has not killed men. I do not understand how these murderers are tolerated walking on the public streets, carrying with them their instruments of death. It is necessary to have them, I suppose, but at least, let them conceal themselves, and not dress up in masquerade, with their red breeches and blue coats. The executioner doesn't dress himself up, does he?"

The woman, without answering, would shrug her shoulders, while the husband, divining the gesture without seeing it, would cry:

"Anybody must be stupid to watch those fellows parade up and down."

Nevertheless, Captain Epivent's reputation for conquests was well established in the whole French army.

Now, in 1868, his regiment, the One Hundred and Second Hussars, came into garrison at Rouen.

He was soon known in the town. He appeared every evening, toward five o'clock, upon the Boieldieu mall, to take his absinthe and coffee at the Comedy; and, before entering the establishment, he would always take a turn upon the promenade, to show his leg, his figure, and his mustaches.

The merchants of Rouen who also promenaded there with their hands behind their backs, preoccupied with business affairs, speaking in high and low voices, would sometimes throw him a glance and murmur:

"Egad! that's a handsome fellow!"

But when they knew him, they remarked:

"Look! Captain Epivent! But he's a rascal all the same!"

The women on meeting him had a very queer little movement of the head, a kind of shiver of modesty, as if they felt themselves grow weak or unclothed before him. They would lower their heads a little, with a smile upon their lips, as if they had a desire to be found charming and have a look from him. When he walked with a comrade the comrade never failed to murmur with jealous envy, each time that he saw the sport:

"This rascal of an Epivent has the chances!"

Among the licensed girls of the town it was a struggle, a race, to see who would carry him off. They all came at five o'clock, the officers' hour, to the Boieldieu mall, and dragged their skirts up and down the length of the walk, two by two, while the lieutenants, captains, and commanders, two by two, dragged their swords along the ground before entering the *café*.

One evening the beautiful Irma, the mistress, it was said, of M. Templier-Papon, the rich manufacturer, stopped her carriage in front of the Comedy and, getting out, made a pretense of buying some paper or some visiting cards of M. Paulard, the engraver, in order to pass before the officers' tables and cast a look at Captain Epivent which seemed to say: "When you will," so clearly that Colonel Prune, who was drinking the green liquor with his lieutenant-colonel, could not help muttering:

"Confound that fellow! But he has the chances, that scamp!"

The remark of the Colonel was repeated, and Captain Epivent, moved by this approbation of his superior, passed the next day and many times after that under the windows of the beauty, in his most captivating attitude.

She saw him, showed herself, and smiled.

That same evening he was her lover.

They attracted attention, made an exhibition of their attachment, and mutually compromised themselves, both of them proud of their adventure.

Nothing was so much talked of in town as the beautiful Irma and the officer. M. Templier-Papon alone was ignorant of their relation.

Captain Epivent beamed with glory; every instant he would say:

"Irma happened to say to me—Irma told me tonight—or, yesterday at dinner Irma said—"

For a whole year they walked with and displayed in Rouen this love like a flag taken from the enemy. He felt himself aggrandized by this conquest, envied, more sure of the future, surer of the decoration

so much desired, for the eyes of all were upon him, and he was satisfied to find himself well in sight, instead of being forgotten.

But here war was declared, and the Captain's regiment was one of
the first to be sent to the front. The adieux were lamentable. They
lasted the whole night long.

Sword, red breeches, cap, and jacket were all overturned from the
back of a chair upon the floor; robes, skirts, silk stockings, also fallen
down, were spread around and mingled with the uniform in distress
upon the carpet; the room upside down as if there had been a battle;
Irma wild, her hair unbound, threw her despairing arms around the
officer's neck, straining him to her; then, leaving him, rolled upon
the floor, overturning the furniture, catching the fringes of the arm-
chairs, biting their feet, while the Captain, much moved, but not
skillful at consolation, repeated:

"Irma, my little Irma, do not cry so, it is necessary."

He occasionally wiped a tear from the corner of his eye with the
end of his finger. They separated at daybreak. She followed her lover
in her carriage as far as the first stopping-place. Then she kissed him
before the whole regiment at the moment of separation. They even
found this very genteel, worthy, and very romantic; and the comrades pressed the Captain's hand and said to him:

"Confound you, rogue, she has a heart, all the same, the little one."

They seemed to see something patriotic in it.

The regiment was sorely proved during the campaign. The Captain
conducted himself heroically and finally received the cross of honor.
Then, the war ended, he returned to Rouen and the garrison.

Immediately upon his return he asked of news of Irma, but no one
was able to give him anything exact. Some said she was married to a
Prussian major. Others, that she had gone to her parents, who were
farmers in the suburbs of Yvetot.

He even sent his orderly to the mayor's office to consult the reg-
istry of deaths. The name of his mistress was not to be found.

He was very angry, which fact he paraded everywhere. He even took the enemy to task for his unhappiness, attributing to the Prussians, who had occupied Rouen, the disappearance of the young girl, declaring:

"In the next war, they shall pay well for it, the beggars!"

Then, one morning as he entered the mess-room at the breakfast hour, an old porter, in a blouse and an oilcloth cap, gave him a letter, which he opened and read:

"My Dearie:

"I am in the hospital, very ill, very ill. Will you not come and see me? It would give me so much pleasure!

"Irma."

The Captain grew pale and, moved with pity, declared:

"It's too bad! The poor girl! I will go there as soon as breakfast."

And during the whole time at the table, he told the officers that Irma was in the hospital, and that he was going to see her that blessed morning. It must be the fault of those unspeakable Prussians. She had doubtless found herself alone without a sou,* broken down with misery, for they must certainly have stolen her furniture.

"Ah! the dirty whelps!"

Everybody listened with great excitement. Scarcely had he slipped his napkin in his wooden ring, when he rose and, taking his sword from the peg, and swelling out his chest to make him thin, hooked his belt and set out with hurried step to the city hospital.

But entrance to the hospital building, where he expected to enter immediately, was sharply refused him, and he was obliged to find his Colonel and explain his case to him in order to get a word from him to the director.

This man, after having kept the handsome Captain waiting some time in his anteroom, gave him an authorized pass and a cold and disapproving greeting.

Inside the door he felt himself constrained in this asylum of misery

---

* French coin worth one-twentieth of a franc (that is, very little).

and suffering and death. A boy in the service showed him the way. He walked upon tiptoe, that he might make no noise, through the long corridors, where floated a slight, moist odor of illness and medicines. A murmur of voices alone disturbed the silence of the hospital.

At times, through an open door, the Captain perceived a dormitory, with its rows of beds whose clothes were raised by the forms of the bodies.

Some convalescents were seated in chairs at the foot of their couches, sewing, and clothed in the uniform gray cloth dress with white cap.

His guide suddenly stopped before one of these corridors filled with patients. He read on the door, in large letters: "Syphilis." The Captain started; then he felt that he was blushing. An attendant was preparing a medicine at a little wooden table at the door.

"I will show you," said she, "it is bed 29."

And she walked ahead of the officer. She indicated a bed: "There it is."

There was nothing to be seen but a bundle of bedclothes. Even the head was concealed under the coverlet. Everywhere faces were to be seen on the couches, pale faces, astonished at the sight of a uniform, the faces of women, young women and old women, but all seemingly plain and common in the humble, regulation garb.

The Captain, very much disturbed, supporting his sword in one hand and carrying his cap in the other, murmured:

"Irma."

There was a sudden motion in the bed and the face of his mistress appeared, but so changed, so tired, so thin, that he would scarcely have known it.

She gasped, overcome by emotion, and then said:

"Albert!—Albert! It is you! Oh! I am so glad—so glad." And the tears ran down her cheeks.

The attendant brought a chair. "Be seated, sir," she said.

He sat down and looked at the pale, wretched countenance, so little like that of the beautiful, fresh girl he had left. Finally he said:

"What seems to be the matter with you?"

She replied, weeping: "You know well enough, it is written on the door." And she hid her eyes under the edge of the bedclothes.

Dismayed and ashamed, he continued: "How have you caught it, my poor girl?"

She answered: "It was those beasts of Prussians. They took me almost by force and then poisoned me."

He found nothing to add. He looked at her and kept turning his cap around on his knees.

The other patients gazed at him, and he believed that he detected an odor of putrefaction, of contaminated flesh, in this corridor full of girls tainted with this ignoble, terrible malady.

She murmured: "I do not believe that I shall recover. The doctor says it is very serious."

Then she perceived the cross upon the officer's breast and cried:

"Oh! you have been honored; now I am content. How contented I am! If I could only embrace you!"

A shiver of fear and disgust ran along the Captain's skin at the thought of this kiss. He had a desire to make his escape, to be in the clear air and never see this woman again. He remained, however, not knowing how to make the adieux, and finally stammered:

"You took no care of yourself, then."

A flame flashed in Irma's eyes: "No, the desire to avenge myself came to me when I should have broken away from it. And I poisoned them too, all, all that I could. As long as there were any of them in Rouen, I had no thought for myself."

He declared, in a constrained tone in which there was a little note of gaiety: "So far, you have done some good."

Getting animated, and her cheek-bones getting red, she answered:

"Oh! yes, there will more than one of them die from my fault. I tell you I had my vengeance."

Again he said: "So much the better." Then rising, he added: "Well, I must leave you now, because I have only time to meet my appointment with the Colonel—"

She showed much emotion, crying out: "Already! You leave me already! And when you have scarcely arrived!"

But he wished to go at any cost, and said:

"But you see that I came immediately; and it is absolutely necessary that I be at the Colonel's at an appointed time."

She asked: "Is it still Colonel Prune?"

"Still Colonel Prune. He was twice wounded."

She continued: "And your comrades? Have some of them been killed?"

"Yes. Saint-Timon, Savagnat, Poli, Saprival, Robert, De Courson, Pasafil, Santal, Caravan, and Poivrin are dead. Sahel had an arm carried off and Courvoisin a leg amputated. Paquet lost his right eye."

She listened, much interested. Then suddenly she stammered:

"Will you kiss me, say? before you leave me; Madame Langlois is not there."

And, in spite of the disgust which came to his lips, he placed them against the wan forehead, while she, throwing her arms around him, scattered random kisses over his blue jacket.

Then she said: "You will come again? Say that you will come again— Promise me that you will."

"Yes, I promise."

"When, now. Can you come Thursday?"

"Yes, Thursday—"

"Thursday at two o'clock?"

"Yes, Thursday at two o'clock."

"You promise?"

"I promise."

"Adieu, my dearie."

"Adieu."

And he went away, confused by the staring glances of those in the dormitory, bending his tall form to make himself seem smaller. And when he was in the street he took a long breath.

That evening his comrades asked him: "Well, how is Irma?"

He answered in a constrained voice: "She has a trouble with the lungs; she is very ill."

But a little lieutenant, scenting something from his manner, went to headquarters, and, the next day, when the Captain went into mess, he was welcomed by a volley of laughter and jokes. They had found vengeance at last.

It was learned further that Irma had made a spite marriage with the staff-major of the Prussians, that she had gone through the country on horseback with the colonel of the Blue Hussars, and many others, and that, in Rouen, she was no longer called anything but the "wife of the Prussians."

For eight days the Captain was the victim of his regiment. He received by post and by messenger, notes from those who can reveal the past and the future, circulars of specialists, and medicines, the nature of which was inscribed on the package.

And the Colonel, catching the drift of it, said in a severe tone:

"Well, the Captain had a pretty acquaintance! I send him my compliments."

At the end of twelve days he was appealed to by another letter from Irma. He tore it up with rage and made no reply to it.

A week later she wrote him again that she was very ill and wished to see him to say farewell.

He did not answer.

After some days more he received a note from a chaplain of the hospital.

"The girl Irma Pavolin is on her deathbed and begs you to come."

He dared not refuse to oblige the chaplain, but he entered the hospital with a heart swelling with wicked anger, with wounded vanity, and humiliation.

He found her scarcely changed at all and thought that she had deceived him. "What do you wish of me?" he asked.

"I wish to say farewell. It appears that I am near the end."

He did not believe it.

"Listen," said he, "you have made me the laughing stock of the regiment, and I do not wish it to continue."

She asked: "What have I done?"

He was irritated at not knowing how to answer. But he said:

"Is it nothing that I return here to be joked by everybody on your account?"

She looked at him with languid eyes, where shone a pale light of anger, and answered:

"What can I have done? I have not been genteel with you, perhaps! Is it because I have sometimes asked for something? But for you, I would have remained with M. Templier-Papon, and would not have found myself here to-day. No, you see, if anyone has reproaches to make it is not you."

He answered in a clear tone: "I have not made reproaches, but I cannot continue to come to see you, because your conduct with the Prussians has been the shame of the town."

She sat up, with a little shake, in the bed, as she replied:

"My conduct with the Prussians? But when I tell you that they took me, and when I tell you that if I took no thought of myself, it was because I wished to poison them! If I had wished to cure myself, it would not have been so difficult, I can tell you! But I wished to kill them, and I have killed them, come now! I have killed them!"

He remained standing: "In any case," said he, "it was a shame."

She had a kind of suffocation, and then replied:

"Why is it a shame for me to cause them to die and try to exterminate them, tell me? You did not talk that way when you used to come to my house in Jeanne-d' Arc street. Ah! it is a shame! You have not done as much, with your cross of honor! I deserve more merit than you, do you understand, more than you, for I have killed more Prussians than you!"

He stood stupefied before her, trembling with indignation. He stammered: "Be still—you must—be still—because those things—I cannot allow—anyone to touch upon—"

But she was not listening: "What harm have you done the Prussians? Would it ever have happened if you had kept them from coming to Rouen? Tell me! It is you who should stop and listen. And I have done more harm than you, I, yes, more harm to them than you, and I am going to die for it, while you are singing songs and making yourself fine to inveigle women—"

Upon each bed a head was raised and all eyes looked at this man in uniform, who stammered again:

"You must be still—more quiet—you know—"

But she would not be quiet. She cried out:

"Ah! yes, you are a pretty *poseur!** I know you well. I know you. And I tell you that I have done them more harm than you—I—and that I have killed more than all your regiment together—come now, you coward."

He went away, in fact he fled, stretching his long legs as he passed between the two rows of beds where the syphilitic patients were becoming excited. And he heard the gasping, stifled voice of Irma pursuing him:

"More than you—yes—I have killed more than you—"

He tumbled down the staircase four steps at a time, and ran until he was shut fast in his room.

The next day he heard that she was dead.

---

* Showoff.

A PECULIAR CASE

WHEN CAPTAIN HECTOR MARIE de Fontenne married Miss Laurine d'Estelle the parents and friends feared it would be a bad match.

Miss Laurine, pretty, thin, blond and confident, had at twelve the assurance of a woman of thirty. She was one of those precocious little Parisians who seem born with a full knowledge of life and of feminine tricks, with that audacity of thought, with that profound astuteness and suppleness of mind which make certain beings seem destined by fate to play with and deceive others, as they do. All their actions seem premeditated, their manner calculated, their words weighed with care, their whole existence a rôle which they are playing with people like themselves.

She was very charming and lively, with the liveliness that cannot restrain itself nor be calm, when something seems amusing or queer. She would laugh in the face of people in almost an impudent fashion, but with so much grace that they were never angered. Then she was rich, very rich.

A priest served as intermediary when she married Captain de Fontenne. Brought up in a religious house, in a most austere fashion, this officer brought to his regiment the morals of the cloister, and very strict, intolerant principles. He was one of those men who invariably become either a saint or a nihilist, in whom ideas install themselves as absolute mistresses, whose beliefs are inflexible, whose resolutions are not to be shaken.

He was a large, dark, young man, serious, severe, ingenuous, of simple mind, curt, and obstinate, one of those men who pass through life without comprehending anything beneath them in variety or subtlety, who divine nothing, suspect nothing, and admit only what they think, what they judge, and what they believe, when some one differs from them.

Miss Laurine saw him, understood him immediately, and accepted him for her husband. They made an excellent pair. She was yielding, skillful, and wise, knowing how to show herself to best advantage, always ready in good works and at festivals, assiduous at church and at the theater, at once worldly and religious, with a little air of irony, and a twinkle in her eye when chatting gravely with her grave husband. She would relate to him all her charitable enterprises with all the priests of the parish and the vicinity, and she made use of these pious occupations in order to remain away from morning until night.

But sometimes, in the midst of the recital of some act of beneficence, a foolish laugh would seize her suddenly, a nervous laugh impossible to check. The captain would look surprised, then disturbed, then a little shocked, as his wife would continue to laugh. When she became a little calm, he would ask: "What is the matter, Laurine?" And she would answer: "Nothing. It is only the memory of such a funny thing that happened to me!" And she would relate some story.

Then, during the summer of 1883, Captain Hector de Fontenne took part in the grand maneuvers of the thirty-second regiment of the army. One evening, as they camped on the edge of a town, after ten days of tent and open field, ten days of fatigue and privation, the comrades of the captain resolved to have a good dinner.

At first, Captain de Fontenne refused to accompany them; then, as his refusal surprised them, he consented. His neighbor at table, the governor of Favré, talking continually of military operations, the only thing that interested the captain, turned to him to drink glass after glass with him. It had been very hot, a heavy, parching, thirst-inspiring heat; and the captain drank without thinking or perceiving that a new gaiety had entered into him, a certain lively, burning joy, a happiness of being, full of awakened desires, of unknown appetites, and undefined hopes.

At the dessert he was tipsy. He talked and laughed and moved about, seized by a noisy drunkenness, the foolish drunkenness of a man ordinarily wise and tranquil.

Some one proposed to finish the evening at the theater. He accompanied his comrades. One of them recognized one of the actresses as some one he had formerly loved, and a supper was planned where a part of the feminine *personnel* of the troupe assisted.

The captain awoke the next day in an unknown room, in the arms of a pretty little blond woman who said to him, on seeing him open his eyes: "Good morning, sweetheart!"

He could not comprehend, at first; then, little by little his memory returned, somewhat cloudy, however. Then he got up without saying a word, dressed himself, and emptied his purse on the chimney-piece. A shame seized him when he found himself standing up in position, his sword at his side, in this furnished room, where the rumpled curtains and sofa, marbleized with spots, had a suspicious appearance, and he dared not go out, since in descending the staircase he might meet some one, nor dared he pass before the *concierge* nor go out in the street in the eyes of neighbors and passers-by.

The woman kept saying: "What has come over you? Have you lost your tongue? You had it fast enough last evening! Oh! what a muzzle!"

He bowed to her ceremoniously and, deciding upon flight, reached his abode with great steps, persuaded that one could guess from his manner and his bearing and his countenance that he had come out of the house of some girl.

And then remorse tortured him; the harassing remorse of a rigid, scrupulous man. He confessed and went to communion, but he still was ill at ease, followed ever by the memory of his fall and by a feeling of debt, a sacred debt contracted against his wife.

He did not see her again until the end of the month, because she went to visit her parents during the encampment of the troops. She came back to him with open arms and a smile upon her lips. He received her with an embarrassed attitude, the attitude of a guilty man; and until evening, he scarcely talked with her.

When they found themselves alone, she asked him: "What is the matter with you, my dear; I find you very much changed."

He answered in a constrained tone: "Oh! nothing, my dear, absolutely nothing."

"Pardon me, but I know you so well, and I feel sure there is something, some care, some angry feeling, something, I know not what!"

"Oh! well, yes, there is something."

"And what is it?"

"It is impossible for me to tell you."

"To tell me? Why so? You disturb me."

"I have no reasons to give you. It is impossible for me to tell you."

She was seated upon a divan and he walked up and down before her with his hands behind his back, avoiding the look of his wife.

Then she said: "Let us see. It is necessary for me to make you confess, it is my duty that I exact from you the truth; it is also my right. You should no more have a secret from me than I should from you."

His back was turned to her, framed in the high window, as he said:

"My dear, there are some things which are better not told. That which vexes me is one of them."

She got up, crossed the room, took him by the arm, and, having forced him to turn around, placed her two hands upon his shoulders, then, smiling and cajoling, raised her eyes as she said:

"You see, Marie [she called him Marie in moments of tenderness] you could never conceal anything from me. I should believe you had done something bad."

He answered: "I have done something very bad."

She said gaily: "Oh! is it so bad as that? I am very much astonished at you!"

He responded quickly: "I shall say nothing further. It is useless to insist."

But she drew him to an armchair, forced him to sit down in it, then seated herself on his right knee and began kissing him with light, rapid kisses which just brushed the curled end of his mustache. Then she said:

"If you don't tell me, we shall always be angry."

Pierced by remorse and tortured by his anguish, he answered: "If I should tell you what I have done, you would never pardon me."

"On the contrary, my friend. I would pardon you immediately."

"No, it is impossible."

"I promise you."

"I tell you it is impossible!"

"I swear that I will pardon you."

"No, my dear Laurine, you never could."

"How simple you are, my friend, you cannot deny it! In refusing to tell me what you have done, you allow me to think you have done something abominable, and I shall think constantly about it, regretting your silence as much as your unknown crime. While, if you speak frankly, I shall forget it all by tomorrow."

"It is because——"

"What?"

He blushed up to the ears and said: "I shall confess to you as I would to a priest, Laurine."

On her lips was the sudden smile that she had sometimes in listening, and with a little mocking tone she said: "I am all ears."

He began: "You know, my dear, that I am a sober man. I drink only red wine, and never liquors, as you know."

"Yes, I know."

"Well, imagine how I allowed myself to drink a little, one evening toward the end of our encampment, when I was very thirsty, very much worn out with fatigue, weary, and——"

"And you got tipsy? Oh! how hideous!"

"Yes, I was intoxicated," he replied, with a severe air.

"And now, were you wholly intoxicated, so that you couldn't walk?"

"Oh! no, not so much as that. But I lost my reason if not my equilibrium. I talked and laughed and made a fool of myself."

As he kept silent, she asked: "Is that all?"

"No."

"Ah! and after that?"

"After that I committed an infamous deed."

She looked at him, disturbed and troubled as well as somewhat excited.

"What then, my friend?"

"We had supper with—with some actresses—and I do not know how it was done, but—I have deceived you, Laurine!"

He made the statement in a grave, solemn tone. She gave a little toss to her head and her eye brightened with a sudden gaiety, a profound, irresistible gaiety. Then she said:

"You—you—you have—"

And a little dry, nervous laugh broke forth and glided between her teeth two or three times and prevented her from speaking. She tried to take him seriously, but each time she tried to pronounce a word, the laugh trembled at the bottom of her throat, leaped forth, was quickly stopped, but constantly reappeared, like gas in a bottle of champagne, pushing for escape until the froth can no longer be retained. She put her hands on her lips to calm herself, that she might restrain this unfortunate gaiety. But the laugh ran through her fingers, shaking her chest and bursting forth in spite of her. She stammered: "You—you—have deceived me— Ha—ha! ha!—ha! ha!—ha! ha!"

And then she looked at him with a singular air, so mocking in spite of herself, that he was speechless, stupefied. And suddenly, as if able to contain herself no longer, she burst forth again, laughing with the kind of laugh that seemed like an attack of nerves. Little jerking cries issued from her mouth, coming, it seemed, from the depths of her lungs. His two hands supported her bosom, and she was almost suffocated with long whoops like the cough in whooping-cough.

With each effort that she made to calm herself a new paroxysm would begin, and each word that she tried to utter was only a greater contortion.

"My—my—my—poor friend—ha! ha!—ha! ha! ha!—ha!"

He got up, leaving her alone upon the armchair, and becoming suddenly very pale, he said: "Laurine, this is more than unbecoming."

She stammered, in a delirium of laughter:

"What—do you want—I—I—I cannot—but—but you are so funny—ha! ha! ha!—ha! ha!"

He became livid and looked at her now with fixed eye, a strange thought awakening within him. Suddenly he opened his mouth as if to say something, but said nothing, then, turning on his heel, he went out and shut the door.

Laurine, doubled up, weak, and fainting, still laughed with a dying laugh, which occasionally took on new life, like the flame of a candle almost ready to go out.

YVETTE

CHAPTER I

The Initiation of Saval

As THEY WERE LEAVING the Café Riche, Jean de Servigny said to Léon Saval: "If you don't object, let us walk. The weather is too fine to take a cab."

His friend answered: "I would like nothing better."

Jean replied: "It is hardly eleven o'clock. We shall arrive much before midnight, so let us go slowly."

A restless crowd was moving along the boulevard, that throng peculiar to summer nights, drinking, chatting, and flowing like a river, filled with a sense of comfort and joy. Here and there a *café* threw a flood of light upon a knot of patrons drinking at little tables on the sidewalk, which were covered with bottles and glasses, hindering the passing of the hurrying multitude. On the pavement the cabs with their red, blue, or green lights dashed by, showing for a second, in the glimmer, the thin shadow of the horse, the raised profile of the coachman, and the dark box of the carriage. The cabs of the Urbaine Company made clear and rapid spots when their yellow panels were struck by the light.

The two friends walked with slow steps, cigars in their mouths, in evening dress and overcoats on their arms, with a flower in their buttonholes, and their hats a trifle on one side, as men will carelessly wear them sometimes, after they have dined well and the air is mild.

They had been linked together since their college days by a close, devoted, and firm affection. Jean de Servigny, small, slender, a trifle bald, rather frail, with elegance of mien, curled mustache, bright eyes, and fine lips, was a man who seemed born and bred upon the boulevard. He was tireless in spite of his languid air, strong in spite of his pallor, one of those slight Parisians to whom gymnastic exercise, fencing, cold shower and hot baths give a nervous, artificial strength. He was known by his marriage as well as by his wit, his fortune, his connections, and by that sociability, amiability, and fashionable gallantry peculiar to certain men.

A true Parisian, furthermore, light, sceptical, changeable, captivating, energetic, and irresolute, capable of everything and of nothing; selfish by principle and generous on occasion, he lived moderately upon his income, and amused himself with hygiene. Indifferent and passionate, he gave himself rein and drew back constantly, impelled by conflicting instincts, yielding to all, and then obeying, in the end, his own shrewd man-about-town judgment, whose weather-vane logic consisted in following the wind and drawing profit from circumstances without taking the trouble to originate them.

His companion, Léon Saval, rich also, was one of those superb and colossal figures who make women turn around in the streets to look at them. He gave the idea of a statue turned into a man, a type of a race, like those sculptured forms which are sent to the Salons. Too handsome, too tall, too big, too strong, he sinned a little from the excess of everything, the excess of his qualities. He had on hand countless affairs of passion.

As they reached the Vaudeville theater, he asked: "Have you warned that lady that you are going to take me to her house to see her?"

Servigny began to laugh: "Forewarn the Marquise Obardi! Do you warn an omnibus driver that you shall enter his stage at the corner of the boulevard?"

Saval, a little perplexed, inquired: "What sort of person is this lady?"

His friend replied: "An upstart, a charming hussy, who came from no one knows where, who made her appearance one day, nobody knows how, among the adventuresses of Paris, knowing perfectly well how to take care of herself. Besides, what difference does it make to us? They say that her real name, her maiden name—for she still has every claim to the title of maiden except that of innocence—is Octavia Bardin, from which she constructs the name Obardi by prefixing the first letter of her first name and dropping the last letter of the last name.

"Moreover, she is a lovable woman, and you, from your physique, are inevitably bound to become her lover. Hercules is not introduced into Messalina's home without making some disturbance. Nevertheless I make bold to add that if there is free entrance to this house, just as there is in bazaars, you are not exactly compelled to buy what is for sale. Love and cards are on the programme, but nobody compels you to take up with either. And the exit is as free as the entrance.

"She settled down in the Etoile district, a suspicious neighborhood, three years ago, and opened her drawing-room to that froth of the continents which comes to Paris to practice its various formidable and criminal talents.

"I don't remember just how I went to her house. I went as we all go, because there is card playing, because the women are compliant, and the men dishonest. I love that social mob of buccaneers with decorations of all sorts of orders, all titled, and all entirely unknown at their embassies, except to the spies. They are always dragging in the subject of honor, quoting the list of their ancestors on the slightest provocation, and telling the story of their life at every opportunity, braggarts, liars, sharpers, dangerous as their cards, false as their names, brave because they have to be, like the assassins who can not pluck their victims except by exposing their own lives. In a word, it is the aristocracy of the bagnio.

"I like them. They are interesting to fathom and to know, amusing to listen to, often witty, never commonplace as the ordinary French guests. Their women are always pretty, with a little flavor of foreign knavery, with the mystery of their past existence, half of which, perhaps, spent in a House of Correction. They generally have fine eyes and glorious hair, the true physique of the profession, an intoxicating grace, a seductiveness which drives men to folly, an unwholesome, irresistible charm! They conquer like the highwaymen of old. They are rapacious creatures, true birds of prey. I like them, too.

"The Marquise Obardi is one of the type of these elegant good-for-nothings. Ripe and pretty, with a feline charm, you can see that she is vicious to the marrow. Everybody has a good time at her house, with cards, dancing, and suppers; in fact there is everything which goes to make up the pleasures of fashionable society life."

"Have you ever been or are you now her lover?" Léon Saval asked.

"I have not been her lover, I am not now, and I never shall be. I only go to the house to see her daughter."

"Ah! She has a daughter, then?"

"A daughter! A marvel, my dear man. She is the principal attraction of the den to-day. Tall, magnificent, just ripe, eighteen years old, as fair as her mother is dark, always merry, always ready for an entertainment, always laughing, and ready to dance like mad. Who will be the lucky man to capture her, or who has already done so? Nobody can tell that. She has ten of us in her train, all hoping.

"Such a daughter in the hands of a woman like the Marquise is a fortune. And they play the game together, the two charmers. No one knows just what they are planning. Perhaps they are waiting for a better bargain than I should prove. But I tell you that I shall close the bargain if I ever get a chance.

"That girl Yvette absolutely baffles me, moreover. She is a mystery. If she is not the most complete monster of astuteness and perversity that I have ever seen, she certainly is the most marvelous phenomenon of innocence that can be imagined. She lives in that atmosphere of infamy with a calm and triumphing ease which is either wonderfully profligate or entirely artless. Strange scion of an adventuress, cast upon the muck-heap of that set, like a magnificent plant nurtured upon corruption, or rather like the daughter of some noble race, of some great artist, or of some grand lord, of some prince or dethroned king, tossed some evening into her mother's arms, nobody can make out what she is nor what she thinks. But you are going to see her."

Saval began to laugh and said: "You are in love with her."

"No. I am on the list, which is not precisely the same thing. I will introduce you to my most serious rivals. But the chances are in my favor. I am in the lead, and some little distinction is shown to me."

"You are in love," Saval repeated.

"No. She disquiets me, seduces and disturbs me, attracts and frightens me away. I mistrust her as I would a trap, and I long for her as I long for a sherbet when I am thirsty. I yield to her charm, and I only approach her with the apprehension that I would feel concerning a man who was known to be a skillful thief. In her presence I have an irrational impulse toward belief in her possible purity and a very reasonable mistrust of her not less probable trickery. I feel myself in contact with an abnormal being, beyond the pale of natural laws, an exquisite or detestable creature—I don't know which."

For the third time Saval said: "I tell you that you are in love. You speak of her with the magniloquence of a poet and the feeling of a troubadour. Come, search your heart, and confess."

Servigny walked a few steps without answering. Then he replied:

"That is possible, after all. In any case, she fills my mind almost continually. Yes, perhaps I am in love. I dream about her too much. I think of her when I am asleep and when I awake—that is surely a grave indication. Her face follows me, accompanies me ceaselessly, ever before me, around me, with me. Is this love, this physical infatuation? Her features are so stamped upon my vision that I see her the moment I shut my eyes. My heart beats quickly every time I look at her, I don't deny it.

"So I am in love with her, but in a queer fashion. I have the strongest desire for her, and yet the idea of making her my wife would seem to me a folly, a piece of stupidity, a monstrous thing. And I have a little fear of her, as well, the fear which a bird feels over which a hawk is hovering.

"And again I am jealous of her, jealous of all of which I am ignorant in her incomprehensible heart. I am always wondering: 'Is she a charming youngster or a wretched jade?' She says things that would make an army shudder; but so does a parrot. She is at times so indiscreet and yet modest that I am forced to believe in her spotless purity, and again so incredibly artless that I must suspect that she has never been chaste. She allures me, excites me, like a woman of a certain category, and at the same time acts like an impeccable virgin. She seems to love me and yet makes fun of me; she deports herself in public as if she were my mistress and treats me in private as if I were her brother or footman.

"There are times when I fancy that she has as many lovers as her mother. And at other times I imagine that she suspects absolutely nothing of that sort of life, you understand. Furthermore, she is a great novel reader. I am at present, while awaiting something better, her book purveyor. She calls me her 'librarian.' Every week the New Book Store sends her, on my orders, everything new that has appeared, and I believe that she reads everything at random. It must make a strange sort of mixture in her head.

"That kind of literary hasty-pudding accounts perhaps for some of the girl's peculiar ways. When a young woman looks at existence through the medium of fifteen thousand novels, she must see it in a strange light, and construct queer ideas about matters and things in general. As for me, I am waiting. It is certain at any rate that I never have had for any other woman the devotion which I have had for her. And still it is quite certain that I shall never marry her. So if she has had numbers, I shall swell the number. And if she has not, I shall take the first ticket, just as I would do for a street car.

"The case is very simple. Of course, she will never marry. Who in the world would marry the Marquise Obardi's daughter, the child of Octavia Bardin? Nobody, for a thousand reasons. Where would they ever find a husband for her? In society? Never. The mother's house is a sort of liberty-hall whose patronage is attracted by the daughter. Girls don't get married under those conditions.

"Would she find a husband among the tradespeople? Still less would that be possible. And besides the Marquise is not the woman to make a bad bargain; she will give Yvette only to a man of high position, and that man she will never discover.

"Then perhaps she will look among the common people. Still less likely. There is no solution of the problem, then. This young lady belongs neither to society, nor to the tradesmen's class, nor to the common people, and she can never enter any of these ranks by marriage.

"She belongs through her mother, her birth, her education, her inheritance, her manners, and her customs, to the vortex of the most rapid life of Paris. She can never escape it, save by becoming a nun, which is not at all probable with her manners and tastes. She has only one possible career, a life of pleasure. She will come to it sooner or later, if indeed she has not already begun to tread its primrose path. She cannot escape her fate. From being a young girl she will take the inevitable step, quite simply. And I would like to be the pivot of this transformation.

"I am waiting. There are many lovers. You will see among them a Frenchman, Monsieur de Belvigne; a Russian, called Prince Kravalow, and an Italian, Chevalier Valreali, who have all announced their candidacies and who are consequently maneuvering to the best of their ability. In addition to these there are several freebooters of less importance. The Marquise waits and watches. But I think that she has views about me. She knows that I am very rich, and she makes less of the others.

"Her drawing-room is, moreover, the most astounding that I know of, in such exhibitions. You even meet very decent men there, like ourselves. As for the women, she has culled the best there is from the basket of pickpockets. Nobody knows where she found them. It is a set apart from Bohemia, apart from everything. She has had one inspiration showing genius, and that is the knack of selecting especially those adventuresses who have children, generally girls. So that a fool might believe that in her house he was among respectable women!"

They had reached the avenue of the Champs-Elysées. A gentle breeze softly stirred the leaves and touched the faces of passers-by, like the breaths of a giant fan, waving somewhere in the sky. Silent shadows wandered beneath the trees; others, on benches, made a dark spot. And these shadows spoke very low, as if they were telling each other important or shameful secrets.

"You can't imagine what a collection of fictitious titles are met in this lair," said Servigny. "By the way, I shall present you by the name of Count Saval; plain Saval would not do at all."

"Oh, no, indeed!" cried his friend; "I would not have anyone think me capable of borrowing a title, even for an evening, even among those people. Ah, no!"

Servigny began to laugh.

"How stupid you are! Why, in that set they call me the Duke de Servigny. I don't know how nor why. But at any rate the Duke de Servigny I am and shall remain, without complaining or protesting. It does not worry me. I should have no footing there whatever without a title."

But Saval would not be convinced.

"Well, you are of rank, and so you may remain. But, as for me, no. I shall be the only common person in the drawing-room. So much the worse, or, so much the better. It will be my mark of distinction and superiority."

Servigny was obstinate.

"I tell you that it is not possible. Why, it would almost seem monstrous. You would have the effect of a ragman at a meeting of emperors. Let me do as I like. I shall introduce you as the Vice-Roi du 'Haut-Mississippi,' and no one will be at all astonished. When a man takes on greatness, he can't take too much."

"Once more, no, I do not wish it."

"Very well, have your way. But, in fact, I am very foolish to try to convince you. I defy you to get in without some one giving you a title, just as they give a bunch of violets to the ladies at the entrance to certain stores."

They turned to the right in the Rue de Barrie, mounted one flight of stairs in a fine modern house, and gave their overcoats and canes into the hands of four servants in knee-breeches. A warm odor, as of a festival assembly, filled the air, an odor of flowers, perfumes, and women; and a composed and continuous murmur came from the adjoining rooms, which were filled with people.

A kind of master of ceremonies, tall, erect, wide of girth, serious, his face framed in white whiskers, approached the newcomers, asking with a short and haughty bow: "Whom shall I announce?"

"Monsieur Saval," Servigny replied.

Then with a loud voice, the man opening the door cried out to the crowd of guests:

"Monsieur the Duke de Servigny.

"Monsieur the Baron Saval."

The first drawing-room was filled with women. The first thing which attracted attention was the display of bare shoulders, above a flood of brilliant gowns.

The mistress of the house, who stood talking with three friends, turned and came forward with a majestic step, with grace in her mien and a smile on her lips. Her forehead was narrow and very low, and was covered with a mass of glossy black hair, encroaching a little upon the temples.

She was tall, a trifle too large, a little too stout, over ripe, but very pretty, with a heavy, warm, potent beauty. Beneath that mass of hair, full of dreams and smiles, rendering her mysteriously captivating, were enormous black eyes. Her nose was a little narrow, her mouth large and infinitely seductive, made to speak and to conquer.

Her greatest charm was in her voice. It came from that mouth as water from a spring, so natural, so light, so well modulated, so clear, that there was a physical pleasure in listening to it. It was a joy for the ear to hear the flexible words flow with the grace of a babbling brook, and it was a joy for the eyes to see those pretty lips, a trifle too red, open as the words rippled forth.

She gave one hand to Servigny, who kissed it, and dropping her fan on its little gold chain, she gave the other to Saval, saying to him: "You are welcome, Baron, all the Duke's friends are at home here."

Then she fixed her brilliant eyes upon the Colossus who had just been introduced to her. She had just the slightest down on her upper lip, a suspicion of a mustache, which seemed darker when she spoke. There was a pleasant odor about her, pervading, intoxicating, some perfume of America or of the Indies. Other people came in, mar-

quesses, counts or princes. She said to Servigny, with the gracious-
ness of a mother: "You will find my daughter in the other parlor.
Have a good time, gentlemen, the house is yours."

And she left them to go to those who had come later, throwing at
Saval that smiling and fleeting glance which women use to show that
they are pleased. Servigny grasped his friend's arm.

"I will pilot you," said he. "In this parlor where we now are,
women, the temples of the fleshly, fresh or otherwise. Bargains as
good as new, even better, for sale or on lease. At the right, gaming,
the temple of money. You understand all about that. At the lower
end, dancing, the temple of innocence, the sanctuary, the market
for young girls. They are shown off there in every light. Even legitimate marriages are tolerated. It is the future, the hope, of our evenings. And the most curious part of this museum of moral diseases
are these young girls whose souls are out of joint, just like the
limbs of the little clowns born of mountebanks. Come and look at
them."

He bowed, right and left, courteously, a compliment on his lips,
sweeping each low-gowned woman whom he knew with the look of
an expert.

The musicians, at the end of the second parlor, were playing a
waltz; and the two friends stopped at the door to look at them. A
score of couples were whirling—the men with a serious expression,
and the women with a fixed smile on their lips. They displayed a good
deal of shoulder, like their mothers; and the bodices of some were
only held in place by a slender ribbon, disclosing at times more than
is generally shown.

Suddenly from the end of the room a tall girl darted forward, gliding through the crowd, brushing against the dancers, and holding her
long train in her left hand. She ran with quick little steps as women
do in crowds, and called out: "Ah! How is Muscade? How do you do,
Muscade?"

Her features wore an expression of the bloom of life, the illumination of happiness. Her white flesh seemed to shine, the golden-
white flesh which goes with red hair. The mass of her tresses, twisted

on her head, fiery, flaming locks, nestled against her supple neck, which was still a little thin.

She seemed to move just as her mother was made to speak, so natural, noble, and simple were her gestures. A person felt a moral joy and physical pleasure in seeing her walk, stir about, bend her head, or lift her arm.

"Ah! Muscade, how do you do, Muscade?" she repeated.

Servigny shook her hand violently, as he would a man's, and said: "Mademoiselle Yvette, my friend, Baron Saval."

"Good evening, Monsieur. Are you always as tall as that?"

Servigny replied in that bantering tone which he always used with her, in order to conceal his mistrust and his uncertainty:

"No, Mam'zelle. He has put on his greatest dimensions to please your mother, who loves a colossus."

And the young girl remarked with a comic seriousness: "Very well! But when you come to see me you must diminish a little if you please. I prefer the medium height. Now Muscade has just the proportions which I like."

And she gave her hand to the newcomer. Then she asked: "Do you dance, Muscade? Come, let us waltz." Without replying, with a quick movement, passionately, Servigny clasped her waist and they disappeared with the fury of a whirlwind.

They danced more rapidly than any of the others, whirled and whirled, and turned madly, so close together that they seemed but one, and with the form erect, the legs almost motionless, as if some invisible mechanism, concealed beneath their feet, caused them to twirl. They appeared tireless. The other dancers stopped from time to time. They still danced on, alone. They seemed not to know where they were nor what they were doing, as if they had gone far away from the ball, in an ecstasy. The musicians continued to play, with their looks fixed upon this mad couple; all the guests gazed at them, and when finally they did stop dancing, everyone applauded them.

She was a little flushed, with strange eyes, ardent and timid, less daring than a moment before, troubled eyes, blue, yet with a pupil so black that they seemed hardly natural. Servigny appeared giddy. He leaned against a door to regain his composure.

"You have no head, my poor Muscade, I am steadier than you," said Yvette to Servigny.

He smiled nervously, and devoured her with a look. His animal feelings revealed themselves in his eyes and in the curl of his lips. She stood beside him looking down, and her bosom rose and fell in short gasps as he looked at her.

Then she said softly: "Really, there are times when you are like a tiger about to spring upon his prey. Come, give me your arm, and let us find your friend."

Silently he offered her his arm and they went down the long drawing-room together.

Saval was not alone, for the Marquise Obardi had rejoined him. She conversed with him on ordinary and fashionable subjects with a seductiveness in her tones which intoxicated him. And, looking at her with his mental eye, it seemed to him that her lips uttered words far different from those which they formed. When she saw Servigny her face immediately lighted up, and turning toward him she said:

"You know, my dear Duke, that I have just leased a villa at Bougival for two months, and I count upon your coming to see me there, and upon your friend also. Listen. We take possession next Monday, and shall expect both of you to dinner the following Saturday. We shall keep you over Sunday."

Perfectly serene and tranquil Yvette smiled, saying with a decision which swept away hesitation on his part:

"Of course Muscade will come to dinner on Saturday. We have only to ask him, for he and I intend to commit a lot of follies in the country."

He thought he divined the birth of a promise in her smile, and in her voice he heard what he thought was invitation.

Then the Marquise turned her big, black eyes upon Saval: "And you will, of course, come, Baron?"

With a smile that forbade doubt, he bent toward her, saying, "I shall be only too charmed, Madame."

Then Yvette murmured with malice that was either naïve or traitorous: "We will set all the world by the ears down there, won't we, Muscade, and make my regiment of admirers fairly mad." And with a look, she pointed out a group of men who were looking at them from a little distance.

Said Servigny to her: "As many follies as *you* may please, Mam'zelle."

In speaking to Yvette, Servigny never used the word "Mademoiselle," by reason of his close and long intimacy with her.

Then Saval asked: "Why does Mademoiselle always call my friend Servigny 'Muscade'?"

Yvette assumed a very frank air and said:

"I will tell you: It is because he always slips through my hands. Now I think I have him, and then I find I have not."

The Marquise, with her eyes upon Saval, and evidently preoccupied, said in a careless tone: "You children are very funny."

But Yvette bridled up: "I do not intend to be funny; I am simply frank. Muscade pleases me, and is always deserting me, and that is what annoys me."

Servigny bowed profoundly, saying: "I will never leave you any more, Mam'zelle, neither day nor night."

She made a gesture of horror:

"My goodness! no—what do you mean? You are all right during the day, but at night you might embarrass me."

With an air of impertinence he asked: "And why?"

Yvette responded calmly and audaciously, "Because you would not look well en *déshabillé*."

The Marquise, without appearing at all disturbed, said: "What extraordinary subjects for conversation. One would think that you were not at all ignorant of such things."

And Servigny jokingly added: "That is also my opinion, Marquise."

Yvette turned her eyes upon him, and in a haughty, yet wounded, tone said: "You are becoming very vulgar—just as you have been several times lately." And turning quickly she appealed to an individual standing by:

"Chevalier, come and defend me from insult."

A thin, brown man, with an easy carriage, came forward.

"Who is the culprit?" said he, with a constrained smile.

Yvette pointed out Servigny with a nod of her head:

"There he is, but I like him better than I do you, because he is less of a bore."

The Chevalier Valreali bowed:

"I do what I can, Mademoiselle. I may have less ability, but not less devotion."

A gentleman came forward, tall and stout, with gray whiskers, saying in loud tones: "Mademoiselle Yvette, I am your most devoted slave."

Yvette cried: "Ah, Monsieur de Belvigne." Then turning toward Saval, she introduced him.

"My last adorer—big, fat, rich, and stupid. Those are the kind I like. A veritable drum-major—but of the *table d'hôte*.* But see, you are still bigger than he. How shall I nickname you? Good! I have it. I shall call you 'M. Colossus of Rhodes, Junior,' from the Colossus who certainly was your father. But you two ought to have very interesting things to say to each other up there, above the heads of us all—so, by-bye."

And she left them quickly, going to the orchestra to make the musicians strike up a quadrille.

Madame Obardi seemed preoccupied. In a soft voice she said to Servigny:

"You are always teasing her. You will warp her character and bring out many bad traits."

Servigny replies: "Why, haven't you finished her education?"

She appeared not to understand, and continued talking in a friendly way. But she noticed a solemn looking man, wearing a

---

* Literally, a common dining table for patrons at a hotel; here the phrase suggests blue-collar tastes.

perfect constellation of crosses and orders, standing near her, and she ran to him:

"Ah! Prince, Prince, what good fortune!"

Servigny took Saval's arm and drew him away:

"That is the latest serious suitor, Prince Kravalow. Isn't she superb?"

"To my mind they are both superb. The mother would suffice for me perfectly," answered Saval.

Servigny nodded and said: "At your disposal, my dear boy."

The dancers elbowed them aside, as they were forming for a quadrille.

"Now let us go and see the sharpers," said Servigny. And they entered the gambling-room.

Around each table stood a group of men, looking on. There was very little conversation. At times the clink of gold coins, tossed upon the green cloth or hastily seized, added its sound to the murmur of the players, just as if the money was putting in its word among the human voices.

All the men were decorated with various orders, and odd ribbons, and they all wore the same severe expression, with different countenances. The especially distinguishing feature was the beard.

The stiff American with his horseshoe, the haughty Englishman with his fan-beard open on his breast, the Spaniard with his black fleece reaching to the eyes, the Roman with that huge mustache which Italy copied from Victor Emmanuel, the Austrian with his whiskers and shaved chin, a Russian general whose lip seemed armed with two twisted lances, and a Frenchman with a dainty mustache, displayed the fancies of all the barbers in the world.

"You won't join the game?" asked Servigny.

"No, shall you?"

"Not now. If you are ready to go, we will come back some quieter day. There are too many people here to-day, and we can't do anything."

"Well, let us go."

And they disappeared behind a door-curtain into the hall. As soon as they were in the street Servigny asked: "Well, what do you think of it?"

"It certainly is interesting, but I fancy the women's side of it more than the men's."

"Indeed! Those women are the best of the tribe for us. Don't you find that you breathe the odor of love among them, just as you scent the perfumes at a hairdresser's?"

"Really such houses are the place for one to go. And what experts, my dear fellow! What artists! Have you ever eaten bakers' cakes? They look well, but they amount to nothing. The man who bakes them only knows how to make bread. Well! the love of a woman in ordinary society always reminds me of these bake-shop trifles, while the love you find at houses like the Marquise Obardi's, don't you see, is the real sweetmeat. Oh! they know how to make cakes, these charming pastry-cooks. Only you pay five sous, at their shops, for what costs two sous elsewhere."

"Who is the master of the house just now?" asked Saval.

Servigny shrugged his shoulders, signifying his ignorance.

"I don't know, the latest one known was an English peer, but he left three months ago. At present she must live off the common herd, or the gambling, perhaps, and on the gamblers, for she has her caprices. But tell me, it is understood that we dine with her on Saturday at Bougival, is it not? People are more free in the country, and I shall succeed in finding out what ideas Yvette has in her head!"

"I should like nothing better," replied Saval. "I have nothing to do that day."

Passing down through the Champs-Elysées, under the steps they disturbed a couple making love on one of the benches, and Servigny muttered: "What foolishness and what a serious matter at the same time! How commonplace and amusing love is, always the same and always different! And the beggar who gives his sweetheart twenty sous gets as much return as I would for ten thousand francs from some Obardi, no younger and no less stupid perhaps than this nondescript. What nonsense!"

He said nothing for a few minutes; then he began again: "All the same, it would be good to become Yvette's first lover. Oh! for that I would give—"

He did not add what he would give, and Saval said good night to him as they reached the corner of the Rue Royale.

CHAPTER II

Bougival and Love

THEY HAD SET THE table on the veranda which overlooked the river. The Printemps villa, leased by the Marquise Obardi, was halfway up this hill, just at the corner of the Seine, which turned before the garden wall, flowing toward Marly.

Opposite the residence, the island of Croissy formed a horizon of tall trees, a mass of verdure, and they could see a long stretch of the big river as far as the floating *café* of La Grenouillère hidden beneath the foliage.

The evening fell, one of those calm evenings at the waterside, full of color yet soft, one of those peaceful evenings which produces a sensation of pleasure. No breath of air stirred the branches, no shiver of wind ruffled the smooth clear surface of the Seine. It was not too warm, it was mild—good weather to live in. The grateful coolness of the banks of the Seine rose toward a serene sky.

The sun disappeared behind the trees to shine on other lands, and one seemed to absorb the serenity of the already sleeping earth, to inhale, in the peace of space, the life of the infinite.

As they left the drawing-room to seat themselves at the table everyone was joyous. A softened gaiety filled their hearts, they felt that it would be so delightful to dine there in the country, with that great river and that twilight for a setting, breathing that pure and fragrant air.

The Marquise had taken Saval's arm, and Yvette, Servigny's. The four were alone by themselves. The two women seemed entirely different persons from what they were at Paris, especially Yvette. She talked but little, and seemed languid and grave.

Saval, hardly recognizing her in this frame of mind, asked her:

"What is the matter, Mademoiselle? I find you changed since last week. You have become quite a serious person."

"It is the country that does that for me," she replied. "I am not the same, I feel queer; besides I am never two days alike. To-day I have the air of a mad woman, and to-morrow shall be as grave as an elegy. I change with the weather, I don't know why. You see, I am capable of anything, according to the moment. There are days when I would like to kill people,—not animals, I would never kill animals,—but people, yes, and other days when I weep at a mere thing. A lot of different ideas pass through my head. It depends, too, a good deal on how I get up. Every morning, on waking, I can tell just what I shall be in the evening. Perhaps it is our dreams that settle it for us, and it depends on the book I have just read."

She was clad in a white flannel suit which delicately enveloped her in the floating softness of the material. Her bodice, with full folds, suggested, without displaying and without restraining, her free chest, which was firm and already ripe. And her superb neck emerged from a froth of soft lace, bending with gentle movements, fairer than her gown, a pilaster of flesh, bearing the heavy mass of her golden hair.

Servigny looked at her for a long time: "You are adorable this evening, Mam'zelle," said he, "I wish I could always see you like this."

"Don't make a declaration, Muscade. I should take it seriously, and that might cost you dear."

The Marquise seemed happy, very happy. All in black, richly dressed in a plain gown which showed her strong, full lines, a bit of red at the bodice, a cincture of red carnations falling from her waist like a chain, and fastened at the hips, and a red rose in her dark hair, she carried in all her person something fervid,—in that simple costume, in those flowers which seemed to bleed, in her look, in her slow speech, in her peculiar gestures.

Saval, too, appeared serious and absorbed. From time to time he stroked his pointed beard, trimmed in the fashion of Henri III., and seemed to be meditating on the most profound subjects.

Nobody spoke for several minutes. Then as they were serving the trout, Servigny remarked:

"Silence is a good thing, at times. People are often nearer to each other when they are keeping still than when they are talking. Isn't that so, Marquise?"

She turned a little toward him and answered:

"It is quite true. It is so sweet to think together about agreeable things."

She raised her warm glance toward Saval, and they continued for some seconds looking into each other's eyes. A slight, almost inaudible movement took place beneath the table.

Servigny resumed: "Mam'zelle Yvette, you will make me believe that you are in love if you keep on being as good as that. Now, with whom could you be in love? Let us think together, if you will; I put aside the army of vulgar sighers. I'll only take the principal ones. Is it Prince Kravalow?"

At this name Yvette awoke: "My poor Muscade, can you think of such a thing? Why, the Prince has the air of a Russian in a wax-figure museum, who has won medals in a hairdressing competition."

"Good! We'll drop the Prince. But you have noticed the Viscount Pierre de Belvigne?"

This time she began to laugh, and asked: "Can you imagine me hanging to the neck of 'Raisiné'?" She nicknamed him according to the day, Raisiné, Malvoisie, Argenteuil, for she gave everybody nicknames. And she would murmur to his face: "My dear little Pierre," or "My divine Pedro, darling Pierrot, give your bow-wow's head to your dear little girl, who wants to kiss it."

"Scratch out number two. There still remains the Chevalier Valreali whom the Marquise seems to favor," continued Servigny.

Yvette regained all her gaiety: " 'Teardrop'? Why he weeps like a Magdalene. He goes to all the first-class funerals. I imagine myself dead every time he looks at me."

"That settles the third. So the lightning will strike Baron Saval, here."

"Monsieur the Colossus of Rhodes, Junior? No. He is too strong. It would seem to me as if I were in love with the triumphal arch of L'Etoile."

"Then Mam'zelle, it is beyond doubt that you are in love with me, for I am the only one of your adorers of whom we have not yet spoken. I left myself for the last through modesty and through discretion. It remains for me to thank you."

She replied with happy grace: "In love with you, Muscade? Ah! no. I like you, but I don't love you. Wait—I—I don't want to discourage you. I don't love you—yet. You have a chance—perhaps. Persevere, Muscade, be devoted, ardent, submissive, full of little attentions and considerations, docile to my slightest caprices, ready for anything to please me, and we shall see—later."

"But, Mam'zelle, I would rather furnish all you demand afterward than beforehand, if it be the same to you."

She asked with an artless air: "After what, Muscade?"

"After you have shown me that you love me, by Jove!"

"Well, act as if I loved you, and believe it, if you wish."

"But you—"

"Be quiet, Muscade; enough on the subject."

The sun had sunk behind the island, but the whole sky still flamed like a fire, and the peaceful water of the river seemed changed to blood. The reflections from the horizon reddened houses, objects, and persons. The scarlet rose in the Marquise's hair had the appearance of a splash of purple fallen from the clouds upon her head.

As Yvette looked on from her end, the Marquise rested, as if by carelessness, her bare hand upon Saval's hand; but the young girl made a motion and the Marquise withdrew her hand with a quick gesture, pretending to readjust something in the folds of her corsage.

Servigny, who was looking at them, said:

"If you like, Mam'zelle, we will take a walk on the island after dinner."

"Oh, yes! That will be delightful. We will go all alone, won't we, Muscade?"

"Yes, all alone, Mam'zelle!"

The vast silence of the horizon, the sleepy tranquillity of the evening captured heart, body, and voice. There are peaceful, chosen hours when it becomes almost impossible to talk.

The servants waited on them noiselessly. The firmamental conflagration faded away, and the soft night spread its shadows over the earth.

"Are you going to stay long in this place?" asked Saval.

And the Marquise answered, dwelling on each word: "Yes, as long as I am happy."

As it was too dark to see, lamps were brought. They cast upon the table a strange, pale gleam beneath the great obscurity of space; and very soon a shower of gnats fell upon the tablecloth—the tiny gnats which immolate themselves by passing over the glass chimneys, and, with wings and legs scorched, powder the table-linen, dishes, and cups with a kind of gray and hopping dust.

They swallowed them in the wine, they ate them in the sauces, they saw them moving on the bread, and had their faces and hands tickled by the countless swarm of these tiny insects. They were continually compelled to throw away the beverages, to cover the plates, and while eating to shield the food with infinite precautions.

It amused Yvette. Servigny took care to shelter what she bore to her mouth, to guard her glass, to hold his handkerchief stretched out over her head like a roof. But the Marquise, disgusted, became nervous, and the end of the dinner came quickly. Yvette, who had not forgotten Servigny's proposition, said to him:

"Now we'll go to the island."

Her mother cautioned her in a languid tone: "Don't be late, above all things. We will escort you to the ferry."

And they started in couples, the young girl and her admirer walking in front, on the road to the shore. They heard, behind them, the Marquise and Saval speaking very rapidly in low tones. All was dark, with a thick, inky darkness. But the sky swarmed with grains of fire, and seemed to sow them in the river, for the black water was flecked with stars.

The frogs were croaking monotonously upon the bank, and numerous nightingales were uttering their low, sweet song in the calm and peaceful air.

Yvette suddenly said: "Gracious! They are not walking behind us any more, where are they?" And she called out: "Mamma!" No voice replied. The young girl resumed: "At any rate, they can't be far away, for I heard them just now."

Servigny murmured: "They must have gone back. Your mother was cold, perhaps." And he drew her along.

Before them a light gleamed. It was the tavern of Martinet, restaurant-keeper and fisherman. At their call a man came out of the house, and they got into a large boat which was moored among the weeds of the shore.

The ferryman took his oars, and the unwieldy barge, as it advanced, disturbed the sleeping stars upon the water and set them into a mad dance, which gradually calmed down after they had passed. They touched the other shore and disembarked beneath the great trees. A cool freshness of damp earth permeated the air under the lofty and clustered branches, where there seemed to be as many nightingales as there were leaves. A distant piano began to play a popular waltz.

Servigny took Yvette's arm and very gently slipped his hand around her waist and gave her a slight hug.

"What are you thinking about?" he said.

"I? About nothing at all. I am very happy!"

"Then you don't love me?"

"Oh, yes, Muscade, I love you, I love you a great deal; only leave me alone. It is too beautiful here to listen to your nonsense."

He drew her toward him, although she tried, by little pushes, to extricate herself, and through her soft flannel gown he felt the warmth of her flesh. He stammered:

"Yvette!"

"Well, what?"

"I do love you!"

"But you are not in earnest, Muscade."

"Oh, yes I am. I have loved you for a long time."

She continually kept trying to separate herself from him, trying to release the arm crushed between their bodies. They walked with difficulty, trammeled by this bond and by these movements, and went zigzagging along like drunken folk.

He knew not what to say to her, feeling that he could not talk to a young girl as he would to a woman. He was perplexed, thinking what he ought to do, wondering if she consented or did not understand, and curbing his spirit to find just the right, tender, and decisive words. He kept saying every second:

"Yvette! Speak! Yvette!"

Then, suddenly, risking all, he kissed her on the cheek. She gave a little start aside, and said with a vexed air:

"Oh! you are absurd. Are you going to let me alone?"

The tone of her voice did not at all reveal her thoughts nor her wishes; and, not seeing her too angry, he applied his lips to the beginning of her neck, just beneath the golden hair, that charming spot which he had so often coveted.

Then she made great efforts to free herself. But he held her strongly, and placing his other hand on her shoulder, he compelled her to turn her head toward him and gave her a fond, passionate kiss, squarely on the mouth.

She slipped from his arms by a quick undulation of the body, and, free from his grasp, she disappeared into the darkness with a great swishing of skirts, like the whir of a bird as it flies away.

He stood motionless a moment, surprised by her suppleness and her disappearance, then hearing nothing, he called gently: "Yvette!"

She did not reply. He began to walk forward, peering through the shadows, looking in the underbrush for the white spot her dress should make. All was dark. He cried out more loudly:

"Mam'zelle Yvette! Mam'zelle Yvette!"

Nothing stirred. He stopped and listened. The whole island was still; there was scarcely a rustle of leaves over his head. The frogs alone continued their deep croakings on the shores. Then he wandered from thicket to thicket, going where the banks were steep and bushy and returning to places where they were flat and bare as a dead man's arm. He proceeded until he was opposite Bougival and reached the establishment of La Grenouillère, groping the clumps of trees, calling out continually:

"Mam'zelle Yvette, where are you? Answer. It is ridiculous! Come, answer! Don't keep me hunting like this."

A distant clock began to strike. He counted the hours: twelve. He had been searching through the island for two hours. Then he thought that perhaps she had gone home; and he went back very anxiously, this time by way of the bridge. A servant dozing on a chair was waiting in the hall.

Servigny awakened him and asked: "Is it long since Mademoiselle Yvette came home? I left her at the foot of the place because I had a call to make."

And the valet replied: "Oh! yes, Monsieur, Mademoiselle came in before ten o'clock."

He proceeded to his room and went to bed. But he could not close his eyes. That stolen kiss had stirred him to the soul. He kept wondering what she thought and what she knew. How pretty and attractive she was!

His desires, somewhat wearied by the life he led, by all his procession of sweethearts, by all his explorations in the kingdom of love, awoke before this singular child, so fresh, irritating, and inexplicable. He heard one o'clock strike, then two. He could not sleep at all. He was warm, he felt his heart beat and his temples throb, and he rose to open the window. A breath of fresh air came in, which he inhaled deeply. The thick darkness was silent, black, motionless. But suddenly he perceived before him, in the shadows of the garden, a shining point; it seemed a little red coal.

"Well, a cigar!" he said to himself. "It must be Saval," and he called softly: "Léon!"

"Is it you, Jean?"

"Yes. Wait. I'll come down." He dressed, went out, and rejoining his friend who was smoking astride an iron chair, inquired: "What are you doing here at this hour?"

"I am resting," Saval replied. And he began to laugh.

Servigny pressed his hand: "My compliments, my dear fellow. And as for me, I—am making a fool of myself."

"You mean—"

"I mean that—Yvette and her mother do not resemble each other."

"What has happened? Tell me."

Servigny recounted his attempts and their failure. Then he resumed:

"Decidedly, that little girl worries me. Fancy my not being able to sleep! What a queer thing a girl is! She appears to be as simple as anything, and yet you know nothing about her. A woman who has lived and loved, who knows life, can be quickly understood. But when it comes to a young virgin, on the contrary, no one can guess anything about her. At heart I begin to think that she is making sport of me."

Saval tilted his chair. He said, very slowly:

"Take care, my dear fellow, she will lead you to marriage. Remember those other illustrious examples. It was just by this same process that Mademoiselle de Montijo, who was at least of good family, became empress. Don't play Napoleon."

Servigny murmured: "As for that, fear nothing. I am neither a simpleton nor an emperor. A man must be either one or the other to make such a move as that. But tell me, are you sleepy?"

"Not a bit."

"Will you take a walk along the river?"

"Gladly."

They opened the iron gate and began to walk along the river bank toward Marly.

It was the quiet hour which precedes dawn, the hour of deep sleep, of complete rest, of profound peacefulness. Even the gentle sounds of the night were hushed. The nightingales sang no longer; the frogs had finished their hubbub; some kind of an animal only, probably a bird, was making somewhere a kind of sawing sound, feeble, monotonous, and regular as a machine. Servigny, who had moments of poetry and of philosophy too, suddenly remarked:

"Now this girl completely puzzles me. In arithmetic, one and one make two. In love one and one ought to make one but they make two just the same. Have you ever felt that? That need of absorbing a woman in yourself or disappearing in her? I am not speaking of the animal embrace, but of that moral and mental eagerness to be but one with a being, to open to her all one's heart and soul, and to fathom her thoughts to the depths.

"And yet you can never lay bare all the fluctuations of her wishes, desires, and opinions. You can never guess, even slightly, all the unknown currents, all the mystery of a soul that seems so near, a soul hidden behind two eyes that look at you, clear as water, transparent as if there were nothing beneath a soul which talks to you by a beloved mouth, which seems your very own, so greatly do you desire it; a soul which throws you by words its thoughts, one by one, and which, nevertheless, remains further away from you than those stars are from each other, and more impenetrable. Isn't it queer, all that?"

"I don't ask so much," Saval rejoined. "I don't look behind the eyes. I care little for the contents, but much for the vessel."

And Servigny replied: "What a singular person Yvette is! How will she receive me this morning?"

As they reached the works at Marly they perceived that the sky was brightening. The cocks began to crow in the poultry-yards. A bird twittered in a park at the left, ceaselessly reiterating a tender little theme.

"It is time to go back," said Saval.

They returned, and as Servigny entered his room, he saw the horizon all pink through his open windows.

Then he shut the blinds, drew the thick, heavy curtains, went back to bed and fell asleep. He dreamed of Yvette all through his slumber. An odd noise awoke him. He sat on the side of the bed and listened, but heard nothing further. Then suddenly there was a crackling against the blinds, like falling hail. He jumped from the bed, ran to the window, opened it, and saw Yvette standing in the path and throwing handfuls of gravel at his face. She was clad in pink, with a wide-brimmed straw hat ornamented with a mousquetaire plume, and was laughing mischievously.

"Well! Muscade, are you asleep? What could you have been doing all night to make you wake so late? Have you been seeking adventures, my poor Muscade?"

He was dazzled by the bright daylight striking him full in the eyes, still overwhelmed with fatigue, and surprised at the jesting tranquillity of the young girl.

"I'll be down in a second, Mam'zelle," he answered. "Just time to splash my face with water, and I will join you."

"Hurry," she cried, "it is ten o'clock, and besides I have a great plan to unfold to you, a plot we are going to concoct. You know that we breakfast at eleven."

He found her seated on a bench, with a book in her lap, some novel or other. She took his arm in a familiar and friendly way, with a frank and gay manner, as if nothing had happened the night before, and drew him toward the end of the garden.

"This is my plan," she said. "We will disobey mamma, and you shall take me presently to La Grenouillère restaurant. I want to see it. Mamma says that decent women cannot go to the place. Now it is all the same to me whether persons can go there or cannot. You'll take me, won't you, Muscade? And we will have a great time—with the boatmen."

She exhaled a delicious fragrance, although he could not exactly define just what light and vague odor enveloped her. It was not one of those heavy perfumes of her mother, but a discreet breath in which he fancied he could detect a suspicion of iris powder, and perhaps a suggestion of vervain.

Whence emanated that indiscernible perfume? From her dress, her hair, or her skin? He puzzled over this, and as he was speaking very close to her, he received full in the face her fresh breath, which seemed to him just as delicious to inhale.

Then he thought that this evasive perfume which he was trying to recognize was perhaps only evoked by her charming eyes, and was merely a sort of deceptive emanation of her young and alluring grace.

"That is agreed, isn't it, Muscade? As it will be very warm after breakfast, mamma will not go out. She always feels the heat very much. We will leave her with your friend, and you shall take me. They will think that we have gone into the forest. If you knew how much it will amuse me to see La Grenouillère!"

They reached the iron gate opposite the Seine. A flood of sunshine fell upon the slumberous, shining river. A slight heat-mist rose from it, a sort of haze of evaporated water, which spread over the surface of the stream a faint gleaming vapor.

From time to time, boats passed by, a quick yawl or a heavy passage boat, and short or long whistles could be heard, those of the trains which every Sunday poured the citizens of Paris into the suburbs, and those of the steamboats signaling their approach to pass the locks at Marly.

But a tiny bell sounded. Breakfast was announced, and they went back into the house. The repast was a silent one. A heavy July noon overwhelmed the earth, and oppressed humanity. The heat seemed thick, and paralyzed both mind and body. The sluggish words would not leave the lips, and all motion seemed laborious, as if the air had become a resisting medium, difficult to traverse. Only Yvette, although silent, seemed animated and nervous with impatience. As soon as they had finished the last course she said:

"If we were to go for a walk in the forest, it would be deliciously cool under the trees."

The Marquise murmured with a listless air: "Are you mad? Does anyone go out in such weather?"

And the young girl, delighted, rejoined: "Oh, well! We will leave the Baron to keep you company. Muscade and I will climb the hill and sit on the grass and read."

And turning toward Servigny she asked: "That is understood?"

"At your service, Mam'zelle," he replied.

Yvette ran to get her hat. The Marquise shrugged her shoulders with a sigh. "She certainly is mad," she said.

Then with an indolence in her amorous and lazy gestures, she gave her pretty white hand to the Baron, who kissed it softly. Yvette and Servigny started. They went along the river, crossed the bridge and went on to the island, and then seated themselves on the bank, beneath the willows, for it was too soon to go to La Grenouillère.

The young girl at once drew a book from her pocket and smilingly said: "Muscade, you are going to read to me." And she handed him the volume.

He made a motion as if of fright. "I, Mam'zelle? I don't know how to read!"

She replied with gravity: "Come, no excuses, no objections; you are a fine suitor, you! All for nothing, is that it? Is that your motto?"

He took the book, opened it, and was astonished. It was a treatise on entomology. A history of ants by an English author. And as he remained inert, believing that he was making sport of her, she said with impatience: "Well, read!"

"Is it a wager, or just a simple fad?" he asked.

"No, my dear. I saw that book in a shop. They told me that it was the best authority on ants and I thought that it would be interesting to learn about the life of these little insects while you see them running over the grass; so read, if you please."

She stretched herself flat upon the grass, her elbows resting upon the ground, her head between her hands, her eyes fixed upon the ground. He began to read as follows:

"The anthropoid apes are undoubtedly the animals which approach nearest to man by their anatomical structure, but if we consider the habits of the ants, their organization into societies, their vast communities, the houses and roads that they construct, their custom of domesticating animals, and sometimes even of making slaves of them, we are compelled to admit that they have the right to claim a place near to man in the scale of intelligence."

He continued in a monotonous voice, stopping from time to time to ask: "Isn't that enough?"

She shook her head, and having caught an ant on the end of a severed blade of grass, she amused herself by making it go from one end to the other of the sprig, which she tipped up whenever the insect reached one of the ends. She listened with mute and contented attention to all the wonderful details of the life of these frail creatures: their subterranean homes; the manner in which they seize, shut up, and feed plant-lice to drink the sweet milk which they secrete, as we keep cows in our barns; their custom of domesticating little blind insects which clean the anthills, and of going to war to capture slaves who will take care of their victors with such tender solicitude that the latter even lose the habit of feeding themselves.

And little by little, as if a maternal tenderness had sprung up in her heart for the poor insect which was so tiny and so intelligent, Yvette made it climb on her finger, looking at it with a moved expression, almost wanting to embrace it.

And as Servigny read of the way in which they live in communities, and play games of strength and skill among themselves, the young girl grew enthusiastic and sought to kiss the insect which escaped her and began to crawl over her face. Then she uttered a piercing cry, as if she had been threatened by a terrible danger, and with frantic gestures tried to brush it off her face. With a loud laugh Servigny caught it near her tresses and imprinted on the spot where he had seized it a long kiss without Yvette withdrawing her forehead.

Then she exclaimed as she rose: "That is better than a novel. Now let us go to La Grenouillère."

They reached that part of the island which is set out as a park and shaded with great trees. Couples were strolling beneath the lofty foliage along the Seine, where the boats were gliding by.

The boats were filled with young people, working-girls and their sweethearts, the latter in their shirtsleeves, with coats on their arms, tall hats tipped back, and a jaded look. There were tradesmen with their families, the women dressed in their best and the children flocking like little chicks about their parents. A distant, continuous sound of voices, a heavy, scolding clamor announced the proximity of the establishment so dear to the boatmen.

Suddenly they saw it. It was a huge boat, roofed over, moored to the bank. On board were many men and women drinking at tables, or else standing up, shouting, singing, bandying words, dancing, capering, to the sound of a piano which was groaning—out of tune and rattling as an old kettle.

Two tall, russet-haired, half-tipsy girls, with red lips, were talking coarsely. Others were dancing madly with young fellows half clad, dressed like jockeys, in linen trousers and colored caps. The odors of a crowd and of rice-powder were noticeable.

The drinkers around the tables were swallowing white, red, yellow, and green liquids, and vociferating at the top of their lungs, feeling as it were, the necessity of making a noise, a brutal need of having their ears and brains filled with uproar. Now and then a swimmer, standing on the roof, dived into the water, splashing the nearest guests, who yelled like savages.

On the stream passed the flotillas of light craft, long, slender wherries, swiftly rowed by bare-armed oarsmen, whose muscles played beneath their bronzed skin. The women in the boats, in blue or red flannel skirts, with umbrellas, red or blue, opened over their heads and gleaming under the burning sun, leaned back in their chairs at the stern of the boats, and seemed almost to float upon the water, in motionless and slumberous pose.

The heavier boats proceeded slowly, crowded with people. A collegian, wanting to show off, rowed like a windmill against all the other boats, bringing the curses of their oarsmen down upon his head, and disappearing in dismay after almost drowning two swimmers, followed by the shouts of the crowd thronging in the great floating *café*.

Yvette, radiantly happy, taking Servigny's arm, went into the midst of this noisy mob. She seemed to enjoy the crowding, and stared at the girls with a calm and gracious glance.

"Look at that one, Muscade," she said. "What pretty hair she has! They seem to be having such fun!"

As the pianist, a boatman dressed in red with a huge straw hat, began a waltz, Yvette grasped her companion and they danced so long and madly that everybody looked at them. The guests, standing on the tables, kept time with their feet; others threw glasses, and the musician, seeming to go mad, struck the ivory keys with great bangs, swaying his whole body and swinging his head covered with that immense hat. Suddenly he stopped and, slipping to the deck, lay flat, beneath his head-gear, as if dead with fatigue. A loud laugh arose and everybody applauded.

Four friends rushed forward, as they do in cases of accident, and lifting up their comrade, they carried him by his four limbs, after carefully placing his great hat on his stomach. A joker following them intoned the "De Profundis," and a procession formed and threaded the paths of the island, guests and strollers and everyone they met falling into line.

Yvette darted forward, delighted, laughing with her whole heart, chatting with everybody, stirred by the movement and the noise. The young men gazed at her, crowded against her, seeming to devour her with their glances; and Servigny began to fear lest the adventure should terminate badly.

The procession still kept on its way, hastening its step; for the four bearers had taken a quick pace, followed by the yelling crowd. But suddenly, they turned toward the shore, stopped short as they reached the bank, swung their comrade for a moment, and then, all four acting together, flung him into the river.

A great shout of joy rang out from all mouths, while the poor pianist, bewildered, paddled, swore, coughed, and spluttered, and though sticking in the mud managed to get to the shore. His hat which floated down the stream was picked up by a boat.

Yvette danced with joy, clapping and repeating: "Oh! Muscade, what fun! what fun!"

Servigny looked on, having become serious, a little disturbed, a little chilled to see her so much at her ease in this common place. A sort of instinct revolted in him, that instinct of the proper, which a well-born man always preserves even when he casts himself loose, that instinct which avoids too common familiarities and too degrading contacts. Astonished, he muttered to himself:

"Egad! Then *you* are at home here, are you?" And he wanted to speak familiarly to her, as a man does to certain women the first time he meets them. He no longer distinguished her from the russet-haired, hoarse-voiced creatures who brushed against them. The language of the crowd was not at all choice, but nobody seemed shocked or surprised. Yvette did not even appear to notice it.

"Muscade, I want to go in bathing," she said. "We'll go into the river together."

"At your service," said he.

They went to the bath-office to get bathing-suits. She was ready the first, and stood on the bank waiting for him, smiling on everyone who looked at her. Then side by side they went into the lukewarm water.

She swam with pleasure, with intoxication, caressed by the wave, throbbing with a sensual delight, raising herself at each stroke as if she were going to spring from the water. He followed her with difficulty, breathless, and vexed to feel himself mediocre at the sport.

But she slackened her pace, and then, turning over suddenly, she floated, with her arms folded and her eyes wide open to the blue sky. He observed, thus stretched out on the surface of the river, the undulating lines of her form, her firm neck and shoulders, her slightly submerged hips, and bare ankles, gleaming in the water, and the tiny foot that emerged.

He saw her thus exhibiting herself, as if she were doing it on purpose, to lure him on, or again to make sport of him. And he began to long for her with a passionate ardor and an exasperating impatience. Suddenly she turned, looked at him, and burst into laughter.

"You have a fine head," she said.

He was annoyed at this bantering, possessed with the anger of a baffled lover. Then yielding brusquely to a half felt desire for retaliation, a desire to avenge himself, to wound her, he said:

"Well, does this sort of life suit you?"

She asked with an artless air: "What do you mean?"

"Oh, come, don't make game of me. You know well enough what I mean!"

"No, I don't, on my word of honor."

"Oh, let us stop this comedy! Will you or will you not?"

"I do not understand you."

"You are not as stupid as all that; besides I told you last night."

"Told me what? I have forgotten!"

"That I love you."

"You?"

"Yes."

"What nonsense!"

"I swear it."

"Then prove it."

"That is all I ask."

"What is?"

"To prove it."

"Well, do so."

"But you did not say so last night."

"You did not ask anything."

"What absurdity!"

"And besides it is not to me to whom you should make your proposition."

"To whom, then?"

"Why, to mamma, of course."

He burst into laughter. "To your mother. No, that is too much!"

She had suddenly become very grave, and looking him straight in the eyes, said:

"Listen, Muscade, if you really love me enough to marry me, speak to mamma first, and I will answer you afterward."

He thought she was still making sport of him, and angrily replied: "Mam'zelle, you must be taking me for somebody else."

She kept looking at him with her soft, clear eyes. She hesitated and then said:

"I don't understand you at all."

Then he answered quickly with somewhat of ill nature in his voice:

"Come now, Yvette, let us cease this absurd comedy, which has already lasted too long. You are playing the part of a simple little girl, and the rôle does not fit you at all, believe me. You know perfectly well that there can be no question of marriage between us, but merely of love. I have told you that I love you. It is the truth. I repeat, I love you. Don't pretend any longer not to understand me, and don't treat me as if I were a fool."

They were face to face, treading water, merely moving their hands a little, to steady themselves. She was still for a moment, as if she could not make out the meaning of his words, then she suddenly blushed up to the roots of her hair. Her whole face grew purple from her neck to her ears, which became almost violet, and without answering a word she fled toward the shore, swimming with all her strength with hasty strokes. He could not keep up with her and panted with fatigue as he followed. He saw her leave the water, pick up her cloak, and go to her dressing-room without looking back.

It took him a long time to dress, very much perplexed as to what he ought to do, puzzled over what he should say to her, and wondering whether he ought to excuse himself or persevere. When he was ready, she had gone away all alone. He went back slowly, anxious and disturbed.

The Marquise was strolling, on Saval's arm, in the circular path around the lawn. As she observed Servigny, she said, with that careless air which she had maintained since the night before:

"I told you not to go out in such hot weather. And now Yvette has come back almost with a sun stroke. She has gone to lie down. She was as red as a poppy, the poor child, and she has a frightful headache. You must have been walking in the full sunlight, or you must have done something foolish. You are as unreasonable as she."

The young girl did not come down to dinner. When they wanted to send her up something to eat she called through the door that she was not hungry, for she had shut herself in, and she begged that they would leave her undisturbed. The two young men left by the ten o'clock train, promising to return the following Thursday, and the Marquise seated herself at the open window to dream, hearing in the distance the orchestra of the boatmen's ball, with its sprightly music, in the deep and solemn silence of the night.

Swayed by love as a person is moved by a fondness for horses or boating, she was subject to sudden tendernesses which crept over her like a disease. These passions took possession of her suddenly, penetrated her entire being, maddened her, enervated or overwhelmed her, in measure as they were of an exalted, violent, dramatic, or sentimental character.

She was one of those women who are created to love and to be loved. Starting from a very low station in life, she had risen in her adventurous career, acting instinctively, with inborn cleverness, accepting money and kisses, naturally, without distinguishing between them, employing her extraordinary ability in an unthinking and simple fashion. From all her experiences she had never known either a genuine tenderness or a great repulsion.

She had had various friends, for she had to live, as in traveling a person eats at many tables. But occasionally her heart took fire, and she really fell in love, which state lasted for some weeks or months, according to conditions. These were the delicious moments of her life, for she loved with all her soul. She cast herself upon love as a person throws himself into the river to drown himself, and let herself be carried away, ready to die, if need be, intoxicated, maddened, infinitely happy. She imagined each time that she never had experienced anything like such an attachment, and she would have been greatly astonished if some one had told her of how many men she had dreamed whole nights through, looking at the stars.

Saval had captivated her, body and soul. She dreamed of him, lulled by his face and his memory, in the calm exaltation of consummated love, of present and certain happiness.

A sound behind her made her turn around. Yvette had just entered, still in her daytime dress, but pale, with eyes glittering, as sometimes is the case after some great fatigue. She leaned on the sill of the open window, facing her mother.

"I want to speak to you," she said.

The Marquise looked at her in astonishment. She loved her like an egotistical mother, proud of her beauty, as a person is proud of a fortune, too pretty still herself to become jealous, too indifferent to plan the schemes with which they charged her, too clever, nevertheless, not to have full consciousness of her daughter's value.

"I am listening, my child," she said; "what is it?"

Yvette gave her a piercing look, as if to read the depths of her soul and to seize all the sensations which her words might awake.

"It is this. Something strange has just happened."

"What can it be?"

"Monsieur de Servigny has told me that he loves me."

The Marquise, disturbed, waited a moment, and, as Yvette said nothing more, she asked:

"How did he tell you that? Explain yourself!"

Then the young girl, sitting at her mother's feet, in a coaxing attitude common with her, and clasping her hands, added:

"He asked me to marry him."

Madame Obardi made a sudden gesture of stupefaction and cried:

"Servigny! Why! you are crazy!"

Yvette had not taken her eyes off her mother's face, watching her thoughts and her surprise. She asked with a serious voice:

"Why am I crazy? Why should not Monsieur de Servigny marry me?"

The Marquise, embarrassed, stammered:

"You are mistaken, it is not possible. You either did not hear or did not understand. Monsieur de Servigny is too rich for you, and too much of a Parisian to marry."

Yvette rose softly. She added: "But if he loves me as he says he does, mamma?"

Her mother replied, with some impatience: "I thought you big enough and wise enough not to have such ideas. Servigny is a man-about-town and an egotist. He will never marry anyone but a woman of his set and his fortune. If he asked you in marriage, it is only that he wants——"

The Marquise, incapable of expressing her meaning, was silent for a moment, then continued: "Come now, leave me alone and go to bed."

And the young girl, as if she had learned what she sought to find out, answered in a docile voice: "Yes, mamma!"

She kissed her mother on the forehead and withdrew with a calm step. As she reached the door, the Marquise called out: "And your sunstroke?" she said.

"I did not have one at all. It was that which caused everything."

The Marquise added: "We will not speak of it again. Only don't stay alone with him for some time from now, and be very sure that he will never marry you, do you understand, and that he merely means to—compromise you."

She could not find better words to express her thought. Yvette went to her room. Madame Obardi began to dream. Living for years in an opulent and loving repose, she had carefully put aside all reflections which might annoy or sadden her. Never had she been willing to ask herself the question—What would become of Yvette? It would be soon enough to think about the difficulties when they arrived. She well knew, from her experience, that her daughter could not marry a man who was rich and of good society, excepting by a totally improbable chance, by one of those surprises of love which place adventuresses on thrones.

She had not considered it, furthermore, being too much occupied with herself to make any plans which did not directly concern herself.

Yvette would do as her mother, undoubtedly. She would lead a gay life. Why not? But the Marquise had never dared ask when, or how. That would all come about in time.

And now her daughter, all of a sudden, without warning, had asked one of those questions which could not be answered, forcing her to take an attitude in an affair, so delicate, so dangerous in every respect, and so disturbing to the conscience which a woman is expected to show in matters concerning her daughter.

Sometimes nodding but never asleep, she had too much natural astuteness to be deceived a minute about Servigny's intentions, for she knew men by experience, and especially men of that set. So at the first words uttered by Yvette, she had cried almost in spite of herself: "Servigny, marry you? You are crazy!"

How had he come to employ that old method, he, that sharp man of the world? What would he do now? And she, the young girl, how should she warn her more clearly and even forbid her, for she might make great mistakes. Would anyone have believed that this big girl had remained so artless, so ill informed, so guileless?

And the Marquise, greatly perplexed and already wearied with her reflections, endeavored to make up her mind what to do without finding a solution of the problem, for the situation seemed to her very embarrassing. Worn out with this worry, she thought:

"I will watch them more clearly, I will act according to circumstances. If necessary, I will speak to Servigny, who is sharp and will take a hint."

She did not think out what she should say to him, nor what he would answer, nor what sort of an understanding could be established between them, but happy at being relieved of this care without having had to make a decision, she resumed her dreams of the handsome Saval, and turning toward that misty light which hovers over Paris, she threw kisses with both hands toward the great city, rapid kisses which she tossed into the darkness, one after the other, without counting; and, very low, as if she were talking to Saval still, she murmured:

"I love you, I love you!"

CHAPTER III

Enlightenment

YVETTE, ALSO, COULD NOT sleep. Like her mother, she leaned upon the sill of the open window, and tears, her first bitter tears, filled her eyes. Up to this time she had lived, had grown up, in the heedless and serene confidence of happy youth. Why should she have dreamed, reflected, puzzled? Why should she not have been a young girl, like all other young girls? Why should a doubt, a fear, or painful suspicion have come to her?

She seemed posted on all topics because she had a way of talking on all subjects, because she had taken the tone, demeanor, and words of the people who lived around her. But she really knew no more than a little girl raised in a convent; her audacities of speech came from her memory, from that unconscious faculty of imitation and assimilation which women possess, and not from a mind instructed and emboldened.

She spoke of love as the son of a painter or a musician would, at the age of ten or twelve years, speak of painting or music. She knew or rather suspected very well what sort of mystery this word concealed,—too many jokes had been whispered before her, for her innocence not to be a trifle enlightened,—but how could she have drawn the conclusion from all this, that all families did not resemble hers?

They kissed her mother's hand with the semblance of respect; all their friends had titles; they all were rich or seemed to be so; they all spoke familiarly of the princes of the royal line. Two sons of kings had even come often, in the evening, to the Marquise's house. How should she have known?

And, then, she was naturally artless. She did not estimate or sum up people as her mother did. She lived tranquilly, too joyous in her life to worry herself about what might appear suspicious to creatures more calm, thoughtful, reserved, less cordial, and sunny.

But now, all at once, Servigny, by a few words, the brutality of which she felt without understanding them, awakened in her a sudden disquietude, unreasoning at first, but which grew into a tormenting apprehension. She had fled home, had escaped like a wounded animal, wounded in fact most deeply by those words which she ceaselessly repeated to get all their sense and bearing: "You know very well that there can be no question of marriage between us—but only of love."

What did he mean? And why this insult? Was she then in ignorance of something, some secret, some shame? She was the only one ignorant of it, no doubt. But what could she do? She was frightened, startled, as a person is when he discovers some hidden infamy, some treason of a beloved friend, one of those heart-disasters which crush.

She dreamed, reflected, puzzled, wept, consumed by fears and suspicions. Then her joyous young soul reassuring itself, she began to plan an adventure, to imagine an abnormal and dramatic situation, founded on the recollections of all the poetical romances she had read. She recalled all the moving catastrophes, or sad and touching stories; she jumbled them together, and concocted a story of her own with which she interpreted the half-understood mystery which enveloped her life.

She was no longer cast down. She dreamed, she lifted veils, she imagined unlikely complications, a thousand singular, terrible things, seductive, nevertheless, by their very strangeness. Could she be, by chance, the natural daughter of a prince? Had her poor mother, betrayed and deserted, made Marquise by some king, perhaps King Victor Emmanuel, been obliged to take flight before the anger of the family? Was she not rather a child abandoned by its relations, who were noble and illustrious, the fruit of a clandestine love, taken in by the Marquise, who had adopted and brought her up?

Still other suppositions passed through her mind. She accepted or rejected them according to the dictates of her fancy. She was moved to pity over her own case, happy at the bottom of her heart, and sad also, taking a sort of satisfaction in becoming a sort of a heroine of a book who must assume a noble attitude, worthy of herself.

She laid out the part she must play, according to events at which she guessed. She vaguely outlined this rôle, like one of Scribe's or of George Sand's. It should be endued with devotion, self-abnegation, greatness of soul, tenderness, and fine words. Her pliant nature almost rejoiced in this new attitude. She pondered almost till evening what she should do, wondering how she should manage to wrest the truth from the Marquise.

And when night came, favorable to tragic situations, she had thought out a simple and subtle trick to obtain what she wanted: it was, brusquely, to say that Servigny had asked for her hand in marriage.

At this news, Madame Obardi, taken by surprise, would certainly let a word escape her lips, a cry which would throw light into the mind of her daughter. And Yvette had accomplished her plan.

She expected an explosion of astonishment, an expansion of love, a confidence full of gestures and tears. But, instead of this, her mother, without appearing stupefied or grieved, had only seemed bored; and from the constrained, discontented, and worried tone in which she had replied, the young girl, in whom there suddenly awaked all the astuteness, keenness, and sharpness of a woman, understanding that she must not insist, that the mystery was of another nature, that it would be painful to her to learn it, and that she must puzzle it out all alone, had gone back to her room, her heart oppressed, her soul in distress, possessed now with the apprehensions of a real misfortune, without knowing exactly either whence or why this emotion came to her. So she wept, leaning at the window.

She wept long, not dreaming of anything now, not seeking to discover anything more, and little by little, weariness overcoming her, she closed her eyes. She dozed for a few minutes, with that deep sleep of people who are tired out and have not the energy to undress and go to bed, that heavy sleep, broken by dreams, when the head nods upon the breast.

She did not go to bed until the first break of day, when the cold of the morning, chilling her, compelled her to leave the window.

The next day and the day after, she maintained a reserved and melancholy attitude. Her thoughts were busy; she was learning to spy out, to guess at conclusions, to reason. A light, still vague, seemed to illumine men and things around her in a new manner; she began to entertain suspicions against all, against everything that she had believed, against her mother. She imagined all sorts of things during these two days. She considered all the possibilities, taking the most extreme resolutions with the suddenness of her changeable and unrestrained nature. Wednesday she hit upon a plan, an entire schedule of conduct and a system of spying. She rose Thursday morning with the resolve to be very sharp and armed against everybody.

She determined even to take for her motto these two words: "Myself alone," and she pondered for more than an hour how she should arrange them to produce a good effect engraved about her crest, on her writing paper.

Saval and Servigny arrived at ten o'clock. The young girl gave her hand with reserve, without embarrassment, and in a tone, familiar though grave, she said:

"Good morning, Muscade, are you well?"

"Good morning, Mam'zelle, fairly, thanks, and you?" He was watching her. "What comedy will she play me," he said to himself.

The Marquise having taken Saval's arm, he took Yvette's, and they began to stroll about the lawn, appearing and disappearing every minute, behind the clumps of trees.

Yvette walked with a thoughtful air, looking at the gravel of the pathway, appearing hardly to hear what her companion said and scarcely answering him.

Suddenly she asked: "Are you truly my friend, Muscade?"

"Why, of course, Mam'zelle."

"But truly, truly, now?"

"Absolutely your friend, Mam'zelle, body and soul."

"Even enough of a friend not to lie to me once, just once?"

"Even twice, if necessary."

"Even enough to tell me the absolute, exact truth?"

"Yes, Mam'zelle."

"Well, what do you think, way down in your heart, of the Prince of Kravalow?"

"Ah, the devil!"

"You see that you are already preparing to lie."

"Not at all, but I am seeking the words, the proper words. Great Heavens, Prince Kravalow is a Russian, who speaks Russian, who was born in Russia, who has perhaps had a passport to come to France, and about whom there is nothing false but his name and title."

She looked him in the eyes: "You mean that he is—?"

"An adventurer, Mam'zelle."

"Thank you, and Chevalier Valreali is no better?"

"You have hit it."

"And Monsieur de Belvigne?"

"With him it is a different thing. He is of provincial society, honorable up to a certain point, but only a little scorched from having lived too rapidly."

"And you?"

"I am what they call a butterfly, a man of good family, who had intelligence and who has squandered it in making phrases, who had good health and who has injured it by dissipation, who had some worth perhaps and who has scattered it by doing nothing. There is left to me a certain knowledge of life, a complete absence of prejudice, a large contempt for mankind, including women, a very deep sentiment of the uselessness of my acts and a vast tolerance for the mob.

"Nevertheless, at times, I can be frank, and I am even capable of affection, as you could see, if you would. With these defects and qualities I place myself at your orders, Mam'zelle, morally and physically, to do what you please with me."

She did not laugh; she listened, weighing his words and his intentions; then she resumed:

"What do you think of the Countess de Lammy?"

He replied, vivaciously: "You will permit me not to give my opinion about the women."

"About none of them?"

"About none of them."

"Then you must have a bad opinion of them all. Come, think; won't you make a single exception?"

He sneered with that insolent air which he generally wore; and with that brutal audacity which he used as a weapon, he said: "Present company is always excepted."

She blushed a little, but calmly asked: "Well, what do you think of me?"

"You want me to tell. Well, so be it. I think you are a young person of good sense, and practicalness, or if you prefer, of good practical sense, who knows very well how to arrange her pastime, to amuse people, to hide her views, to lay her snares, and who, without hurrying, awaits events."

"Is that all?" she asked.

"That's all."

Then she said with a serious earnestness: "I shall make you change that opinion, Muscade."

Then she joined her mother, who was proceeding with short steps, her head down, with that manner assumed in talking very low, while walking, of very intimate and very sweet things. As she advanced she drew shapes in the sand, letters perhaps, with the point of her sun-shade, and she spoke, without looking at Saval, long, softly, leaning on his arm, pressed against him.

Yvette suddenly fixed her eyes upon her, and a suspicion, rather a feeling than a doubt, passed through her mind as a shadow of a cloud driven by the wind passes over the ground.

The bell rang for breakfast. It was silent and almost gloomy. There was a storm in the air. Great solid clouds rested upon the horizon, mute and heavy, but charged with a tempest. As soon as they had taken their coffee on the terrace, the Marquise asked:

"Well, darling, are you going to take a walk to-day with your friend Servigny? It is a good time to enjoy the coolness under the trees."

Yvette gave her a quick glance.

"No, mamma, I am not going out to-day."

The Marquise appeared annoyed, and insisted. "Oh, go and take a stroll, my child, it is excellent for you."

Then Yvette distinctly said: "No, mamma, I shall stay in the house to-day, and you know very well why, because I told you the other evening."

Madame Obardi gave it no further thought, preoccupied with the thought of remaining alone with Saval. She blushed and was annoyed, disturbed on her own account, not knowing how she could find a free hour or two. She stammered:

"It is true. I was not thinking of it. I don't know where my head is."

And Yvette taking up some embroidery, which she called "the public safety," and at which she worked five or six times a year, on dull days, seated herself on a low chair near her mother, while the two young men, astride folding-chairs, smoked their cigars.

The hours passed in a languid conversation. The Marquise fidgety, cast longing glances at Saval, seeking some pretext, some means, of getting rid of her daughter. She finally realized that she would not succeed, and not knowing what ruse to employ, she said to Servigny:

"You know, my dear Duke, that I am going to keep you both this evening. To-morrow we shall breakfast at the Fournaise restaurant, at Chaton."

He understood, smiled, and bowed: "I am at your orders, Marquise."

The day wore on slowly and painfully under the threatenings of the storm. The hour for dinner gradually approached. The heavy sky was filled with slow and heavy clouds. There was not a breath of air stirring. The evening meal was silent, too. An oppression, an embarrassment, a sort of vague fear, seemed to make the two men and the two women mute.

When the covers were removed, they sat long upon the terrace; only speaking at long intervals. Night fell, a sultry night. Suddenly the horizon was torn by an immense flash of lightning, which illumined with a dazzling and wan light the four faces shrouded in darkness. Then a far-off sound, heavy and feeble, like the rumbling of a carriage upon a bridge, passed over the earth; and it seemed that the heat of the atmosphere increased, that the air suddenly became more oppressive, and the silence of the evening deeper.

Yvette rose. "I am going to bed," she said, "the storm makes me ill."

And she offered her brow to the Marquise, gave her hand to the two young men, and withdrew.

As her room was just above the terrace, the leaves of a great chestnut-tree growing before the door soon gleamed with a green hue, and Servigny kept his eyes fixed on this pale light in the foliage, in which at times he thought he saw a shadow pass. But suddenly the light went out. Madame Obardi gave a great sigh.

"My daughter has gone to bed," she said.

Servigny rose, saying: "I am going to do as much, Marquise, if you will permit me." He kissed the hand she held out to him and disappeared in turn.

She was left alone with Saval, in the night. In a moment she was clasped in his arms. Then, although he tried to prevent her, she kneeled before him murmuring: "I want to see you by the lightning flashes."

But Yvette, her candle snuffed out, had returned to her balcony, barefoot, gliding like a shadow, and she listened, consumed by an unhappy and confused suspicion. She could not see, as she was above them, on the roof of the terrace.

She heard nothing but a murmur of voices, and her heart beat so fast that she could actually hear its throbbing. A window closed on the floor above her. Servigny, then, must have just gone up to his room. Her mother was alone with the other man.

A second flash of lightning, clearing the sky, lighted up for a second all the landscape she knew so well, with a startling and sinister gleam, and she saw the great river, with the color of melted lead, as a river appears in dreams in fantastic scenes.

Just then a voice below her uttered the words: "I love you!" And she heard nothing more. A strange shudder passed over her body, and her soul shivered in frightful distress. A heavy, infinite silence, which seemed eternal, hung over the world. She could no longer breathe, her breast oppressed by something unknown and horrible. Another flash of lightning illumined space, lighting up the horizon for an instant, then another almost immediately came, followed by still others. And the voice, which she had already heard, repeated more loudly: "Oh! how I love you! how I love you!" And Yvette recognized the voice; it was her mother's.

A large drop of warm rain fell upon her brow, and a slight and almost imperceptible motion ran through the leaves, the quivering of the rain which was now beginning. Then a noise came from afar, a confused sound, like that of the wind in the branches: it was the deluge descending in sheets on earth and river and trees. In a few minutes the water poured about her, covering her, drenching her like a shower-bath. She did not move, thinking only of what was happening on the terrace.

She heard them get up and go to their rooms. Doors were closed within the house; and the young girl, yielding to an irresistible desire to learn what was going on, a desire which maddened and tortured her, glided downstairs, softly opened the outer door, and, crossing the lawn under the furious downpour, ran and hid in a clump of trees, to look at the windows.

Only one window was lighted, her mother's. And suddenly two shadows appeared in the luminous square, two shadows, side by side. Then distracted, without reflection, without knowing what she was doing, she screamed with all her might, in a shrill voice: "Mamma!" as a person would cry out to warn people in danger of death.

Her desperate cry was lost in the noise of the rain, but the couple separated, disturbed. And one of the shadows disappeared, while the other tried to discover something, peering through the darkness of the garden.

Fearing to be surprised, or to meet her mother at that moment, Yvette rushed back to the house, ran upstairs, dripping wet, and shut herself in her room, resolved to open her door to no one.

Without taking off her streaming dress, which clung to her form, she fell on her knees, with clasped hands, in her distress imploring some superhuman protection, the mysterious aid of Heaven, the unknown support which a person seeks in hours of tears and despair.

The great lightning flashes threw for an instant their livid reflections into her room, and she saw herself in the mirror of her wardrobe, with her wet and disheveled hair, looking so strange that she did not recognize herself. She remained there so long that the storm abated without her perceiving it. The rain ceased, a light filled the sky, still obscured with clouds, and a mild, balmy, delicious freshness, a freshness of grass and wet leaves, came in through the open window.

Yvette rose, took off her wet, cold garments, without thinking what she was doing, and went to bed. She stared with fixed eyes at the dawning day. Then she wept again, and then she began to think.

Her mother! A lover! What a shame! She had read so many books in which women, even mothers, had overstepped the bounds of propriety, to regain their honor at the pages of the climax, that she was not astonished beyond measure at finding herself enveloped in a drama similar to all those of her reading. The violence of her first grief, the cruel shock of surprise, had already worn off a little, in the confused remembrance of analogous situations. Her mind had rambled among such tragic adventures, painted by the novel-writers, that the horrible discovery seemed, little by little, like the natural continuation of some serial story, begun the evening before.

She said to herself: "I will save my mother." And almost reassured by this heroic resolution, she felt herself strengthened, ready at once for the devotion and the struggle. She reflected on the means which must be employed. A single one seemed good, which was quite in keeping with her romantic nature. And she rehearsed the interview which she should have with the Marquise, as an actor rehearses the scene which he is going to play.

The sun had risen. The servants were stirring about the house. The chambermaid came with the chocolate. Yvette put the tray on the table and said:

"You will say to my mother that I am not well, that I am going to stay in bed until those gentlemen leave, that I could not sleep last night, and that I do not want to be disturbed because I am going to try to rest."

The servant, surprised, looked at the wet dress, which had fallen like a rag on the carpet.

"So Mademoiselle has been out?" she said.

"Yes, I went out for a walk in the rain to refresh myself."

The maid picked up the skirts, stockings, and wet shoes; then she went away carrying on her arm, with fastidious precautions, these garments, soaked as the clothes of a drowned person. And Yvette waited, well knowing that her mother would come to her.

The Marquise entered, having jumped from her bed at the first words of the chambermaid, for a suspicion had possessed her heart since that cry: "Mamma!" heard in the dark.

"What is the matter?" she said.

Yvette looked at her and stammered: "I—I—" Then overpowered by a sudden and terrible emotion, she began to choke.

The Marquise, astonished, again asked: "What in the world is the matter with you?"

Then, forgetting all her plans and prepared phrases, the young girl hid her face in both hands and stammered:

"Oh! mamma! Oh! mamma!"

Madame Obardi stood by the bed, too much affected thoroughly to understand, but guessing almost everything, with that subtle instinct whence she derived her strength. As Yvette could not speak, choked with tears, her mother, worn out finally and feeling some fearful explanation coming, brusquely asked:

"Come, will you tell me what the matter is?"

Yvette could hardly utter the words: "Oh! last night—I saw— your window."

The Marquise, very pale, said: "Well? what of it?"

Her daughter repeated, still sobbing: "Oh! mamma! Oh! mamma!"

Madame Obardi, whose fear and embarrassment turned to anger, shrugged her shoulders and turned to go.

"I really believe that you are crazy. When this ends, you will let me know."

But the young girl suddenly took her hands from her face, which was streaming with tears.

"No, listen, I must speak to you, listen. You must promise me— we must both go away, very far off, into the country, and we must live like the country people; and no one must know what has become of us. Say you will, mamma; I beg you, I implore you; will you?"

The Marquise, confused, stood in the middle of the room. She had in her veins the irascible blood of the common people. Then a sense of shame, a mother's modesty, mingled with a vague sentiment of fear and the exasperation of a passionate woman whose love is threatened, and she shuddered, ready to ask for pardon, or to yield to some violence.

"I don't understand you," she said.

Yvette replied:

"I saw you, mamma, last night. You cannot—if you knew—we will both go away. I will love you so much that you will forget—"

Madame Obardi said in a trembling voice: "Listen, my daughter, there are some things which you do not yet understand. Well, don't forget—don't forget—that I forbid you ever to speak to me about those things."

But the young girl, brusquely taking the rôle of savior which she had imposed upon herself, rejoined:

"No, mamma, I am no longer a child, and I have the right to know.

I know that we receive persons of bad repute, adventurers, and I know that, on that account, people do not respect us. I know more. Well, it must not be, any longer, do you hear? I do not wish it. We will go away: you will sell your jewels; we will work, if need be, and we will live as honest women, somewhere very far away. And if I can marry, so much the better."

She answered: "You are crazy. You will do me the favor to rise and come down to breakfast with all the rest."

"No, mamma. There is some one whom I shall never see again, you understand me. I want him to leave, or I shall leave. You shall choose between him and me."

She was sitting up in bed, and she raised her voice, speaking as they do on the stage, playing, finally, the drama which she had dreamed, almost forgetting her grief in the effort to fulfill her mission.

The Marquise, stupefied, again repeated: "You are crazy——" not finding anything else to say.

Yvette replied with a theatrical energy: "No, mamma, that man shall leave the house, or I shall go myself, for I will not weaken."

"And where will you go? What will you do?"

"I do not know, it matters little—I want you to be an honest woman."

These words which recurred, aroused in the Marquise a perfect fury, and she cried:

"Be silent. I do not permit you to talk to me like that. I am as good as anybody else, do you understand? I lead a certain sort of life, it is true, and I am proud of it; the 'honest women' are not as good as I am."

Yvette, astonished, looked at her, and stammered: "Oh! mamma!"

But the Marquise, carried away with excitement, continued:

"Yes, I lead a certain life—what of it? Otherwise you would be a cook, as I was once, and earn thirty sous a day. You would be washing dishes, and your mistress would send you to market—do you understand—and she would turn you out if you loitered, just as you loiter now because I am—because I lead this life. Listen. When a person is only a nursemaid, a poor girl, with fifty francs saved up, she must know how to manage, if she does not want to starve to death;

and there are not two ways for us, there are not two ways, do you understand, when we are servants. We cannot make our fortune with
official positions, nor with stockjobbing tricks. We have only one
way—only one way."

She struck her breast as a penitent at the confessional, and flushed
and excited, coming toward the bed, she continued: "So much the
worse. A pretty girl must live or suffer—she has no choice!" Then returning to her former idea: "Much they deny themselves, your 'honest women.' They are worse, because nothing compels them. They
have money to live on and amuse themselves, and they choose vicious
lives of their own accord. They are the bad ones in reality."

She was standing near the bed of the distracted Yvette, who
wanted to cry out "Help," to escape. Yvette wept aloud, like children
who are whipped. The Marquise was silent and looked at her daughter, and, seeing her overwhelmed with despair, felt, herself, the pangs
of grief, remorse, tenderness, and pity, and throwing herself upon
the bed with open arms, she also began to sob and stammered:

"My poor little girl, my poor little girl, if you knew how you were
hurting me." And they wept together, a long while.

Then the Marquise, in whom grief could not long endure, softly
rose, and gently said:

"Come, darling, it is unavoidable; what would you have? Nothing
can be changed now. We must take life as it comes to us."

Yvette continued to weep. The blow had been too harsh and too
unexpected to permit her to reflect and to recover at once.

Her mother resumed: "Now, get up and come down to breakfast,
so that no one will notice anything."

The young girl shook her head as if to say, "No," without being
able to speak. Then she said, with a slow voice full of sobs:

"No, mamma, you know what I said, I won't alter my determination. I shall not leave my room till they have gone. I never want to see
one of those people again, never, never. If they come back, you will
see no more of me."

The Marquise had dried her eyes, and wearied with emotion, she
murmured:

"Come, reflect, be reasonable."

Then, after a moment's silence:

"Yes, you had better rest this morning. I will come up to see you this afternoon." And having kissed her daughter on the forehead, she went to dress herself, already calmed.

Yvette, as soon as her mother had disappeared, rose, and ran to bolt the door, to be alone, all alone; then she began to think. The chambermaid knocked about eleven o'clock, and asked through the door:

"Madame the Marquise wants to know if Mademoiselle wishes anything, and what she will take for her breakfast."

Yvette answered: "I am not hungry, I only ask not to be disturbed."

And she remained in bed, just as if she had been ill. Toward three o'clock, some one knocked again. She asked:

"Who is there?"

It was her mother's voice which replied: "It is I, darling, I have come to see how you are."

She hesitated what she should do. She opened the door, and then went back to bed. The Marquise approached, and, speaking in low tones, as people do to a convalescent, said:

"Well, are you better? Won't you eat an egg?"

"No, thanks, nothing at all."

Madame Obardi sat down near the bed. They remained without saying anything, then, finally, as her daughter stayed quiet, with her hands inert upon the bedclothes, she asked:

"Don't you intend to get up?"

Yvette answered: "Yes, pretty soon."

Then in a grave and slow tone she said: "I have thought a great deal, mamma, and this—this is my resolution. The past is the past, let us speak no more of it. But the future shall be different or I know what is left for me to do. Now, let us say no more about it."

The Marquise, who thought the explanation finished, felt her impatience gaining a little. It was too much. This big goose of a girl ought to have known about things long ago. But she did not say anything in reply, only repeating:

"You are going to get up?"

"Yes, I am ready."

Then her mother became maid for her, bringing her stockings, her corset, and her skirts. Then she kissed her.

"Will you take a walk before dinner?"

"Yes, mamma."

And they took a stroll along the water, speaking only of commonplace things.

THE WRECK

It was yesterday, the 31st of December.

I had just finished breakfast with my old friend Georges Garin when the servant brought him in a letter covered with seals and foreign stamps.

Georges said:

"Will you excuse me?"

"Certainly."

And so he began to read eight pages in a large English handwriting, crossed in every direction. He read them slowly, with serious attention and the interest which we only pay to things which touch our hearts.

Then he put the letter on a corner of the mantle-piece, and he said:

"That was a curious story! I've never told you about it, I think. And yet it was a sentimental adventure, and it happened to me. Aha! That was a strange New-year's Day indeed! It must be twenty years ago, since I was then thirty, and am now fifty years old.

"I was then an inspector in the Maritime Insurance Company, of which I am now director. I had arranged to pass the fête of New-year's in Paris—since it is a convention to make that day a fête—when I received a letter from the manager, directing me to proceed at once to the island of Ré, where a three-masted vessel from Saint-Nazaire, insured by us, had just gone ashore. It was then eight o'clock in the morning. I arrived at the office at ten, to get my instructions; and the same evening I took the express, which put me down in La Rochelle the next day, December 31st.

"I had two hours to spare before going aboard the boat for Ré. So

I made a tour in the town. It is certainly a fantastic city, La Rochelle, with a strong character of its own—streets tangled like a labyrinth, sidewalks running under endless arcaded galleries like those of the Rue de Rivoli, but low, mysterious, built as if to form a fit scene for conspirators, and making an ancient and striking background for those old-time wars, the savage heroic wars of religion. It is indeed the typical old Huguenot city, grave, discreet, with no fine art to show, with no wonderful monuments, such as make Rouen so grand; but it is remarkable for its severe, somewhat cunning look; it is a city of obstinate fighters, a city where fanaticisms might well blossom, where the faith of the Calvinists became exalted, and where the plot of the 'Four Sergeants' was born.

"After I had wandered for some time about these curious streets, I went aboard the black, fat-bellied little steamboat which was to take me to the island of Ré. It was called the *Jean Guiton*. It started with angry puffings, passed between the two old towers which guard the harbor, crossed the roadstead, and issued from the mole built by Richelieu, the great stones of which are visible at the water's edge, enclosing the town like an immense necklace. Then the steamboat turned off to the right.

"It was one of those sad days which oppress and crush the thoughts, tighten the heart, and extinguish in us all energy and force—a gray, icy day, salted by a heavy mist which was as wet as rain, as cold as frost, as bad to breathe as the lye of a washtub.

"Under this low ceiling of sinister fog, the shallow, yellow, sandy sea of all gradually receding coasts lay without a wrinkle, without a movement, without life, a sea of turbid water, of greasy water, of stagnant water. The *Jean Guiton* passed over it, rolling a little from habit, dividing the smooth, opaque sheet, and leaving behind a few waves, a little chopping sea, a few undulations, which were soon calm.

"I began to talk to the captain, a little man almost without feet, as round as his boat and balancing himself like it. I wanted some details about the disaster on which I was to deliver a report. A great square-rigged three-master, the *Marie Joseph*, of Saint-Nazaire, had gone ashore one night in a hurricane on the sands of the island of Ré.

"The owner wrote us that the storm had thrown the ship so far ashore that it was impossible to float her, and that they had had to remove everything which could be detached, with the utmost possible haste. Nevertheless, I was to examine the situation of the wreck, estimate what must have been her condition before the disaster, and decide whether all efforts had been used to get her afloat. I came as an agent of the company in order to bear contradictory testimony, if necessary, at the trial.

"On receipt of my report, the manager would take what measures he judged necessary to protect our interests.

"The captain of the *Jean Guiton* knew all about the affair, having been summoned with his boat to assist in the attempts at salvage.

"He told me the story of the disaster, and very simply too. The *Marie Joseph*, driven by a furious gale, lost her bearings completely in the night, and steering by chance over a heavy foaming sea—'a milk-soup sea,' said the captain—had gone ashore on those immense banks of sand which make the coasts of this region seem like limitless Saharas at hours when the tide is low.

"While talking I looked around and ahead. Between the ocean and the lowering sky lay a free space where the eye could see far. We were following a coast. I asked:

"'Is that the island of Ré?'

"'Yes, sir.'

"And suddenly the captain stretched his right hand out before us, pointed to something almost invisible in the middle of the sea, and said:

"'There's your ship!'

"'The *Marie Joseph?*'

"'Yes.'

"I was stupefied. This black, almost imperceptible speck, which I should have taken for a rock, seemed at least three miles from land.

"I continued:

"'But, captain, there must be a hundred fathoms of water in that place?'

"He began to laugh.

" 'A hundred fathoms, my boy! Well, I should say about two!'

"He was from Bordeaux. He continued:

" 'It's now 9.40, just high tide. Go down along the beach with your hands in your pockets after you've had your lunch at the Hôtel du Dauphin, and I'll engage that at ten minutes to three, or three o'clock, you'll reach the wreck without wetting your feet, and have from an hour and three-quarters to two hours aboard of her; but not more, or you'll be caught. The farther the sea goes out the faster it comes back. This coast is as flat as a bed-bug! But start away at ten minutes to five, as I tell you, and at half-past seven you will be aboard of the *Jean Guiton* again, which will put you down this same evening on the quay at La Rochelle.'

"I thanked the captain, and I went and sat down in the bow of the steamer to get a good look at the little city of Saint-Martin, which we were now rapidly approaching.

"It was just like all the miniature seaports which serve as the capitals of the barren islands scattered along the coast—a large fishing village, one foot on sea and one on shore, living on fish and wild-fowl, vegetables and shell-fish, radishes and mussels. The island is very low, and little cultivated, yet seems to be filled with people. However, I did not penetrate into the interior.

"After having breakfasted, I climbed across a little promontory, and then, as the tide was rapidly falling, I started out across the sands towards a kind of black rock which I could just perceive above the surface of the water, far out, far down.

"I walked quickly over the yellow plain; it was elastic, like flesh, and seemed to sweat beneath my foot. The sea had been there very lately; now I perceived it at a distance, escaping out of sight, and I no longer distinguished the line which separated the sands from ocean. I felt as though I were assisting at a gigantic supernatural work of en-chantment. The Atlantic had just now been before me, then it had disappeared into the strand, just as does scenery through a trap; and I now walked in the midst of a desert. Only the feeling, the breath of the salt-water, remained in me. I perceived the smell of the wrack, the smell of the wide sea, the rough good smell of sea-coasts. I walked fast; I was no longer cold; I looked at the stranded wreck, which grew in size as I approached, and came now to resemble an enormous shipwrecked whale.

"It seemed fairly to rise out of the ground, and on that great, flat, yellow stretch of sand assumed surprising proportions. After an hour's walk I reached it at last. Bulging out and crushed, it lay upon its side, which, like the flanks of an animal, displayed its broken bones, its bones of tarry wood pierced with enormous bolts. The sand had already invaded it, entered it by all the crannies, and held it, possessed it, refused to let it go. It seemed to have taken root in it. The bow had entered deep into this soft, treacherous beach; while the stern, high in air, seemed to cast at heaven, like a cry of despairing appeal, the two white words on the black planking, *Marie Joseph*.

"I scaled this carcass of a ship by the lowest side; then, having reached the deck, I went below. The daylight, which entered by the stove-in hatches and the cracks in the sides, showed sadly enough a species of long sombre cellar full of demolished woodwork. There was nothing here but the sand, which served as foot-soil in this cavern of planks.

"I began to take some notes about the condition of the ship. I was seated on a broken empty cask, writing by the light of a great crack, through which I could perceive the boundless stretch of the strand. A strange shivering of cold and loneliness ran over my skin from time to time; and I would often stop writing for a moment to listen to the vague mysterious noises in the wreck: the noise of the crabs scratching the planking with their hooked claws; the noise of a thousand little creatures of the sea already installed on this dead body; the noise, so gentle and regular, of the worms, who, with their gimlet-like, grinding sound, gnaw ceaselessly at the old timber, which they hollow out and devour.

"And, suddenly, very near me, I heard human voices; I started as though I had seen a ghost. For a second I really thought I was about to see two drowned men rise from the sinister depths of the hold, who would tell me about their death. At any rate, it did not take me long to swing myself on deck with all the strength I had in my wrists.

There, below the bow, I found standing a tall gentleman with three young girls, or rather a tall Englishman with three young misses. Certainly, they were a good deal more frightened at seeing this sudden apparition on the abandoned three-master than I had been at seeing them. The youngest girl turned round and ran; the two others caught their father by the arms; as for him, he opened his mouth—that was the sole sign of his emotion which he showed.

"Then, after several seconds, he spoke:

"'Aw, *môsieu*, are you the owner of this ship?'

"'I am.'

"'May I go over it?'

"'You may.'

"Then he uttered a long sentence in English, in which I only distinguished the word 'gracious,' repeated several times.

"As he was looking for a place to climb up, I showed him the best, and lent him a hand. He ascended. Then we helped up the three little girls, who were now quite reassured. They were charming, especially the oldest, a blonde of eighteen, fresh as a flower, and so dainty, so pretty! Ah yes! the pretty Englishwomen have indeed the look of tender fruits of the sea. One would have said of this one that she had just risen from the sands and that her hair had kept their tint. They all, with their exquisite freshness, make you think of the delicate colors of pink sea-shells, and of shining pearls rare and mysterious, hidden in the unknown deeps of ocean.

"She spoke French a little better than her father, and she acted as interpreter. I must tell all about the shipwreck, to the very least details, and I romanced as though I had been present at the catastrophe. Then the whole family descended into the interior of the wreck. As soon as they had penetrated into this sombre, dim-lit gallery, they uttered cries of astonishment and admiration. And suddenly the father and his three daughters were holding sketch-books in their hands, which they had doubtless carried hidden somewhere in their heavy weather-proof clothes, and were all beginning at once to make pencil sketches of this melancholy and fantastic place.

"They had seated themselves side by side on a projecting beam, and the four sketch-books on the eight knees were being rapidly covered with little black lines which were intended to represent the half-opened stomach of the *Marie Joseph*.

"I continued to inspect the skeleton of the ship, and the oldest girl talked to me while she worked.

"I learned that they were spending the winter at Biarritz, and that they had come to the island of Ré expressly to see the stranded three-master. They had none of the usual English arrogance; they were simple honest hearts of that class of constant wanderers with which England covers the globe. The father was long and thin, with a red face framed in white whiskers, and looking like a living sandwich, a slice of ham cut in the shape of a head, placed between two wedges of hair. The daughters, like little wading-birds in embryo, had long legs and were also thin—except the oldest. All three were pretty, especially the tallest.

"She had such a droll way of speaking, of talking, of laughing, of understanding and of not understanding, of raising her eyes to ask a question (eyes blue as deep water), of stopping her drawing a moment to make a guess at what you meant, of returning once more to work, of saying 'yes' or 'no'—that I could have listened and looked indefinitely.

"Suddenly she murmured:

" 'I hear a little movement on this boat.'

"I lent an ear; and I immediately distinguished a low, steady, curious sound. What was it? I rose and looked out of the crack, and I uttered a violent cry. The sea had come back; it was about to surround us!

"We were on deck in an instant. It was too late. The water circled us about, and was running towards the coast with prodigious swiftness. No, it did not run, it slipped, it crawled, it grew longer, like a kind of great limitless blot. The water on the sands was barely a few centimetres deep; but the rising flood had gone so far that we no longer saw the flying line of its edge.

"The Englishman wanted to jump. I held him back. Flight was impossible because of the deep places which we had been obliged to go round on our way out, and into which we should certainly fall on our return.

"There was a minute of horrible anguish in our hearts. Then the little English girl began to smile, and murmured:

" 'So we too are shipwrecked.'

"I tried to laugh; but fear caught me tight, a fear which was cowardly and horrid and base and mean, like the tide. All the dangers which we ran appeared to me at once. I wanted to shriek 'Help!' But to whom?

"The two younger girls were cowering against their father, who regarded, with a look of consternation, the measureless sea which hedged us round about.

"And the night fell as swiftly as the ocean rose—a lowering, wet, icy night.

"I said:

" 'There's nothing to do but to stay on the ship.'

"The Englishman answered:

" 'Oh yes!'

"And we waited there a quarter of an hour, half an hour, indeed I don't know how long, watching that yellow water which grew deep about us, whirled round and round, and seemed to bubble, and seemed to sport over the reconquest of the vast sea-strand.

"One of the little girls was cold, and we suddenly thought of going below to shelter ourselves from the light but freezing wind which blew upon us and pricked our skins.

"I leaned over the hatchway. The ship was full of water. So we must cower against the stern planking, which shielded us a little.

"The shades were now inwrapping us, and we remained pressed close to one another, surrounded by the darkness and by the sea. I felt trembling against my shoulder the shoulder of the little English girl, whose teeth chattered from time to time. But I also felt the gentle warmth of her body through her ulster, and that warmth was as delicious to me as a kiss. We no longer spoke; we sat motionless, mute, cowering down like animals in a ditch when a hurricane is raging. And, nevertheless, despite the night, despite the terrible and increasing danger, I began to feel happy that I was there, to be glad of the cold and the peril, to rejoice in the long hours of darkness and anguish which I must pass on this plank so near this dainty and pretty little girl.

"I asked myself, 'Why this strange sensation of well-being and of joy?'

"Why! Does one know? Because she was there? Who? She, a little unknown English girl? I did not love her, I did not even know her. And for all that I was touched and conquered. I should have liked to save her, to sacrifice myself for her, to commit a thousand follies! Strange thing! How does it happen that the presence of a woman overwhelms us so? Is it the power of her grace, which infolds us? Is it the seduction in her beauty and youth, which intoxicates us like wine?

"Is it not rather, as it were, the touch of Love, of Love the Mysterious, who seeks constantly to unite two beings, who tries his strength the instant he has put a man and a woman face to face, and who suffuses them with a confused, secret, profound emotion just as you water the earth to make the flowers spring?

"But the silence of the shades and of the sky became dreadful, because we could thus hear vaguely about us an infinite low roar, the dull rumor of the rising sea, and the monotonous dashing of the current against the ship.

"Suddenly I heard the sound of sobs. The youngest of the little girls was crying. Then her father tried to console her, and they began to talk in their own tongue, which I did not understand. I guessed that he was reassuring her, and that she was still afraid.

"I asked my neighbor:

"'You are not too cold, are you, miss?'

"'Oh yes. I am very cold.'

"I wanted to give her my cloak; she refused it. But I had taken it off, and I covered her with it against her will. In the short struggle her hand touched mine. It made a charming shiver run over my body.

"For some minutes the air had been growing brisker, the dashing of the water stronger against the flanks of the ship. I raised myself; a great gust blew in my face. The wind was rising!

"The Englishman perceived this at the same time that I did, and said, simply:

" 'That is bad for us, this——'

"Of course it was bad, it was certain death if any breakers, however feeble, should attack and shake the wreck, which was already so loose and broken that the first big sea would carry it off in a jelly.

"So our anguish increased from second to second as the squalls grew stronger and stronger. Now the sea broke a little, and I saw in the darkness white lines appearing and disappearing, which were lines of foam; while each wave struck the *Marie Joseph,* and shook her with a short quiver which rose to our hearts.

"The English girl was trembling; I felt her shiver against me. And I had a wild desire to take her in my arms.

"Down there before and behind us, to left and right, light-houses were shining along the shore—light-houses white and yellow and red, revolving like the enormous eyes of giants who were staring at us, watching us, waiting eagerly for us to disappear. One of them in especial irritated me. It went out every thirty seconds and it lit up again as soon. It was indeed an eye, that one, with its lid ceaselessly lowered over its fiery look.

"From time to time the Englishman struck a match to see the hour; then he put his watch back in his pocket. Suddenly he said to me, over the heads of his daughters, with a gravity which was supreme:

" 'I wish you a Happy New Year, *môsieu.*'

"It was midnight. I held out my hand, which he pressed. Then he said something in English, and suddenly he and his daughters began to sing 'God save the Queen,' which rose through the black and silent air and vanished into space.

"At first I felt a desire to laugh; then I was seized by a strong, fantastic emotion.

"It was something sinister and superb, this chant of the shipwrecked, the condemned, something like a prayer, and also like something grander, something comparable to the ancient sublime *'Ave Cæsar morituri te salutamus.'*

"When they had finished I asked my neighbor to sing a ballad alone, a legend, anything she liked, to make us forget our terrors. She consented, and immediately her clear young voice flew off into the night. She sang something which was doubtless sad, because the notes were long drawn out, issued slowly from her mouth, and hovered, like wounded birds, above the waves.

"The sea was rising now and beating upon our wreck. As for me, I thought only of that voice. And I thought also of the sirens. If a ship had passed near by us what would the sailors have said? My troubled spirit lost itself in the dream! A siren! Was she not really a siren, this daughter of the sea, who had kept me on this worm-eaten ship, and who was soon about to go down with me deep into the waters?

"But suddenly we were all five rolling on the deck, because the *Marie Joseph* had sunk on her right side. The English girl had fallen across me, and before I knew what I was doing, thinking that my last moment was come, I had caught her in my arms and kissed her cheek, her temple, and her hair.

"The ship did not move again, and we, we also, remained motionless.

"The father said, 'Kate!' The one whom I was holding answered, 'Yes,' and made a movement to free herself. And at that moment I should have wished the ship to split in two and let me fall with her into the sea.

"The Englishman continued:

" 'A little rocking; it's nothing. I have my three daughters safe.'

"Not having seen the oldest, he had thought she was lost overboard!

"I rose slowly, and suddenly I made out a light on the sea quite near us. I shouted; they answered. It was a boat sent out in search of us by the hotel-keeper, who had guessed at our imprudence.

"We were saved. I was in despair. They picked us up off our raft, and they brought us back to Saint-Martin.

"The Englishman was now rubbing his hands and murmuring:

" 'A good supper! A good supper!'

"We did sup. I was not gay. I regretted the *Marie Joseph*.

"We had to separate, the next day, after much handshaking and many promises to write. They departed for Biarritz. I was not far from following them.

"I was hard hit; I wanted to ask this little girl in marriage. If we had passed eight days together, I should have done so! How weak and incomprehensible a man sometimes is!

"Two years passed without my hearing a word from them. Then I received a letter from New York. She was married, and wrote to tell me. And since then we write to each other every year, on New-year's Day. She tells me about her life, talks of her children, her sisters, never of her husband! Why? Ah! why? . . . And as for me, I only talk of the *Marie Joseph*. That was perhaps the only woman I have ever loved. No—that I ever should have loved. . . . Ah, well! who can tell? Facts master you. . . . And then—and then—all passes. . . . She must be old now; I should not know her. . . . Ah! she of the by-gone time, she of the wreck! What a creature! . . . Divine! She writes me her hair is white. . . . That caused me terrible pain. . . . Ah! her yellow hair. . . . No, *my* English girl exists no longer. . . . They are sad, such things as that!"

LOVE

Three Pages from a Sportsman's Book

I HAVE JUST READ among the general news in one of the papers a drama of passion. He killed her and then he killed himself, so he must have loved her. What matters He or She? Their love alone matters to me; and it does not interest me because it moves me or astonishes me, or because it softens me or makes me think, but because it recalls to my mind a remembrance of my youth, a strange recollection of a hunting adventure where Love appeared to me, as the Cross appeared to the early Christians, in the midst of the heavens.

I was born with all the instincts and the senses of primitive man, tempered by the arguments and the restraints of a civilized being. I am passionately fond of shooting, yet the sight of the wounded animal, of the blood on its feathers and on my hands, affects my heart so as almost to make it stop.

That year the cold weather set in suddenly toward the end of autumn, and I was invited by one of my cousins, Karl de Rauville, to go with him and shoot ducks on the marshes, at daybreak.

My cousin was a jolly fellow of forty, with red hair, very stout and bearded, a country gentleman, an amiable semi-brute, of a happy disposition and endowed with that Gallic wit which makes even mediocrity agreeable. He lived in a house, half farmhouse, half château, situated in a broad valley through which a river ran. The hills right and left were covered with woods, old manorial woods where magnificent trees still remained, and where the rarest feathered game in that part of France was to be found. Eagles were shot there occasionally, and birds of passage, such as rarely venture into our over-populated part of the country, invariably lighted amid these giant oaks, as if they knew or recognized some little corner of a primeval forest which had remained there to serve them as a shelter during their short nocturnal halt.

In the valley there were large meadows watered by trenches and separated by hedges; then, further on, the river, which up to that point had been kept between banks, expanded into a vast marsh. That marsh was the best shooting ground I ever saw. It was my cousin's chief care, and he kept it as a preserve. Through the rushes that covered it, and made it rustling and rough, narrow passages had been cut, through which the flat-bottomed boats, impelled and steered by poles, passed along silently over dead water, brushing up against the reeds and making the swift fish take refuge in the weeds, and the wild fowl, with their pointed, black heads, dive suddenly.

I am passionately fond of the water: of the sea, though it is too vast, too full of movement, impossible to hold; of the rivers which are so beautiful, but which pass on, and flee away; and above all of the marshes, where the whole unknown existence of aquatic animals palpitates. The marsh is an entire world in itself on the world of earth—a different world, which has its own life, its settled inhabitants and its passing travelers, its voices, its noises, and above all its mystery. Nothing is more impressive, nothing more disquieting, more terrifying occasionally, than a fen. Why should a vague terror hang over these low plains covered with water? Is it the low rustling of the rushes, the strange will-o'-the-wisp lights, the silence which prevails on calm nights, the still mists which hang over the surface like a shroud; or is it the almost inaudible splashing, so slight and so gentle, yet sometimes more terrifying than the cannons of men or the thunders of the skies, which make these marshes resemble countries one has dreamed of, terrible countries holding an unknown and dangerous secret?

No, something else belongs to it—another mystery, profounder and graver, floats amid these thick mists, perhaps the mystery of the creation itself! For was it not in stagnant and muddy water, amid the heavy humidity of moist land under the heat of the sun, that the first germ of life pulsated and expanded to the day?

I arrived at my cousin's in the evening. It was freezing hard enough to split the stones.

During dinner, in the large room whose sideboards, walls, and ceiling were covered with stuffed birds, with wings extended or perched on branches to which they were nailed,—hawks, herons, owls, nightjars, buzzards, tiercels, vultures, falcons,—my cousin who, dressed in a sealskin jacket, himself resembled some strange animal from a cold country, told me what preparations he had made for that same night.

We were to start at half past three in the morning, so as to arrive at the place which he had chosen for our watching-place at about half past four. On that spot a hut had been built of lumps of ice, so as to shelter us somewhat from the trying wind which precedes daybreak, a wind so cold as to tear the flesh like a saw, cut it like the blade of a knife, prick it like a poisoned sting, twist it like a pair of pincers, and burn it like fire.

My cousin rubbed his hands: "I have never known such a frost," he said; "it is already twelve degrees below zero at six o'clock in the evening."

I threw myself on to my bed immediately after we had finished our meal, and went to sleep by the light of a bright fire burning in the grate.

At three o'clock he woke me. In my turn, I put on a sheepskin, and found my cousin Karl covered with a bearskin. After having each swallowed two cups of scalding coffee, followed by glasses of liqueur brandy, we started, accompanied by a gamekeeper and our dogs, Plongeon and Pierrot.

From the first moment that I got outside, I felt chilled to the very marrow. It was one of those nights on which the earth seems dead with cold. The frozen air becomes resisting and palpable, such pain does it cause; no breath of wind moves it, it is fixed and motionless; it bites you, pierces through you, dries you, kills the trees, the plants, the insects, the small birds themselves, who fall from the branches on to the hard ground, and become stiff themselves under the grip of the cold.

The moon, which was in her last quarter and was inclining all to one side, seemed fainting in the midst of space, so weak that she was unable to wane, forced to stay up yonder, seized and paralyzed by the severity of the weather. She shed a cold, mournful light over the world, that dying and wan light which she gives us every month, at the end of her period.

Karl and I walked side by side, our backs bent, our hands in our pockets and our guns under our arms. Our boots, which were wrapped in wool so that we might be able to walk without slipping on the frozen river, made no sound, and I looked at the white vapor which our dogs' breath made.

We were soon on the edge of the marsh, and entered one of the lanes of dry rushes which ran through the low forest.

Our elbows, which touched the long, ribbonlike leaves, left a slight noise behind us, and I was seized, as I had never been before, by the powerful and singular emotion which marshes cause in me. This one was dead, dead from cold, since we were walking on it, in the middle of its population of dried rushes.

Suddenly, at the turn of one of the lanes, I perceived the ice-hut which had been constructed to shelter us. I went in, and as we had nearly an hour to wait before the wandering birds would awake, I rolled myself up in my rug in order to try and get warm. Then, lying on my back, I began to look at the misshapen moon, which had four horns through the vaguely transparent walls of this polar house. But the frost of the frozen marshes, the cold of these walls, the cold from the firmament penetrated me so terribly that I began to cough. My cousin Karl became uneasy.

"No matter if we do not kill much to-day," he said: "I do not want you to catch cold; we will light a fire." And he told the gamekeeper to cut some rushes.

We made a pile in the middle of our hut which had a hole in the middle of the roof to let out the smoke, and when the red flames rose up to the clear, crystal blocks they began to melt, gently, imperceptibly, as if they were sweating. Karl, who had remained outside, called out to me: "Come and look here!" I went out of the hut and remained struck with astonishment. Our hut, in the shape of a cone, looked like an enormous diamond with a heart of fire, which had been suddenly planted there in the midst of the frozen water of the marsh. And inside, we saw two fantastic forms, those of our dogs, who were warming themselves at the fire.

But a peculiar cry, a lost, a wandering cry, passed over our heads, and the light from our hearth showed us the wild birds. Nothing moves one so much as the first clamor of a life which one does not see, which passes through the somber air so quickly and so far off, just before the first streak of a winter's day appears on the horizon. It seems to me, at this glacial hour of dawn, as if that passing cry which is carried away by the wings of a bird is the sigh of a soul from the world!

"Put out the fire," said Karl, "it is getting daylight."

The sky was, in fact, beginning to grow pale, and the flights of ducks made long, rapid streaks which were soon obliterated on the sky.

A stream of light burst out into the night; Karl had fired, and the two dogs ran forward.

And then, nearly every minute, now he, now I, aimed rapidly as soon as the shadow of a flying flock appeared above the rushes. And Pierrot and Plongeon, out of breath but happy, retrieved the bleeding birds, whose eyes still, occasionally, looked at us.

The sun had risen, and it was a bright day with a blue sky, and we were thinking of taking our departure, when two birds with extended necks and outstretched wings, glided rapidly over our heads. I fired, and one of them fell almost at my feet. It was a teal, with a silver breast, and then, in the blue space above me, I heard a voice, the voice of a bird. It was a short, repeated, heart-rending lament; and the bird, the little animal that had been spared, began to turn round in the blue sky, over our heads, looking at its dead companion which I was holding in my hand.

Karl was on his knees, his gun to his shoulder watching it eagerly, until it should be within shot. "You have killed the duck," he said, "and the drake will not fly away."

He certainly did not fly away; he circled over our heads continually, and continued his cries. Never have any groans of suffering pained me so much as that desolate appeal, as that lamentable reproach of this poor bird which was lost in space.

Occasionally he took flight under the menace of the gun which followed his movements, and seemed ready to continue his flight alone, but as he could not make up his mind to this, he returned to find his mate.

"Leave her on the ground," Karl said to me, "he will come within shot by and by." And he did indeed come near us, careless of danger, infatuated by his animal love, by his affection for his mate, which I had just killed.

Karl fired, and it was as if somebody had cut the string which held the bird suspended. I saw something black descend, and I heard the noise of a fall among the rushes. And Pierrot brought it to me.

I put them—they were already cold—into the same game-bag, and I returned to Paris the same evening.

THE HORLA

May 8th.

WHAT A MAGNIFICENT DAY! I spent the whole morning stretched on the grass, before my house, under the great plane-tree which entirely covers, shelters, and shades it. I love this country, and I love to live here, because here I have my roots, those deep, fine roots which attach a man to the soil where his forefathers were born and buried, which attach him to what is thought there and to what is eaten, to its customs as to its dishes, to its localisms of speech, to the peculiar intonation of its peasants, to the smell of its earth, of its villages, of its very air.

I love the house where I have grown up. From my windows I see the Seine, flowing by my garden; on the other side of the road, almost on my own property:——the great, wide Seine that goes to Havre from Rouen, covered with the passing boats.

To the left, down there, Rouen——the great city of blue roofs swarming far and wide below a crowd of pointed Gothic bell-towers. These, ponderous or slender, are innumerable, overtowered by the cathedral's cast-iron spire, and filled with bells which ring in the blue air on fine mornings. Their sweet and distant iron humming, their brazen chant, reaches out to me, brought by the breeze, and now louder, now lower, as the breeze now wakes, now drowses.

How fine it was this morning!

About eleven o'clock, I remember, a long tow of ships defiled past my garden railings. They were pulled by a tug the size of a fly; it groaned and vomited forth a thick, black smoke.

Just behind two English schooners, whose red flag waved against the sky, came a superb Brazilian three-master, quite white, admirably clean and shining. This ship gave me so much pleasure that I saluted her, I don't know why.

May 12th.

For some days I have had a little fever; I feel unwell, or rather, properly speaking, I feel depressed.

Whence come these mysterious influences which change our happiness into discouragement and our confidence into distress? One would almost say that the air, the invisible air, was full of unknowable Powers, to whose mysterious proximity we submit. I awake full of gayety, with desires to sing in my throat. Why? I go down to the waterside, and suddenly, after a short walk, return distressed, as though some misfortune awaited me at home. Why? Is it a shiver of cold which, brushing across my skin, has unsettled my nerves and darkened my soul? Is it the shapes of the clouds, or the colors of the day, or the changeable colors of things which have passed in through my eyes, and have troubled my thoughts? Do we know? Everything about us, everything which we see without observing, everything which we brush against without recognizing, everything which we touch without feeling, everything which we encounter without clearly distinguishing, may have upon us, upon our senses, and, through them, upon our minds and upon our hearts, instant effects which are wonderful and not to be explained.

Ah! but it is deep, this mystery of the Invisible! No, we may not sound it with our wretched senses, with our eyes—which can perceive neither what is too small nor too great, nor too near nor too far, nor the inhabitants of a planet nor the inhabitants of a drop of water. And we may not sound it with our ears—which deceive us, transmitting air-waves in the form of sonorous notes. They are the fairies who perform the miracle of changing movement into sound, and by this metamorphosis they give birth to music and to Nature's dumb agitation the power of singing. No, we may not sound it with our sense of smell—feebler than that of the dog; nor with our taste—which can hardly discern the age of wine!

Ah, if we had only other organs which would perform in our favor other miracles like that miracle of music, what new things we should discover all about our lives!

May 16th.

I am certainly ill. Last month I was so well! I have a fever, a dreadful fever, or rather a feeling of feverish enervation which causes my mind to suffer as much as my body. I experience that awful sense of some menacing danger, that apprehension of coming misfortune or approaching death, that curious presentiment which is no doubt really the stroke of a still unrecognized sickness germinating in body and in blood.

May 18th.

I have just been to consult my physician, for I was not able to sleep. He found my pulse rapid, my eye dilated, my nerves disturbed, but no alarming symptoms. I must take shower-baths and drink a little bromide of potassium.

May 25th.

No change. My condition is truly curious. With the approach of evening a strange anxiety invades me, as if the night concealed for me some dreadful menace. I dine quickly, then try to read, but I do not comprehend the words. I barely distinguish the letters. Then I pace my drawing-room backward and forward, under the oppression of a confused and resistless fear, the fear of sleep and the fear of my bed.

Towards ten o'clock I go up-stairs to my room. As soon as I get inside the door I double-lock it and I push the bolts; I am afraid . . . of what? . . . Hitherto I feared nothing. . . . I open my closets, I look under my bed; I listen. . . . I listen for what? . . . Is it not strange that a simple indisposition, a difficulty in the circulation perhaps, an irritated nerve, a slight congestion, a little disturbance of the works of my delicate, imperfect human machinery, can out of a merry man make a melancholy one—out of a brave man make a coward? Then I go to bed, and I await sleep as one might await an executioner. I wait with terror for its coming. And my heart beats, and my limbs quiver, and my whole body trembles under the warmth of the bedclothes, until the moment when I fall suddenly into slumber, as a man might fall, to drown himself, into a gulf of stagnant water. I do not feel sleep coming in the way I used to feel it coming—calmly. For this sleep, hidden somewhere near me, is perfidious, and it watches and will soon seize me by the head, and close my eyes, and destroy me.

I sleep long—two or three hours—then a dream—no, a nightmare grips me in its arms. I feel that I am in bed and that I am sleeping . . . I feel it and I know it. . . . and I also feel that some one approaches me, looks at me, touches me, mounts upon my bed, kneels upon my breast, seizes my neck in his hands and presses . . . presses . . . with all his force, to strangle me.

I—I writhe, bound fast by that awful powerlessness which paralyzes us in dreams. I desire to shout,—I cannot;—to move,—I cannot;—I try, with fearful efforts, panting, to turn myself, to throw off this being who is crushing and suffocating me;—I cannot.

And suddenly I awake, wild, covered with perspiration. I light a candle. I am alone.

After this crisis, which recurs every night, I sleep at last calmly until dawn.

June 2d.

My condition is still worse. What is the matter with me? The bromide has no effect; the shower-baths have no effect. Just now, in order to tire myself out (though Heaven knows I am languid enough already!) I went to walk in the forest of Roumare. I thought at first that the fresh, buoyant, balmy air, full of the perfume of herbs and leaves, was pouring new blood into my veins, new energy into my heart. I took a wide glade. Then I turned towards La Bouille, along a narrow *allée*,* between two armies of great trees which built a thick, green, almost black roof between the sky and myself.

---

* Pathway.

Suddenly a shiver seized me—not a shiver of cold, but a strange shiver of anguish.

I quickened my pace, uneasy at being alone in the wood, terrified without reason, stupidly, by the profound loneliness. All at once it seemed to me that I was being followed, that some one was treading on my heels, on the point—on the point—on the point of touching me.

I turned abruptly. I was alone. I saw behind me only the straight, wide glade—empty, high, fearfully empty; and in front of me also it stretched out of sight just the same—dreadful!

I closed my eyes. Why? And I began to turn round and round on my heel, quickly, like a top. I came near falling. I opened my eyes again; the trees danced; the earth swam; I was obliged to sit down. Then, of course, I no longer knew from which direction I had come! Fantastic thought! Strange! Fantastic thought! I set off to the right, and happened into the same avenue which had led me to the middle of the forest.

June 3d.

The night was horrible. I shall go away for a few weeks. A little journey will no doubt set me on my feet again.

July 2d.

At home again. I am cured; and, besides that, I have made a charming trip. I have visited Mont Saint Michel, where I had never been.

What a vision, when one arrives, as I did, at Avranches towards the end of the day! The city is on a little hill; a guide took me to the public garden at the end of the town. A great bay stretched away before me out of sight, between two lonely shores which lost themselves far off in the mists; and in the midst of this immense yellow bay, beneath a golden and glittering sky, rose, sombre and pointed, a strange mount in the midst of the sands. The sun had just disappeared, and against the still flaming horizon there was designed the profile of that fantastic rock which bears upon its summit a fantastic monument.

By daybreak I was on my way towards it. The tide was low, as yesterday at evening, and I watched that wonder-arousing abbey growing taller and taller before me as I approached. After several hours of walking I reached the enormous block of stones which bears the little town dominated by the great church. Having ascended the narrow and steep street, I entered the most admirable Gothic dwelling which has ever been constructed for God on earth, vast as a city, full of low passages borne down by heavy arches, of high galleries borne up by slender columns. I entered that gigantic granite jewel, light as a bit of lace, covered with towers and with slender belfries linked one to the other by fine-carved arches. They are climbed by twisting stair-ways, and they dart into the blue sky of day and into the black sky of night, their fantastic heads bristling with chimeras, with Devils, and with strange Beasts.

When I reached the top I said to the monk who accompanied me, "Father, you must be well off here."

He answered: "There's a great deal of wind, Monsieur;" and we fell into conversation while we watched the rising sea spread over the sand and cover it with a steely cuirass.

And the monk told me stories—all the old stories of the place— legends, always legends.

One of them impressed me very strongly. The country people, those of the mount, pretend that talking is heard on the sands by night, then the bleating of two goats, the one with a voice which is high, the other with a voice which is deep. Unbelievers maintain it is the sea-birds' crying, which resembles now a bleat, and now a human wail; but belated fishermen swear that they have met, wandering on the sands, between two tides, about the little city cast out so far from the rest of the world, an old shepherd whose head, shrouded in a cloak, is always invisible, and who leads behind him a he-goat with the face of a man, and a she-goat with the face of a woman. They have long white hair, and they talk incessantly, quarrelling together in an unknown tongue; then suddenly they cease crying and begin to bleat with all their might.

I said to the monk: "Do you believe it?"

He murmured: "I do not know."

I continued: "If there really existed on the earth any other beings beside ourselves, how is it possible that we should not have known them long ago? How should you have seen them, you? How should I not have seen them, I?"

He answered: "Do we see the hundred-thousandth part of what exists? For instance, take the wind, which is the greatest force in nature, which knocks down men, lays low buildings, tears up trees by the roots, heaps the sea into mountains of water, destroys coasts, and hurls great ships upon the breakers,—the Wind which kills, which whistles, which moans, which roars,—have you ever seen it? Can you see it? It exists, nevertheless."

I was silent before this simple reasoning. This man was a wise man or perhaps a fool. I could not have decided which; but I was silent. What he had just said I had often thought.

July 3d.

I have slept badly; there is certainly something feverish in the air here, for my coachman suffers from the same complaint as myself. On my return yesterday I noticed that he was looking curiously pale. I asked him:—

"What is the matter, Jean?"

"It is that I cannot sleep, Monsieur; my nights eat up my days. Since Monsieur went away, it holds me like a charm."

The other servants, however, are well; but I myself am in great fear of a relapse.

July 4th.

Yes, I have had a relapse. My old nightmares have returned. Last night I felt some one squatting on my chest with his mouth to mine, drinking my life out through my lips. Yes, like a leech he drew it out of my throat. Then when he was satiated he arose, and I, I awoke, so nearly murdered, so exhausted, so broken, that I had no longer power to move. If this continues many days more I shall certainly go away again.

July 5th.

Have I lost my reason? That which has happened, that which I saw last night, is so strange that my head turns when I think of it!

I had, as I now do every evening, locked my door; then, being thirsty, I drank half a glass of water, and I noticed by mere chance that the water-bottle was full up to the glass stopper.

After that I went to bed and fell into one of my dreadful slumbers, from which, two hours later, I was drawn by a shock more awful yet.

Imagine a man who sleeps, who is being murdered, and who awakes with a knife in his breast, and who groans covered with blood, and who cannot breathe, and who is dying, and who does not understand. It was like that!

Having at last recovered my reason, I again felt thirsty; I lit a candle and I went to the table where the water-bottle stood. I raised it, tipping it over the glass; nothing came out. It was empty! It was completely empty! At first I did not understand; then, all at once, I experienced so terrible an emotion that I had to sit down, or rather that I simply fell, upon a chair! Then, with a start, I jumped to my feet, and looked about me! Then, again, I sat down, dazed with astonishment and with fear, before the transparent glass! I glared at it with staring eyes, trying to understand. My hands trembled! Had some one really drunk that water? Who——I? I, without a doubt. It could only be I. Then I was a somnambulist, I was living, without knowing it, that mysterious double life which makes us wonder whether we are in ourselves two beings, or whether some strange being, unknowable and invisible, may not animate, at moments when our will is weak, our bodies captive and more obedient to this stranger than to us.

Ah! who will understand my abominable anguish? Who will understand the emotion of a man, perfectly sane, well educated, full of reason, and yet contemplating in terror, through the glass of a water-bottle, the disappearance, while he slept, of a little water! And I remained there until morning, not daring to go back to bed.

July 6th.

I am going mad. The water was again drunk by some one last night; or, rather, I drank it!

But, is it—is it I? Who should it be? Who? Oh, my God! I am going mad. Who shall save me?

July 10th.

I have just established the most wonder-arousing proofs.

Yes, I am mad! And yet?

On the 6th of July, before going to bed, I placed some wine, some milk, some water, some bread, and some strawberries on my table.

Some one drank—I drank—all the water, and a little milk. The wine, the bread, and the strawberries were not touched.

On the 7th of July I made the same experiment, with the same result.

On the 8th of July I suppressed the water and the milk. Nothing was touched at all.

Finally, on the 9th of July, I put only the milk and the water on my table, being careful to wrap up the bottles in cloths of white muslin and to tie down the stoppers. Then I rubbed my lips, my beard, my hands, with black-lead, and I retired.

The invincible slumber seized me, soon followed by the dreadful awaking. I had not stirred; my very sheets bore no stains. I rushed to the table. The cloths covering the bottles were immaculate. I untied the cords, trembling with fear. Some one had drunk all the water! Some one had drunk all the milk! Oh, my God! . . .

I leave to-day for Paris.

July 12th.

Paris. I must have lost my head completely these last days. I have been undoubtedly the plaything of a nervous imagination, unless, that is, I am really a somnambulist, or that I have been subjected to one of those influences, admitted but not yet explained, which are called "suggestions." In any case my perturbation came near insanity, and twenty-four hours of Paris have sufficed to put me on my feet again.

Yesterday, after taking a drive and making some visits which caused a new, revivifying air to pass into my soul, I finished the evening at the Théâtre Français. They were playing a piece by Alexandre Dumas *fils;* and that strong, alert spirit completed my cure. Solitude is certainly dangerous for an active intelligence. We need around us men who think and talk. When we are long alone, we people the void with phantoms.

I returned to the hotel in great good spirits, along the boulevards. Reminded by the jostling of the crowd, I thought, not without irony, of my terrors and imaginings of last week, when I believed, yes, really believed, that an invisible being was dwelling under my roof. How easily we lose our heads, how weakly and quickly we become wild with fear the moment we encounter some little incident which cannot be explained!

Instead of concluding with the words: "The reason I do not understand is that the cause as yet escapes me," we immediately proceed to imagine some dreadful mystery, some supernatural power.

July 14th.

Fête de la République.* I took a walk in the streets. The flags and the fireworks amused me like a child. Nevertheless, it is simply an absurdity—this being joyous on a fixed date, by Government decree. The people is an imbecile herd, now stupidly patient, now ferociously rebellious. Some one says to it: "Make merry." It makes merry. Some one says to it: "Go and fight with your neighbors." It goes and fights. Some one says to it: "Vote for the Emperor." It votes for the Emperor. Then some one says to it: "Vote for the Republic." And it votes for the Republic.

---

* Bastille Day, French national holiday celebrating the storming of the Bastille in 1789 and the beginning of the French Revolution.

Those who give it these orders are fools, also; but instead of obeying men, they obey principles, things whose stupidity, whose barrenness, whose falsity appears in the very name—Principles! Ideas supposed certain and immutable in this world where one is sure of nothing, where even light, even sound are illusions, merely states in the brain, merely states in the brain!

July 16th.

Yesterday I saw something which disturbed me very much.

I was dining with my cousin Mme. Sablé, whose husband commands the 76th Chasseurs at Limoges. At dinner there were two young ladies, and the husband of one of them, a Doctor Parent, a nerve-specialist, much interested in the extraordinary developments brought to light by the experiments now making in Hypnotism and Suggestion.

He gave us a long account of the prodigious results obtained by English scientists and by the physicians of the school at Nancy.

The facts which he advanced appeared to me so extremely fantastic that I declared myself entirely sceptical.

"We are," he maintained, "on the point of discovering one of Nature's most important secrets—I mean to say, one of her most important terrestrial secrets; since, of course, she hides forever others quite as important up there in the stars. Ever since Man has been able to think, ever since he has been able to speak and write his thoughts, he has from time to time felt brushing against him the touch of a mystery which is impenetrable to his gross, imperfect senses; and he has tried to supplement this weakness of his bodily organs by an effort of his mind. While his intelligence remained in the rudimentary state this notion of phenomena, all about him, yet invisible, took on shapes of the most vulgar terror. From it were born popular beliefs in the supernatural, legends of wandering spirits, of fairies, of gnomes, of ghosts—I might even add, the vulgar idea of God; for the ordinary conception of a workman-creator, in whatever religion it springs up, is, of all the inventions of the human brain, the most common, the most stupid, the most unacceptable. Nothing is truer than Voltaire's epigram: 'God made man in his own image, and man has returned the compliment.'

"But about a century ago people began to have dim forebodings of something new. Mesmer and several others started us on an unexpected track, and now, and especially in the last three or four years, we have arrived at wonderful results."

My cousin, as unbelieving as myself, smiled. Doctor Parent said to her: "May I try to hypnotize you, madame?"

"Certainly you may."

She seated herself in an arm-chair, and, trying to fascinate her gaze, he looked at her fixedly. As for me, I felt suddenly troubled— my heart beating, a choking in my throat. I saw the eyes of Mme. Sablé droop, her mouth work, her breast heave. At the end of ten minutes she slept.

"Put yourself behind her," said the physician.

And I seated myself behind her. In her hands he placed a visiting-card, saying: "This is a mirror; what do you see in it?"

She answered: "I see my cousin."

"What is he doing?"

"He is twisting his mustache."

"What now?"

"He is taking a photograph out of his pocket."

"A photograph of whom?"

"Of himself."

It was true! And the photograph had been sent home only that evening to my hotel.

"How does he look in the photograph?"

"He is standing up, with his hat in his hand."

So then she saw in this card, in this white card, as well as she would have seen in a glass!

The young ladies, very much frightened, cried: "Enough! Enough! Enough!"

But the doctor gave her an order: "You will rise at eight o'clock to-morrow morning; and you will go to find your cousin at his hotel; and you will beg him to lend you five thousand francs, which your husband has said he needs, and hopes to get from you when he comes up shortly to town."

Then he awoke her.

While returning to the hotel I meditated on this curious *séance*, and I was assailed by doubts, not of the absolute, the indubitable good faith of my cousin, whom I have known like a sister from childhood up, but of a possible trick on the part of the doctor. Might he not, at the same time with his visiting-card, have held before the sleeping lady a mirror hidden in his hand? Professional prestidigitators perform equally extraordinary feats.

So I went home and to bed.

But this morning, about half after eight, I was awaked by my man, who said:

"It is Mme. Sablé. She asks to speak with you, sir, immediately."

I dressed in all haste, and I bid him show her in.

Very much embarrassed, she sat down, lowering her eyes, not lifting her veil; and she said:

"My dear cousin, I have to ask you for a great favor."

"What is it, cousin?"

"I hate to ask you, and yet I must. I need—I need five thousand francs; I need it very much."

"Oh, come now!—You?"

"Yes, I. Or, rather, my husband. He says I must get the money for him somehow."

I was so stupefied that I stammered. I asked myself if this were not a joke on me which she was playing with Doctor Parent; if this were not a simple farce rehearsed in advance, and very well acted.

But, when I looked at her carefully, all my doubts vanished. She trembled with anguish, the proceeding was so painful for her; and I saw that her throat was full of sobs.

I knew she was very rich, and I continued:

"What! Your husband has not five thousand francs at his disposal? Come! Think a little. Are you sure he told you to ask me for it?"

For some seconds she hesitated as though making a great effort to remember, then she answered:

"Yes. . . . Yes. . . . I am sure of it."

"Has he written?"

Again she hesitated, reflecting. I divined how she was tortured by the working of her thoughts. She did not know. She knew simply that she must borrow from me, for her husband, five thousand francs. But she gained the courage to lie.

"Yes, he wrote to me."

"When, then? You said nothing to me of it yesterday."

"I got the letter this morning."

"Can you show it me?"

"No . . . no . . . no . . . it had private matters in it . . . too personal . . . I . . . I burnt it."

"Oh! I suppose then he's been getting into debt."

Again she hesitated; then murmured:

"I do not know."

I announced, abruptly:

"The fact is at the moment I haven't five thousand francs to my hand, cousin."

She uttered a kind of suffering cry.

"Oh, oh! I beg you, I beg you to get it somehow, somehow." . . .

She grew excited, clasped her hands before me as though she were praying! I heard her voice change tone; she wept and stammered; she was tormented, overpowered, dominated by the irresistible order which had been laid upon her.

"Oh, oh! I beg you . . . if you knew how I suffer. . . . I must have it to-day."

I took pity on her.

"You shall have it, and very soon, I promise."

"Oh, thank you! thank you! You are good."

I continued:—"Do you remember what happened at your house last night?"

"Yes."

"Do you remember that Doctor Parent put you to sleep?"

"Yes."

"Well, he ordered you to come to me this morning, and borrow

five thousand francs. And at this moment you are obeying his suggestion."

She reflected for a few seconds, and answered:

"But it's my husband who wants it."

For an hour I tried in vain to convince her.

As soon as she had gone, I hurried to the Doctor. He was on the
point of going out; and he listened to me with a smile. Then he said:—

"Do you believe now?"

"Yes, I must."

"Let us go to your cousin."

She was already dozing in a long chair, exhausted with fatigue. The
physician felt her pulse, looked at her for a time, his raised hand
pointing towards her eyes. Little by little she closed them, submitting
to the resistless strength of the magnetic power.

When she slumbered:

"Your husband has no longer any need of five thousand francs. You
will therefore forget that you have asked your cousin to lend you
them; and if he speaks to you of it, you will not understand him."

Then he awoke her. I drew out a pocket-book.

"Here, my dear cousin, here is what you asked me for this morning."

She was so surprised that I did not dare to insist. Nevertheless, I tried
to arouse her memory; but she denied everything with vehemence,
thought I was making fun of her, and at last came near being angry.

There it is!—I have just returned; and I was so disturbed by this experience that at luncheon I could eat nothing.

July 19th.

Several people to whom I have related this adventure have made fun
of me. I do not know what to think. The wise man says: "It may be."

July 21st.

I've been to dine at Bougival; afterwards I went to the Water-
men's Ball. Decidedly everything depends on circumstance and

place. To believe in the supernatural on the island of La Grenouil-lière would be the height of folly indeed. . . . But on the top of Mont St. Michel? . . . But in the Far East? We are subject fear-somely to the influence of what surrounds us. Next week I shall go home.

July 30th.

I arrived yesterday. All well.

August 2d.

Nothing new. Beautiful weather. I pass my days watching the Seine flow.

August 4th.

Quarrels among the servants. They say that some one breaks the glass at night in the closets. My man accuses the cook, who accuses the laundress, who accuses the two maids. Which one is guilty? It would take a wise man to say.

August 6th.

This time I am not mad. I have seen. . . . I have seen! . . . I have seen! . . . I can doubt no more. . . . I have seen! . . . I am still chilled to my very finger-nails. . . . I am still afraid to the very mar-row. . . . I have seen! . . .

I was taking a walk about two o'clock, in broad daylight, in my rose-garden, . . . along a row of autumn roses which are already be-ginning to bloom.

Pausing to look at a Géant des Batailles, which bore three magnif-icent buds, I saw, I distinctly saw, quite near me the stem of one of these roses bend as though twisted by an invisible hand, then break, as though that hand had plucked it! Then the flower lifted itself, fol-lowing the curve which would have been described by an arm carry-ing it to a mouth; and it remained hanging in the empty air, alone, motionless, a terrifying red stain three paces from my eyes.

Maddened, I threw myself forward to seize it! I found nothing; it had disappeared. Then I was overcome with violent anger against myself, since a man who is serious and reasonable should not allow himself to have such hallucinations as this.

But was it really an hallucination? I turned to look for the stem, and I discovered it almost immediately, on the plant, freshly broken, between the two other roses which remained upon the tree.

So I went back to the house with a troubled soul; for now I am certain that near me there exists an invisible being who lives on milk and on water; who can touch objects; can take them up and change their places; whose nature, therefore, though imperceptible to our sense, is material, and who, like myself, dwells under my roof. . . .

August 7th.

I slept quietly. He drank all the water in my bottle, but did not disturb my sleep.

I ask myself if I am mad. While walking just now along the river, doubts about my reason came to me; not vague doubts such as I have hitherto experienced, but doubts precise and absolute. I have seen lunatics, I have known some who remained intelligent, clear-headed, lucid on every subject save one. They talked clearly, easily, profoundly, then suddenly their intelligence, striking on the rock of their monomania, there ground itself to pieces, was broken up and foundered in that terrible, furious sea, full of heaving waves and mists and squalls, the sea which we call "Madness."

I should certainly believe that I was mad, quite mad, if I were not so entirely self-conscious, if I did not recognize my condition so perfectly, if I were not always sounding it by an analysis which is so completely clear. I am, then, only a man who suffers from an hallucination, but who is in full possession of his reason? Some trouble has occurred in my brain, one of those troubles which psychologists nowadays endeavor to note and particularize? And this trouble has induced a profound lapse in my intellect, in the order and logic of my thoughts? A similar phenomenon occurs in dreams, where we are led through the most improbable of phantasmagoria without feeling a shadow of surprise, simply for the reason that the verifying apparatus, our sense of control, is asleep, while our imaginative faculty wakes and is active. May it not be, therefore, that one of the invisible keys of my cerebral piano is paralyzed? People very often, in consequence of an accident, lose their memory of proper names, or of verbs, or of figures, or simply of dates. That the various little bundles of thought are specially localized is now considered proved. Hence what is there surprising if my power of controlling the unreality of certain hallucinations finds itself at the present moment torpid?

I pondered on all this as I followed the bank of the river. The sun covered the stream with radiance, made the earth delicious, filled my eyes with love for life, for the swallows whose swift motions are a joy to look at, for the grasses by the water's edge whose rustling is a joy to me when I listen.

Little by little, however, I was penetrated by a strange uneasiness. It seemed to me that a force, an occult force, benumbed me, checked me, prevented me from going farther, called me back. I experienced a mournful feeling that I must return, a feeling like that which oppresses us when, having left at home some sick person whom we love, we are suddenly seized by a presentiment that she is worse.

So I turned back, against my will, certain that I should find bad news at home, a letter, or a telegram. There was nothing, and I remained more surprised and uneasy than if I had again seen some fantastic vision.

August 8th.

I passed a dreadful evening yesterday. He no longer makes his presence evident, but I feel him near me, spying, watching, penetrating me, dominating me, more terrible while thus concealed than if he manifested by supernatural phenomena his invisible and constant presence.

I slept, however.

August 9th.

Nothing. But I am afraid.

August 10th.

Nothing. What will happen to-morrow?

August 11th.

Still nothing; I cannot stay at home any longer with this fear and these thoughts in my soul; I shall go away.

August 12th: 10 P.M.

All day I have wanted to be off; I could not go. I wished to perform an act of free will, very easy and very simple:—going out of my door—getting into my carriage—driving to Rouen. I was not able. Why?

August 13th.

When one is attacked by certain maladies all the powers of the physical being seem broken, all the energies destroyed, all the muscles relaxed, the bones becoming soft as flesh and the flesh liquid as water. I experience this in my moral state after a strange and appalling fashion. I have no longer any strength, courage, self-control, no power to put in motion my own will. I can no longer will; but some one wills for me, and I obey.

August 14th.

I am lost! Some one is in possession of my soul and governs it. Some one orders all my acts, all my movements, all my thoughts. I am no longer anything in myself; I am nothing but an enslaved and terrified spectator of the things which I accomplish. I desire to go out; I cannot—he does not wish it, and I remain, frightened, trembling, in the arm-chair where he holds me seated. I desire simply to rise, to get up, so as to prove that I am still my own master. I cannot! I am riveted to my seat, and my seat adheres to the ground with such force that no power could lift us up.

Then, on a sudden, I must, I must, I must go to the end of the garden and pick some strawberries and eat them. And I go. I pick the berries and I eat them. Oh, my God!—my God! If there be a God, deliver me, save me, help me! Pardon! Pity! Grace! Save me! Oh, what suffering! what torture! what horror!

August 15th.

Yes, this is the way in which my poor cousin was possessed and dominated when she came to me to borrow five thousand francs. She submitted to a strange will which had entered into her like a new soul—like a new parasite and dominant soul. Is the world ending?

But this being who governs me—what is he, this invisible? Who is he, this unknowable, this prowler of a supernatural race?

And so the Invisibles exist! How is it, then, that since the beginning of the world they have never manifested themselves as they have to me? I never read of any such things as have happened here in my house. Oh, if I could leave it!—if I could go away—flee and never return—I should be saved! But I cannot.

August 16th.

I was able to make my escape to-day for two hours, like a prisoner who finds the door of his dungeon, by chance, open. I suddenly felt that I was free, and that he was far away. I ordered the carriage instantly, and I got as far as Rouen. Oh, what joy to say to a man who obeys you—"Go to Rouen."

I had myself driven to the library, and I took out Hermann Herestauss's great treatise, *The Unrecognized Inhabitants of the Ancient and Modern World*.

Then, as I was getting back into my brougham I wanted to say: "To the station!" but cried—I did not say, I shouted—with a voice so loud that the people in the street turned round—"Home!" and I fell, mad with despair, on the cushions of the carriage. He had found and captured me again.

August 17th.

Ah! what a night!—what a night! And yet it occurs to me that I ought to rejoice. I read till one o'clock in the morning. Hermann Herestauss is a doctor of philosophy and of theogony; he has written a complete history of the manifestations of those beings which wander mostly invisible about mankind, or are imagined by him as so doing; he treats exhaustively of their origin, of their domain, of the power which they exercise; and not one of them resembles the one who haunts me. One would say that ever since man could think he has had dim forebodings and fears of a new being, stronger than himself, his successor in the world; and that, feeling him near at hand, and being unable to foresee the real nature of this new master, he has in terror created all that fantastic crowd of occult beings—vague phantoms born of fear.

But to continue. Having read till one o'clock, I went and seated myself at an open window to refresh brow and brain in the calm air of darkness.

The night was gentle and warm. How I should have loved this kind of a night long ago!

No moon. The stars at the back of the black sky glittered and trembled. Who dwell in those worlds up there? What forms? what living things? what animals? what plants? That which thinks in those distant universes, what knows it more than we? What power has it more than we? What sees it that we know not? And some day or another will not one of those beings, traversing space, appear upon the earth and conquer it, just as the Normans of old crossed the sea to subdue more feeble races?

We are so weak, so defenceless, so ignorant, so little, we here on this revolving speck of mud and water.

Thus dozing in the fresh evening breeze, I drowsed off.

But after I had slept about forty minutes, I opened my eyes, making no other movement, awoke by some confused fantastical emotion. At first I saw nothing; then, on a sudden, it seemed to me that a page of the open book lying on my table had just turned by itself. No breath of air came through the window. I was surprised, and I waited. At the end of about four minutes I saw, I saw, yes, I saw with my eyes another page lift itself and fold over down on the preceding one as though a finger had turned it. My arm-chair was empty, seemed empty; but I understood that he was there, he, seated in my place, and that he was reading. With one furious leap, with the bound of a beast who has rebelled at last, and fallen on his master to tear him open, I crossed the room to seize, to grip him in my hands, to kill him! . . . But my chair, before I had reached it, was overturned, as though some one fled before me . . . my table tottered, my lamp fell and was extinguished, and my window shut itself as though a detected thief had leaped out into the night by catching both the sashes in his hands.

So, he fled! He was afraid, he was afraid of me!

Then . . . then . . . to-morrow . . . or the day after . . . or some day . . . I shall be able to get him down under my hands, and to crush him against the earth! Do not dogs sometimes bite and throttle their masters?

August 18th.

I have reflected all day. Oh yes, I shall obey him, follow his suggestions, accomplish all his desires, appear humble, submissive, cowardly! He is the strongest. But an hour will come. . . .

August 19th.

I know . . . I know . . . I know all! I have read as follows in the *Revue du Monde Scientifique:*[11] "Information of a curious nature comes to us from Rio de Janeiro. An epidemic of madness, comparable to those contagious crazes which attacked the European peoples during the Middle Ages, is, it seems, at present, raging in the province of San Paulo. The inhabitants are leaving their houses in dismay, deserting their villages, and abandoning their crops, maintaining that they are being pursued, taken possession of, governed like a human herd of cattle, by certain invisible but tangible beings, resembling vampires, who suck upon their life-blood during their sleep, and who, besides that, take water and milk, but no other nourishment.

"Professor Don Pedro Henriquez, accompanied by several other scientists of the medical profession, is on his way to the province of San Paulo, to study on the spot the causes and the manifestations of this curious mania; he will then propose to the Emperor whatever measures he decides best for recalling these unhappy lunatics to their reason."

Ah! Ah! I remember, I remember the beautiful Brazilian three-master which passed up the Seine under my windows on the 8th of last May! I thought it so beautiful, so white, so gay! The Being was aboard it, coming from that distant country where his race was born! And he saw me! He saw that my dwelling was white, likewise; and he leaped from the ship to the river-banks. Oh, my God!

And now, I know, I divine. The kingdom of man is ended.

He has come. He whom primitive peoples dreaded with a naïve terror, He who was exorcised by anxious priests, He whom sorcerers invoked in vain on sombre nights, He to whom the forebodings of man, the transitory master of the earth, have given the monstrous or gracious forms of gnomes and ghosts, of genii, of fairies, and of familiar spirits. After the vulgar conceptions of primitive fear came the clearer presentations of more highly developed minds. Mesmer first divined Him; and the doctors, as long as ten years ago, discovered the exact nature of His power before He himself had ever used it. They have played with this weapon of the new Lord, this domination of a mysterious will over a human soul made captive. They have called it magnetism, hypnotism, suggestion . . . what not? I have seen them, like careless children, amusing themselves with that dreadful power! Woe to us! Woe to Man! He is come, the . . . the . . . how calls he himself . . . the . . . it seems to me that he is crying out his name, and that I cannot hear it . . . the . . . yes . . . he is crying it . . . I am listening . . . I cannot . . . I repeat . . . the . . . Horla . . . I heard . . . the Horla . . . it is he . . . the Horla . . . he has come! . . .

Ah! the vulture has devoured the dove, and the wolf has devoured the sheep, the lion has devoured the buffalo with the pointed horns; and the man has slain the lion by arrows and by his knife and by powder. But the Horla will make of man what man has made of the horse, and of the ox: his thing, his servant, his food, by the sole power of his will. Woe unto us!

Nevertheless, the animal sometimes revolts and kills his master . . . and I, too, I wish . . . I shall be able . . . but I must first know what he is like, I must touch him, see him! Scientists say that the eyes of animals are different from ours, and do not distinguish things as ours do. . . . Just so my eyes cannot distinguish this newcomer who oppresses me.

Why? Oh! now I remember the words of the monk of Mont St. Michel: "Do we see the hundred-thousandth part of what exists? For instance, take the wind, which is the greatest force in nature, which knocks down men, lays low buildings, tears up trees by the roots, heaps the sea into mountains of water, destroys coasts, and hurls great ships upon the breakers,—the Wind which kills, which whistles, which moans, which roars,—have you ever seen it? Can you see it? It exists, nevertheless."

And I continued to reflect: "My eye is so feeble, so imperfect, that it does not even distinguish solid bodies, if they are transparent— such as glass! . . . And if a mirror without a quicksilver back bars the way, my eye allows me to throw myself up against it like a bird which, straying into a room, dashes its head to pieces against the window-panes. A thousand things beside deceive and confuse it. Then what wonder if it cannot see this new transparent body?"

A new being! Why not? Inevitably he must have arisen! Why should we be the last. We cannot see him as we do other beings created before ourselves. That is simply because his nature is more perfect, because his body is more subtlely and highly developed than ours, than ours so feeble, than ours conceived so roughly, encumbered with organs like over-complex springs, always fatigued, and always straining. For our body lives like a plant and like a beast, gaining a painful sustenance from air, from grasses, and from flesh. A living machine, the prey to sickness, to deformity, and to decay, it is of dust; a work at once coarse and delicate, irregular, pitifully simple, fantastic, and ill-made ingeniously; the first rough sketch of a being which might sometime be developed into something intelligent and perfect.

There are, after all, from the oyster up to the man, so few of us here on the earth. Why not one more, once the period which separates the appearances of different successive species has been accomplished?

Why not one more? Why not other trees with immense flowers dazzling and suffusing entire regions with their perfume? Why not other elements besides Fire, Air, Earth, and Water? They are four, only four, these nursing fathers of being! What a pity! Why are they not forty, four hundred, four thousand? How poor, how mean, how wretched is everything! Granted, but not freely; conceived, but without genius; executed, but with no lightness of touch! The elephant, forsooth, the hippopotamus, how graceful! The camel, how elegant!

But what say you of the butterfly, that flying flower? I dream of one large as a hundred worlds, with wings whose shape, whose beauty, whose color, and whose manner of motion I cannot even describe. But I see it . . . it is going from star to star refreshing and perfuming each with the light and harmonious breathing of its course! . . . And whole peoples, high up there, watch, in ecstasy and ravishment, its passing! . . .

What is the matter with me? It is he, he, the Horla, who haunts me and makes me dream such follies! He is within me. He has become my soul; I shall kill him!

August 20th.

I shall kill him. I have seen him. I sat down last night at my table, and I pretended to be absorbed in writing. I knew very well that he would come and prowl round me, very near, so near that perhaps I should be able to touch him, to seize him. And then! . . . then I should have the strength of desperation; I should have hands and knees, breast, and brow, and teeth, to strangle, to crush, to bite, to tear.

And, straining every sense, I watched for him.

I had lit my two lamps and the eight candles on my mantel, exactly as though the light would help me to discover him!

Before me was my bed, an old oak bedstead with columns. On my right the chimney-piece. On my left the door, which I had carefully shut, after leaving it open for a while in order to attract him. Behind me, a tall wardrobe, with a looking-glass which I used every day for shaving and for dressing, and in which, every time I passed it, I had a habit of looking myself over from head to foot.

So I pretended to write in order to deceive him; for he, too, was watching. And suddenly I felt, I was certain, that he was reading over my shoulder, that he was there almost brushing my ear.

I jumped up with out-stretched hands, and turned round so quickly that I almost fell. Well? In my chamber it was as light as day, but I did not see myself in the glass! . . . It was empty, clear, deep, full of light! My image was not in it . . . and I stood there right in front of it, I! The great glass was clear from top to bottom. And with wild eyes I stared at this thing; and I did not dare to advance, I did not dare to move, feeling indeed that he was there, but that he would escape me, he, whose invisible body had absorbed the reflection of mine.

What fear I suffered! Then, all of a sudden, I began to perceive myself in a mist at the back of the mirror, in a mist as though through a sheet of water; and it seemed to me that this water glided from left to right, slowly, making my figure clearer, from second to second. It was like the ending of an eclipse. That which concealed me did not appear to possess sharp outlines, but merely a kind of opaque transparence, rarefying itself little by little.

At last I could distinguish my whole figure, just as I do each day when I look.

I had seen him! The terror of it remains still on me, causing me still to shiver.

August 21st.

Kill him? How? Since I cannot reach him? Poison? But he would see me mixing it in the water; and, besides, would our poisons have any effect on his supersensual body? No . . . no . . . of course not. . . . What then? . . . what then? . . .

August 22d.

I have had up a locksmith from Rouen, and I have ordered for my room some iron shutters like those which certain private houses in Paris have on the ground-floor as a protection against robbers. He is also to make me an iron door. I am appearing like a great coward, but at that I laugh! . . .

Sept. 10th.

Rouen. Hôtel Continental. It is accomplished . . . it is accomplished . . . but is he dead? My soul is overwhelmed by what I have seen.

Yesterday the locksmith, having fitted my shutters and my iron door, I left everything open until midnight, although it began to be very cold.

All of a sudden I felt that he was there, and a joy, a mad joy seized me. I rose gently, and I walked up and down for a long time in order to put him off his guard. Then I carelessly took off my boots and put on my slippers. Then I closed my iron shutters, and, returning tranquilly to the door, I closed that also and double-locked it. Again returning to the window, I secured the shutter with a padlock, and put the key in my pocket.

All of a sudden I understood that he was stirring anxiously round me; that, in his turn now, he was afraid; that he was commanding me to open. I came near yielding; I did not yield, but, setting my back against the door, I opened it on a crack just wide enough for me to pass through backward; and as I am very tall, my head touched the lintel. I was sure that he could not have escaped, and I shut him in all alone—all alone! What happiness! I had him fast! Then I went down-stairs, running. In the drawing-room under my bedchamber I took the two lamps, and I poured oil over the carpet, over the furniture, over everything; then I set fire to it and I escaped from the house after having double-locked on the outside the great hall door.

And I hid myself at the bottom of the garden in a thicket of laurels. How long it was! How long it was! All remained black, silent, immobile; not a breath of air, not a star in the great mountains of clouds which I could not see, but which rested on my soul so heavily, so heavily.

I watched my house and I waited. How long it was! I had begun to think that the fire had gone out of itself, or that he—He had extinguished it. Then one of the windows on the ground-floor cracked under the pressure of the inner conflagration, and a tongue of flame—a great tongue of red and yellow flame—long and soft and caressing, climbed up along the white wall and kissed the very roof. A glow ran over the trees, the branches, the leaves, and a shiver—a shiver of fear also! The birds awoke; a dog began to howl; it seemed to me that the day itself was getting up! Soon two other windows burst open, and I saw that the whole ground-floor of my house was nothing but a dreadful brazier. But a cry—an awful cry—sharp, heart-rending—a woman's shriek—came out into the night, and two windows in the garret opened! I had forgotten my servants! I saw their wild faces, their waving arms! . . .

Then, mad with horror, I set off running to the village, shouting "Help!—help! Fire!—fire!" I met people already hastening to the scene, and I returned with them—to look!

The house was now simply a horrible and magnificent stake—a monstrous stake—illuminating all the country—a stake at which men were burning, and at which he burned also—He, He, my prisoner, the new Being, the new master, the Horla!

Suddenly the entire roof fell in between the walls, and a volcano of flame shot upward to the sky. Through the windows open upon the furnace I saw the fiery vat, and I thought: he is there in that burning oven—dead. . . .

Dead? Perhaps. . . . But his body? His body, which the light of day could pass through, is it not perhaps indestructible by such means as destroy our bodies?

What if he be not dead? . . . Time alone, perhaps, has power over the Being Invisible, the Being Terrible. Why a transparent body? why an imperceptible body? why the body of a Spirit, if he too must fear misfortunes, wounds, infirmities, premature destruction?

Premature destruction? All human terror springs from the idea of that. After Man, the Horla. After him who can die any day, any hour, any moment, by any accident, has come He who shall die only on his appointed day, at his appointed hour, at his appointed minute, having touched the appointed limit of existence!

No . . . no . . . there is no doubt, there is no doubt. . . . I have not killed him. . . . Then . . . then . . . I see . . . it is plain . . . yes, it is plain that I must . . . kill . . . myself! . . .

ALLOUMA

CHAPTER I

ONE OF MY FRIENDS had said to me: "If you happen to be near Bordj-Ebbaba while you are in Algeria, be sure and go to see my old friend Auballe, who has settled there."

I had forgotten the name of Auballe and of Ebbaba, and I was not thinking of the man, when I arrived at his house by pure accident. For a month, I had been wandering on foot through that magnificent district which extends from Algiers to Cherchel, Orléansville, and Tiaret. It is at the same time wooded and bare, grand and charming. Between two hills, you come across large pine forests, in narrow valleys through which torrents rush in the winter. Enormous trees, which have fallen across the ravine, serve as bridges for the Arabs, and also for the tropical creepers, which twine round the dead stems, and adorn them with new life. There are hollows, in little known recesses of the mountains, terrible, yet beautiful in character, and the banks of the brooks, which are covered with oleanders, are indescribably lovely.

But the most pleasant recollections of that excursion are the long after-dinner walks, along the slightly wooded roads on those undulating hills from which one can see an immense tract of country stretching from the blue sea as far as the chain of the Ouarsenis, on whose summit is the cedar forest of Teniet-el-Haad.

On that day I lost my way. I had just climbed to the top of a hill, whence, beyond a long extent of rising ground, I could see the extensive plain of Metidja, and then, on the summit of another chain, almost invisible in the distance, that strange monument called "The

Tomb of the Christian Woman," which is said to be the burial-place of the kings of Mauritania. I descended again, heading southward, with a yellow landscape before me, extending as far as the fringe of the desert, as yellow as if all the hills were covered with lions' skins sewn together. Sometimes a pointed yellow peak would rise out of them, like the hump of a camel.

I walked quickly and lightly, as one does when following tortuous paths on a mountain slope. Nothing seems to weigh on you in those short, quick walks through the invigorating air of those heights, neither body, nor heart, nor thoughts, nor cares. On that day I felt nothing of all that crushes and tortures our life; I only felt the pleasure of that descent. In the distance I saw an Arab encampment, brown pointed tents which seemed fixed to the earth like limpets to a rock, or else *gourbis*, huts made of branches, from which a gray smoke rose. White figures, men and women, were walking slowly about, and the bells of the flocks sounded vaguely through the evening air.

The arbutus trees on my road hung down under the weight of the purple fruit, which was falling on the ground. They looked like martyred trees, from which a blood-colored sweat was falling, for at the top of every tier there was a red spot, like a drop of blood.

The ground all round them was covered with it, and as my feet crushed the fruit, they left blood-colored traces behind them. Sometimes, as I went along, I would reach and pick one and eat it.

By this time all the valleys were filled with a white vapor, which rose slowly, like the steam from the flanks of an ox, and on the chain of mountains that bordered the horizon, on the outskirts of the desert of Sahara, the sky was in flames. Long streaks of gold alternated with streaks of blood—blood again! Blood and gold, the whole of human history—and sometimes between the two there was a small opening in the greenish azure, far away like a dream.

How far away I was from all those persons and things with which one occupies oneself on the boulevards! Far from myself also, for I had become a kind of wandering being, without thought or consciousness; far from any road, too, indeed not troubling about one, for as night came on, I found that I had lost my way.

The shades of night were falling on the earth like a darkling shower, and I saw nothing before me but the mountain, in the far distance. Presently, however, I saw some tents in the valley, into which I descended, and tried to make the first Arab I met understand in which direction I wanted to go. I do not know whether he understood me, but he gave me a long answer, which I did not in the least understand. In despair, I was about to make up my mind to pass the night wrapped up in a cloak near the encampment, when among the strange words that he uttered, I fancied that I heard the name, "Bordj-Ebbaba," and so I repeated:

"Bordj-Ebbaba."

"Yes, yes."

I showed him two francs—a fortune to him, and he started off, while I followed—yes, followed that pale phantom striding barefooted before me along stony paths, on which I stumbled continually, for a long time. Suddenly I saw a light, and we soon reached the door of a white house, a kind of fortress with straight walls, without any outside windows. When I knocked, dogs began to bark inside, and a voice asked in French:

"Who is there?"

"Does Monsieur Auballe live here?" I asked.

"Yes."

The door was opened for me, and I found myself face to face with Monsieur Auballe himself, a tall man in slippers, with a pipe in his mouth and the looks of a good-natured Hercules.

As soon as I mentioned my name, he put out both his hands and said:

"Consider yourself at home here, Monsieur."

A quarter of an hour later I was dining ravenously, opposite to my host, who went on smoking.

I knew his history. After having wasted a great amount of money on women, he had invested the remnants of his fortune in Algerian landed property and had taken to money-making. It turned out prosperously; he was happy and had the calm look of a contented man. I could not understand how this gay Parisian could have grown accustomed to that monstrous life in such a lonely spot, and I asked him about it.

"How long have you been here?" I asked.

"Nine years."

"And have you not been intolerably dull and miserable?"

"No, one gets used to this country, and ends by liking it. You cannot imagine how it lays hold of you by those small, animal instincts that we are ignorant of, ourselves. We first become attached to it by our organs, to which it affords a secret gratification that we cannot define. The air and the climate dominate the body, in spite of ourselves, and the bright light with which the country is inundated keeps the mind clear and fresh, at but little cost. It penetrates you continually by the inlet of vision, and one might really say that it cleanses the somber nooks of the soul."

"But what about women?"

"Ah! There is rather a dearth of them!"

"Only *rather?*"

"Well, yes, rather. For one can always, even among the Arabs, find some complaisant, native women, who think of the nights of Roumi."

He turned to the Arab who was waiting on me, a tall, dark fellow, with bright, black eyes that flashed beneath his turban, and said to him:

"I will call you when I want you, Mohammed." Then, turning to me, he said:

"He understands French, and I am going to tell you a story in which he plays a leading part."

As soon as the man had left the room, he began:

"I had been here about four years, and scarcely felt quite settled yet in this country, whose language I was beginning to speak. I was forced, in order not to break too suddenly away from those passions that had been fatal to me in other places, to go to Algiers for a few days, from time to time.

"I had bought this farm, this *bordj,** which had been a fortified

---

* Fort (Arabic).

post, and was within a few hundred yards of the native encampment, whose men I employ to cultivate my land. Among the tribe that had settled here, and which formed a portion of the Oulad-Taadja, I chose, as soon as I arrived here, the tall fellow whom you have just seen, Mohammed ben Lam'har, who soon became greatly attached to me. As he would not sleep in a house, not being accustomed to it, he pitched his tent a few yards from my house, so that I might be able to call him from my window.

"You can guess what my life was, I dare say? Every day I was busy with cleanings and plantings. I hunted a little, and used to go and dine with the officers of the neighboring fortified posts, or else they came and dined with me. As for pleasures—I have told you what they consisted in. Algiers offered me some which were rather more refined, and from time to time a complaisant and compassionate Arab would stop me when I was out for a walk and offer to bring one of the women of his tribe to my house at night. Sometimes I accepted, but more frequently I refused, from fear of the disagreeable consequences and troubles it might entail upon me.

"One evening, at the beginning of summer, as I was going home after inspecting the farm, I wanted Mohammed. I went into his tent without calling him, as I frequently did, and there I saw a woman, a girl sleeping almost naked, with her arms crossed under her head, on one of those thick, red carpets, made of the fine wool of Djebel-Amour, which are as soft and as thick as a feather bed. Her body, which was beautifully white under the ray of light that came in through the raised covering of the tent, appeared to me to be one of the most perfect specimens of the human race that I had ever seen, though most of the women about here are beautiful and tall and are a rare combination of feature and shape. I let the edge of the tent fall in some confusion, and returned home.

"I love women! The sudden flash of this vision had penetrated and scorched me, had rekindled in my veins that old, formidable ardor to which I owe my being here. It was very hot, for it was July, and I spent nearly the whole night at my window with my eyes fixed on the black spot Mohammed's tent made on the ground.

"When he came into my room the next morning, I looked him closely in the face, and he hung his head, like a man who was guilty and in confusion. Did he guess that I knew? I, however, asked him, suddenly:

" 'So you are married, Mohammed?' I saw that he got red; then he stammered out: 'No, mo'ssieuia!'

"I used to make him speak French to me, and to give me Arabic lessons, which was often productive of a most incoherent mixture of languages. However, I went on:

" 'Then why is there a woman in your tent?'

" 'She comes from the South,' he said, in a low, apologetic voice.

" 'Oh! So she comes from the South? But that does not explain to me how she comes to be in your tent.'

"Without answering my question, he continued:

" 'She is very pretty.'

" 'Oh! Indeed. Another time, please, when you happen to receive a pretty woman from the South, you will take care that she comes to my *gourbi*,* and not to yours. You understand me, Mohammed?'

" 'Yes, mo'ssieuia,' he repeated, seriously.

"I must acknowledge that during the whole day I was in a state of aggressive excitement at the recollection of that Arab girl lying on the red carpet, and when I went in at dinner time, I felt very strongly inclined to go to Mohammed's tent again. During the evening, he waited on me just as usual, hovering round me with his impassive face, and several times I was very nearly asking him whether he intended to keep that pretty girl from the South in his camel skin tent for a long time.

"Toward nine o'clock, still troubled with that longing for female society which is as tenacious as the hunting instinct in dogs, I went out to get some fresh air, and to stroll for a little while round that cone of brown skin through which I could see a brilliant speck of light. I did not remain long, however, for fear of being surprised by Mohammed in the neighborhood of his dwelling. When I went in an

---

* Thatched hut.

hour later, I clearly saw his outline in the tent. Then taking the key out of my pocket, I went into the *bordj*, where, besides myself, there slept my steward, two French laborers, and an old cook whom I had picked up in Algiers. As I went upstairs, I was surprised to see a streak of light under my door. When I opened it, I saw a girl with the face of a statue sitting on a straw chair by the side of the table, on which a wax candle was burning. She was bedizened with all those silver gew-gaws which women in the South wear on their legs, arms, breasts, and even on their stomachs. Her eyes, which were tinged with kohl, to make them look larger, looked at me earnestly, and four little blue spots, finely tattooed on her skin, marked her forehead, her cheeks, and her chin. Her arms, which were loaded with bracelets, were resting on her hips, which were covered by the long, red silk skirt that she wore.

"When she saw me come in, she got up and remained standing in front of me, covered with her barbaric jewels, in an attitude of proud submission.

" 'What are you doing here?' I said to her in Arabic.

" 'I am here because Mohammed told me to come.'

" 'Very well, sit down.'

"So she sat down and lowered her eyes while I examined her attentively.

"She had a strange, regular, delicate, yet rather sensual face, as mysterious as that of a Buddha. Her lips, which were rather thick, were covered with a reddish efflorescence, which I discovered on the rest of her body as well. This indicated a slight admixture of negro blood, although her hands and arms were of an irreproachable whiteness.

"I hesitated what to do with her, and felt excited, tempted, and rather confused. So in order to gain time and to give myself opportunity for reflection, I put other questions to her—about her birth, how she came into this part of the country, and what her connection with Mohammed was. But she only replied to those that interested me the least, and it was impossible for me to find out why she had come, with what intention, by whose orders, or what had taken place between her and my servant. However, just as I was about to say to her: 'Go back to Mohammed's tent,' she seemed to guess my intention, for getting up suddenly, and raising her two bare arms, on which the jingling bracelets slipped down to her shoulders, she crossed her hands behind my neck and drew me toward her with an irresistible air of suppliant longing.

"Her eyes, which were bright from emotion, from that necessity of conquering man which makes the looks of an impure woman as seductive as those of the feline tribe, allured me, enchained me, deprived me of all power of resistance, and filled me with impetuous ardor. It was a short, sharp struggle of the eyes only, that eternal struggle between the two human brutes, the male and the female, in which the male is always beaten.

"Her hands, which were clasped behind my head, drew me irresistibly, with the gentle, increasing pressure of a mechanical force, toward her red lips, on which I suddenly laid mine, while, at the same moment, I clasped her waist, which was covered with jingling silver rings, in an ardent embrace.

"She was as strong, as healthy, and as supple as a wild animal, with all the motions, the ways, the grace, and even something of the look of a gazelle, which made me find a rare, unknown zest in her kisses, as strange to my senses as the taste of tropical fruits.

"Soon—I say soon, although it may have been toward morning— I wished to send her away, as I thought that she would go in the same way that she had come. I did not even, at the moment, ask myself what I should do with her, or what she would do with me, but as soon as she guessed my intention, she whispered:

" 'What do you expect me to do, if you get rid of me now? I shall have to sleep on the ground in the open air, at night. Let me sleep on the carpet at the foot of your bed.'

"What answer could I give her, or what could I do? I thought that Mohammed would no doubt be watching the window of my room, in which a light was burning, and questions of various natures, that I had not put to myself during the first minutes, formulated themselves clearly in my brain.

" 'Stop here,' I replied, 'and we will talk.'

"My resolution was taken in a moment. As this girl had been thrown into my arms, in this manner, I would keep her; I would make her a kind of slave-mistress, hidden in my house, like women in a harem are. When the time should come that I no longer cared for her, it would be easy for me to get rid of her in some way or another, for on African soil this sort of creatures almost belong to us, body and soul. So I said to her:

" 'I wish to be kind to you, and I will treat you so that you shall not be unhappy, but I want to know who you are and where you come from?'

"She saw clearly that she must say something, and she told me her story, or rather a story, for no doubt she was lying from beginning to end, as Arabs always do, with or without any motive.

"That is one of the most surprising and incomprehensible signs of the native character—the Arabs always lie. Those people in whom Islam has become incarnate, has become part of themselves, to such an extent as to model their instincts, to mold the entire race, and differentiate it from others in morals just as much as the color of the skin differentiates a negro from a white man, are liars to the backbone, so that one can never trust a word that they say. I do not know whether they owe this to their religion, but one must have lived among them in order to know the extent to which lying forms part of their being, of their heart and soul. It has become a kind of second nature, a very necessity of life, with them.

"Well, she told me that she was the daughter of a *Caidi* of the *Ouled Sidi Cheik,* and of a woman whom he had carried off in a raid against the Touaregs. The woman must have been a black slave, or, at any rate, have sprung from a first cross of Arab and negro blood. It is well known that negro women are in great request for harems, where they act in various capacities. Nothing of such an origin was to be noticed, however, except the purple color of her lips, and the dark blush of her elongated breasts, which were as supple as if they were on springs. Nobody who knew anything about the matter could be mistaken in that. But all the rest of her belonged to the beautiful race from the South, fair, supple, and with a delicate face formed on straight and simple lines like those of a Hindoo figure. Her eyes, which were very far apart, still further heightened the somewhat goddess-like looks of this desert marauder.

"I knew nothing exact about her real life. She related it to me in incoherent fragments, that seemed to rise up at random from a disordered memory, and she mixed up deliciously childish observations with them—a vision of a nomad world, born in a squirrel's brain, that had leaped from tent to tent, from encampment to encampment, from tribe to tribe. And all this was done with the grave aspect which this reserved people always preserve—the appearance of a brass idol, and rather comic in itself.

"When she had finished, I perceived that I had not remembered anything of the long story, full of insignificant events, that she had stored up in her flighty brain. I asked myself whether she had not simply been making fun of me by her empty and would-be serious chatter, which told me nothing about her, nor of any real facts connected with her life.

"And I thought of the conquered race, among whom our race has encamped, or, rather, who are camping among us, whose language we are beginning to speak, whom we see every day, living under the transparent linen of their tents—a race on whom we have imposed our laws, our regulations, and our customs, about whom we know nothing, nothing more whatever, I assure you, than if we had not been here, and solely occupied in looking at them, for nearly sixty years. We know no more about what is going on in those huts made of branches, and under those small canvas cones fastened to the ground by stakes, within twenty yards of our doors, than we know what the so-called civilized Arabs of the Moorish houses in Algiers do, think, and are. Behind the whitewashed walls of their town houses, behind the partitions of their *gourbis,* made of branches, or behind that thin, brown, camel-hair curtain which the wind moves, they live close to us, unknown, mysterious, cunning, submissive, smiling, impenetrable. What if I were to tell you that when I look at the neighboring encampment through my field glasses, I surmise that there are superstitions, customs, ceremonies, a thousand practices, of which we know nothing, and which we do not even suspect! Never previously, in all probability, did a conquered race escape so completely from the real domination, the moral influence, and the inveterate, but useless, investigations of the conquerors.

"I now suddenly felt the insurmountable, secret barrier which incomprehensible nature had set up between the two races, felt it more than ever before, between this girl and myself, between this woman who had just given herself to me, who had yielded herself to my caresses, and, thinking of it for the first time, I said to her: 'What is your name?'

"She did not speak for some moments. I saw her start, as if she had forgotten that I was there, and then, in her eyes, which were raised to mine, I saw that that moment had sufficed for her to be overcome by sleep, by irresistible, sudden, almost overwhelming sleep, like everything that lays hold of the mobile senses of women, and she answered, carelessly, suppressing a yawn:

" 'Allouma.'

" 'Do you want to go to sleep?'

" 'Yes,' she replied.

" 'Very well then, go to sleep!'

"She stretched herself out tranquilly by my side, lying on her stomach, with her forehead resting on her folded arms. I felt almost immediately that her fleeting, untutored thoughts were lulled in repose, while I began to ponder, as I lay by her side, and tried to understand it all. Why had Mohammed given her to me? Had he acted the part of a loyal servant, who sacrifices himself for his master, even to the extent of resigning the woman he had brought into his own tent, to him? Or had he, on the other hand, obeyed a more complex and more practical, though less generous, impulse, in handing over this girl who had taken my fancy to my use? An Arab, when it is a question of women, is rigorously modest and unspeakably complaisant, and you can no more understand his rigorous yet easy morality, than you can all the rest of his sentiments. Perhaps, when I accidentally went into his tent, I had merely forestalled the benevolent intentions of this thoughtful servant, who had intended this woman, who might be his friend and accomplice, or perhaps even his mistress, for me.

"All these suppositions assailed me, and fatigued me so much that, at last, in my turn, I fell into a profound sleep, from which I was roused by the creaking of my door. Mohammed had come in to call me as usual. He opened the window, through which a flood of light streamed in and fell on to Allouma, who was still asleep; then he picked up my trousers, coat, and waistcoat from the floor in order to brush them. He did not look at the woman who was lying by my side, did not seem to know or to remark that she was there, preserving his ordinary gravity, demeanor, and looks. But the light, the movement, the slight noise which his bare feet made, the feeling of the fresh air on her skin and in her lungs, roused Allouma from her lethargy. She stretched out her arms, turned over, opened her eyes, and looked at me and then Mohammed with the same indifference; then she sat up and said: 'I am hungry.'

" 'What would you like?'

" 'Kahoua.'

" 'Coffee and bread and butter?'

" 'Yes.'

"Mohammed remained standing close to the bed, with my clothes under his arm, waiting for my orders.

" 'Bring breakfast for Allouma and me,' I said to him.

"He went out, without his face betraying the slightest astonishment or anger, and as soon as he had left the room, I said to the girl:

" 'Will you live in my house?'

" 'I should like to, very much.'

" 'I will give you a room to yourself and a woman to wait on you.'

" 'You are very generous, and I am grateful to you.'

" 'But if you behave badly, I shall send you away immediately.'

" 'I will do everything that you wish me to.'

"She took my hand and kissed it as a token of submission, and just then Mohammed came in carrying a tray with our breakfast on it. I said to him:

" 'Allouma is going to live here. You must spread a carpet on the floor of the room at the end of the passage, and get Abd-el-Kader-el-Hadara's wife to come and wait on her.'

" 'Yes, *mo'ssieuia*.'

"That was all. An hour later, my beautiful Arab was installed in a large, airy, light room, and when I went in to see that everything was in order, she asked me in a supplicating voice, to give her a wardrobe with a looking-glass in the doors. I promised her one, and then I left her squatting on the carpet from Djebel-Amour, with a cigarette in her mouth, and gossiping with the old Arab woman I had sent for, as if they had known each other for years."

CHAPTER II

"For a month I was very happy with her, and got strangely attached to this creature of another race, who seemed to me to belong to some other species, and to have been born on a neighboring planet.

"I did not love her; no, one does not love the women of that primitive continent. The small, pale blue flower of Northern countries never unfolds between them and us, or even between them and their natural counterparts, the Arabs. They are too near to human animalism, their hearts are too rudimentary, their feelings are not refined enough to rouse that sentimental exaltation in us which is the poetry of love. Nothing intellectual, no intoxication of thought or of feeling is mingled with that sensual desire which those charming nonentities excite in us. Nevertheless, they captivate us like the others do, but in different fashion, less tenacious, and, at the same time, less cruel and painful.

"I cannot even now explain precisely what I felt for her. I said to you just now that this country, this bare land of Africa, without any arts, void of all intellectual pleasures, gradually captivates us by its climate, by the continual mildness of the dawn and sunset, by its delightful light, and by the feeling of absolute health with which it fills our organs. Well, then! Allouma captivated me in the same manner, by a thousand hidden, physical, alluring charms, and by the procreative seductiveness, not of her embraces, for she was of thoroughly oriental supineness in that respect, but of her sweet self-surrender.

"I left her absolutely free to come and go as she liked, and she certainly spent one afternoon out of two with the wives of my native agricultural laborers. Often also, she would remain for nearly a whole day admiring herself in front of a mahogany wardrobe with a large looking-glass in its doors, that I had got from Miliana.

"She examined herself with serious care, standing before the glass doors and following her own movements with profound and serious attention. She walked with her head somewhat thrown back, in order to be able to see whether her hips and loins swayed properly; went away, came back again, and then, tired with her own movements, sat down on a cushion opposite to her own reflection, with her eyes fixed on her face in the glass and her whole soul absorbed in that picture.

"Soon, I began to notice that she went out nearly every morning after breakfast, and that she disappeared altogether until evening. As I felt rather anxious about this, I asked Mohammed whether he knew what she could be doing during all those long hours of absence—but he replied very calmly:

" 'Do not be uneasy. It will be the Feast of Ramadan[12] soon, and so she goes to say her prayers.'

"He seemed delighted at having Allouma in the house, but I never once saw anything suspicious between them. So I accepted the situation as it was, and let time, accident, and life act for themselves.

"Often, after I had inspected my farm, my vineyards, and my clearings, I used to take long walks. You know the magnificent forests there are in this part of Algeria, and those almost impenetrable ravines, where fallen pine-trees dam the mountain torrents, and yet again those little valleys filled with oleanders, which look like oriental carpets stretching along the banks of the streams. You know that now and again in these woods and on these hills, where you would think the foot of man had never penetrated, you suddenly see the white dome of a shrine that contains the bones of a humble, solitary Marabout.

"Now one evening as I was going home, I passed one of these

Mohammedan chapels, and looking in through the door, which is always open, I saw a woman praying before the altar—an Arab woman, sitting on the ground in that dilapidated building, into which the wind entered as it pleased, heaping up the fine, dry pine needles in yellow heaps in the corners. I went near to see better and recognized Allouma. She neither saw nor heard me, so absorbed was she with the saint, to whom she was speaking in a low voice. She thought that she was alone with him, and was telling this servant of God all her troubles. Sometimes she stopped for a moment to think, trying to recollect what more she had to say, so that she might not forget anything that she wished to confide to him. Then, again, she would grow animated, as if he had replied to her, as if he had advised her to do something that she did not want to do, and the reasons for which she was impugning. I went away as I had come, without making any noise, and returned home to dinner.

"That evening, when I sent for her, I saw that she had a thoughtful look, which was not usual with her.

" 'Sit down there,' I said, pointing to her place on the couch by my side. As soon as she had sat down, I stooped to kiss her, but she drew her head away quickly, and, in great astonishment, I said to her:

" 'Well, what is the matter?'

" 'It is the Ramadan,' she replied.

"I began to laugh, and said: 'And the Marabout has forbidden you to allow yourself to be kissed during the Ramadan?'

" 'Oh, yes; I am an Arab woman, and you are a Roumi!' *

" 'And it would be a great sin?'

" 'Oh, yes!'

" 'So you ate nothing all day, until sunset?'

" 'No, nothing.'

" 'But you had something to eat after sundown?'

" 'Yes.'

" 'Well, then, as it is quite dark now, you ought not to be more strict about the rest than you are about your food.'

---

* That is, a European, not a Muslim (*Roumi* is Arabic for "Roman").

"She seemed irritated, wounded, and offended, and replied with an amount of pride that I had never noticed in her before:

" 'If an Arab girl were to allow herself to be kissed by a Roumi during the Ramadan, she would be cursed forever.'

" 'And that is to continue for a whole month?'

" 'Yes, for the whole of the month of Ramadan,' she replied, with great determination.

"I assumed an irritated manner and said: 'Very well, then, you can go and spend the Ramadan with your family.'

"She seized my hands, and, laying them on her heart, she said:

" 'Oh! Please do not be unkind, and you shall see how nice I will be. We will keep Ramadan together, if you like. I will look after you, and spoil you, but don't be unkind.'

"I could not help smiling at her funny manner and her unhappiness. I sent her to sleep at home, but, an hour later, just as I was thinking about going to bed, there came two little taps at my door, so slight, however, that I scarcely heard them. When I said, 'Come in,' Allouma appeared carrying a large tray covered with Arab dainties—fried balls of rice, covered with sugar, and a variety of other strange, nomad pastry.

"She laughed, showing her white teeth, and repeated: 'Come, we will keep Ramadan together.'

"You know that the fast, which begins at dawn and ends at twilight, at the moment the eye can no longer distinguish a black from a white thread, is followed every evening by small, friendly entertainments, at which eating is kept up until the morning. The result is that for such of the natives as are not very scrupulous, Ramadan consists of turning day into night, and night into day. But Allouma carried her delicacy of conscience further than this. She placed her tray between us on the divan, and taking a small, sugared ball between her long, slender fingers, she put it into my mouth, and whispered: 'Eat it, it is very good.'

"I munched the light cake, which was really excellent, and asked her: 'Did you make that?'

" 'Yes.'

" 'For me?'

" 'Yes, for you.'

" 'To enable me to support Ramadan?'

" 'Oh! Don't be so unkind! I will bring you some every day.'

"Oh! the terrible month that I spent! A sugared, insipidly sweet month; a month that nearly drove me mad; a month of spoiling and of temptation, of anger and of vain efforts against an invincible resistance. But at last the three days of Beiram came, which I celebrated in my own fashion, and Ramadan was forgotten.

"The summer went on, and it was very hot. In the first days of autumn, Allouma appeared to me to be preoccupied and absent-minded, and seemingly took no interest in anything. At last, when I sent for her one evening, she was not to be found in her room. I thought that she was roaming about the house, and I gave orders to look for her. She had not come in, however, and so I opened my window, and called out:

" 'Mohammed,' and the voice of the man, who was in his tent, replied:

" 'Yes, *mo'ssieuia*.'

" 'Do you know where Allouma is?'

" 'No, *mo'ssieuia*—it is not possible—is Allouma lost?'

"A few moments later, my Arab came into my room so agitated that he could not master his feelings, and I said:

" 'Is Allouma lost?'

" 'Yes, she is lost.'

" 'It is impossible. Go and look for her,' I said.

"He remained standing where he was, thinking, seeking for her motives, and unable to understand anything about it. Then he went into the empty room, where Allouma's clothes were lying about in oriental disorder. He examined everything, as if he had been a police officer, or, rather, he scented them like a dog, and then, incapable of any lengthened effort, he murmured, resignedly:

" 'She has gone, she has gone!'

"I was afraid that some accident had happened to her; that she had fallen into some ravine and sprained herself, and I immediately sent all the men about the place off with orders to look for her until they should find her. They hunted for her all that night, all the next day, and all the week long, but nothing was discovered that could put us upon her track. I suffered, for I missed her very much; my house seemed empty, and my existence a void. And then, disgusting thoughts entered my mind. I feared that she might have been carried off, or even murdered; but when I spoke about it to Mohammed, and tried to make him share my fears, he invariably replied:

" 'No; gone away.'

"Then he added the Arab word *r'ezale*, which means gazelle, as if he meant to say that she could run quickly, and that she was far away.

"Three weeks passed, and I had given up all hopes of seeing my Arab mistress again, when one morning Mohammed came into my room, with every sign of joy in his face, and said to me:

" '*Mo'ssieuia*, Allouma has come back.'

"I jumped out of bed and said:

" 'Where is she?'

" 'She does not dare to come in! There she is, under the tree.'

"And stretching out his arm, he pointed out to me, through the window, a whitish spot at the foot of an olive-tree.

"I got up immediately, and went out to where she was. As I approached what looked like a mere bundle of linen thrown against the gnarled trunk of the tree, I recognized the large, dark eyes, the tattooed stars, and the long, regular features of that semi-wild girl who had so captivated my senses. As I advanced toward her, I felt inclined to strike her, to make her suffer—to have revenge, and so I called out to her from a little distance:

" 'Where have you been?'

"She did not reply, but remained motionless and inert, as if scarcely alive, resigned to my violence, and ready to receive my blows. I was standing up close to her, looking in stupefaction at the rags with which she was covered, at those bits of silk and muslin, covered with dust, torn and dirty, and I repeated, raising my hand, as if she had been a dog:

" 'Where have you come from?'

" 'From yonder,' she said, in a whisper.

" 'Where is that?'

" 'From the tribe.'

" 'What tribe?'

" 'Mine.'

" 'Why did you go away?'

"When she saw that I was not going to beat her, she grew rather bolder, and said in a low voice:

" 'I was obliged to do it. I was forced to go, I could not stop in the house any longer.'

"I saw tears in her eyes, and immediately felt softened. I leaned over her, and when I turned round to sit down, I noticed Mohammed, who was watching us at a distance, and I went on, very gently:

" 'Come, tell me why you ran away?'

"Then she told me that for a long time in her nomad's heart she had felt the irresistible desire to return to the tents, to lie, to run, to roll on the sand; to wander about the plains with the flocks, to feel nothing over her head between the yellow stars in the sky and the blue stars in her face, except the thin, threadbare, patched stuff, through which she could see spots of fire in the sky, when she awoke during the night.

"She made me understand all that in such simple and powerful words, that I felt quite sure that she was not lying, and pitied her, and I asked her:

" 'Why did you not tell me that you wished to go away for a time?'

" 'Because you would not have allowed me.'

" 'If you had promised to come back, I should have consented.'

" 'You would not have believed me.'

"Seeing that I was not angry, she began to laugh, and said:

" 'You see that is all over; I have come home again, and here I am. I only wanted a few days there. I have had enough of it now, it is finished and passed; the feeling is cured. I have come back, and have not that longing any more. I am very glad, and you are very kind.'

" 'Come into the house,' I said to her.

"She got up, and I took her hand, her delicate hand, with its slender fingers, and triumphant in her rags, with her bracelets and her necklace ringing, she went gravely toward my house, where Mohammed was waiting for us. But before going in, I said:

" 'Allouma, whenever you want to return to your own people, tell me, and I will allow you to go.'

" 'You promise?'

" 'Yes, I promise.'

" 'And I will make you a promise also. When I feel ill or unhappy'—and here she put her hand to her forehead, with a magnificent gesture—'I shall say to you: "I must go yonder," and you will let me go.'

"I went with her to her room, followed by Mohammed who was carrying some water, for there had been no time to tell the wife of Abd-el-Kader-el-Hadara that her mistress had returned. As soon as she got into the room, and saw the wardrobe with the looking-glass in the door, she ran up to it, like a child does when it sees its mother. She looked at herself for a few seconds, made a grimace, and then, in a rather cross voice, she said to the looking-glass:

" 'Just you wait a moment; I have some silk dresses in the wardrobe. I shall be beautiful in a few minutes.'

"And I left her alone, to act the coquette to herself.

"Our life began its usual course again, and I felt more and more under the influence of the strange, merely physical attractions of the girl, for whom, at the same time, I felt a kind of paternal contempt. For two months all went well, and then I felt that she was again becoming nervous, agitated, and low-spirited. So one day I said to her:

" 'Do you want to return home again?'

" 'Yes.'

" 'And you did not dare to tell me?'

" 'I did not venture to.'

" 'Go, if you wish to; I give you leave.'

"She seized my hands and kissed them, as she did in all her outbursts of gratitude, and the same morning she disappeared.

"She came back, as she had come the first time, at the end of about three weeks, in rags, covered with dust, and satiated with her nomad life of sand and liberty. In two years she returned to her own people four times in this fashion.

"I took her back, gladly, without any feelings of jealousy, for with me jealousy can only spring from love, as we Europeans understand it. I might very likely have killed her if I had surprised her in the act of deceiving me, but I should have done it just as one half kills a disobedient dog, from sheer violence. I should not have felt those torments, that consuming fire—Northern jealousy. I have just said that I should have killed her like a disobedient dog, and, as a matter of fact, I loved her somewhat in the same manner as one loves some very highly bred horse or dog, which it is impossible to replace. She was a splendid animal, a sensual animal, an animal made for pleasure in the shape of a woman.

"I cannot tell you what an immeasurable distance separated our two souls, although our hearts perhaps occasionally warmed toward each other. She was something belonging to my house, she was part of my life, she had become an agreeable and regular requirement with me, to which I clung, and which the sensual man in me loved.

"Well, one morning, Mohammed came into my room with a strange look on his face, that uneasy look of the Arabs, which resembles the furtive look of a cat face to face with a dog, and when I noticed his expression, I said:

" 'What is the matter, now?'

" 'Allouma has gone away.'

"I began to laugh, and said: 'Where has she gone to?'

" 'Gone away altogether, *mo'ssieuia!*'

" 'What do you mean by *gone away altogether?* You are mad, my man.'

" 'No, *mo'ssieuia.*'

" 'Why has she gone away? Just explain yourself; come!'

"He remained motionless, and evidently did not wish to speak; then he had one of those explosions of Arab rage which make us stop in streets in front of two demoniacs, whose oriental silence and gravity suddenly give place to the most violent gesticulations and the most ferocious vociferations. I gathered, amid his shouts, that Allouma had run away with my shepherd, and when I had partially succeeded in calming him, I managed to extract the facts, one by one.

"It was a long story, but at last I gathered that he had been watching my mistress, who used to meet a sort of vagabond, whom my steward had hired the month before, behind the neighboring cactus woods, or in the ravine where the oleanders flourished. The night before, Mohammed had seen her go out without seeing her return, and he repeated, in an exasperated manner: 'Gone, mo'ssieuia; she has gone away!'

"I do not know why, but his conviction, the conviction that she had run away with this vagabond, laid hold of me irresistibly in a moment. It was absurd—unlikely, and yet certain in virtue of that very unreasonableness which constitutes feminine logic.

"Boiling over with indignation, I tried to recall the man's features, and I suddenly remembered having seen him the previous week, standing on a mound amid his flock, and watching me. He was a tall Bedouin, the color of whose bare limbs was blended with that of his rags; he was a type of a barbarous nomad, with high cheek-bones, and hooked nose, a retreating chin, thin legs, and a lean body in rags, with the shifty eyes of a jackal.

"I did not doubt for a moment that she had run away with that beggar. Why? Because she was Allouma, a daughter of the desert. A girl from the pavement in Paris would have run away with my coachman, or some thief in the suburbs.

" 'Very well,' I said to Mohammed. Then I got up, opened my window, and began to draw in the stifling south wind, for the sirocco was blowing, and I thought to myself:

" 'Good heavens! she is a woman, like so many others. Does anybody know what makes them act, what makes them love, what makes them follow, or throw over a man? You certainly do know occasionally; but often you don't, and sometimes you are in doubt. Why did she run away with that repulsive brute? Why? Perhaps, because the wind had been blowing regularly from the south for a month; that was enough; a breath of wind! Does *she* know, do *they* know, even the cleverest of them, why they act? No more than a weathercock that turns with the wind. An imperceptible breeze makes the iron, brass, zinc, or wooden arrow revolve, just in the same manner as some imperceptible influence, some undiscernible impression, moves the female heart and urges it on to resolutions, no matter whether it belongs to town or country, to the suburbs, or to the desert.

" 'They can then feel, provided that they reason and understand, why they have done one thing rather than another, but, for the moment, they do not know. They are the playthings of their own feelings, the thoughtless, giddy-headed slaves of events, of surroundings, of chance meetings, and of all the sensations with which their soul and their body tremble!' "

Monsieur Auballe had risen, and, after walking up and down the room once or twice, he looked at me, and said, with a smile:

"That is love in the desert!"

"Suppose she were to come back?" I asked him.

"Horrid girl!" he replied. "But I should be very glad if she did return to me."

"And you would pardon the shepherd?"

"Good heavens, yes! With women, one must always pardon—or else pretend not to see things."

THE RENDEZVOUS

Although she had her bonnet and jacket on, with a black veil over her face, and another in her pocket, which would be put on over the other as soon as she had got into a cab, she was tapping the top of her little boot with the point of her parasol, and remained sitting in her room, unable to make up her mind to keep this appointment.

And yet how many times within the last two years had she dressed herself thus, when she knew that her husband would be on the Stock Exchange, in order to go to the bachelor chambers of handsome Viscount de Martelet.

The clock behind her was ticking loudly, a book which she had half read was lying open on a little rosewood writing-table, between the windows, and a strong sweet smell of violets from two bunches in Dresden china vases mingled with a vague smell of verbena which came through the half-open door of her dressing-room.

The clock struck three, she rose up from her chair, turned round to look at herself in the glass and smiled. "He is already waiting for me, and will be getting tired."

Then she left the room, told her footman that she would be back in an hour, at the latest—which was a lie—went downstairs, and ventured into the street on foot.

It was toward the end of May, that delightful time of the year when spring seems to be besieging Paris, flowing over its roofs, invading its houses through their walls, and making the city look gay, shedding brightness over its granite *façades*, the asphalt of its pavements, the stones on its streets, bathing and intoxicating it with new life, like a forest putting on its spring vesture.

Madame Haggan went a few steps to the right, intending, as usual, to go along the Parade Provence, where she would hail a cab. But the soft air, that feeling of summer which penetrates our breasts on some days, now took possession of her so suddenly that she changed her mind and went down the Rue de la Chaussée d'Antin, without knowing why, but vaguely attracted by a desire to see the trees in the Place de la Trinité.

"He may just wait ten minutes longer for me," she said to herself. And the idea pleased her as she walked slowly through the crowd. She fancied that she saw him growing impatient, looking at the clock, opening the window, listening at the door, sitting down for a few moments, getting up again, not daring to smoke, as she had forbidden him to do so when she was coming to him, and throwing despairing looks at his box of cigarettes.

She walked slowly, interested in what she saw, the shops and the people she met, walking slower and slower, and so little eager to get to her destination, that she only sought for some pretext for stopping. At the end of the street, in the little square, the green lawns attracted her so much that she went in, took a chair, and, sitting down, watched the hands of the clock as they moved.

Just then, the half hour struck, and her heart beat with pleasure when she heard the chimes. She had gained half-an-hour, then it would take her a quarter of an hour to reach the Rue de Miromesnil, and a few minutes more in strolling along—an hour! a whole hour saved from her rendezvous! She would not stop three-quarters of an hour, and that business would be finished once more.

She disliked going there as a patient dislikes going to the dentist. She had an intolerable recollection of all their past meetings, one a week on an average, for the last two years; and the thought that another was to take place immediately made her shiver with misery from head to foot. Not that it was exactly painful, like a visit to the dentist, but it was wearisome, so wearisome, so complicated, so long, so unpleasant, that anything, even a visit to the dentist, would have seemed preferable to her.

She went on, however, but very slowly, stopping, sitting down, going hither and thither, but she went. Oh! how she would have liked to miss this meeting, but she had left the unhappy Viscount in the lurch, twice running, during the last month, and she did not dare to do it again so soon. Why did she go to see him? Oh! why? Because she had acquired the habit of doing it, and had no reason to give poor Martelet when he wanted to know *the why!* Why had she begun it? Why? She did not know herself, any longer. Had she been in love with him? Very possibly! Not very much, but a little, a long time ago! He was very nice, much sought after, perfectly dressed, most courteous, and after the first glance, he was a perfect lover for a fashionable woman.

He had courted her for three months—the normal period, an honorable strife and sufficient resistance—and then she had consented. What emotion, what nervousness, what terrible, delightful fear, attended that first meeting in his small, ground-floor bachelor rooms, in the Rue de Miromesnil. Her heart? What did her little heart of a woman who had been seduced, vanquished, conquered, feel when she for the first time entered the door of the house which was her nightmare? She really did not know! She had quite forgotten. One remembers a fact, a date, a thing, but one hardly remembers, after the lapse of two years, what an emotion, which soon vanished because it was very slight, was like. But she had certainly not forgotten the others, that rosary of meetings, that road to the cross of love and its stations, which were so monotonous, so fatiguing, so similar to each other, that she felt nauseated.

The very cabs were not like the other cabs which you use for ordinary purposes! Certainly, the cabmen guessed. She felt sure of it, by the very way they looked at her, and the eyes of these Paris cabmen are terrible! When you realize that these jehus constantly identify in the Courts of Justice, after a lapse of several years, the faces of criminals whom they have only driven once, in the middle of the night, from some street or other to a railway station, and that they carry daily almost as many passengers as there are hours in the day, and that their memory is good enough for them to declare: "That is the man whom I took up in the Rue des Martyrs, and put down at the Lyons Railway Station, at 12 o'clock at night, on July 10, last year!" Is it not terrible to risk what a young woman risks when she is going to meet her lover, and has to trust her reputation to the first cabman she meets? In two years she had employed at least one hundred or more of them in that drive to the Rue de Miromesnil, reckoning only one a week. They were so many witnesses, who might appear against her at a critical moment.

As soon as she was in the cab, she took another veil, as thick and dark as a domino mask, out of her pocket, and put it on. That hid her face, but what about the rest, her dress, her bonnet, and her parasol? They might be remarked—they might, in fact, have been seen already. Oh! What misery she endured in this Rue de Miromesnil! She thought she recognized the foot-passengers, the servants, everybody, and almost before the cab had stopped, she jumped out and ran past the porter who was standing outside his lodge. He must know everything, everything!—her address, her name, her husband's profession,—everything, for those porters are the most cunning of policemen! For two years she had intended to bribe him, to give him (to throw at him one day as she passed him) a hundred franc bank-note, but she had never dared to do it. She was frightened. What of? She did not know! Of his calling her back, if he did not understand? Of a scandal? Of a crowd on the stairs? Of being arrested, perhaps? To reach the Viscount's door, she had only to ascend half a flight of stairs, but it seemed to her as high as the tower of Saint Jacques's Church.

As soon as she had reached the vestibule, she felt as if she were caught in a trap. The slightest noise before or behind her nearly made her faint. It was impossible for her to go back, because of that porter who barred her retreat; and if anyone came down at that moment she would not dare to ring at Martelet's door, but would pass it as if she had been going elsewhere! She would have gone up, and up, and up! She would have mounted forty flights of stairs! Then, when everything seemed quiet again down below, she would run down feeling terribly frightened, lest she should not recognize the apartment.

He would be there in a velvet coat lined with silk, very stylish, but rather ridiculous, and for two years he had never altered his manner of receiving her, not in a single movement! As soon as he had shut the door he used to say: "Let me kiss your hands, my dear, dear friend!" Then he would follow her into the room, where with closed shutters and lighted candles, out of refinement, no doubt, he would kneel down before her and look at her from head to foot with an air of adoration. On the first occasion that had been very nice and very successful; but now it seemed to her as if she saw Monsieur Delaunay acting the last scene of a successful piece for the hundred and twentieth time. He might really change his manner of acting. But no, he never altered his manner of acting, poor fellow. What a good fellow he was, but so commonplace!

And how difficult it was to undress and dress without a lady's maid! Perhaps that was the moment when she began to take a dislike to him. When he said: "Do you want me to help you?" she could have killed him. Certainly there were not many men as awkward as he was, or as uninteresting. Certainly little Baron de Isombal would never have asked her in such a manner: "Do you want me to help you?" He would have helped her, he was so witty, so funny, so active. But there! He was a diplomatist, he had been about in the world, and had roamed everywhere, and, no doubt, had dressed and undressed women arrayed in every possible fashion!

The church clock struck the three-quarters. She looked at the dial, and said: "Oh, how anxious he will be!" and then she quickly left the square. But she had not taken a dozen steps outside, when she found herself face to face with a gentleman who bowed profoundly to her.

"Why! Is that you, Baron?" she said, in surprise. She had just been thinking of him.

"Yes, madame." And then, after asking how she was, he continued: "Do you know that you are the only one—you will allow me to say of my lady friends, I hope—who has not yet seen my Japanese collection?"[13]

"But, my dear Baron, a lady cannot go to a bachelor's room like this."

"What do you mean? That is a great mistake, when it is a question of seeing a rare collection!"

"At any rate, she cannot go alone."

"And why not? I have received a number of ladies alone, only for the sake of seeing my collection! They come every day. Shall I tell you their names? No—I will not do that, one must be discreet, even when one is not guilty. As a matter of fact, there is nothing improper in going to the house of a well-known seriously minded man who holds a certain position, unless one goes for an improper reason!"

"Well, what you have said is certainly correct, at bottom."

"So you will come and see my collection?"

"When?"

"Well, now, immediately."

"Impossible, I am in a hurry."

"Nonsense, you have been sitting in the square for this last half hour."

"You were watching me?"

"I was looking at you."

"But I am sadly in a hurry."

"I am sure you are not. Confess that you are in no particular hurry."

Madame Haggan began to laugh, and said: "Well, no—not very."

A cab passed close by them, and the little Baron called out: "Cabman!" The vehicle stopped, and opening the door, he said: "Get in, madame."

"But, Baron! No, it is impossible to-day; I really cannot."

"Madame, you are acting very imprudently. Get in! People are beginning to look at us, and you will collect a crowd; they will think I am trying to carry you off, and we shall both be arrested; please get in!"

She got in, frightened and bewildered, and he sat down by her side, saying to the cabman: "Rue de Provence."

But suddenly she exclaimed: "Good heavens! I have forgotten a very important telegram; please drive to the nearest telegraph office first of all."

The cab stopped a little farther on, in the Rue de Châteaudun, and she said to the Baron: "Would you kindly get me a fifty-centimes telegraph form? I promised my husband to invite Martelet to dinner tomorrow, and had quite forgotten it."

When the Baron returned and gave her the blue telegraph form, she wrote in a pencil:

> "My dear friend, I am not at all well. I am suffering terribly from neuralgia, which keeps me in bed. Impossible to go out. Come and dine to-morrow night, so that I may obtain my pardon.
>
> "Jeanne."

She wetted the gum, fastened it carefully, and addressed it to "Viscount de Martelet, 240 Rue de Miromesnil," and then, giving it back to the Baron, she said: "Now, will you be kind enough to throw this into the telegram box?"

USELESS BEAUTY

CHAPTER I

A VERY ELEGANT VICTORIA,* with two beautiful black horses, was drawn up in front of the mansion. It was a day in the latter end of June, about half past five in the afternoon, and the sun shone warm and bright into the large courtyard.

The Countess de Mascaret came down just as her husband, who was coming home, appeared in the carriage entrance. He stopped for a few moments to look at his wife and grew rather pale. She was very beautiful, graceful, and distinguished looking, with her long oval face, her complexion like gilt ivory, her large gray eyes, and her black hair; and she got into her carriage without looking at him, without even seeming to have noticed him, with such a particularly high-bred air, that the furious jealousy by which he had been devoured for so long again gnawed at his heart. He went up to her and said: "You are going for a drive?"

She merely replied disdainfully: "You see I am!"

"In the Bois de Boulogne?"

"Most probably."

"May I come with you?"

"The carriage belongs to you."

Without being surprised at the tone of voice in which she answered him, he got in and sat down by his wife's side, and said: "Bois de Boulogne." The footman jumped up by the coachman's side, and the horses as usual pawed the ground and shook their heads until they

---

*Four-wheeled carriage.

were in the street. Husband and wife sat side by side, without speaking. He was thinking how to begin a conversation, but she maintained such an obstinately hard look, that he did not venture to make the attempt. At last, however, he cunningly, accidentally as it were, touched the Countess's gloved hand with his own, but she drew her arm away, with a movement which was so expressive of disgust, that he remained thoughtful, in spite of his usual authoritative and despotic character. "Gabrielle!" said he at last.

"What do you want?"

"I think you are looking adorable."

She did not reply, but remained lying back in the carriage, looking like an irritated queen. By that time they were driving up the Champs-Elysées, toward the Arc de Triomphe. That immense monument, at the end of the long avenue, raised its colossal arch against the red sky, and the sun seemed to be sinking on to it, showering fiery dust on it from the sky.

The streams of carriages, with the sun reflecting from the bright, plated harness and the shining lamps, were like a double current flowing, one toward the town and one toward the wood, and the Count de Mascaret continued: "My dear Gabrielle!"

Then, unable to bear it any longer, she replied in an exasperated voice: "Oh! do leave me in peace, pray; I am not even at liberty to have my carriage to myself, now." He, however, pretended not to hear her, and continued: "You have never looked so pretty as you do to-day."

Her patience was decidedly at an end, and she replied with irrepressible anger: "You are wrong to notice it, for I swear to you that I will never have anything to do with you in that way again." He was stupefied and agitated, and his violent nature gaining the upper hand, he exclaimed: "What do you mean by that?" in such a manner as revealed rather the brutal master than the amorous man. But she replied in a low voice, so that the servants might not hear, amid the deafening noise of the wheels:

"Ah! What do I mean by that? What do I mean by that? Now I recognize you again! Do you want me to tell everything?"

"Yes."

"Everything that has been on my heart, since I have been the victim of your terrible selfishness?"

He had grown red with surprise and anger, and he growled between his closed teeth: "Yes, tell me everything."

He was a tall, broad-shouldered man, with a big, red beard, a handsome man, a nobleman, a man of the world, who passed as a perfect husband and an excellent father, and now for the first time since they had started she turned toward him, and looked him full in the face: "Ah! You will hear some disagreeable things, but you must know that I am prepared for everything, that I fear nothing, and you less than anyone, to-day."

He also was looking into her eyes, and already was shaking with passion; then he said in a low voice: "You are mad."

"No, but I will no longer be the victim of the hateful penalty of maternity, which you have inflicted on me for eleven years! I wish to live like a woman of the world, as I have the right to do, as all women have the right to do."

He suddenly grew pale again, and stammered: "I do not understand you."

"Oh! yes; you understand me well enough. It is now three months since I had my last child, and as I am still very beautiful, and as, in spite of all your efforts you cannot spoil my figure, as you just now perceived, when you saw me on the outside flight of steps, you think it is time that I should become *enceinte* again."

"But you are talking nonsense!"

"No, I am not; I am thirty, and I have had seven children, and we have been married eleven years, and you hope that this will go on for ten years longer, after which you will leave off being jealous."

He seized her arm and squeezed it, saying: "I will not allow you to talk to me like that, for long."

"And I shall talk to you till the end, until I have finished all I have to say to you, and if you try to prevent me, I shall raise my voice so that the two servants, who are on the box, may hear. I only allowed you to come with me for that object, for I have these witnesses, who will oblige you to listen to me, and to contain yourself; so now, pay attention to what I say. I have always felt an antipathy for you, and I have always let you see it, for I have never lied, Monsieur. You married me in spite of myself; you forced my parents, who were in embarrassed circumstances, to give me to you, because you were rich, and they obliged me to marry you, in spite of my tears.

"So you bought me, and as soon as I was in your power, as soon as I had become your companion, ready to attach myself to you, to forget your coercive and threatening proceedings, in order that I might only remember that I ought to be a devoted wife and to love you as much as it might be possible for me to love you, you became jealous—you—as no man has ever been before, with the base, ignoble jealousy of a spy, which was as degrading for you as it was for me. I had not been married eight months, when you suspected me of every perfidiousness, and you even told me so. What a disgrace! And as you could not prevent me from being beautiful, and from pleasing people, from being called in drawing-rooms, and also in the newspapers, one of the most beautiful women in Paris, you tried everything you could think of to keep admirers from me, and you hit upon the abominable idea of making me spend my life in a constant state of motherhood, until the time when I should disgust every man. Oh! do not deny it! I did not understand it for some time, but then I guessed it. You even boasted about it to your sister, who told me of it, for she is fond of me and was disgusted at your boorish coarseness.

"Ah! Remember our struggles, doors smashed in, and locks forced! For eleven years you have condemned me to the existence of a brood mare. Then as soon as I was pregnant, you grew disgusted with me, and I saw nothing of you for months, and I was sent into the country, to the family mansion, among fields and meadows, to bring forth my child. And when I reappeared, fresh, pretty, and indestructible, still seductive and constantly surrounded by admirers, hoping that at last I should live a little like a young rich woman who belongs to society, you were seized by jealousy again, and you recommenced to persecute me with that infamous and hateful desire from which you are suffering at this moment, by my side. And it is not the desire of possessing me—for I should never have refused myself to you—but it is the wish to make me unsightly.

"Besides this, that abominable and mysterious circumstance took place, which I was a long time in penetrating (but I grew acute by dint of watching your thoughts and actions). You attached yourself to your children with all the security which they gave you while I bore them in my womb. You felt affection for them, with all your aversion for me, and in spite of your ignoble fears, which were momentarily allayed by your pleasure in seeing me a mother.

"Oh! how often have I noticed that joy in you! I have seen it in your eyes and guessed it. You loved your children as victories, and not because they were of your own blood. They were victories over me, over my youth, over my beauty, over my charms, over the compliments which were paid me, and over those who whispered round me, without paying them to me. And you are proud of them, you make a parade of them, you take them out for drives in your coach in the Bois de Boulogne, and you give them donkey rides at Montmorency. You take them to theatrical matinées so that you may be seen in the midst of them, and that people may say: 'What a kind father!' and that it may be repeated."

He had seized her wrist with savage brutality, and squeezed it so violently that she was quiet, though she nearly cried out with the pain. Then he said to her in a whisper:

"I love my children, do you hear? What you have just told me is disgraceful in a mother. But you belong to me; I am master—your master. I can exact from you what I like and when I like—and I have the law on my side."

He was trying to crush her fingers in the strong grip of his large, muscular hand, and she, livid with pain, tried in vain to free them from that vise which was crushing them; the agony made her pant, and the tears came into her eyes. "You see that I am the master, and the stronger," he said. And when he somewhat loosened his grip, she asked him: "Do you think that I am a religious woman?"

He was surprised and stammered: "Yes."

"Do you think that I could lie, if I swore to the truth of anything to you, before an altar on which Christ's body is?"

"No."

"Will you go with me to some church?"

"What for?"

"You shall see. Will you?"

"If you absolutely wish it, yes."

She raised her voice and said: "Philip!" And the coachman, bending down a little, without taking his eyes from his horses, seemed to turn his ear alone toward his mistress, who said: "Drive to St. Philip-du-Roule's." And the victoria, which had reached the entrance of the Bois de Boulogne, returned to Paris.

Husband and wife did not exchange a word during the drive. When the carriage stopped before the church, Madame de Mascaret jumped out, and entered it, followed by the Count, a few yards behind her. She went, without stopping, as far as the choir-screen, and falling on her knees at a chair, she buried her face in her hands. She prayed for a long time, and he, standing behind her, could see that she was crying. She wept noiselessly, like women do weep when they are in great and poignant grief. There was a kind of undulation in her body, which ended in a little sob, hidden and stifled by her fingers.

But Count de Mascaret thought that the situation was long drawn out, and he touched her on the shoulder. That contact recalled her to herself, as if she had been burned, and getting up, she looked straight into his eyes.

"This is what I have to say to you. I am afraid of nothing, whatever you may do to me. You may kill me if you like. One of your children is not yours, and one only; that I swear to you before God, who hears me here. That is the only revenge which was possible for me, in return for all your abominable male tyrannies, in return for the penal servitude of childbearing to which you have condemned me. Who was my lover? That you will never know! You may suspect everyone, but you will never find out. I gave myself up to him, without love and without pleasure, only for the sake of betraying you, and he made me a mother. Which is his child? That also you will never know. I have seven; try and find out! I intended to tell you this later, for one cannot completely avenge oneself on a man by deceiving him, unless he knows it. You have driven me to confess it to-day; now I have finished."

She hurried through the church, toward the open door, expecting to hear behind her the quick steps of her husband whom she had de-fied, and to be knocked to the ground by a blow of his fist, but she heard nothing, and reached her carriage. She jumped into it at a bound, overwhelmed with anguish, and breathless with fear; she called out to the coachman, "Home!" and the horses set off at a quick trot.

CHAPTER II

THE COUNTESS DE MASCARET was waiting in her room for dinner time, like a criminal sentenced to death awaits the hour of his execu-tion. What was he going to do? Had he come home? Despotic, pas-sionate, ready for any violence as he was, what was he meditating, what had he made up his mind to do? There was no sound in the house, and every moment she looked at the clock. Her maid had come and dressed her for the evening, and had then left the room again. Eight o'clock struck; almost at the same moment there were two knocks at the door, and the butler came in and told her that dinner was ready.

"Has the Count come in?"

"Yes, Madame la Comtesse; he is in the dining-room."

For a moment she felt inclined to arm herself with a small revolver, which she had bought some weeks before, foreseeing the tragedy which was being rehearsed in her heart. But she remembered that all the children would be there, and she took nothing except a smelling-bottle. He rose somewhat ceremoniously from his chair. They ex-changed a slight bow, and sat down. The three boys, with their tutor, Abbé Martin, were on her right, and the three girls, with Miss Smith, their English governess, were on her left. The youngest child, who was only three months old, remained upstairs with his nurse.

The Abbé said grace, as was usual when there was no company, for the children did not come down to dinner when there were guests present; then they began dinner. The Countess, suffering from emotion which she had not at all calculated upon, remained with her eyes cast down, while the Count scrutinized, now the three boys, and now the three girls with uncertain, unhappy looks, which traveled from one to the other. Suddenly, pushing his wineglass from him, it broke, and the wine was spilt on the tablecloth, and at the slight noise caused by this little accident, the Countess started up from her chair, and for the first time they looked at each other. Then, almost every moment, in spite of themselves, in spite of the irritation of their nerves caused by every glance, they did not cease to exchange looks, rapid as pistol shots.

The Abbé, who felt that there was some cause for embarrassment which he could not divine, tried to get up a conversation, and started various subjects, but his useless efforts gave rise to no ideas and did not bring out a word. The Countess, with feminine tact and obeying the instincts of a woman of the world, tried to answer him two or three times, but in vain. She could not find words, in the perplexity of her mind, and her own voice almost frightened her in the silence of the large room, where nothing else was heard except the slight sound of plates and knives and forks.

Suddenly, her husband said to her, bending forward: "Here, amid your children, will you swear to me that what you told me just now is true?"

The hatred which was fermenting in her veins suddenly roused her, and replying to that question with the same firmness with which she had replied to his looks, she raised both her hands, the right pointing toward the boys and the left toward the girls, and said in a firm, resolute voice, and without any hesitation: "On the heads of my children, I swear that I have told you the truth."

He got up, and throwing his table napkin on to the table with an exasperated movement, turned round and flung his chair against the wall. Then he went out without another word, while she, uttering a deep sigh, as if after a first victory, went on in a calm voice: "You must not pay any attention to what your father has just said, my darlings; he was very much upset a short time ago, but he will be all right again, in a few days."

Then she talked with the Abbé and with Miss Smith, and had tender, pretty words for all her children; those sweet spoiling mother's ways which unlock little hearts.

When dinner was over, she went into the drawing-room with all her little following. She made the elder ones chatter, and when their bedtime came she kissed them for a long time, and then went alone into her room.

She waited, for she had no doubt that he would come, and she made up her mind then, as her children were not with her, to defend her human flesh, as she defended her life as a woman of the world; and in the pocket of her dress she put the little loaded revolver which she had bought a few weeks before. The hours went by, the hours struck, and every sound was hushed in the house. Only the cabs continued to rumble through the streets, but their noise was only heard vaguely through the shuttered and curtained windows.

She waited, energetic and nervous, without any fear of him now, ready for anything, and almost triumphant, for she had found means of torturing him continually, during every moment of his life.

But the first gleams of dawn came in through the fringe at the bottom of her curtains, without his having come into her room, and then she awoke to the fact, much to her surprise that he was not coming. Having locked and bolted her door, for greater security, she went to bed at last, and remained there, with her eyes open, thinking, and barely understanding it all, without being able to guess what he was going to do.

When her maid brought her tea, she at the same time gave her a letter from her husband. He told her that he was going to undertake a longish journey, and in a postscript he added that his lawyer would provide her with such money as she might require for her expenses.

CHAPTER III

It was at the opera, between two of the acts in "Robert the Devil."[14] In the stalls, the men were standing up, with their hats on, their waistcoats cut very low so as to show a large amount of white shirt front, in which the gold and precious stones of their studs glistened.

They were looking at the boxes crowded with ladies in low dresses, covered with diamonds and pearls, women who seemed to expand like flowers in that illuminated hothouse, where the beauty of their faces and the whiteness of their shoulders seemed to bloom for inspection, in the midst of the music and of human voices.

Two friends, with their backs to the orchestra, were scanning those parterres of elegance, that exhibition of real or false charms, of jewels, of luxury, and of pretension which showed itself off all round the Grand Theater. One of them, Roger de Salnis, said to his companion, Bernard Grandin: "Just look how beautiful Countess de Mascaret still is."

Then the elder, in turn, looked through his opera glasses at a tall lady in a box opposite, who appeared to be still very young, and whose striking beauty seemed to appeal to men's eyes in every corner of the house. Her pale complexion, of an ivory tint, gave her the appearance of a statue, while a small, diamond coronet glistened on her black hair like a cluster of stars.

When he had looked at her for some time, Bernard Grandin replied with a jocular accent of sincere conviction: "You may well call her beautiful!"

"How old do you think she is?"

"Wait a moment. I can tell you exactly, for I have known her since she was a child, and I saw her make her *début* into society when she was quite a girl. She is—she is—thirty—thirty-six."

"Impossible!"

"I am sure of it."

"She looks twenty-five."

"She has had seven children."

"It is incredible."

"And what is more, they are all seven alive, as she is a very good mother. I go to the house, which is a very quiet and pleasant one, occasionally, and she presents the phenomenon of the family in the midst of the world."

"How very strange! And have there never been any reports about her?"

"Never."

"But what about her husband? He is peculiar, is he not?"

"Yes and no. Very likely there has been a little drama between them, one of those little domestic dramas which one suspects, which one never finds out exactly, but which one guesses pretty nearly."

"What is it?"

"I do not know anything about it. Mascaret leads a very fast life now, after having been a model husband. As long as he remained a good spouse, he had a shocking temper and was crabbed and easily took offense, but since he has been leading his present, rackety life, he has become quite indifferent; but one would guess that he has some trouble, a worm gnawing somewhere, for he has aged very much."

Thereupon the two friends talked philosophically for some minutes about the secret, unknowable troubles, which differences of character or perhaps physical antipathies, which were not perceived at first, give rise to in families. Then Roger de Salnis, who was still looking at Madame de Mascaret through his opera-glasses, said:

"It is almost incredible that that woman has had seven children!"

"Yes, in eleven years; after which, when she was thirty, she put a stop to her period of production in order to enter into the brilliant period of entertaining, which does not seem near coming to an end."

"Poor women!"

"Why do you pity them?"

"Why? Ah! my dear fellow, just consider! Eleven years of maternity, for such a woman! What a hell! All her youth, all her beauty, every hope of success, every poetical ideal of a bright life, sacrificed to that abominable law of reproduction which turns the normal woman into a mere machine for maternity."

"What would you have? It is only nature!"

"Yes, but I say that Nature is our enemy, that we must always fight against Nature, for she is continually bringing us back to an animal state. You may be sure that God has not put anything on this earth that is clean, pretty, elegant, or accessory to our ideal, but the human brain has done it. It is we who have introduced a little grace, beauty, unknown charm, and mystery into creation by singing about it, interpreting it, by admiring it as poets, idealizing it as artists, and by explaining it as learned men who make mistakes, but who find ingenious reasons, some grace and beauty, some unknown charm and mystery in the various phenomena of nature.

"God only created coarse beings, full of the germs of disease, and who, after a few years of bestial enjoyment, grow old and infirm, with all the ugliness and all the want of power of human decrepitude. He only seems to have made them in order that they may reproduce their species in a repulsive manner, and then die like ephemeral insects. I said, *reproduce their species in a repulsive manner,* and I adhere to that expression. What is there as a matter of fact, more ignoble and more repugnant than that ridiculous act of the reproduction of living beings, against which all delicate minds always have revolted, and always will revolt? Since all the organs which have been invented by this economical and malicious Creator serve two purposes, why did he not choose those that were unsullied, in order to intrust them with that sacred mission, which is the noblest and the most exalted of all human functions? The mouth which nourishes the body by means of material food, also diffuses abroad speech and thought. Our flesh revives itself by means of itself, and at the same time, ideas are communicated by it. The sense of smell, which gives the vital air to the lungs, imparts all the perfumes of the world to the brain: the smell of flowers, of woods, of trees, of the sea. The ear, which enables us to communicate with our fellowmen, has also allowed us to invent music, to create dreams, happiness, the infinite, and even physical pleasure, by means of sounds!

"But one might say that the Creator wished to prohibit man from ever ennobling and idealizing his commerce with women. Nevertheless, man has found love, which is not a bad reply to that sly Deity, and he has ornamented it so much with literary poetry, that woman often forgets the contact she is obliged to submit to. Those among us who are powerless to deceive themselves have invented vice and refined debauchery, which is another way of laughing at God, and of paying homage, immodest homage, to beauty.

"But the normal man makes children; just a beast that is coupled with another by law.

"Look at that woman! Is it not abominable to think that such a jewel, such a pearl, born to be beautiful, admired, fêted, and adored, has spent eleven years of her life in providing heirs for the Count de Mascaret?"

Bernard Grandin replied with a laugh: "There is a great deal of truth in all that, but very few people would understand you."

Salnis got more and more animated. "Do you know how I picture God myself?" he said. "As an enormous, creative organ unknown to us, who scatters millions of worlds into space, just as one single fish would deposit its spawn in the sea. He creates, because it is His function as God to do so, but He does not know what He is doing, and is stupidly prolific in His work, and is ignorant of the combinations of all kinds which are produced by His scattered germs. Human thought is a lucky little local, passing accident, which was totally unforeseen, and is condemned to disappear with this earth, and to recommence perhaps here or elsewhere, the same or different, with fresh combinations of eternally new beginnings. We owe it to this slight accident which has happened to His intellect, that we are very uncomfortable in this world which was not made for us, which had not been prepared to receive us, to lodge and feed us, or to satisfy reflecting beings, and we owe it to Him also that we have to struggle without ceasing against what are still called the designs of Providence, when we are really refined and civilized beings."

Grandin, who was listening to him attentively, as he had long known the surprising outbursts of his fancy, asked him: "Then you believe that human thought is the spontaneous product of blind, divine parturition?"

"Naturally? A fortuitous function of the nerve-centers of our brain, like some unforeseen chemical action which is due to new mixtures, and which also resembles a product of electricity, caused by friction or the unexpected proximity of some substance, and which, lastly, resembles the phenomena caused by the infinite and fruitful fermentations of living matter.

"But, my dear fellow, the truth of this must be evident to anyone who looks about him. If human thought. ordained by an omniscient Creator, had been intended to be what it has become, altogether different from mechanical thoughts and resignation, so exacting, inquiring, agitated, tormented, would the world which was created to receive the beings which we now are have been this unpleasant little dwelling place for poor fools, this salad plot, this rocky, wooded, and spherical kitchen garden where your improvident Providence has destined us to live naked, in caves or under trees, nourished on the flesh of slaughtered animals, our brethren, or on raw vegetables nourished by the sun and the rain.

"But it is sufficient to reflect for a moment, in order to understand that this world was not made for such creatures as we are. Thought, which is developed by a miracle in the nerves of the cells in our brain, powerless, ignorant, and confused as it is, and as it will always remain, makes all of us who are intellectual beings eternal and wretched exiles on earth.

"Look at this earth, as God has given it to those who inhabit it. Is it not visibly and solely made, planted and covered with forests, for the sake of animals? What is there for us? Nothing. And for them? Everything. They have nothing to do but to eat, or go hunting and eat each other, according to their instincts, for God never foresaw gentleness and peaceable manners; He only foresaw the death of creatures which were bent on destroying and devouring each other. Are not the quail, the pigeon, and the partridge the natural prey of the hawk? the sheep, the stag, and the ox that of the great flesh-eating animals, rather than meat that has been fattened to be served up to us with truffles, which have been unearthed by pigs, for our special benefit?

"As to ourselves, the more civilized, intellectual, and refined we are, the more we ought to conquer and subdue that animal instinct, which represents the will of God in us. And so, in order to mitigate our lot as brutes, we have discovered and made everything, beginning with houses, then exquisite food, sauces, sweetmeats, pastry, drink, stuffs, clothes, ornaments, beds, mattresses, carriages, railways, and innumerable machines, besides arts and sciences, writing and poetry.

Every ideal comes from us as well as the amenities of life, in order to make our existence as simple reproducers, for which divine Providence solely intended us, less monotonous and less hard.

"Look at this theater. Is there not here a human world created by us, unforeseen and unknown by Eternal destinies, comprehensible by our minds alone, a sensual and intellectual distraction, which has been invented solely by and for that discontented and restless little animal that we are.

"Look at that woman, Madame de Mascaret. God intended her to live in a cave naked, or wrapped up in the skins of wild animals, but is she not better as she is? But, speaking of her, does anyone know why and how her brute of a husband, having such a companion by his side, and especially after having been boorish enough to make her a mother seven times, has suddenly left her, to run after bad women?"

Grandin replied: "Oh! my dear fellow, this is probably the only reason. He found that always living with her was becoming too expensive in the end, and from reasons of domestic economy, he has arrived at the same principles which you lay down as a philosopher."

Just then the curtain rose for the third act, and they turned round, took off their hats, and sat down.

CHAPTER IV

THE COUNT AND COUNTESS Mascaret were sitting side by side in the carriage which was taking them home from the opera, without speaking. But suddenly the husband said to his wife: "Gabrielle!"

"What do you want?"

"Don't you think that this has lasted long enough?"

"What?"

"The horrible punishment to which you have condemned me for the last six years."

"What do you want? I cannot help it."

"Then tell me which of them it is?"

"Never."

"Think that I can no longer see my children or feel them round me, without having my heart burdened with this doubt. Tell me which of them it is, and I swear that I will forgive you, and treat it like the others."

"I have not the right to."

"You do not see that I can no longer endure this life, this thought which is wearing me out, or this question which I am constantly asking myself, this question which tortures me each time I look at them. It is driving me mad."

"Then you have suffered a great deal?" she said.

"Terribly. Should I, without that, have accepted the horror of living by your side, and the still greater horror of feeling and knowing that there is one among them whom I cannot recognize, and who prevents me from loving the others?"

She repeated: "Then you have really suffered very much?" And he replied in a constrained and sorrowful voice:

"Yes, for do I not tell you every day that it is intolerable torture to me? Should I have remained in that house, near you and them, if I did not love them? Oh! You have behaved abominably toward me. All the affection of my heart I have bestowed upon my children, and that you know. I am for them a father of the olden time, as I was for you a husband of one of the families of old, for by instinct I have remained a natural man, a man of former days. Yes, I will confess it, you have made me terribly jealous, because you are a woman of another race, of another soul, with other requirements. Oh! I shall never forget the things that you told me, but from that day, I troubled myself no more about you. I did not kill you, because then I should have had no means on earth of ever discovering which of our—of your children is not mine. I have waited, but I have suffered more than you would believe, for I can no longer venture to love them, except, perhaps, the two eldest; I no longer venture to look at them, to call them to me, to kiss them; I cannot take them on to my knee without asking myself: 'Can it be this one?' I have been correct in my behavior toward you for six years, and even kind and complaisant; tell me the truth, and I swear that I will do nothing unkind."

He thought, in spite of the darkness of the carriage, that he could perceive that she was moved, and feeling certain that she was going to speak at last, he said: "I beg you, I beseech you to tell me."

"I have been more guilty than you think perhaps," she replied; "but I could no longer endure that life of continual pregnancy, and I had only one means of driving you from my bed. I lied before God, and I lied, with my hand raised to my children's heads, for I have never wronged you."

He seized her arm in the darkness, and squeezing it as he had done on that terrible day of their drive in the Bois de Boulogne, he stammered: "Is that true?"

"It is true."

But he in terrible grief said with a groan: "I shall have fresh doubts that will never end! When did you lie, the last time or now? How am I to believe you at present? How can one believe a woman after that? I shall never again know what I am to think. I would rather you had said to me: 'It is Jacques, or, it is Jeanne.'"

The carriage drove them into the courtyard of their mansion, and when it had drawn up in front of the steps, the Count got down first as usual, and offered his wife his arm, to help her up. And then, as soon as they had reached the first floor he said: "May I speak to you for a few moments longer?"

And she replied: "I am quite willing."

They went into a small drawing-room, while a footman in some surprise, lit the wax candles. As soon as he had left the room and they were alone, he continued: "How am I to know the truth? I have begged you a thousand times to speak, but you have remained dumb, impenetrable, inflexible, inexorable, and now to-day, you tell me that you have been lying. For six years you have actually allowed me to believe such a thing! No, you are lying now, I do not know why, but out of pity for me, perhaps?"

She replied in a sincere and convincing manner: "If I had not done so, I should have had four more children in the last six years!"

And he exclaimed: "Can a mother speak like that?"

"Oh!" she replied, "I do not at all feel that I am the mother of children who have never been born, it is enough for me to be the mother of those that I have, and to love them with all my heart. I am—we are—women who belong to the civilized world, Monsieur, and we are no longer, and we refuse to be, mere females who re-stock the earth."

She got up, but he seized her hands. "Only one word, Gabrielle. Tell me the truth!"

"I have just told you. I have never dishonored you."

He looked her full in the face, and how beautiful she was, with her gray eyes, like the cold sky. In her dark hair dress, on that opaque night of black hair, there shone the diamond coronet, like a cluster of stars. Then he suddenly felt, felt by a kind of intuition, that this grand creature was not merely a being destined to perpetuate his race, but the strange and mysterious product of all the complicated desires which have been accumulating in us for centuries but which have been turned aside from their primitive and divine object, and which have wandered after a mystic, imperfectly seen, and intangible beauty. There are some women like that, women who blossom only for our dreams, adorned with every poetical attribute of civilization, with that ideal luxury, coquetry, and æsthetic charm which should sur-round the living statue who brightens our life.

Her husband remained standing before her, stupefied at the tardy and obscure discovery, confusedly hitting on the cause of his former jealousy, and understanding it all very imperfectly. At last he said: "I believe you, for I feel at this moment that you are not lying, and for-merly, I really thought that you were."

She put out her hand to him: "We are friends then?"

He took her hand and kissed it, and replied: "We are friends. Thank you, Gabrielle."

Then he went out, still looking at her, and surprised that she was still so beautiful, and feeling a strange emotion arising in him, which was, perhaps, more formidable than antique and simple love.

GRAVEYARD SIRENS

THE FIVE FRIENDS HAD finished their dinner; there were two bachelors and three married men, all middle-aged and wealthy. They assembled thus once a month, in memory of old times, and lingered to gossip over their coffee till late at night. Many a happy evening was spent in this way, for they were fond of one another's society, and had remained closely united. Conversation among them was a sort of review of the daily papers, commenting on everything that interests and amuses Parisians. One of the cleverest, Joseph de Bardon, was a bachelor. He lived the life of a boulevardier most thoroughly and fantastically, without being debauched or depraved. It interested him, and as he was still young, being barely forty, he enjoyed it keenly. A man of the world in the broadest and best sense of the word, he possessed a great deal of wit without much depth, a general knowledge without real learning, quick perception without serious penetration; but his adventures and observations furnished him many amusing stories, which he told with so much philosophy and humor that society voted him very intellectual.

He was a favorite after-dinner speaker, always having some story to relate to which his friends looked forward. Presently he began to tell a story without being asked. Leaning on the table with a half-filled glass of brandy in front of his plate, in the smoky atmosphere filled with the fragrance of coffee, he seemed perfectly at ease, just as some beings are entirely at home in certain places and under certain conditions—as a goldfish in its aquarium, for instance, or a nun in her cloister.

Puffing at his cigar, he said:

"A rather curious thing happened to me a little while ago."

All exclaimed at once: "Tell us about it!"

Presently he continued:

"You all know how I love to roam around the city, like a collector in search of antiquities. I enjoy watching people and things. About the middle of September, the weather being very fine, I went for a walk one afternoon, without a definite purpose. Why do we men always have the vague impulse to call on some pretty woman? We review them in our mind, compare their respective charms, the interest they arouse in us, and finally decide in favor of the one that attracts us most.

"But when the sun shines brightly and the air is balmy, sometimes we altogether lose the desire for calling.

"That day the sun was bright and the air balmy, so I simply lighted a cigar and started for the Boulevard Extérieur. As I was sauntering along, I thought I would take a look around the cemetery of Montmartre. Now, I have always liked cemeteries because they sadden and rest me; and I need that influence at times. Besides, many of my friends are laid to rest there, and I go to see them once in a while.

"As it happens, I once buried a romance in this particular cemetery,—an old love of mine, a charming little woman whose memory awakens all kinds of regrets in me—I often dream beside her grave. All is over for her now!

"I like graveyards because they are such immense, densely populated cities. Just think of all the bodies buried in that small space, of the countless generations of Parisians laid there forever, eternally entombed in the little vaults of their little graves marked by a cross or a stone, while the living—fools that they are!—take up so much room and make such a fuss.

"Cemeteries have some monuments quite as interesting as those to be seen in the museums. Cavaignac's tomb I liken, without comparing it, to that masterpiece of Jean Goujon, the tombstone of Louis de Brézé in the subterranean chapel in the cathedral of Rouen. My friends, all so-called modern and realistic art originated there. That reproduction of Louis de Brézé is more life-like and terrible, more convulsed with agony, than any one of the statues that decorate modern tombs.

"In Montmartre is Baudin's monument, and it is quite imposing; also the tombs of Gautier and Mürger, where the other day I found a solitary wreath of yellow immortelles, laid there—by whom do you suppose? Perhaps by the last *grisette*, grown old, and possibly become a janitress in the neighborhood! It's a pretty little statue by Millet, but it is ruined by neglect and accumulated filth. Sing of youth, O Mürger!

"Well, I entered the cemetery, filled with a certain sadness, not too poignant, a feeling suggesting such thoughts as this: The place is not very cheerful, but I'm not to be put here yet.

"The impression of autumn, a warm dampness smelling of dead leaves, the pale, anæmic rays of the sun, intensified and poetized the solitude of this place, which reminds one of death and of the end of all things.

"I walked slowly along the alleys of graves where neighbors no longer visit, no longer sleep together, nor read the papers. I began reading the epitaphs. There is nothing more amusing in the world. Labiche and Meilhac have never made me laugh as much as some of these tombstone inscriptions. I tell you these crosses and marble slabs on which the relatives of the dead have poured out their regrets and their wishes for the happiness of the departed, their hopes of reunion—the hypocrites!—make better reading than Balzac's funniest tales! But what I love in Montmartre are the abandoned plots filled with yew-trees and cypress, the resting-place of those departed long ago. However, the green trees nourished by the bodies will soon be felled to make room for those that have recently passed away, whose graves will be there, under little marble slabs.[15]

"After loitering awhile, I felt tired, and decided to pay my faithful tribute to my little friend's memory. When I reached the grave, my heart was very sad. Poor child! she was so sweet and loving, so fair and white—and now—should her grave be reopened—

"Bending over the iron railing I murmured a prayer, which she probably never heard, and I turned to leave, when I caught sight of a woman in deep mourning kneeling beside a neighboring grave. Her crape veil was thrown back, disclosing her blond hair, which seemed illumined under the darkness of her hat. I forgot to leave.

"She seemed bowed with sorrow. She had buried her face in her hands, apparently lost in deep thought. With closed lids, as rigid as a statue, she was living over torturing memories and seemed herself a corpse mourning a corpse. Presently I saw that she was weeping, as there was a convulsive movement of her back and shoulders. Suddenly she uncovered her face. Her eyes, brimming with tears, were charming. For a moment she gazed around as if awakening from a nightmare. She saw me looking at her and quickly hid her face again, greatly abashed. Now, with convulsive sobs she bent her head slowly over the tombstone. She rested her forehead against it, and her veil, falling around her, covered the whiteness of the beloved sepulcher with a dark shroud. I heard her moan and then saw her fall to the ground in a faint.

"I rushed to her side and began slapping her hands and breathing on her temples, while reading this simple inscription on the tombstone:

" 'Here lies Louis-Théodore Carrel, Captain in the Marine Infantry, killed by the enemy in Tonkin. Pray for his soul.'

"This death was quite recent. I was moved almost to tears, and renewed my efforts to revive the poor girl. At last she came to. I am not so very bad-looking, and my face must have shown how upset I was, for her very first glance showed me that she was likely to be grateful for my care. Between sobs she told me of her marriage to the officer who had been killed in Tonkin within a year after their wedding. He had married her for love, she being an orphan and possessing nothing above the required dowry.

"I consoled her, comforted her, and assisted her to her feet, saying:

" 'You must not stay here. Come away.'

" 'I am unable to walk,' she whispered.

" 'Let me help you,' I said.

" 'Thank you, you are very kind,' she murmured. 'Did you also come to mourn some one?'

" 'Yes, Madame.'

" 'A woman?'

" 'Yes, Madame.'

" 'Your wife?'

" 'A friend.'

" 'One may love a friend just as much as a wife, for passion knows no law,' said the lady.

" 'Yes, Madame,' I replied.

"And so we left the spot together, she leaning on me and I almost carrying her through the alleys. As we came out, she murmured:

" 'I'm afraid that I'm going to faint.'

" 'Wouldn't you like to take something, Madame?' I inquired.

" 'Yes,' she said, 'I would.'

"I discovered a restaurant near at hand, where the friends of the dead gather to celebrate the end of their painful duty. We went in, and I made her drink a cup of hot tea, which appeared to give her renewed strength.

"A faint smile dawned on her lips and she began telling me about herself: how terrible it was to go through life all alone, to be alone at home day and night, to have no one on whom to lavish love, confidence, and intimacy.

"It all seemed sincere and sounded well coming from her. I was softened. She was very young, perhaps twenty. I paid her several compliments that appeared to please her, and as it was growing dark I offered to take her home in a cab. She accepted. In the carriage we were so close to each other that we could feel the warmth of our bodies through our clothing, which really is the most intoxicating thing in the world.

"When the cab stopped in front of her home she said:

" 'I hardly feel able to walk upstairs, for I live on the fourth floor. You have already been so kind, that I am going to ask you to assist me to my rooms.'

"I consented gladly. She walked up slowly, breathing heavily at each step. In front of her door she added:

" 'Do come in for a few minutes, so that I can thank you again for your kindness.'

"And I, of course, followed her.

"Her apartment was modest, even a trifle poor, but well-kept and in good taste.

"We sat down side by side on a small divan, and she again began to speak of her loneliness.

"Then she rang for the maid, so as to offer me some refreshments. But the girl failed to appear, and I joyfully concluded that this maid probably came only in the morning, and was a sort of scrub-woman.

"She had taken off her hat. How pretty she was! Her clear eyes looked steadily at me, so clear and so steady that a great temptation came to me, to which I promptly yielded. Clasping her in my arms, I kissed her again and again on her half-closed lids.

"She repelled me, struggling to free herself and repeating:

" 'Do stop—do end it—'

"What did she mean to imply by this word? Under such conditions, to 'end' could have at least two meanings. In order to silence her, I passed from her eyes to her lips, and gave to the word 'end' the conclusion I preferred. She did not resist very much, and as our eyes met after this insult to the memory of the departed captain, I saw that her expression was one of tender resignation, which quickly dispelled my misgivings.

"Then I grew attentive and gallant. After an hour's chat I asked her:

" 'Where do you dine?'

" 'In a small restaurant near by.'

" 'All alone?'

" 'Why, yes.'

" 'Will you take dinner with me?'

" 'Where?'

" 'In a good restaurant on the Boulevard.'

"She hesitated a little, but at last consented, consoling herself with the argument that she was so desperately lonely, and adding, 'I must put on a lighter gown.'

"She retired to her room, and when she emerged she was dressed in a simple gray frock that made her look exquisitely slender. She apparently had different costumes for street and for cemetery wear!

"Our dinner was most pleasant and cordial. She drank some champagne, thereby becoming very animated and lively, and we returned to her apartment together.

"This *liaison*, begun among tombstones, lasted about three weeks. But man tires of everything and especially of women. So I pleaded an urgent trip and left her. Of course, I managed to be generous, for which she was duly thankful, making me promise and even swear that I would come back, for she really seemed to care a little for me.

"In the meantime I formed other attachments, and a month or so went by without the memory of this love being vivid enough to bring me back to her. Still, I had not forgotten her. She haunted me like a mystery, a psychological problem, an unsolved question.

"I can't tell why, but one day I imagined that I should find her in the cemetery. So I went back. I walked around a long time without meeting anyone but the usual visitors of the place, mourners who had not broken off all relations with their dead. The grave of the captain killed in Tonkin was deserted, without flowers, or wreaths.

"As I was passing through another part of this great city of Death, I suddenly saw a couple in deep mourning coming toward me through one of the narrow paths hedged with crosses. When they drew near, Oh, surprise! I recognized—her! She saw me and blushed. As I brushed past her, she gave me a little wink that meant clearly: Don't recognize me, and also seemed to say: Do come back.

"The man who accompanied her was about fifty years old, fine-looking and distinguished, an officer of the Legion of Honor. He was leading her just as I had, when we left the cemetery together.

"I was utterly nonplussed, reluctant to believe what my eyes had just seen, and I wondered to what strange tribe of creatures this graveyard huntress belonged. Was she merely a clever courtesan, an inspired prostitute, who haunted cemeteries for men disconsolate at the loss of some woman, a mistress or a wife, and hungering for past caresses? Is it a profession? Are the cemeteries worked like the streets? Are there graveyard sirens? Or had she alone the idea—wonderful for its deep philosophy—to profit by the amorous regrets awakened in these awful places? I would have given a great deal to know whose widow she was that day!"

ENDNOTES

1. (p. 4) *The last French soldiers finally came across the Seine . . . and, marching behind, . . . the General, . . . disastrously beaten, in spite of his legendary bravery:* France's disastrous ten-month experience during the Franco-Prussian War (1870–1871) became the unfortunate defining moment of masculinity and national shame for Maupassant's generation of young men. French military forces proved to be woefully inadequate to defend against the invading Prussian army. The conflict forced the political collapse of France's imperialist Second Empire (1852–1870) under Napoléon III, which was seceded with great initial difficulty by the democratic Third Republic (1870–1940). Germany's seizure of Alsace and Lorraine (reclaimed by France in 1918) became a source of continual friction between the two countries and was one of the circumstances that led to World War I (1914–1918) more than forty years later.

2. (p. 10) *the Orléans party in the Department:* Born during the French Revolution (1789–1799), the Orléans political party attempted to mediate between monarchist and democratic factions during the following eighty years. By the era of the Second Empire, however, the party had little significant impact on French politics; it ceased to exist after the Franco-Prussian War.

3. (p. 17) *whereby he gave that "scamp of a Badinguet" a good lashing. Then Ball-of-Fat was angry, for she was a Bonapartist:* Bonapartism was a French political faction that advocated monarchism, supporting in particular the political ambitions of descendants of Napoléon Bonaparte (Napoléon I, 1769–1821). Badinguet was a satirical nickname for Napoléon III.

4. (p. 26) *a Guesclin, or a Joan of Arc, perhaps, or would it be another Napoleon First?:* Bertrand du Guesclin (c.1320–1380) and Joan of

Arc (c.1412–1431) led French military forces during the Hundred Years War between France and England (1337–1453). Napoléon Bonaparte reigned as France's emperor from 1804 to 1814 and briefly again in 1815.

5. (p. 33) *Judith and Holophernes . . . Lucrece and Sextus, and Cleopatra obliging all the generals of the enemy to pass by her couch and reducing them in servility to slaves:* In the Book of Judith, whose canonicity is disputed by various religious sects, the Jewish heroine Judith seduces the Babylonian general Holofernes, whose forces were besieging her city; Judith's beheading of Holofernes ends the assault and saves her people. According to Roman historian Livy (59 B.C.–A.D. 17), the Roman nobleman Sextus Tarquinius (died B.C. 496?) raped his father's wife, Lucretia; her subsequent suicide compelled her family and the people of Rome to seek revenge, leading to an uprising that ended the monarchy and established the Roman Republic. Queen Cleopatra's sexual relationships with Julius Caesar and Marc Antony played a significant role in Roman politics from 48 B.C. to 30 B.C.

6. (p. 41) *began to whistle the "Marseillaise":* The lyrics for "La Marseillaise" were penned by French army officer Claude-Joseph Rouget de Lisle in 1792; he adapted the melody from a composition by Italian violinist and composer Giovanni Battista Viotti (1755–1824). After two abortive previous attempts, the song was finally adopted as the French national anthem in 1879, nine years after the time frame of "Ball-of Fat."

7. (p. 43) *they descended the stream toward La Grenouillère:* La Grenouillère (The Froggery) was an infamous open-air café and bathing and boating resort located west of Paris. For an Impressionist's view of the establishment, see Claude Monet's 1869 painting *La Grenouillère*, held by the Metropolitan Museum of Art in New York.

8. (p. 63) *After visiting Bona, Constantine, Biskara, and Setif, I went to Bougie through the defiles of Chabet:* Bona (now Annaba), Constantine, Biskara (or Biskra), Sétif, and Bougie (now Bejaïa) are cities

in Algeria. Chabet is a gorge through a high plateau of the region.

9. (p. 89) *ought to be worth about six or seven francs:* For centuries, the franc was the basic monetary unit of France, which switched to the euro in 2002.

10. (p. 128) *de Châteauvillard's dueling code:* The Count de Chateauvillard's *Essai sur le duel* was first published in 1836.

11. (p. 261) Revue du Monde Scientifique: The periodical *Revue du monde nouveau: littéraire, artistique, scientifique* has been published since 1874.

12. (p. 282) *"It is the Ramadan":* Observed during the ninth Islamic month, Ramadan commemorates the first revelation of the Koran, which Muslims honor through fasting, prayer, and other rites.

13. (p. 296) *"who has not yet seen my Japanese collection?":* Throughout the second half of the nineteenth century, Japanese wood-block prints, ceramics, and other art objects attracted great interest among French artists, collectors, and aesthetic critics. In 1872, French writer and art critic Jules Claretie coined the word "Japonism" to label the phenomenon, which spread to other Western countries.

14. (p. 307) *between two of the acts in "Robert the Devil":* German composer Giacomo Meyerbeer's opera *Robert le Diable* (1831) follows the downfall and redemption of a protagonist who makes a Faustian bargain with the devil.

15. (p. 319) *the cemetery of Montmartre . . . whose graves will be there, under little marble slabs:* In the preceding paragraphs, Maupassant's narrator, Joseph de Bardon, mentions people associated with Montmartre's famous cemetery, where the gravesites of many French writers, artists, performers, politicians, and military leaders are located. There are four notable members of the Cavaignac family buried there; scholar Louis Forestier identifies the grave highlighted in the story as belonging to Eugène Cavaignac (1802–1857), a general and politician. Other

famous gravesites mentioned are those of explorer Nicolas
Baudin (1754–1803); author Théophile Gautier (1811–1872);
and novelist Henri Mürger (1822–1861). Bardon also mentions playwrights Eugène Labiche (1815–1888), who had been
buried there by the time Maupassant composed the story, and
Henri Meilhac (1831–1897), who died after Maupassant did
but whose resting place prophetically proved to be at Montmartre. Bardon compares Montmartre's elaborate gravesites to
the work of Jean Goujon (1510–c.1572), a Renaissance sculp-
tor who constructed the tomb of Louis de Brézé (d.1531), a
grandson of King Charles VII. He also alludes to the works of
artist Jean-François Millet (1814–1875) and realist novelist
Honoré de Balzac (1799–1850), author of the monumental *La
Comédie humaine.*

ORIGINAL PUBLICATION DATA

The stories in this volume have been arranged by their chronological order of first publication as established by editor Louis Forestier in *Contes et nouvelles,* 2 vols. (Paris: Gallimard, Bibliothèque de la Pléiade, 1974 and 1979). The English translations have been taken from the three collections listed immediately below. In the list of stories that follows, we have named the original publication in French and the English source for each.

The Life Work of Henri René Guy de Maupassant. 17 vols. Edited by M. Walter Dunne. New York and London: M. Walter Dunne, 1903. This collection was the first, albeit unsuccessful, attempt to offer all of Maupassant's fiction to an English-speaking audience. Because of the risqué nature of a good number of the stories, the project had difficulty finding a mainstream publisher. Consequently, the collection was issued a number of times by nontraditional agencies, such as through a limited edition put out by a literary society or through private publication. Plagued by sporadic imprecise translations, the omission of many canonical texts, and the inexplicable erroneous attribution of scores of stories to Maupassant in the project, this anthology nevertheless shaped the American perception of his work during the early decades of the twentieth century. Its translations were subsequently incorporated in later attempts to present Maupassant in English, such as Artine Artinian's *The Complete Short Stories of Guy de Maupassant* (see "For Further Reading").

The Odd Number: Thirteen Tales. Edited and translated by Jonathan Sturges. New York: Harper and Brothers, 1889. With an introduction by Henry James, this volume greatly promoted Maupassant's reputation among writers in the United States during the 1890s and early 1900s.

Modern Ghosts. Edited by George William Curtis. New York: Harper and Brothers, 1890. This anthology collected translations of ghost stories by European writers Guy de Maupassant, Alexander L. Kielland

(1849–1906), Pedro Antonio de Alarcón (1833–1891), Gustavo Adolfo Bécquer (1836–1870), Giovanni Magherini-Graziani (1856?–1925), and Leopold Kompert (1822–1886). The two Maupassant stories in the volume were translated by Jonathan Sturges.

"Ball-of-Fat" (p. 3). "Boule de suif," first published in the anthology *Les Soirées de Médan* (*Evenings at Médan*) in 1880. The translation is from the Dunne edition.

"Paul's Mistress" (p. 43). "La Femme de Paul," first published in Maupassant's anthology *La Maison Tellier* (*The Tellier House*) in 1881. The translation is from the Dunne edition.

"Marroca" (p. 62). "Marroca," first published by the French newspaper *Gil Blas* in 1882 and collected in the anthology *Mademoiselle Fifi* that same year. The translation is from the Dunne edition.

"Moonlight" (p. 70). "Clair de lune," first published by *Gil Blas* in 1882 and collected in the anthology *Clair de lune* in 1884. The translation is from Sturges's *The Odd Number*.

"The Will" (p. 76). "Le Testament," first published by *Gil Blas* in 1882 and collected in *Contes de la bécasse* (*Tales of the Goose*) the following year. The translation is from the Dunne edition.

"The Awakening" (p. 81). "Réveil," first published by *Gil Blas* in 1883 and collected in a reissue of *Mademoiselle Fifi* that same year. Maupassant often added new stories to his short-story collections when they were republished. The translation is from the Dunne edition.

"The False Gems" (p. 87). "Les Bijoux," first published by *Gil Blas* in 1883 and collected in *Clair de lune* the following year. The translation is from the Dunne edition.

"The Confession" (p. 94). "La Confession," first published by the French newspaper *Le Gaulois* in 1883 and collected in *Contes du jour et de la nuit* (*Stories of Day and Night*) in 1885. The translation is from Sturges's *The Odd Number*.

"Regret" (p. 100). "Regret," first published by *Le Gaulois* in 1883 and collected in *Miss Harriet* in 1884. The translation is from the Dunne edition.

"The Avenger" (p. 107). "Le Vengeur," first published by *Gil Blas* in 1883. Maupassant did not include the story in any collection published during his lifetime. The translation is from the Dunne edition.

"The Artist's Wife" (p. 114). "Le Modèle," first published by *Le Gaulois* in 1883 and collected in *Le Rosier de Madame Husson* (*Madame Husson's Rosebush*) in 1888. The translation is from the Dunne edition.

"A Coward" (p. 121). "Un Lâche," first published by *Le Gaulois* in 1884 and collected in *Contes du jour et de la nuit* the following year. The translation is from Sturges's *The Odd Number*.

"The Necklace" (p. 130). "La Parure," first published by *Le Gaulois* in 1884 and collected in *Contes du jour et de la nuit* the following year. The translation is from Sturges's *The Odd Number*.

"A Meeting" (p. 140). "Rencontre," first published by *Gil Blas* in 1884 and collected in *Les Soeurs Rondoli* (*The Rondoli Sisters*) that same year. The translation is from the Dunne edition.

"Bed No. 29" (p. 149). "Le Lit 29," first published by *Gil Blas* in 1884 and collected in *Toine* the following year. The translation is from the Dunne edition.

"A Peculiar Case" (p. 161). "La Confession," first published by *Gil Blas* in 1884 and collected in *Le Rosier de Madame Husson* in 1888. Maupassant published two stories using the title "La Confession," both of which are included in this volume. The translation is from the Dunne edition.

"Yvette" (p. 168). "Yvette," first published by the French newspaper *Le Figaro* in 1884 and collected in the anthology *Yvette* the following year. The translation is from the Dunne edition.

"The Wreck" (p. 222). "L'Épave," first published by *Le Gaulois* in 1886 and collected in *La Petite Roque* (*Little Roque*) that same year. The translation is from Sturges's *The Odd Number*.

"Love—Three Pages from a Sportsman's Book" (p. 234). "Amour—Trois pages du livre d'un chasseur," first published by *Gil Blas* in 1886 and collected in the anthology *Le Horla* the following year. The translation is from the Dunne edition.

"The Horla" (p. 240). "Le Horla," first published in the anthology *Le Horla* in 1887. The translation is by Jonathan Sturges and was first published in Curtis's *Modern Ghosts*.

"Allouma" (p. 269). "Allouma," first published by the French newspaper *L'Écho de Paris* in 1889 and collected in *La Main gauche* (*The Left Hand*) that same year. The translation is from the Dunne edition.

"The Rendezvous" (p. 292). "Le Rendez-vous," first published by *L'Écho de Paris* in 1889 and collected in *La Main gauche* that same year. The translation is from the Dunne edition.

"Useless Beauty" (p. 299). "L'Inutile Beauté," first published by *L'Écho de Paris* in 1890 and collected in the anthology *L'Inutile Beauté* that same year. The translation is from the Dunne edition.

"Graveyard Sirens" (p. 317). "Les Tombales," first published by *Gil Blas* in 1891 and collected in a revised edition of *La Maison Tellier* that same year. The translation is from the Dunne edition.

Inspired by the Stories of

GUY DE MAUPASSANT

LITERATURE

A master of the short story, Guy de Maupassant influenced the work of many subsequent writers. Even within his own lifetime, writers no less established than Henry James admired his style. In a February 1889 notebook entry made while James was suffering an artistic slump, he expressed the desire to write more succinctly, invoking the spirit of Maupassant: "I have undertaken to tell and to describe too much. . . . *À la Maupassant* must be my constant motto." Many of the shorter pieces James composed in the early 1890s reflect his efforts to achieve a Maupassant-like brevity.

Later American writers whose work shows the pronounced influence of Maupassant include Kate Chopin and O. Henry. Chopin, author of the short novel *The Awakening* (1899), wrote movingly of her spiritual connection with Maupassant in a draft of her essay "Confidences." Printed posthumously in *The Complete Works of Kate Chopin* (1969), it describes how Maupassant opened the door for Chopin to put trust in her own personal voice and vision of life:

It was at this period of my emerging from the vast solitude in which I had been making my own acquaintance, that I stumbled upon Maupassant. I read his stories and marvelled at them. Here was life, not fiction; for where were the plots, the old fashioned mechanism and stage trapping that in a vague, unthinking way I had fancied were essential to the art of story making? Here was a man who had escaped from tradition and authority, who had entered into himself and looked out upon life through his own being and with his own eyes; and who, in a direct and simple way, told us what he saw.

In her writings Chopin achieves the directness and simplicity she attributed to her predecessor, painting strong, clear portraits of the personalities that inhabit the bayous and beaches of Louisiana. Her most famous novel, *The Awakening*, relates the coming-to-consciousness of a wealthy but unhappily married Louisiana housewife, with frank sexual detail directly inspired by Maupassant. Several of Chopin's short stories—notably the much-anthologized "Désirée's Baby" (1893)—make expert use of the "twist" ending, a technique established by Maupassant. Chopin read Maupassant's tales in the original French and used for her own works English translations of several of his story titles, including, in this volume, "The Awakening" and "Regret."

New York–based William Sydney Porter, better known as O. Henry, wrote more than 100 short stories before his death in 1910 and was one of the most popular storytellers of his day. O. Henry is sometimes called the "Yankee Maupassant," and there are several parallels between the two writers. Even more so than Chopin, O. Henry regularly employed Maupassant's signature twist ending, achieving dramatic effect in his stories through the ingenious use of coincidence and surprise. In no story does O. Henry use the twist to richer ironic purpose than in "The Gift of the Magi" (1905), in which two impoverished young lovers make noble sacrifices for one another that, because they are reciprocal, are to no avail. In much the same way that Maupassant chronicled life in his native Normandy and his experiences in the Franco-Prussian War, O. Henry portrayed the lives of ordinary New Yorkers and denizens of the West with a compassion bred from the author's own rough-and-tumble existence. According to biographer C. Alphonso Smith, O. Henry felt such an affinity for Maupassant that during his final years he carried a volume of his work everywhere he went.

Maupassant's most famous "trick ending" story is "The Necklace," which has inspired many subsequent writers to compose plots centered upon ascertaining the value of jewelry. In 1899, for instance, Henry James published "Paste" in a deliberate attempt to reverse Maupassant's premise by suggesting that a supposedly fake necklace may consist of real pearls. W. Somerset Maugham directly borrowed concepts from both "The Necklace" and "Paste" in his short stories "Mr. Know-All" (1927) and "A String of Beads" (1927). These Maugham texts in turn influenced Raymond Chandler's creation of a pearl necklace as the central metaphor in his short story "Red Wind" (1938).

FILM

Since 1909, more than 100 films have been made from the works of Maupassant in countries around the world. Of the stories in this volume, "Ball-of-Fat" has been adapted most often: as *The Woman Disputed* (1928), directed by Henry King and Sam Taylor and featuring silent film star Norma Talmadge in one of only three talkies she made in her lifetime; *Boule de suif* (1934), sometimes known by its Russian title, *Pyshka*, directed by Mikhail Romm; *Oyuki, the Madonna* (1935), sometimes known as *Oyuki, the Virgin* or *Maria no Oyuki*, by Japanese director Kenji Mizoguchi; *Angel and Sinner* (1945), by French director Christian-Jaque; and *The Flower Girl* (1951), from Chinese director Shilin Zhu. Scholars have also recently noted the plot similarities between "Ball-of-Fat" and American director John Ford's *Stagecoach* (1939). Another Maupassant tale, "Yvette," was filmed in France in 1928, in Germany in 1938, and for French television in 1971. Silent film legend D. W. Griffith directed a version of "The Necklace" in 1909, and director Denison Clift followed in 1921 with his film *The Diamond Necklace*. Finally, the great French film director Jean-Luc Godard borrowed from both "Paul's Mistress" and "The Sign" (the latter not included in this anthology) for his film *Masculin, féminin* (1966), a meandering, politically infused boy-meets-girl tale that jokingly refers to its characters as "the children of Marx and Coca-Cola."

COMMENTS & QUESTIONS

In this section, we aim to provide the reader with an array of perspectives on the text, as well as questions that challenge those perspectives. The commentary has been culled from sources as diverse as reviews contemporaneous with the work, literary criticism of later generations, and appreciations written throughout the work's history. Following the commentary, a series of questions seeks to explore The Collected Stories of Guy de Maupassant *through a variety of perspectives and to promote a richer understanding of these enduring works.*

COMMENTS

Henry James

[Maupassant] produced a hundred short tales and only four regular novels; but if the tales deserve the first place in any candid appreciation of his talent it is not simply because they are so much the more numerous: they are also more characteristic; they represent him best in his originality, and their brevity, extreme in some cases, does not prevent them from being a collection of masterpieces. . . .

For the last ten years our author has brought forth with regularity these condensed compositions, of which, probably, to an English reader, at a first glance, the most universal sign will be their licentiousness. They really partake of this quality, however, in a very differing degree, and a second glance shows that they may be divided into numerous groups. It is not fair, I think, even to say that what they have most in common is their being extremely *lestes* [nimble]. What they have most in common is their being extremely strong, and after that their being extremely brutal. A story may be obscene without being brutal, and *vice versâ*, and M. de Maupassant's contempt for those interdictions which are supposed to be made in the interest of good morals is but an incident—a very large one indeed—of his general contempt. A pessimism so great that its alliance with the love of good work, or even with the calculation of the sort of work that pays best in a country of style, is, as I have intimated, the most puzzling of anomalies (for it would seem in the light of such sentiments that nothing is worth anything). . . . The author fixes a hard eye on some small spot of human life, usually some ugly, dreary, shabby, sordid one, takes up the particle, and squeezes it either till it grimaces or till it bleeds. Sometimes the grimace is very droll, sometimes the wound is very horrible; but in either case the whole thing is real, observed, noted, and represented, not an invention or a castle in the air. M. de Maupassant sees human life as a terribly ugly business relieved by the comical, but even the comedy is for the most part the comedy of misery, of avidity, of ignorance, helplessness, and grossness. When his laugh is not for these things, it is for the little *saletés* [indecencies] (to use one of his own favourite words) of luxurious life, which are intended to be prettier, but which can scarcely be said to brighten the picture.

—from *Fortnightly Review* (March 1888)

Brander Matthews

Here I cancel a casual sentence written in 1885, before Guy de Maupassant had completely revealed his extraordinary gifts and marvellous craftsmanship. His Short-stories are masterpieces of the art of story-telling, because he had a Greek sense of form, a Latin power of construction, and a French felicity of style. They are simple, most of them; direct, swift, inevitable, and inexorable in their straightforward movement. If art consists in the suppression of non-essentials, there have been few greater artists in fiction than Maupassant. In his Short-stories there is never a word wasted, and there is never an excursus. Nor is there any feebleness or fumbling. What he wanted to do he did, with the unerring certainty of Leatherstocking, hitting the bull's-eye again and again. He had the abundance and the ease of the

very great artists; and the half-dozen or the half-score of his best stories are among the very best Short-stories in any language.

—from *Philosophy of the Short-Story* (1901)

Joseph Conrad

Maupassant's conception of his art is such as one would expect
from a practical and resolute mind; but in the consummate simplicity of his technique it ceases to be perceptible. This is one of its
greatest qualities, and like all the great virtues it is based primarily
on self-denial. . . .

If our feelings (which are tender) happen to be hurt because his
talent is not exercised for the praise and consolation of mankind, our
intelligence (which is great) should let us see that he is a very splendid sinner, like all those who in this valley of compromises err by
over-devotion to the truth that is in them. His determinism, barren
of praise, blame and consolation, has all the merit of his conscientious
art. The worth of every conviction consists precisely in the steadfast-
ness with which it is held.

Except for his philosophy, which in the case of so consummate an
artist does not matter (unless to the solemn and naïve mind), Maupassant of all writers of fiction demands least forgiveness from his
readers. He does not require forgiveness because he is never dull.

The interest of a reader in a work of imagination is either ethical
or that of simple curiosity. Both are perfectly legitimate, since there
is both a moral and an excitement to be found in a faithful rendering
of life. And in Maupassant's work there is the interest of curiosity and
the moral of a point of view consistently preserved and never ob-
truded for the end of personal gratification. The spectacle of this immense talent served by exceptional faculties and triumphing over the
most thankless subjects by an unswerving singleness of purpose is in
itself an admirable lesson in the power of artistic honesty, one may
say of artistic virtue. The inherent greatness of the man consists in
this, that he will let none of the fascinations that beset a writer working in loneliness turn him away from the straight path, from the

vouchsafed vision of excellence. He will not be led into perdition by the seductions of sentiment, of eloquence, of humour, of pathos; of all that splendid pageant of faults that pass between the writer and his probity on the blank sheet of paper, like the glittering cortège of deadly sins before the austere anchorite in the desert air of Thebaïde. This is not to say that Maupassant's austerity has never faltered; but the fact remains that no tempting demon has ever succeeded in hurling him down from his high, if narrow, pedestal. . . .

Here is where Maupassant's austerity comes in. He refrains from setting his cleverness against the eloquence of the facts. There is humour and pathos in these stories; but such is the greatness of his talent, the refinement of his artistic conscience, that all his high qualities appear inherent in the very things of which he speaks, as if they had been altogether independent of his presentation. Facts, and again facts are his unique concern. That is why he is not always properly understood. His facts are so perfectly rendered that, like the actualities of life itself, they demand from the reader the faculty of observation which is rare, the power of appreciation which is generally wanting in most of us who are guided mainly by empty phrases requiring no effort, demanding from us no qualities except a vague susceptibility to emotion. Nobody has ever gained the vast applause of a crowd by the simple and clear exposition of vital facts. Words alone strung upon a convention have fascinated us as worthless glass beads strung upon a thread have charmed at all times our brothers the unsophisticated savages of the islands. Now, Maupassant, of whom it has been said that he is the master of the *mot juste*, has never been a dealer in words. His wares have been, not glass beads, but polished gems: not the most rare and precious, perhaps, but of the very first water of their kind.

—from his Introduction to *Yvette, and Other Stories* (1904)

Prosser Hall Frye

Like Flaubert, then, whom he styles "Master," and whom he strikingly resembles in several respects, Maupassant seems to have been dominated exclusively by an obsession of the *bête*, a mixture of vulgarity, ignorance, and fatuity almost impossible of translation, which had for him a snaky horror and fascination. He is like his master also in the practice of a rigid "imperturbability"—heartlessness, we should call it; only, while Flaubert was occasionally carried away by a great enthusiasm, there is never the faintest glimmer of moral sense in all Maupassant's uncleanly pages. And yet his cynicism is not entirely without relief. The constant preoccupation with the mean, the trivial, and the commonplace tends, particularly in the case of a sensitive nature, to induce an undue respect for the petty as well as an undue contempt for it. And in the midst of his contemptuous indifference to the miseries of existence, it is not uncommon to come across some lean streak of feeling—a humour or a pathos so rudimentary and animal that it makes his cynicism appear enlightened in comparison.

—from *Literary Reviews and Criticisms* (1908)

George Saintsbury

The vividness and actuality of [Maupassant's] power of presentation are unquestioned, and there has been complaint rather of the character of his "illusions" than of his failure to convey them to others. It is not merely that nature, helped by the discipline of practice under the severest of masters, had endowed him with a style of the most extraordinary sobriety and accuracy—the style of a more scholarly, reticent, and tightly-girt Defoe. It is not merely that his vision, and his capacity of reproducing that vision, were unsurpassed and rarely equalled for sharpness of outline and perfection of disengagement. He had something else which it is much less easy to put into words— the power of treating an incident or a character (character, it is true, less often and less fully than incident) as if it were a phrase or a landscape, of separating it, carving it out (so to speak), and presenting it isolated and framed for survey. . . .

As for the character of Maupassant's "illusions," there could never be much doubt about some of them. *Boule de Suif* ["Ball-of-Fat"] itself pretty clearly indicated, and *La Maison Tellier* shortly after showed, at the very opening of his literary career, the scenes, the society, and the solaces which he most affected: while it was impossible to read even two or three of his stories without discovering that, to M. de Maupassant, the world was most emphatically *not* the best of all possible worlds. . . .

His preference for the unhappy ending amounts almost to a *tic*, and would amount wholly to a bore—for *toujours* [always] unhappy-ending is just as bad as *toujours* marriage-bells—if it were not re-lieved and lightened by a real presence of humour. With this sovereign preservative for self, and more sovereign charm for others, Guy de Maupassant was more richly provided than any of his French contemporaries, and more than any but a very few of his countrymen at any time. And as humour without tenderness is an impossibility, so, too, he could be and was tender. Yet it was seldom and *malgré lui* [in spite of himself], while he allowed the mere exercise of his hu-mour itself too scantily for his own safety and his readers' pleasure. That there was any more *fanfaronnade* [bluster] either of vice or of misanthropy about him, I do not believe. An unfortunate conformity of innate temperament and acquired theory made such a *fanfaronnade* as unnecessary as it would have been repugnant to him. But illusion, in such cases, is more dangerous, if less disgusting, than imposture. And so it happened that, in despite of the rare and vast faculties just allowed him, he was constantly found applying them to subjects dis-tasteful if not disgraceful, and allowing the results to be sicklied over with a persistent "soot-wash" of pessimism which was always rather monotonous, and not always very impressive. . . .

The limitations of his art have been sufficiently dealt with; the ex-cellences of it within those limitations are unmistakable. He had no tricks—the worst curse of art at all times, and the commonest in these days of what pretends to be art. He had no splash of so-called "style"; no acrobatic contortions of thought or what does duty for thought; no pottering and peddling of the psychological kind, which would fain make up for a faulty product by ostentatiously parading the processes of production. Had he once got free—as more than once it seemed that he might—from the fatal conventionalities of his unconventionalism, from the trammels of his obtrusive negations, there is hardly a height in prose fiction which he might not have attained.

—from *A History of the French Novel* (1919)

QUESTIONS

1. One value of the literary realism that Maupassant practiced was a fierce fidelity to depicting humans as they really are rather than as they would like to be seen. In his essay, Henry James observes that Maupassant "fixes a hard eye on some small spot of human life, usually some ugly, dreary, shabby, sordid one, takes up the particle, and squeezes it either till it grimaces or till it bleeds." Which stories in this volume present life with such uncompromising realism? How do they accomplish this? Why would nineteenth-century readers such as James view Maupassant's perspective on life with both admiration and repulsion?

2. Note the qualities in Maupassant's style that Brander Matthews and Joseph Conrad praise, especially the approach that every word in a good story should have an artistic purpose. For instance, Conrad asserts that Maupassant "refrains from setting his cleverness against the eloquence of the facts." Reread "The Necklace," looking for clues planted throughout the story that would allow a careful reader to guess the last surprise. How does the final revelation stress the essential character flaw in Mathilde Loisel's personality? Although he did not invent the "trick ending" story, Maupassant greatly popularized this plot structure. Can you think of any other writers who composed a story that ends with a surprise? What movies have employed this plot device?

3. Conrad admires Maupassant for possessing "the power of artistic honesty." How does this ability manifest itself throughout

these stories? For example, compare how a moment of intense insight ("an epiphany") can ironically ruin personal happiness in stories such as "Moonlight," "The False Gems," and "Regret." Why does Maupassant occasionally present a circumstance in which a revelation damns rather than enlightens an individual? What does such a circumstance reveal about the possible dangers in pursuing truth?

4. Is the Horla a ghost or a figment of the narrator's imagination? Is that narrator truly haunted or is he growing decidedly insane? Consider how the text supports each of these interpretations. What problems does an unreliable narrator present?

5. Prosser Hall Frye notes several points of comparison between Flaubert and his disciple, Maupassant. If you have read *Madame Bovary*, compare how Flaubert portrays the plight of women in French society to the way Maupassant treats similar topics in stories such as "Yvette" and "Useless Beauty." What social insights does Maupassant borrow from his mentor? Does the disciple ever exceed Flaubert's genius in portraying women? If so, how?

6. Is Maupassant a sexist or a feminist? Which stories in this volume support your position? Which do not? Discuss how individual scenes reveal Maupassant's intentions. Can a writer be both a sexist and a feminist? If so, what does this contradiction say about the complexities of authorship?

FOR FURTHER READING

TEXTUAL STUDIES AND SELECTED TRANSLATIONS

Maupassant, Guy de. *The Complete Short Stories of Guy de Maupassant.* Edited by Artine Artinian. Garden City, NY: Hanover House, 1955. The closest any American publisher has come to printing translations of all of Maupassant's short stories. Many of this volume's translations are culled from the 1903 Dunne edition (see below).

————. *Contes et nouvelles.* 2 vols. Edited by Louis Forestier. Paris: Gallimard, Bibliothèque de la Pléiade, 1974, 1979. The authoritative textual source for Maupassant's stories in their original French.

————. *The Life Work of Henri René Guy de Maupassant.* 17 vols. Edited by M. Walter Dunne. New York and London: M. Walter Dunne, 1903. The first attempt to collect Maupassant's work in an English translation. (See "Original Publication Data" in this volume for a discussion of the project's textual problems.)

————. *The Odd Number: Thirteen Tales.* Translated by Jonathan Sturges; introduction by Henry James. New York: Harper and Brothers, 1889. A collection that had a significant impact upon Maupassant's reputation in the United States during the 1890s and early 1900s.

SELECTED BIOGRAPHIES AND CRITICAL STUDIES AVAILABLE IN ENGLISH

Donaldson-Evans, Mary. *A Woman's Revenge: The Chronology of Dispossession in Maupassant's Fiction.* Lexington, KY: French Forum, 1986.

Dugan, J. Raymond. *Illusion and Reality: A Study of Descriptive Techniques in the Works of Guy de Maupassant*. The Hague: Mouton, 1973.

Fusco, Richard. *Maupassant and the American Short Story: The Influence of Form at the Turn of the Century*. University Park: The Pennsylvania State University Press, 1994.

Gregorio, Laurence A. *Maupassant's Fiction and the Darwinian View of Life*. New York: Peter Lang, 2005.

Ignotus, Paul. *The Paradox of Maupassant*. London: University of London Press, 1967.

James, Henry. *Partial Portraits*. 1888. Reprint: Ann Arbor: University of Michigan Press, 1970.

Steegmuller, Francis. *Maupassant: A Lion in the Path*. New York: Random House, 1949.

Stivale, Charles J. *The Art of Rupture: Narrative Desire and Duplicity in the Tales of Guy de Maupassant*. Ann Arbor: University of Michigan Press, 1994.

Sullivan, Edward D. *Maupassant: The Short Stories*. London: Edward Arnold, 1962.

Look for the following titles, available now from
BARNES & NOBLE CLASSICS

Visit your local bookstore for these and more fine titles.
Or to order online go to: WWW.BN.COM/CLASSICS

Adventures of Huckleberry Finn	Mark Twain	1-59308-112-X	$6.95
The Adventures of Tom Sawyer	Mark Twain	1-59308-139-1	$6.95
The Aeneid	Vergil	1-59308-237-1	$7.95
Aesop's Fables		1-59308-062-X	$5.95
The Age of Innocence	Edith Wharton	1-59308-143-X	$5.95
Agnes Grey	Anne Brontë	1-59308-323-8	$5.95
Alice's Adventures in Wonderland and Through the Looking-Glass	Lewis Carroll	1-59308-015-8	$5.95
Anna Karenina	Leo Tolstoy	1-59308-027-1	$8.95
The Arabian Nights	Anonymous	1-59308-281-9	$9.95
The Art of War	Sun Tzu	1-59308-017-4	$7.95
The Autobiography of an Ex-Colored Man and Other Writings	James Weldon Johnson	1-59308-289-4	$5.95
The Awakening and Selected Short Fiction	Kate Chopin	1-59308-113-8	$6.95
Babbitt	Sinclair Lewis	1-59308-267-3	$7.95
The Beautiful and Damned	F. Scott Fitzgerald	1-59308-245-2	$7.95
Beowulf	Anonymous	1-59308-266-5	$4.95
Billy Budd and The Piazza Tales	Herman Melville	1-59308-253-3	$5.95
Bleak House	Charles Dickens	1-59308-311-4	$9.95
The Bostonians	Henry James	1-59308-297-5	$7.95
The Brothers Karamazov	Fyodor Dostoevsky	1-59308-045-X	$9.95
Bulfinch's Mythology	Thomas Bulfinch	1-59308-273-8	$12.95
The Call of the Wild and White Fang	Jack London	1-59308-200-2	$5.95
Candide	Voltaire	1-59308-028-X	$4.95
The Canterbury Tales	Geoffrey Chaucer	1-59308-080-8	$9.95
A Christmas Carol, The Chimes and The Cricket on the Hearth	Charles Dickens	1-59308-033-6	$5.95
The Collected Oscar Wilde		1-59308-310-6	$9.95
The Collected Poems of Emily Dickinson		1-59308-050-6	$5.95
Common Sense and Other Writings	Thomas Paine	1-59308-209-6	$6.95
The Communist Manifesto and Other Writings	Karl Marx and Friedrich Engels	1-59308-100-6	$5.95
The Complete Sherlock Holmes, Vol. I	Sir Arthur Conan Doyle	1-59308-034-4	$7.95
The Complete Sherlock Holmes, Vol. II	Sir Arthur Conan Doyle	1-59308-040-9	$7.95
Confessions	Saint Augustine	1-59308-259-2	$6.95
A Connecticut Yankee in King Arthur's Court	Mark Twain	1-59308-210-X	$7.95
The Count of Monte Cristo	Alexandre Dumas	1-59308-151-0	$7.95
The Country of the Pointed Firs and Selected Short Fiction	Sarah Orne Jewett	1-59308-262-2	$6.95
Crime and Punishment	Fyodor Dostoevsky	1-59308-081-6	$8.95
Daisy Miller and Washington Square	Henry James	1-59308-105-7	$4.95
Daniel Deronda	George Eliot	1-59308-290-8	$8.95
Dead Souls	Nikolai Gogol	1-59308-092-1	$7.95
The Deerslayer	James Fenimore Cooper	1-59308-211-8	$7.95

(continued)

(continued)

(continued)

Silas Marner and Two Short Stories	George Eliot	1-59308-251-7	$6.95
Sister Carrie	Theodore Dreiser	1-59308-226-6	$7.95
The Souls of Black Folk	W. E. B. Du Bois	1-59308-014-X	$5.95
The Strange Case of Dr. Jekyll and Mr. Hyde and Other Stories	Robert Louis Stevenson	1-59308-131-6	$4.95
Swann's Way	Marcel Proust	1-59308-295-9	$8.95
A Tale of Two Cities	Charles Dickens	1-59308-138-3	$5.95
Tarzan of the Apes	Edgar Rice Burroughs	1-59308-227-4	$5.95
Tess of d'Urbervilles	Thomas Hardy	1-59308-228-2	$7.95
This Side of Paradise	F. Scott Fitzgerald	1-59308-243-6	$6.95
Three Theban Plays	Sophocles	1-59308-235-5	$6.95
Thus Spoke Zarathustra	Friedrich Nietzsche	1-59308-278-9	$7.95
The Time Machine and The Invisible Man	H. G. Wells	1-59308-388-2	$6.95
Tom Jones	Henry Fielding	1-59308-070-0	$8.95
Treasure Island	Robert Louis Stevenson	1-59308-247-9	$4.95
The Turn of the Screw, The Aspern Papers and Two Stories	Henry James	1-59308-043-3	$5.95
Twenty Thousand Leagues Under the Sea	Jules Verne	1-59308-302-5	$5.95
Uncle Tom's Cabin	Harriet Beecher Stowe	1-59308-121-9	$7.95
Vanity Fair	William Makepeace Thackeray	1-59308-071-9	$7.95
The Varieties of Religious Experience	William James	1 59308 072 7	$7.95
Villette	Charlotte Brontë	1-59308-316-5	$7.95
The Virginian	Owen Wister	1-59308-236-3	$7.95
Walden and Civil Disobedience	Henry David Thoreau	1-59308-208-8	$5.95
War and Peace	Leo Tolstoy	1-59308-073-5	$12.95
The War of the Worlds	H. G. Wells	1-59308-362-9	$5.95
Ward No. 6 and Other Stories	Anton Chekhov	1-59308-003-4	$7.95
The Waste Land and Other Poems	T. S. Eliot	1-59308-279-7	$4.95
The Way We Live Now	Anthony Trollope	1-59308-304-1	$9.95
The Wind in the Willows	Kenneth Grahame	1-59308-265-7	$4.95
The Wings of the Dove	Henry James	1-59308-296-7	$7.95
Wives and Daughters	Elizabeth Gaskell	1-59308-257-6	$7.95
The Woman in White	Wilkie Collins	1-59308-280-0	$7.95
Women in Love	D. H. Lawrence	1-59308-258-4	$8.95
The Wonderful Wizard of Oz	L. Frank Baum	1-59308-221-5	$6.95
Wuthering Heights	Emily Brontë	1-59308-128-6	$5.95

ℬ
BARNES & NOBLE CLASSICS

If you are an educator and would like to receive an
Examination or Desk Copy of a Barnes & Noble Classics edition,
please refer to Academic Resources on our website at
WWW.BN.COM/CLASSICS
or contact us at
BNCLASSICS@BN.COM

All prices are subject to change.